CLIMBING MT. CHEAHA:

Emerging Alabama Writers

Edited by

Don Noble

Livingston Press
University of West Alabama

Printed on acid-free paper.
Printed in the United States of America,
Publishers Graphics
Hardcover binding by: Heckman Bindery
Typesetting and page layout: David Smith
Proofreading: Debbie Davis, Margaret Walburn,
Tricia Taylor, Tina Jones, Melissa Newton,
Jennifer Brown
Cover design and layout: Gina Montarsi
Cover art: Sheila & Robbie Limerick
Acknowledgements:
"Aubade," *Dogwood*; "The Last Testament of Major Ludlam," *The Sucarnochee Review;* "Playing Bingo for Money," *The Blessings of Hard-Used Angels* (Texas Review Press); From *Chicken Dreaming Corn* by Roy Hoffman. Copyright 2004 by Roy Hoffman. Reprinted by permission of the University of Georgia Press; "The Green Woman," *Portland Magazine;* "A Classical Education," *The Carolina Quarterly;* "Making It," *Kennesaw Review*

THIS PROJECT WAS FUNDED BY A GENEROUS GRANT FROM
THE SUMTER COUNTY FINE ARTS COUNCIL

These are works of fiction. You know the rest:
any resemblance to persons living or dead is coincidental.
Livingston Press is part of The University of West Alabama,
and thereby has non-profit status.
Donations are tax-deductible:
brothers and sisters, we need 'em.

first edition
6 5 4 3 3 2 1

Table of Contents

This book is for Jennifer Horne.

Introduction

While the soliciting, judging, and printing of a volume of short stories may not be a blindingly original idea, it is, I think, a perennially good idea. A little over a year ago, when I began expressing in various venues around the state my interest in this kind of project and my willingness to choose and introduce a volume of new short fiction, I was very pleased that Joe Taylor of the Livingston Press took me up on it. Livingston Press is a particularly appropriate house for this kind of project, for they are the people who most recently produced *Belles' Letters: Contemporary Fiction by Alabama Women*, edited by Joe Taylor and Tina N. Jones, in 1999. This was a collection of twenty-seven pieces of fiction, by veterans and newcomers, all women.

Prior to this, in 1995, Livingston had published, under the editorship of the late James E. Colquitt, with an introduction by Norman McMillan, the volume *Alabama Bound: Contemporary Stories of a State*. Here were twenty-eight pieces of fiction, all previously published, all written in the mid- to late-twentieth century. Jim Colquitt used a very generous definition of "Alabama writer" in his selections, and so we find Tobias Wolff, Barry Hannah, and Lex Williford, all of whom have real, but tenuous, Alabama credentials. A similar generosity of definition has been followed in this volume, *Climbing Mt. Cheaha*, as well.

In 1996 Allen Wier edited *Walking on Water and Other Stories*, published by the University of Alabama Press, but inclusion in this volume had a specific criterion. These stories, twenty-four in all, had been written by graduates of the wonderfully successful University of Alabama Master of Fine Arts in Fiction Program. This is a natural idea and should be done again, in just the same way, and I think there should also be a companion volume in poetry, of which there has also been a prodigious amount and of high quality.

Although few may remember it, and few purchased it at the time, there was a precedent for these books: a volume of stories, *Alabama Prize Stories*

1970, edited by the late O. B. Emerson of the University of Alabama English Department. In the foreword to the 1970 volume, the publishers, Strode of Huntsville, tell the reader that there were two hundred entries, previously published and unpublished, and that there were three judges, the fiction writers Elise Sanguinetti and Thomas C. Turner, and professor Oxford Stroud. Twenty-nine stories were chosen. The publishers also declared that "we plan more such contests and published anthologies in the future." For a variety of reasons, sadly, there were no more. *Alabama Prize Stories 1970* stands alone.

Comparing the contents of *Alabama Bound* and *Alabama Prize Stories*, it is striking to see only H. E. Francis in both volumes. None of the other twenty-eight from *Prize Stories* is in *Alabama Bound* and, of the women authors, only Carolynne Scott appears in both *Prize Stories* and *Belles' Letters*. Tastes change. Tastes of editors change. New talent appears and some writers quit writing for one reason or another. The prize winners of 1970 are missing in 1995 and 1999.

In any discussion of Alabama fiction, however, the standard reference will be Philip D. Beidler's two-volume collection *The Art of Fiction in the Heart of Dixie* (1986) and *Many Voices, Many Rooms* (1998). Published by the University of Alabama Press, these books are composed of both stories and excerpts from novels with chronological periods introduced by reliable, informative essays which briefly set up the writers of that period and introduce each piece. Of the authors in *Prize Stories* and *Alabama Bound,* only William Cobb appears in Beidler's *The Art of Fiction.* No authors from *Belles' Letters* appear in *The Art of Fiction.* Only Eugene Walter and Mary Ward Brown appear both in *Alabama Bound* and *Many Voices, Many Rooms,* and there are no authors from *Belles' Letters* in *Many Voices, Many Rooms.*

Why bother with the above? Well, because it is a path I found myself going down, and I'm glad I did. Short fiction in Alabama is a fluid, even mercurial genre. The path is littered with names and stories now not known or widely read: that is the bad news. The good news is there are always new writers and a volume to receive them. This remains true in *Climbing Mt. Cheaha.*

And so we come to the present volume. Taylor issued a call for submissions for these stories in the Alabama Writers' Forum publication *First Draft,* in the magazine *Poets and Writers,* on the internet—the internet notice was apparently picked up by some give-away newspapers, because several submitters from North Alabama mentioned it—and extensively by word of mouth. When the submission period was over, I was sent a box with 150 stories in it. Finally, I chose twenty-seven, which you now hold in your hand. The process of choosing was much, much more difficult that I had, in my worst nightmare, imagined. Of the 150 stories about a dozen appeared to me, at once, as first rate, no doubt about it. They went into the "yes" pile. Unfortunately for me, only about a dozen went at once into the "reject" pile, the "no" pile.

Let me digress for a moment about that reject pile. In the late 1960s when the poet John Ciardi was poetry editor of *The Saturday Review of Literature*, and received hundreds of poetry submissions per week, Ciardi infuriated many of the magazine's readers with a column in which he stated that sometimes he could and did reject a poem after reading only the first two or three lines. Letters to the editor howled. How could he? How dare he! Outrageous! Then, a couple of weeks later, Ciardi's column was composed of a large selection of the first two or three lines of poems he had recently received and rejected. They were horrible, hysterical, achingly awful.

I was advised by several friends to follow Ciardi's advice and read only until something in a story struck me as bad, and then stop reading. I did not. I assure all the unsuccessful submitters to this volume that I read every word of every story. I promise. This may smack of compulsive and even, in a sense, masochistic, behavior, but I swear it is true. In all I spent over one hundred hours reading the box of 150 stories I was sent. Most I read more than once. Why?

Because about one hundred of the stories were too good to reject quickly but not wonderful enough to swoon over quickly. Of these, I finally chose about a dozen; readers are free to guess which dozen. I'll never tell. This group of one hundred stories suggests that something good is happening in Alabama short fiction, or at least I guess it is good. Writing programs, workshops, seminars, conferences—somebody is teaching writers how to make an acceptable, not perfect and maybe not inspired, but not stupid short story. Trained teachers of fiction writers have taught their students to manage point of view, include a few details of setting, sometimes generate a little dialogue, all of which make for a competent piece of short fiction. Teachers are unable to give their students that elusive "voice," however, or of course to give them what readers crave to see: spark, genius, the exceptional talent—call it what you will.

So what was in the box? First, there were many more stories by women than by men, perhaps twice as many. (In the final selection, as it turns out, seventeen are by men and nine by women, but that's just how it worked out.) Many of the stories submitted were by women who have written what seem to be autobiographical laments about the unreliable, unfaithful, feckless, drunken, worthless men who used to be their boyfriends or husbands. The Lifetime Channel could go for years on what was in that box.

You will not be surprised to learn that most of the lawyers in Alabama, as with the rest of the nation, think that they are also fiction writers, and several actually are. Mike Stewart and Frank Turner Hollon, for example, are attorneys in Alabama who write wonderful fiction. Richard North Patterson is doing nearly as well at it as John Grisham or Scott Turow. This should come as no surprise, really. Attorneys went to college for seven years; they are smart, educated people. And, in their line of business, they run into a great many colorful, odd characters and unusual situations. Add to that the structure of the actual trial, which gives a nearly perfect dramatic situation in which there is a life-and-death conflict which ends in climax, resolution, and denouement, and you have the best possible recipe. There is only one lawyer story chosen for this volume, but there could have been several others, nearly as good.

Another kind of story in the box was something I want to call "the barely disguised incident from one's life." It may be that the recent rage for memoir has gotten a lot of people thinking and writing about their childhoods and younger lives, and special moments get written up. Usually, however, and sadly, incidents, however important to the person who lived them, are not short stories. As Gertrude Stein said to the young Ernest: "Hemingway, remarks are not literature." These pieces tend to be anecdotes, actual events, rather than imagined or crafted works of literary art. I think I can tell. They don't work. They are the stories one tells after work at the bar at five o'clock—Wow, let me tell you what happened last weekend—or, in a quiet conversation with a significant other, one recalls a trauma from childhood. Even *Look Homeward, Angel* was more imagined than these stories appear to be.

There were, however, a number of naïve, but promising, pieces by middle-aged people, I think, who wrote of their experiences in the world of work, real physical work in textile mills and lumber yards. These pieces were *not* about the kind of work one used to see often on dust jackets: "R. Q. Smith has been a bartender, a shrimper, a long distance trucker, a tattoo artist, etc." *Those* were probably summer jobs. I'm talking about people who worked at jobs for decades and are now perhaps in a writing seminar at the town public library on Saturday mornings. These writers have authentic material to use and one day, as their skills sharpen, their stories will be appearing in print.

As one would expect in the contemporary South, there were lots of stories about contemporary problems. People wrote a good deal about drugs in various ways—production, distribution, effects of, etc.; of these, I included stories by Mike Burrell and Janet Mauney. Looking through the volume, I see I have chosen a half-dozen stories of a strong sexual nature—by Brad Watson, Michael Knight, Suzanne Hudson, Bart Barton, and Michelle Richmond, among others. Several stories take into account varieties of sexuality: male and female homosexuality, transvestism, and interest in transsexual operations. Modern life, in other words.

As one might expect, several submissions were of a violent nature. Of these, I chose stories by Tom Franklin and Beaux Boudreaux, among others. There has also been more interest lately in the short-short, and that subgenre is represented here by Loretta Cobb as well as by Watson and Franklin.

Many stories involved religion in some way, for these are the stories of the Bible Belt. But, surprisingly, there were very few stories of what one might think to be the stock-in-trade of Southern literature: the subject of race. The Erskine Caldwell or William Faulkner story of lynching, cruelty, injustice of whites toward blacks was almost entirely missing. There is some of this in the Beaux Boudreaux piece.

At a recent convocation of journalists at the University of Alabama, on the occasion of the presentation of the Clarence Cason Award for Distinguished Nonfiction, Rick Bragg, Diane McWhorter, Roy Hoffman, and several others were nearly unanimous in declaring that race as a contentious social issue in Alabama is coming to a close. In the near future, the social wars will be fought on the issues of religion and class. Whether and where to hang the ten commandments is on the evening news and the front page. The police dogs, water hoses, and berserk state troopers are now items of the past, to be written about by historians and writers of historical fiction. This idea is implicit in Kirk Curnutt's piece, which is in part about how the civil rights movement itself is fading from Alabamians' minds, especially younger Alabamians.

Reading these dozens of stories was of course a learning experience for me. In much the same way as it is not actually possible to know what you think about a book until you hear what you yourself have to say about it, either in print or out loud, so one does not know what one likes, really, until a situation like this arises: choosing which stories to include and exclude. I discovered that I dislike the stories that seem to me to be simply anecdotes, without resonance, however well-narrated. I also seem not to like the O. Henry ending, in which there is a grand switcheroo. Fantasy and science fiction stories also leave me cold , but there are a few pieces included that might be loosely considered in that genre. Janet Nodar's story is fantastical; Brett Cox's story is a kind of statement from beyond the grave, while Joe Formichella's has a whiff of metafiction and Patricia Mayer's has suggestions of extra-sensory perception.More conventional science fiction or fantasy will have to find publication elsewhere: "What? You spoke with Farmer Jones? But that's impossible! He's been dead for years. Murdered, you know."

A large number of the submissions were chapters from books. This was perfectly within the guidelines, but not, I think, usually a good idea. Most chapters from novels are just that, part of an ongoing narrative development and do not stand alone very well. Only three are represented in this volume with an excerpt.

Put simply, I seem to like stories that are more or less realistic and have characters who develop at least a little or, perhaps, learn something.. The kind of conclusions I seem to favor follow more or less naturally from what came before.

This is all, of course, a matter of judgment. Twenty-six people now think I have pretty fair judgment. About 125 people think my judgment stinks. It will always be this way, I guess, as long as there is art, and subjectivity, and judging. I can only hope that the readers of this book have a little fun with the pieces I *have* picked.

Don Noble, Cottondale, Alabama, July 2004

CLIMBING MT. CHEAHA:

Emerging Alabama Writers

MARLIN BARTON

ANOTHER STORY FOR CATHERINE

We courted on a merry-go-round. A strange place for two grown people to find themselves—but then again I didn't know we were courting. We had met in June in an American history class at the university in Tuscaloosa. I was back in school after dropping out for a year-and-a-half. I'd gone home to Riverfield and worked first in my grandfather's general store, then in a hardware store in nearby Demarville. Now I was back and nervous about school, which is probably why I got to class early that first night. The professor was late, so I had plenty of time to look around. After the year-and-a-half away, somehow the desk I sat in felt as if it were made for a child.

"My husband don't want me in school," I heard a girl say in a hill-country voice that I took for North Alabama. "He don't think I need it. But I told him I did. 'You got to let me go,' I said."

The girl was attractive in a simple and ordinary way—brown eyes, long brown hair, a pleasant face—but it was the woman listening to her who caught my attention. She listened with her head tilted at such a distinct and delicate angle, down and forward and slightly sideways, like some porcelain figure.

She was older. She had those tiny lines around her eyes, but I don't mean she looked old. She was a pretty woman, tall, only a few inches shorter than me, somewhat thin, with long legs and breasts more full than her loose-fitting shirts revealed. Her short reddish hair had a patch of gray in front. She told me later that she left that little bit of gray instead of dyeing it because she'd earned it. Later, after she told me a few things about her husband and her life with him, I decided she was right.

"Well," she said to the girl, "you have to be patient with him. Don't make him feel like he's not intelligent when you talk about class."

"I wouldn't do that," the girl said.

"I know." She smiled at the girl, then at me to let me know she'd noticed my listening. There was almost a question in her smile, as if she wanted to hear my story, too.

After about two weeks of class, the girl didn't show up one night. I leaned across the aisle toward Catherine, whose name I'd finally overheard. "You're nice to listen to the girl every night the way you do," I said. "But does anyone ever listen to you?" Her smile faded and her face showed surprise, as if I'd said something slightly lewd, or told her something about herself that she was trying to keep secret. I surprised myself in saying what I did. I'm usually quiet, especially with women, and for this reason I'd often spent a great deal of time without their company.

"You can speak," she said.

I laughed. After a few minutes of conversation about the class I asked her where she was from. She told me Albany, New York, and she quickly mentioned her husband in that casual way women have, I've since learned, when they're by themselves and meet a man. "We've lived all over," she said, "and we've come South for the first time because my husband is working now for Gulf States Paper Mill." Unlike people I'd grown up with back in Riverfield, he didn't do shift work. I could tell they had money by looking at her and listening to her.

The next night, when the girl didn't show up again, she told me she had two children. "A girl and a boy. Both teenagers," she said hesitantly. "Now, be a southern gentleman and don't ask how old I am." It was later that she told me she was forty, sixteen years older than I was.

By the next week it was clear that the hill-country girl wasn't coming back. "I guess her husband talked her out of it, or simply told her she couldn't," Catherine said on a Monday night, just as the professor walked in. Her voice held a trace of sadness or anger, like notes off key. It was as if Catherine's own fate were somehow tied to that girl and what happened to her, only I didn't understand how deeply, not then, and by the time I did understand, I had already failed her.

Toward the end of June the heat seemed to stick to your skin upon walking outside. After class one night, when Catherine was about to get inside her car, she asked if I'd like to walk over to the cafeteria. "I've hardly eaten all day," she said. She reached then into her purse and pulled out cigarettes and a lighter.

"I didn't know you smoked," I said.

"When you're around people long enough, you learn things about them." She smiled and lit one. "I've been keeping secrets. Actually, I go for long periods when I don't need them."

"But this isn't one of those times?"

"No. It isn't."

We sat toward the back of the cafeteria. She ate a small portion of salad. I drank a glass of tea. She told me about her children. The boy did well in school; the girl didn't. She was worried about her daughter, and other things seemed to be troubling her too, but I didn't pry. When asked, I told her how my parents had divorced when I was young and how my father and I moved to the tiny community of Riverfield, his hometown. It occurred to me then that she was about the same age as my mother when the divorce happened, and that her son was only a little older than I had been. Looking at her, I felt, for a moment, as if I were a child again, and what that made Catherine I did not want to consider.

I told her a few stories about the people in Riverfield, many of whom worked in the nearby paper mill, people who her husband probably had a great deal of power over. She listened carefully. Clearly she'd become used to a certain standard of living, but she was never condescending about others. "I like your stories," she said, taking a bite of salad. "They help me to understand the people down here a little better."

Then she told me something about herself. She'd been an art major when she was younger; she never finished though—she'd gotten married instead. She claimed she wasn't very good. "I only have a basic mastery of skill," she said, "but every few years I sneak out the easel." The few things I eventually saw *were* good. She was talented, just as I'd suspected. She drew people, and that impressed me. "You're learning all kinds of things about me tonight," she said and finally stood up from the table.

We began to frequent the cafeteria after class. Then, one night, that changed. "Let's go somewhere different tonight," she said. We ended up at a park not far from campus. She drove because I didn't have a car. We walked around a little, through some ancient oak trees and along a walkway, then sat down on the merry-go-round next to a set of swings. It wasn't one of those fancy merry-go-rounds you see at a carnival or at the state fair like I used to ride when I was still a small child in Montgomery. There were no colored lights or finely decorated horses mounted on brass poles. It was nothing but a flat piece of metal with galvanized pipe for handrails. The shuffling feet of children had long since worn away whatever bright colors had once adorned it.

I pushed the merry-go-round with my foot and started us moving at a slow pace. We were both quiet until Catherine turned to me. "Tell me a story, Seth," she said. "Quick. Before I start crying."

I did what she asked. I told her about a boat ride up the Tennahpush River that my cousin and I went on years ago. There were a handful of adults who proceeded to get drunk on vodka and the sacramental wine my cousin's mother, Sarah Ann, had provided for the Episcopal church service they'd all been to earlier that day. I told her how we ran out of gas and how we finally got on our way back down the river at midnight with no lights and a driver who wore prescription sunglasses because that was all she had, and how we hit a half-submerged log and almost turned over. She was laughing as hard as I'd ever heard her. It sounded so very feminine. When I finished the story she was quiet for a moment, then said, "Before I left for class tonight my husband picked up our glass coffee table and threw it against the brick wall in our den."

All through the summer we'd sit on the merry-go-round, slowly spin, and talk. One clear night we sat and looked at the stars, and Catherine named some of the constellations she knew, Ursa Major and Minor, Draco, Libra, and Corona Borealis—the Northern Crown. "See how it's shaped?" she said. "Like a tiara with the one bright star in the middle?"

I told her another story then. "Once, years ago, stars fell on Alabama," I said. There'd been a meteor shower in the early 1800s, and some people thought that the world was coming to an end. But the legend is more romantic than that, and I told her about only the legend. It speaks of a spell being cast by the falling stars, creating a land of enchantment. There's even an old song about it. *Moonlight and magnolia, starlight in your hair.* We never saw any stars fall, though. We didn't need to, the same way we didn't need carnival lights or decorated horses. Just talk and friendship was enough. Later, an occasional bottle of wine.

In September, after our class was over with and a new semester had started, I called her at home at ten-thirty one night, something I'd never done. I knew her husband had left town on business that morning. Before I even realized why I called her, she asked if I'd like for her to come over.

I waited outside and spotted the Corona Borealis in the night sky. It had moved some with the change in season, but I saw it clearly. In a little while Catherine pulled up. She got out of the car carrying a bottle of wine, and when we went into the building I could see that there was a stronger hint of make-up on her face than usual—a light shade of lipstick, a touch of blush. She usually wore very little make-up, a testament to how pretty she was.

We sat on the floor in my apartment and drank some of the wine while we talked about the classes we were taking. I told her about my last trip home, where I'd spent some of my time waiting on customers in my grandfather's store, but I didn't have any new stories for her, and she didn't ask for one. We listened to some music on the stereo, and I asked her about her husband. She looked down and shook her head.

"Has he done something?" I said. I suppose I saw myself as being protective of her, even though she was the one who was older.

"He went through my desk yesterday and threw away all of the notebooks I've used for my classes. But I don't really feel like talking about him right now." She fiddled with her now-empty wine glass. "Part of me feels like I shouldn't have come here tonight." She looked away from me again.

"Why not?" I said.

She kept her head turned, hesitated, then said, "I guess you could say I've had less than platonic thoughts about you."

I'd imagined her in my bed, her body warm beneath me. "You're not the only one," I said.

We were both silent then. Her hair hung down and hid the side of her face, and she still wouldn't turn toward me. I could smell the light scent of her perfume. Slowly, I leaned toward her and tried to kiss her, but she pulled away.

"Please don't turn from me," I said. I leaned my head onto her shoulder, really just wanting to be close to her, then kissed the soft flesh where her sweater left her shoulder exposed. Once. Twice. I kissed her cheek. She still kept turning from me, and I gently pushed her back onto the floor, kissing finally each corner of her mouth. She turned toward me, and I could smell the wine on her breath. Her mouth was warm, soft, responsive. We made love there on the floor. And later, in the bedroom, the small mattress, which didn't fit the too-large bed frame, kept dipping dangerously toward the floor. Neither of us cared.

My classes were usually in the mornings or at night, and I worked at the library on campus but was often through early enough to meet Catherine back at my apartment for a few hours in the afternoon. She'd leave in time to be home when her children arrived after school, unless she had a class. We usually had either part of a Friday or Saturday night together, too. I didn't ask her how she managed it. We'd still go to the park on those nights, before it got too cold. Sometimes she'd point out a new constellation. Then we'd go back to my apartment.

One afternoon she was sitting in her car waiting for me when I came home. "Hope you've got a story ready," she said when she got out. She was wearing a long blue car coat, a nice thing. She followed me up to my apartment, staying a few steps behind. We never touched in public. She was afraid someone she knew might see us. Once we were inside she sat down on the sofa, still huddled in her coat. "So tell me a story," she said.

I told her about my cousin Ralph, who ran away from home once when he was a boy. He hopped a freight train, rode it twelve miles to Valhia, then discovered he was hungry and hopped one back. He was gone all day, but his mother pretended she hadn't missed him, so when their old tom cat came slinking into the kitchen, Ralph said, "Mama, is that the same old cat we had around here before I left?"

She smiled after I told her the story.

"Is it your husband?" I said then.

"Yes."

"Does he hit you?"

"No. Years ago he did. Once. Not since then. But he scares me sometimes. He threw that table against the wall. He tells me he doesn't want me in school. He says that's why our daughter's having problems. I'm not at home enough for her. After we fight the only way he knows how to apologize is to give me money. The day after he threw the table he gave me two hundred dollars. There were tears in his eyes. I took it. What else could I do? And this morning he told Lisa to get a job, told her to quit sulking around the damn house and do something besides bring home Ds and Fs from school. We'd talked about trying to persuade her to get a job, thought that it might be good for her. Why did he have to bring it up like that? She already hates herself, thinks she's not lovable if her own father can't love her. She's been in therapy, already taken sleeping pills once. If she survives her father it'll be a miracle."

"What about you?" I said.

"What do you mean?"

"Can you survive him?"

Her answer didn't come in words, only in the slight shaking of her body as I held her. Then, without a word, she pushed me down on the sofa, turned off the light, and slipped out of her clothes. She climbed onto me and clung to me not unlike some lonely frightened teenage girl. It wasn't desire, nor love—not then. It was closer to desperation.

Christmas came and I went home to Riverfield for two weeks. I spent some time in Montgomery, too, with my mother. A few days before I was to head back to Tuscaloosa, a letter came. "I can't keep on with you," she said, "because it's going to have to end sometime. Even if I wasn't married, I'm still sixteen years older than you, Seth. You can't pretend that sixteen years don't make a difference. You're not going to want some old woman."

On the bus back to Tuscaloosa I kept imagining her being there to pick me up as we'd planned weeks ago. I knew she wouldn't be, but when the bus pulled into the terminal and the air brakes squealed, there she stood, just as I'd imagined her. She wore her blue car coat, and her hair, which had grown a little longer, blew slightly in the cold breeze.

On the way home we talked as if she'd never sent me the letter. "How was your trip?" she said. "Did you have a good time?" Somehow her questions didn't make the situation any easier to handle.

"Do you want to come inside?" I asked when we pulled into the parking lot.

She hesitated, then said, "Yes."

We went in. "This is the last time," she said. "I mean it. But I couldn't not see you."

We undressed and made love. Then again, but this time she stopped suddenly, held me still. The words came. "I love you." A simple declaration. There was no question in her tone, no "Do you love me?"

I held her tight. "Tell me again," I said. Then I waited before I spoke so that my own words would not sound like an echo of hers.

Several weeks passed in that slow and monotonous way one feels, I've since learned, after discovering again what loss means. Then one evening I walked home from a bar on a week night, drunk, and passed the large white antebellum home just off campus that the university owns. Some kind of social function was letting out. I spotted Catherine and the man who I knew must be her husband. They stood on the lawn talking to a small group of people. She wore a long black dress and a string of pearls around her slender neck. He had on a dark suit, probably tailored, I thought. He was a little heavy, with thinning gray hair, but handsome in a way that most women probably find older, successful men. They began to walk away from the group, and I detected, or perhaps imagined, a hint of arrogance in his stride. They were not walking arm in arm. She didn't see me, and I was glad for that, because I felt suddenly like a spy.

I knew that what I had just glimpsed was her *other* life, the one she had gone back to. I imagined them going home and telling their children goodnight, then undressing. Before I could stop myself, I pictured the two of them in bed together, then wondered if there had ever been times when she'd come to me right after having been with him.

A few days later I found her parked beside my apartment building waiting on me to get home. "Come take a ride with me," she said before I could begin to imagine why she was there. As I got in the car smoke stung my throat, and she put out the cigarette that I hadn't noticed at first.

She drove faster than usual, but she wouldn't tell me where we were going. "He's been having affairs," she said. "A friend told me." Her voice was harder than I'd heard before. "When he got home I confronted him. He didn't even try to deny it. You think he would have at least done that. He just got mad, real mad. 'It's your fault,' he said. He told me he'd *had* to go to other women, said maybe he wouldn't have done it if I hadn't been spending all my time with school." She began to slow the car down and look for a turn, as if she weren't sure where it was. "Then I bluffed," she said. "'Years,' I told him. 'You've been doing it for years.' He got furious then."

He didn't hit her, which is what I was afraid she was going to tell me. Instead, he hit the window in the kitchen door and shattered one of the small panes there.

"'Get out,' I told him. I know I was being a hypocrite." She looked at me for the first time. "He said he wasn't leaving, that I could move out if I wanted, he'd even fucking pay for it, but that he damn well wasn't leaving."

We stopped then.

"So this is it." She looked up. "My apartment."

She'd done it out of anger. She said she didn't really stop to think about her children, that she'd just gone out that very day and rented it. The tone in her voice told me that the guilt of leaving her kids was already bothering her.

We went upstairs and I helped her move some of her furniture. It was really the kind of place a student would rent, and I wondered why she hadn't gotten something nicer. We went out to eat, and by the time we made it back up the stairs to her apartment, both of us knew that we had started again. This was to be our longest stretch of time together, and it was also the point when I would, ultimately, fail her.

For some time there she stopped suddenly asking me to tell her stories. We spent every weekend with each other, but always at her apartment, in case there was some kind of emergency with one of her children. She didn't talk about what was going to happen with her marriage, but I felt that it couldn't last, and that going back with her husband would be a mistake. Besides, I wanted her with me. What I intended for us I didn't know. I wouldn't let myself think about the future.

We were eating supper one night at the little glasstop table she'd bought when she told me in a measured voice that she'd filed for divorce. "He can have his money," she said, "but I want my kids. I have to have them with me." She sat silent a moment, shook her head, and pushed away her plate. "I know he's going to say that I deserted them." She looked down at the floor. "He'd be right, too."

"No," I told her. "You didn't." But I could see from the way she wouldn't face me that she didn't believe me. She said her daughter was getting along better than usual with her father. Catherine was glad, but she said she knew that their relationship could turn ugly at any time. And I'm sure that her daughter's attempt at suicide must have been on her mind, but she did not mention it, just as she said nothing about how her divorce might change our relationship.

The next morning Catherine wasn't in bed. I found her in the living room sitting on a small bench in front of an easel. Her hands moved quickly, with a kind of certainty and strength. Already the painting was taking shape. The figure in its center was that of a woman standing naked, her arms folded across her breasts. She was tall, built thin. Standing all around her was a roomful of people dressed for a party and staring. At the foot of the figure lay a small naked child who looked only days old.

"Is that you?" I said. "And your daughter?"

"It's from the dream I had last night," she said finally.

I walked closer to the easel and saw the wet shine in her eyes. She was suddenly so still and beautiful that she looked, for a moment, as if she were her own portrait. I put my arms around her, not knowing what else to do.

She worked on the painting for weeks and the sharp smell of mineral spirits often filled the apartment. "I can't get all the faces right," she kept saying. "I'm not sure what they make of her, or maybe I mean how they judge her."

One night not long afterward we were watching television and a program about raising children came on. None of the children behaved very well, and their parents didn't seem to care. "I'll never let my kids act like that," I said. "I wasn't raised to behave like that and no child of mine will either. I won't let their mama spoil them."

We watched the end of the program in silence. Then she turned off the television. "I want to be alone tonight," she said suddenly. "I think maybe you'd best go home."

"Why? I said. "What's wrong?"

She kept saying "nothing," but finally she told me. "It's what you said."

"What did I say?"

"About having children. I know this will sound crazy to you, but I've dreamed of having a child with you, of giving you that, even though we both know that I'm too old to have your child."

"It doesn't sound crazy," I said.

"But it's not going to happen. It can't." She pulled a pillow toward her and hugged it to her body. "*Even* if we stayed together," she said then. There was the sound of a question in her voice, and she looked up at me as if she were waiting on something. After a moment she turned away in a quiet reproach, as if I'd failed to give her what she wanted.

She took me home. It had rained earlier and the roads had iced. She told me when she pulled into my drive that she'd see me tomorrow. That was all.

I couldn't sleep, and about twelve o'clock I picked up the phone. She answered on the second ring. "I wish you'd let me come back over," I said.

"If you want to come over, you can walk. I'll leave the door unlocked." With that, she hung up.

The walk was a mile-and-a-half. The wind blew hard from the west, and my fingers ached from the cold so much they felt mashed. Even my face hurt. *Penance,* I thought. I found myself looking for the Corona Borealis, but this time I couldn't find it. The winter sky was shifted far beyond my recognition.

The lights were off when I got to her apartment, but the door was open, as promised. I called her name, and in the darkness went to her bedroom, undressed, and crawled into bed. The warmth there beneath the covers was womb-like, and after a time it took away even the deepest part of my chill.

Her moods grew dark. Often I would wake up at night and find her sitting in the living room, a shadow against shadows. Some weekends she'd call and say she wanted to be alone, then call back a few hours later and ask me to come over. She would not let go of the notion that she'd deserted her children. Her divorce was almost final, too, and even though she felt it was for the best, she couldn't help but grieve the end of a twenty-year marriage. There was also the question of us, which I didn't want to answer.

Late in the spring I went home to Riverfield for a week. She took me to the bus station and waited with me. We hadn't made love the night before, but that morning when I woke up she was already awake, and she took me in her hand and was on me then, quickly and passionately. It was almost as if she were fighting me.

At the station we stood beside her car, neither of us saying very much. When the bus came I hugged her. "I want you to kiss me," she said. Her voice was flat, cold.

"Here?" I said, surprised. I told her I shouldn't.

She looked directly at me and said an odd thing. "You're going to regret not kissing me goodbye."

Later in the week I called her from home. She told me that the day after I left she gave away most of her clothes and drove to a pawnshop. "I bought a revolver," she said. "The man told me it was the easiest to use."

I was horrified. She'd ended up calling her husband. He went to her immediately, then took her to a shrink, which was an unusual thing for him to do. "He's not all bad," she said.

"I'll come back today," I told her.

"No, a few more days will be soon enough."

Suddenly I felt angry at her. "Do you have any idea what it would have been like for me to lose you that way?"

Her silence was not enough to make me realize the selfishness of my question.

By the summer the shrink told her she was making progress. Those were the kinds of words he used, "making progress," "turning point." Her divorce was final, and she'd moved into a larger apartment and now had her children with her. She had bad days sometimes and leaned on me when she did. She still asked for stories from time to time, and I had them for her, as always.

One warm night after we'd started going back to the merry-go-round she asked for a story. I kept spinning us slowly with my foot for a time, then stopped and decided to tell her a story that had been in my mind lately, a story my father had once told me about a black man who killed, or thought he killed, another man with a knife. There was something about gambling involved. The man ran away before anyone could tell him that the other man hadn't died. He wasn't seen again. His wife, whose name was Jennie, and who I can remember as an old woman, never heard a word from him. After he left she started to drink and drank bad for years. Then, not too long before she died, she took up religion. But hers had been a mostly miserable life.

When I finished telling the story, Catherine looked at me as if she were accusing me of something. "I didn't like that story," she said. And that was all she said before she walked away to the car.

I knew then that I'd told the story wrong. It was the life the man had lived after he ran away that I wondered about, how he managed to keep living with his guilt and loneliness. But the story didn't come out right. Just as I was about to get up and follow her to the car, I spotted the Corona Borealis in the night sky. It was as if the sky had moved back into place, had completed a turn.

A few weeks later, and just a night after we'd last been together, she called and said that she couldn't keep seeing me, that it was too hard on her.

I tried to talk her into keeping our relationship going, but she stood strong. For once I wanted her weak, crying even, asking for a story.

I dropped out of my summer classes, went home, and spent much of my time down on the bank of the Tennahpush River, trying to decide if there was any way I could convince her that we should continue together. Mostly I wondered if I had the courage to stay with a woman who was sixteen years older than I. But what did I mean by *stay with?* Marry? Could I handle the things people would say, what my family would say? And what would they say exactly, that I was making a big mistake? She couldn't give me children? She would die before me?

When I got back to Tuscaloosa I called and asked her to come over. We sat on the floor in my living room. This time there was no bottle of wine, no music playing, only a wide space of ugly brown carpet between us. "I don't want to lose you," I said. I mentioned marriage, too, and I think a part of me expected gratitude for that.

She moved close to me and took me in her arms and held me in her lap, like a child. "I can't do it," she said in a whisper. Looking back now, I wonder if she felt that it couldn't work, or if she had simply decided that it was over between us, the decision made and final at last. I have learned that this is what a woman has to do sometimes with a man in order to survive him. The one thing I am certain of now is that she knew my words, my pleas to stay together, weren't something I meant, that I simply *wanted* to mean them.

While I lay there, still in her arms, I thought back to the night we'd been watching television, when she told me she'd dreamed of having my child. I remembered how she said she knew that it couldn't happen. *Even if we stayed together,* she'd said, and then looked at me. It was a question. Not about children, but about us. That was the moment I lost her, the moment I failed her. I could have said, "Yes, we'll stay together," but I didn't.

I finished school the next semester and saw Catherine only once, at a bookstore off campus not long before I was set to leave Tuscaloosa. She was looking at a magazine, and when I spoke her name she looked up quickly, as if she were afraid someone was about to scold her for reading in the store. She told me how her children were doing and about how busy she'd been lately. She also said that she was thinking of leaving Alabama. I asked her to call me so that we could have lunch together right before I left, and I told her I was leaving on a Friday. I never heard from her. I was hurt and wondered if maybe I'd never really meant anything to her, if maybe I'd just been someone who'd helped her through a rough time, but I know better than that now.

The one memory I keep coming back to is when I walked to her apartment that winter night and went to her bed. I remember how she held me and how warm her bed and her body were, but what strikes me most now isn't how warm she felt, but the fact that she could bear to hold my freezing body next to her, how painful that must have been while I lay there humbled and cold to the bone.

BEAUX BOUDREAUX

BAPTISM

Aidan watched the old man put on a pair of leather work boots that had seen better days, thinking that the smell of the house—a mixture of sweat, garlic, and pipe tobacco, but not the sweet stuff his dad smoked— would stick to him for a week. Or two. The old man's cracked and red knuckles had a crust of dead skin like psoriasis around them. Most of his nails had neat splits running down the middle, like somebody had cut them with a razor blade. Aidan thought they looked insectile and ugly. He cringed.

"Used to know your daddy, when I worked at MacMillan," the old man said. He looked at Aidan in a way that irritated him, like he was waiting for Aidan to jump with excitement at the fact.

"Oh," Aidan said.

"Yeah, I reckon that mill beat and stunk the life out of me," the old man said. "It's why I got arthritis, and it's why I cain't breathe right no more." He looked at Aidan for another moment, and then he got up, walked across the room, and took an orange hunting cap from the mantle over the fireplace. He put on the cap and said, "Well, ready when you are, bud." The old man had been calling him "bud" since their first phone conversation when Aidan had called him from the *Times* office. Aidan fucking hated it.

"Sure," Aidan said. He put the strap of his digital camera over his head and stood up.

"That one of them new cameras where you can see the picture on that little screen after you take it?" the old man said.

"Yep," Aidan said.

The old man looked at him in the way that irritated him again. Aidan started towards the front door.

"We'll go out the back," the old man said. He pointed through the door into the kitchen to the back door.

"Oh," Aidan said. He motioned with his hand for the old man to lead the way.

The old man led him through the house, his boots rubbing on the hideous yellow and green carpet in a way that made Aidan grimace, to a sliding glass door that looked out over the old man's back yard.

"Watch your step comin' down," the old man said. A set of wooden stairs, steep and rickety, rose five feet from the ground. The old man made his way down swiftly, and Aidan thought he would fall off of the wobbly stairs, but he didn't.

Aidan could barely tell where the old man's yard ended and the woods began. Big pine trees rose from the rough ground, which was littered with fallen branches and shrubs. A stand of four trees had been taken over by kudzu, swallowed into one green mass. An old shed, rusty brown with white double doors, stood at the back of the yard.

The old man led him past the shed and stopped at the back corner, pointing at a piece of rock that was mostly buried in the ground.

"That there is part of the foundation of the house that was originally on this land," he said.

Aidan looked at it, not saying anything.

"That house belonged to my granddaddy, Earl T. Booker," he said. Aidan thought the old man was looking at him again, but he refused to look up from the rock to see.

"Oh," he said. He turned the camera on. The mechanical noise of the lens extending was like a rape in this quiet place. He pointed and made a shot of the rock, knowing that it wouldn't be used.

"Yeah," the old man said. "I never saw the house before it was tore down. I think it was . . . oh, ten years or so before I was born."

"Oh," Aidan said.

"But I guess that's not what you're here to see, is it?"

"Not really."

"Well, let's head on down there."

The old man started walking away from the house, through the trees.

Past the line where the woods became thicker, the ground took a hard downward slope. Hardwood trees becamse more frequent as they walked.

"Got to be careful now," the old man said. Aidan could hear his breath beginning to be labored. "I've always wondered why they even built it down in this hollow, with it being so hard to get down there."

Rhea was thinking, *I should not be doing this.*

It had been hard to descend the hill earlier today when she'd come to be baptized, and it hadn't gotten any easier in the four hours that had passed. She could no longer hear the noises at the house, but that didn't lessen her fear of being caught. No—she thought the quiet made it a little worse. But if anybody did notice that she was gone, they wouldn't come down here, she thought. Surely they wouldn't.

She wasn't only scared of being caught, though. She was thinking about what Charlotte, her sister, had told her after she got married.

"You don't want to be in any hurry," Charlotte had said. "It hurts like the devil the first time you do it. Put it off as long as you can. You bleed."

The Lord Jesus said, "He who believeth in Me—"

As she stepped over a fallen log, her dress caught on a limb and she nearly fell. The limb ripped a small tear in the bottom of her dress. *I wonder how I'll explain that,* she thought.

"—shall never die."

Rhea came to the ridge that overlooked the spring and the baptistery. The spring was at the corner where two ridges came together to form the hollow. A long iron pipe extended from the spring's opening down to the baptistery, where the water poured out and filled the reservoir. Rhea remembered how cold the water had been and shivered.

The baptistery, a brick pool about four feet high and six feet square, rested near the edge where the hollow dropped off and the water fed into Fredrick Creek. The iron pipe kept the reservoir filled with water, and on the side opposite of the pipe there were three bricks missing where the water overflowed and poured into the stream that fed the creek.

Rhea started down the path that negotiated the ridge, zigzagging back and forth through the trees. She ducked under branches and batted at the spider webs that had sprung up to replace the ones she and Brother Bill had torn down earlier.

Always be vigilant, Sister Rhea, for the Devil will never give up on you.

It was dark down here where the dense woods blocked the sun. Rhea swatted at the mosquitoes and gnats buzzing around her, but there were too many to kill. Three mosquito bumps on her arms started to itch.

Near the bottom, where the path ended, Rhea tripped on her dress and fell. She heard the dress tear as she went tumbling off the ridge, and she landed on the ground beside the iron pipe with a wet *smack*.

Behind her, on the ridge, she heard a voice laughing.

Aidan and the old man walked down the ridge that formed the boundary of the hollow, stepping carefully on railroad ties that were partially buried in the dirt, forming a staircase down to the spring at the bottom of the ridge.

"I put these ties here a couple three years after my momma died and I moved back into that house," the old man said. "It was pretty hard to get down here before. Me and my son got them from Scotch Lumber Company after they tore up that old line that ran out of that mill over by Whatley, and he helped me lay 'em down. It was pretty hard work, but it sure makes it a lot easier to get down here."

"Yeah," Aidan said. He waved his hand at the gnats and mosquitoes that swarmed around his face. One of them flew up his nose, and he sneezed.

"These bugs are bad 'round this time of year," the old man said.

"Yeah," Aidan said.

They were halfway to the bottom of the ridge when Aidan could see the baptistery rising up from the underbrush.

"Well, bud," the old man said. "There it is."

The baptistery was made of red brick and filled with green water. Moss and lichen had grown up one corner. A PVC pipe ran from the spring to the reservoir, supported by metal stakes that jutted out from the muddy earth, and water poured out of the end of it. The baptistery leaned, only slightly, but visibly, in the direction of the creek. The green water trickled over the edge of the pool, through an opening in the top where three bricks were missing.

"Watch your step down here," the old man said as they reached the bottom of the ridge. "You kinda gotta hop down."

Aidan jumped down and the ground, a muddy mixture of water and dead leaves, sank beneath his feet. Water splashed onto his jeans. He noticed how his white tennis shoes had turned gray and brown.

The spring was a triangular hole at the point where two ridges came together to form the hollow. Roots and vines hung over the opening, and water trickled out. Aidan couldn't see the end of the PVC pipe. It simply disappeared into the darkness.

"This was an old iron pipe, originally," the old man said. He swatted a mosquito on his arm. Aidan saw a little smear of bright red blood on the old man's wrinkled, bruised skin. "I replaced it with the PVC 'bout the same time I put in those railroad ties 'cause it was rusted and there was holes in it. It wouldn't hardly keep the reservoir filled 'cause it lost so much water through rust-holes."

"Oh," Aidan said.

"But that's it," the old man said, gesturing to the baptistery.

Aidan started taking shots of the pool, the little *beep* of the camera echoing in the hollow, and the old man continued to talk.

Rhea picked herself up and turned to look up the ridge. Warren leaned against a pine tree that jutted out of the embankment and cast a shadow across the baptistery.

"You act like you're nervous about somethin'," he said, laughing. He started down the ridge, smiling as he maneuvered effortlessly, not stumbling or tripping as she had. "I can't figure out why you're *nervous.*" He still wore the shirt and pants he'd worn at the baptism this morning, the top two buttons of his shirt undone. Rhea remembered seeing him this morning at the top of the hill with the rest of the congregation as she stood in the cold water of the baptistery. Even as Brother Bill stood over her, praying that she would lead her life in the name of the Lord Jesus Christ, she had imagined herself writhing in the cold water, her nipples hard, and Warren kneeling over her, his pelvis between her thighs, breathing on her throat, running his tongue along her collarbone.

"I ain't nervous," she said.

"Your dress is torn."

Rhea looked down at her dress, which was ripped and streaked with gray mud, and said, "I'm never going to get away with this."

"You'll think of something to tell them," Warren said.

Noah ran along the edge of Fredrick Creek, panting, his legs ready to give out, but he was not about to stop now—not when he could still hear shouts of *Come back here, nigger!* coming through the woods behind him. He had long since dropped the coffee grinder—which belonged to *him*, anyway —onto the creek bank, hoping that if they found it they wouldn't follow him farther, but still the calls came, echoing off of the pine trees and through the ditch that the creek had carved into the earth.

A large moss and vine-covered log had fallen across the creek, resting on the bank of either side and leaving a three-foot gap beneath it. He fell to his hands and knees and crawled under it to the other side, digging trenches with his knees through the sand that lined the creek and scraping his back on the stump of a broken limb that hung from the underside of the log. He barely noticed the pain of the scratch, which made a tear in his shirt from just below the collar halfway down his back. He scrambled to his feet, tripped, and fell into the creek.

"You get back here, nigger!" Armstead's voice was closer now. Noah ran on, wiping the sweat from his eyes. *"We're gonna get you!"* the voice of the other man called. Noah didn't know his name. He'd been the one who had come through the door of the house first, followed by Armstead and his wife, and seen Noah standing there in Armstead's kitchen with his reclaimed coffee grinder, and come tearing after him as he ran out Armstead's back door. Armstead had taken the coffee grinder after breaking one of his wagon wheels on a brick in the road in front of Noah's cabin. He had walked right into Noah's cabin, looked around at his few belongings, and taken the coffee grinder even as Noah's wife looked on, silent.

"You niggers need to keep that road clear," Armstead had told Noah's wife. "I'll take this as payment for my wheel."

The ground began to slope upwards as he ran upstream, the creek becoming narrower. Noah saw a cottonmouth bathing in a little pool of sunlight on the other side of the creek. It bared its fangs and hissed as he ran by. He was likely to step on one, frantically as he was running, but he thought that a cottonmouth's venom might be a mercy compared to Armstead and the other man.

Warren came close to Rhea and put his hands on her hips. Little beads of sweat shone on his forehead and glistened in his eyebrows. He pulled her against him, and she felt him through her dress. He groped at her breasts with one hand, still pressing her to him with the other.

"I been wantin' to," he said. "I been wantin' to."

He rubbed her right breast roughly, and the way his hand felt through the cloth of her dress, the way his calluses felt as they rubbed against the cotton, made her shiver. This wasn't how she'd imagined it would start. His other hand groped lower, and simultaneously she felt a sudden burst of warmness and revulsion, nausea.

"I don't know . . ." she said, and trailed off. "If we get caught . . ."

He shook his head and began to kiss her throat, but not as she had imagined. He sucked on her neck, making noises like her little brother made when he ate, and yet it excited her. No, it was not like she had thought—it was dirty, ugly, but still she let him. Not really because she *wanted* it, but because she was here, and he was here, and now he was touching her— touching her in a place and in a way that only *she* had before—and she couldn't stand not to.

Warren pulled her dress up, his hands wandering beneath it eagerly, searching, fumbling.

"Wait," she said, pressing her hand to his chest.

"No," Warren replied, panting.

Rhea looked over his shoulder as he sucked on her neck and worked at her underclothes. A red squirrel ran up the embankment, stopped, looked down at the baptistery, and then ran to the tree that Warren had leaned against and scurried up its trunk. The sun was high overhead now, and lines of light, like rain, filtered through the pines and oaks and elms. She and Warren stood in one of the few rays that reached the deepest part of the hollow. Even as she said no, knowing that she meant yes *and* no, Warren pulled her dress over her head, dropped it onto the wet ground, and led her towards the baptistery, which was nestled in the shadow of the pine that jutted out over the hollow.

Aidan walked around to the other side of the baptistery, still taking pictures. He stepped up onto the ridge opposite the one they'd come down, crouched, and took a down-angle shot. Mosquito bites covered his arms, neck, and even his legs, despite the fact that he was wearing jeans. He scratched his arms and neck, thinking that he was about to go crazy.

"I try to clean this place up about twice a year," the old man said.

Aidan stepped off of the ridge and went down the hill towards the creek to get a shot from below the baptistery.

"When I first moved here," the old man said, "it was all growed up and covered with limbs and vines. I did have it lookin' like new. There wasn't no moss, or anything. I'm just too old to be foolin' with it anymore."

Aidan came back up the hill, nearly slipping on wet leaves.

"My daddy and momma never kept it up," the old man said. "At least, not after I was born. They may've done a little with it before I came along, but I always remember it being growed up back here, almost to where you couldn't see it 'cause of all the trees and such."

Aidan peered into the water of the reservoir and saw his face reflected back, tinted green.

"I did keep that water clear," said the old man. "You could see the bottom of it just as good as you can see your face there. You can still see the steps over there in that corner of it, just barely."

Aidan looked and saw two concrete steps just beneath the surface of the algae-saturated water. He couldn't see the bottom of the reservoir— only steps that continued on into a green oblivion.

"Me and my wife, Nina—we come down here and cleaned this *whole* place up. I had all the vines cut out with a machete and we got all the limbs, and I diverted the water from the spring and got all of the dirty water out of the pool and cleaned it out. . . ."

But Aidan wasn't paying attention. He was still staring at his face in the pool, thinking that all he'd come down here to do was get a couple of fucking pictures, not listen to this old man blab on about how he and his wife had done this, and done that, and all he wanted was to get the hell out of this place.

"But I guess you don't know about that, do you?" the old man said.

"Yeah," Aidan said.

"Oh—I almost forgot," the old man said, digging into the pocket of his faded Dickies. "Well, I thought I . . ." He switched pockets. "There it is." He produced a dingy chain that had probably once been shiny silver and handed it to Aidan. It was a silver cross and necklace. "I found that on the bottom when I was bucketing all that dirty water out. Wouldn't have ever found it if I hadn't cleaned the thing out—you couldn't see the bottom like you cain't now."

Aidan turned the necklace over in his hand. The face of the cross had turned gray and black. The chain was broken near the clasp and kinked in a few places. He stretched it out on the edge of the baptistery and took a picture of it. In the image that showed up on the camera's LCD screen, the black stain was darker and the whole cross appeared black.

"I don't know how old it is," the old man said. "Nobody might've found it if I hadn't come down here and cleaned up. I had the strength and energy to do it back then. I ain't now."

Charlotte had been right—it did hurt like the devil.

Rhea's her back and stomach muscles hurt from fighting to keep from falling into the water behind her. Warren rocked her back and forth, and the bricks were beginning to rub her buttocks raw. She could feel grains of sand and dirt between her skin and the bricks, burning and itching her as she slid back and forth, back and forth.

But the bricks were nothing compared to the pain between her legs, the pain inside her. It stung and burned and rubbed as he shoved. It was the same feeling—the same heat—that you might feel when you rub your hands together too hard, only much worse, and yet she wanted it, if for no other reason than because he was in her, and now it had to finish because he was in her.

Warren stood with his knees bent and against the side of the baptistery so that he was level with her, his shirt still buttoned and his pants down around his ankles. His right hand was on her lower back, pushing her towards him as he rocked. He began to push harder, grunting and breathing like a bull, and Rhea felt the fullness in her eyes that meant tears. No, this was not the way she had imagined it. Warren kept shoving harder and harder, pushing on her lower back with one hand and grabbing her breasts awkwardly with the other, and part of her wanted the dirtiness, the hurt—not *liked* it, but *wanted* it, nonetheless.

"It feels good," Warren moaned. "It feels good. . . ."

His eyes were squinted and angry, his eyebrows curling over them and his forehead wrinkled. His mouth turned down and he showed his top row of teeth, as though he was about to bite her. His breath, sour, old tobacco and coffee, blew into her face in hot, stinking waves. Sweat poured off of his face. A single drop of it dripped off of his nose and fell between her breasts. It tickled her as it ran down the center of her belly and into her navel. Despite the pain, the feeling of that sweat bead was acute, and, for a second, all she could be aware of.

"I can't do it like this anymore," he said, pulling back from her.

Rhea waved her arms for balance when he let go and she tumbled backwards. As she fell, she flailed for something to grasp and snatched Warren's necklace from around his neck just before hitting the water. The cold shocked the breath out of her (just as it had earlier, when Brother Bill had said *I baptize you in the name of the Father, and the Son, and the Holy Ghost*), but she was glad for it, glad for something besides heat and burning. Warren took her arm and pulled her out.

"Just got baptized twice," he said, still panting, not smiling. His face was strained and yearning. "Turn around." He gripped her shoulders, turned her around, and bent her over the edge of the pool. She placed her hands on the bricks and did not have time to be glad to not be sitting on them anymore before he began again, and she let out a small moan that was partially in pain and partially in something better than pain. He began to thrust harder.

"That's . . . *better* . . ." he croaked.

Through the woods, Rhea thought she heard a faint voice over Warren's huffing.

"I think . . . I think I hear something," she said, her voice quivering.

"No," Warren said, not stopping. "You ain't h-heard nothing."

Rhea stared at her reflection in the water, which waved slowly back and forth, disturbed by her intrusion, sending the sky and trees above them swinging and stretching. Through her face she could see Warren's necklace lying on the gray mortar bottom of the reservoir. She watched her mouth tremble, her nose wrinkle, and her eyes glisten as she felt his thighs pound against hers and the stinging begin to slowly turn into something else.

For a moment Noah thought that he had lost Armstead and the other man, and he began to slow down, but then he heard splashes in the creek, and Armstead yelling something.

Jesus, he thought. *Help me outen this.*

He pressed on, his legs aching in protest. He wouldn't be able to go on much farther, but maybe that meant that the two men would be getting tired, too. Maybe they would give up on him soon. No, that wouldn't happen. And even if they did, Armstead's wagon would roll into his yard today, or tomorrow. And then what?

Turning to cross to the other side of the creek, he tripped on the root of an oak that was exposed and fell to his hands and knees. He scrambled up, nearly slipping on the wet rocks in the bed of the creek, splashed to the other side, and kept running. He could hear Armstead's voice again, and it sounded a little farther behind him. Maybe they were giving up. Still, he would not take his chances.

Ahead he saw a small stream that fed into the creek, rolling off of a steep hill. There were thin pines that lined the stream, and he thought he could hold on to those and climb his way up. If he could be quick enough, maybe the two men wouldn't realize what he'd done and keep following the creek.

He reached the stream, grabbed the lowest pine and pulled himself up the embankment, but in his panic he lost his footing and slid down onto the wet bank of the creek. A broken limb cut into his right side, halfway up his ribcage, and he saw a red bloom spreading on his shirt.

"We're coming, nigger!"

They sounded very close now. Noah stood and began to climb the hill, digging his hands into the wet dirt and holding on to trees when he could. His feet slipped on the moss-covered rocks. His nose and cheeks rubbed against the ground as he crawled, and the smell of the wet dirt was nauseating.

This time Rhea was sure that she heard a voice. She had been able to pick out two of the words: *coming* and *nigger*.

"That *was* somebody," she said, and she started to pull away from him.

"No!" Warren said. He grabbed her shoulders and bent her over again. He pressed on, grunting with each push. She closed her eyes and threw her head back and forth, unable to control herself. She felt as though her insides were being ripped out of her.

And then it stopped, and Warren withdrew. Rhea fell to her knees and leaned over the edge of the baptistery, panting and struggling against tears. It couldn't be over yet. She was empty now—empty and throbbing.

"What—" she began, and then she stopped. She heard what Warren had heard: splashing in the stream that poured over the hill, and then she heard Warren's hurried footsteps behind her. She turned and saw him running up the ridge, holding his pants round his waist.

"Warren, wait!"

Rhea stood and ran, naked, towards where her dress lay. She heard more splashes behind her, and she turned to see a colored man coming over the hill, crawling in the stream. He stood up and began to run, but he stopped when he saw her standing there. Their eyes locked, the colored man's wide and absurdly white against his dark skin. He was covered with mud from his feet to his face. For a moment Rhea couldn't move—couldn't even reach down to get her dress and cover herself. Nothing moved except for the cool water that poured out of the hole where the two ridges met and ran over Rhea's muddy feet. She felt the muscles inside her tighten.

He left me here with this nigger, she thought. *He left me.*

Then there were voices and more splashes coming from past the drop-off. The colored man broke his gaze to look over the edge, and then started running towards her. Rhea's knees gave out, and she collapsed onto her side.

He left me.

She began to scream.

Jesus, *naw, girl,* Noah thought, running towards the ridge where the screaming girl lay. *Don't do that.* She was lying in the mud, pushing herself back towards the spring with her feet. Her clothes were lying at the foot of the ridge.

"I ain't gonna hurt you," Noah said. "I ain't gonna—"

"We got you, nigger!" It was Armstead. Noah ran past the girl, who was huddling into a fetal position, crossing her hands to cover her breasts. He leapt onto the ridge, hearing Armstead and the other man splashing in the stream behind him.

I can make it, Noah thought. *I can make it.*

But then a strong arm latched to his leg and pulled him down onto the muddy, leaf-covered ground. One of the two white men rolled him onto his back and punched him in the face before he could see who it was. There was a burst of white pain and then blood began pouring out of his nose.

"I'll teach you to come into *my* house, nigger," Armstead said, and he kicked Noah in the stomach. Noah doubled, sure that he was about to vomit, and moaned. He looked towards the girl and saw the other man crouched by her. She covered herself with the muddy white dress. She wasn't screaming anymore, but weeping.

"Did he do somethin' to you?" the man said, but he wasn't looking at her. He was looking at Noah.

"I never did *nothing* to that girl," Noah said, his voice muffled and nasal. He looked at Armstead. "You *know* I didn't, 'cause you was—"

Armstead slapped him. *"Shut up!"*

The girl looked at the water, rocking back and forth and hugging the dress to her breast with one hand. The other hand was under the dress and between her legs. Noah thought that she was rubbing herself. Slowly, she began to nod.

"He took me," she whispered. "He got me dirty."

Armstead grabbed Noah's shirt and dragged him to his feet.

"I think we'll hang him," Armstead said.

"You *know* I didn't do nothin' to her," Noah said.

"Fletcher," the other man said. "Let's drown 'im in that pool over yonder."

Armstead looked at Noah, nodding. Noah flailed his arms and broke loose from Armstead's grip and turned to run, but then both of them were on him. They each grabbed an arm and dragged him to the baptistery. Noah kicked his legs and screamed. The girl continued to stare at the water with her hand under her dress, weeping.

The white men dragged him over the edge of the baptistery and he felt a flare of pain as the top corner brick dug a gash in his back.

"I didn't do noth—" he began, and then he was under the water, still screaming out the words. He struggled, convulsing and kicking, but the two men were strong. He managed to bring his face above the surface and take a deep breath, but they pushed him back under as he inhaled, and he took in water. It felt cold.

Then Armstead was sitting on his chest, pushing down on his shoulders with his hands, and the other man was holding his arms down above his head. Noah tried to lift his legs and wrap his ankles around Armstead's neck, but then the other man was holding his legs. Armstead grabbed his wrists and held them down, leaning over him so that all he could see was Armstead's chest and arms, which were distorted by the water.

Rhea rocked back and forth, touching herself like she had done before, but now nothing would happen. She no longer even felt the heat that she had felt before, and she knew that the wetness that she felt was her blood.

He left me, Rhea thought. *He got me dirty and he took me and then he ran off and he left me for that nigger.*

She watched the stream that ran along under the iron pipe as the splashing sounds coming from the baptistery began to quiet.

Empty.

"**You** say these pictures are for the *Democrat?*" the old man said. He looked at the baptistery, one hand on his hip. He rubbed his finger under his nose.

"The *Times,*" Aidan corrected, irritated.

"The *Times,*" the old man said, nodding. "I keep forgetting. I'm from over in Sandflat, originally, and we all used to read the *Democrat.*"

Aidan said nothing. He was thinking that Mr. Huckabee was going to kill him for taking so long.

"Well, I reckon it's a good thing pictures are going to be in the paper of it. I reckon it'll eventually crumble away and be forgot about, after I'm gone. My son won't keep it up, even if he stays around here, which he probably won't." He looked into the water. Aidan could see the old man's reflected eyes looking out at the woods. "Don't nobody around here know anybody that was baptized here. They all died too long ago. I think that they stopped using it around 1903—that's the best that I can figure out. Supposedly, a girl was raped here, right in the baptistery. In the water of the baptistery. They say the girl killed herself."

The old man looked at him. "That's a thing, ain't it?" He shook his head. "To rape a girl in the saving waters of the Lord."

SONNY BREWER

TRAVELING LIGHT
(Inspired by a John Cleverdon wood-block
print of a pair of sneakers.)

Eugene was on a northbound train 135 kilometers out of Cadiz, Spain, when his daddy died and a week passed before he got word. His sister finally thought to send an email. When he caught the southbound, he took a window seat and slung his backpack on the floor and put his feet on it, resting his forehead against the frosted glass, feeling all over the buzz of the steel wheels on the rails. By the time he got home, the old man was in the ground. His house had been cleaned out. Everybody got what they wanted. Figuring him good for a few more years traveling light, they left Eugene out of the "settlement."

"Be a long time before that boy grows up, if he *ever* grows up," his brother had said, and then gave the family an update on his "dot-com phenom."

Eugene's hollow footfalls down the hall toward the back bedroom echoed like the clocking of time toward his own mortgaged future. The last place he'd seen the old man, sitting on his bed, fumbling to untie the frazzled shoelaces in his Target store house-brand sneakers. Cherokees, maybe. Eugene had done a lot of looking at the sneakers that night, not wanting to get into it with the old man's eyes. They could look a hole in you.

"So you spend four damn years in Tuscaloosa getting your ticket punched to be a hobo? I told you a diploma in English is about as useful as tits on a boar hog. Son, I don't know what the hell to make of you anymore."

Eugene nodded slow, noticing the glue was breaking loose on the toe of the left sneaker as his dad gave a soft, sighing groan while bent over tugging off the shoe. And then Eugene looked at his father's thin hair falling forward, watched until his reddened face tilted back and his eyes rose like a gray dawn. Then, without a word, the son walked out. Hit the road. Almost a year ago to the day.

Eugene opened the door into his father's bedroom, stripped bare of the bed and the dresser and the pictures on the wall. Full to ringing with memories of cautious approaches to the old man. "Come in here, boy!"

Then Eugene saw them. The sneakers at right angles, toe-to-toe, one turned over on its side, in the middle of the floor, looking soft like they'd been lived in. They were the only things left in the entire house. The old man always said Hell's a stylish shoe. "Heels jacked up and toes squeezed in, it's gotta be true. The devil's own invention."

Now you are dead, Eugene said, his words bouncing off the silent walls. Cloud-tripping barefoot, and drinking Scotch whisky with Uncle Ed. Eugene looked around at the emptiness. Except for the sneakers. I guess your heirs and assigns are funny about secondhand shoes, he thought. Their powdered toes refuse.

Eugene looked at the shoes. Odd, he thought, I don't know what size he wore. Then he kicked off his Birkenstocks and sat cross-legged on the floor. His bare feet caterpillared into his father's sneakers, a perfect fit. He stood up, looked at the worn out shoes on his feet. The prodigal son had come home to claim his prize. Eugene felt it only fair to leave his sandals in exchange. His brother would say, "See what I tell you about that kid!" And he would be right.

Wendy Reed Bruce

AUBADE

Death is no different whined at than withstood
—Philip Larkin

Martin was upstairs looking for body disposal choices online when he heard the UPS truck stop at the Cunningham's house. His house would be the next stop. Excarnation proved to be a fascinating option. What better way than for a wild animal to devour her body? Lilly walked in to let him know the UPS truck was coming.

"I know," he said. "I saw the Cunningham's get a Styrofoam box. Probably a spiral ham. Nice robe," he said. "New?"

She nodded. "I think I look good in spots," she said.

He pulled her to him and rubbed his hand over her hips. They used to be rock hard when she was able to run.

"Very smooth," he said.

She glanced at the monitor. "Excarnation?" she asked.

"Yeah, if you get this started, no more Zoo-bilee fundraisers necessary. With 'Lease a Lion,' people can simultaneously save money on funeral expenses and contribute to the expansion of the primate exhibit."

Lilly blinked hard at the screen. Since starting chemo, sometimes she didn't comprehend quickly. She blinked faster as if that might help.

"Excarnation is where wild animals are given the corpse to eat," he said.

Lilly chewed her top lip.

"I meant the zoo could lease out their lions to eat the bodies."

"Was it only an ancient practice or is still done today?"

"The Parees still practice it." He read from the screen, "They believe that demons take over the body at death and if you burn them, you pollute the air. If you bury them, you contaminate the earth. But since wild animals represent the goodness of creation, feed the body to them, and goodness consumes evil."

"Hmmm." She kept blinking. "Only the Parees?"

"Some tribes in Australia hang the bodies in trees. A sorta human piñata for the wild kingdom, I guess."

Her eyelids began to twitch. Sometimes she wanted to sew her eyelids shut.

"No hanging. But," and she raised her eyebrows up and down a few times and grinned, "lets keep the wild thing option open." She leaned down and kissed him. "You are a very lucky man. How many husbands have dying wives with raging libidos?"

Martin's erection was synchronized with the doorbell.

"Four days. Just like Amazon.com promised," he said.

He took the stairs two at a time. She held the handrail and stopped between some of them.

"You open it," she said, "while I pour some tequila."

One good thing about dying: you don't wait 'til five o'clock. Five o'clock may never come.

"Pour me a shot, too," Martin said.

As he suspected, *Book of the Dead* was daunting. How could a comprehensive compilation of ancient Egyptian burial customs not be? It had a faux leather cover with a crumbling pyramid and was thicker than their large print *King James Bible*.

"Here." She'd put a slice of lime on the side of his glass. "Cheers."

She'd poured him four ounces, not one. Which was good because he was suddenly parched.

So they got wasted before 9am on an ordinary Thursday in their ordinary house they'd lived in for twenty-some odd ordinary years.

"What time's hospice coming?" he asked. He was hard again. Tequila effect.

"Not for another hour." He listened for the doorbell. Maybe it wouldn't ring.

And so they had sex, though not the ordinary kind, but the kind a woman, tired from walking steps, and sore from needles, and tender from soft tissue edema could have; and though more of a whisper than a scream, it was oddly satisfying for Martin.

When the shadow of death moved in, Martin and Lilly spent the first week hunkered down in one hell of a pity party. It wasn't fair. They couldn't imagine life apart. They weren't young anymore, but they weren't old enough for black-caped, scythe-bearing reapers, either. But then Lilly dreamed of her death and woke Martin at 2am to tell him it was okay.

"It wasn't scary. It didn't hurt. It wasn't quiet and warm and white like on commercials and funeral plot brochures, but it wasn't grim reaper-ish. It was less of a visual thing, more of a humming. Yeah, it was a humming. Definitely not quiet or still. Humming."

From then on Lilly attacked everything. Borrowing time gently wasn't her style.

She bought stocks. "You'll enjoy the dividends," she said. She planted cedars and sang "Evergreen" like she was Barbara Streisand. Then she began to plan for her body.

"I don't want a stranger draining my fluids," she said.

"So burn 'em."

Some thought she should've put her energy into trying to fight the cancer. Maybe so. But Lilly knew the stats. You might dance with it for an extra round, but this was a duel not a tango, and when the right number of paces had been covered, it would take its fatal shot. Not one case-study with aggressive or experimental treatments survived more than a few weeks longer than the rest.

"Four to five months tops," the oncologist said three months ago.

Martin kept his job at the phone company until Lilly called one day.

"I've got it. I know what I want done with my body. I want you to prepare it," she said.

"You want what?" Martin couldn't believe his fucking ears. "Have you been mixing your meds with beer again?"

"I'm deadly, I mean dyingly, serious." Then she made some hysterical cackling sound that she tried to pass off as a laugh. "Get it? Deathly? Dyingly?"

"That I get. It's the other I'm having a bit of a problem with."

"You know my body. You know my stretch marks, my birth marks."

Martin couldn't see through the phone but he knew she had tilted her head to the right and was holding her chin in that self-righteous position she did when preparing to argue. "I don't want some stranger undressing me and de-gassing me. I want you to."

Martin took a leave of absence that day.

"Not only is my wife dying, she's gone nuts," he told his boss.

"Come back when you're ready," they said. "Telephone bill paying data will be here when you get back."

Unlike many men, Martin didn't mind female body stuff.

He and Lilly had started out partners and been through a lot: irregular periods, tampons, infertility suppositories, vaginal sperm plugs, amniocentesis, Lamaze classes, birth, umbilical cord cutting, breast-feeding, hysterectomy, hair dye, hemorrhoids, Preparation H, and vaginal dryness.

But this was another matter altogether. What he could tolerate with a live Lilly was much different than with a dead Lilly.

He held her in his arms that night after they finished off a large stuffed-crust, double cheese pizza. That was another good thing about dying right away. You don't count calories. There's not time enough to get fat. He couldn't imagine being without her. Twenty-nine years of marriage. She was a habit but not in a bad way. Every morning after the alarm went off, they'd scratched each other's back. Then he'd get her coffee and sometimes have a quickie before the day got started good. Even after Billy was born, they kept up the routine. Now he was trying to imagine the bed without her.

"We could roast me," Lilly said after discovering suttee, the Indian tradition where the widows throw themselves on the funeral pyre of their husbands. "A regular wife kebab."

"Yes, but then you'd expect me to hop on the fire after you."

"History suggests you've never minded hopping on me before," she countered.

"History never required skin grafts." Martin knew she'd been kidding. Kinda.

"If we get you a pacemaker before we light you, you can be your own fireworks show." Lilly began to blink hard. Damn chemo.

"They explode in fire, Lilly."

"Oh."

Anything would be better than having to prepare her body. But she was serious about the whole thing.

"Please promise me," she begged.

But he couldn't. Instead he promised to think about it and research alternatives in the meantime.

"I'm not dead set yet on it," she said. She loved her morbid puns.

And so he had a little time yet to talk her out of it.

Autumn is a season for turning loose, of shifting colors, of preparing for the hardness of winter. But autumn is not, Martin thought, a season to learn basic mortician skills.

"You helped pump breast milk when I was engorged," Lilly reminded him.

"That was different. You were warm."

"But I screamed. You won't have to put up with that when I'm dead."

This wasn't going to be easy. So he humored her. He spoke with a funeral director and signed up for the Evelyn Wood speed-embalming course.

She was waiting on the front steps with a spiral bound book of 4x6 note cards after his first lesson.

"Tell me everything. I want to take notes." She tried reading some of the books herself. But a side effect of the meds was inconsistent pupil dilation. Focusing could be a chore.

"Let me just put you in the compost heap," he begged. "I won't have to go to class for that. According to this book, a body your size would take 12 years to decompose. That's a dozen years of fertilizer."

But she was insistent. Though his suggestion about freezing her was considered for the better part of a day, until she discovered some cryogenic companies charge 128,000 dollars and many have gone bankrupt. A literal pulling of the freezer plugs. Talk about a big thaw.

"It'd be hard to imagine me frigid, wouldn't it?" That time she wore a striped thong, with her mesh robe. Her body wasn't badly swollen and Martin found he liked the softness of the edema especially around her ankles. He'd always had a thing for calves and ankles and now hers were sexier.

"You're lying. You're just trying to get lucky."

"I am not. You have sexy calves."

He couldn't imagine draining the fluid out of those calves. He knew it wouldn't be like a balloon losing air. But still he couldn't help imagine her calves deflating. He ran his thumb along the curve. What would they feel like? Cold? Would she feel strange? Or like a stranger?

Once he'd fondled a stripper. It was on Bourbon Street in New Orleans, Sin City for God's sake, he reasoned, and the conference had been a bust. He and some colleagues drank too much and wound up with women in their laps. He'd thought of doing more than a little fondling, not because he was bored with Lilly or unhappy, but for no other reason than she was there, on his lap. It wasn't his morals or his conscience that stopped him. The woman fell over. Fell right off his lap onto the floor. Someone yelled, "Get her some orange juice," and as he was making his way out the door, he thought he heard the word "diabetes." He'd gone straight to the hotel room and called Lilly. It was the first time they had phone sex.

"That's one hell of a book we got," Lilly said. "Tell me about the Egyptians."

The smell of tequila lingered on the pillow. They probably smelled of sex, too. He propped against the headboard and situated the monstrous book on one side of his lap so Lilly's head could rest on the other side. Betsy, the hospice nurse, would be here soon. She was as predictable as UPS.

Martin began, "These texts are a collection of magic spells and incantations meant to change the minds of those who wish their spouses to embalm them."

"Very funny."

"Egyptians followed the processes for mummification from about 3,000 BCE until conversion to Islam 3,500 years later. A person's kaò or vital life energy needs to be reunited with its spiritual energy the baò inside the tomb. Pyramids are the largest tombs in the world with the Great Pyramid of Khufa at Giza standing 480 feet high and containing over 2,300 stone blocks."

"God, I didn't even like designing this house. Can you imagine if I had to design a tomb?"

He placed a fingertip on her temple and felt the pulse. He'd gotten into the habit of checking her vitals. She'd bitched that whole year of building. Contractors were late or didn't show. The doorknobs didn't work. The plumber had not connected the bathtub drain pipe, and the first shower dumped water onto the dining room ceiling making it bulge like a water balloon. But it had been home for two decades now. One year of hell for twenty years of heaven seemed a decent trade.

Martin actually could imagine Lilly designing her own tomb. What he couldn't imagine was her inside the tomb, a mass of dried skin over skeleton.

He skimmed some mummification facts. "The good news is that mummification-economy style—costs about $75 in current dollars."

"What do we get for that?"

"Cedar oil up the anus, a seventy-day drying out period, and a generous covering of Natron, a sodium carbonate compound. But you don't get the cloth covering or any other amenities like you do in the $1200 package. The $1200 pkg. includes aromatic herbs, myrrh, organ preservation, cosmetics and/or hot pitch. But if you'd like the economy package, I suppose I could glue some sheets onto you and sprinkle you with some oregano for a nominal fee."

He waited for her comment. But she was asleep.

He closed *Book of the Dead* and stared at her. Her brown hair was flecked with gray now that Miss Clairol seemed a waste of time. He'd always admired her skin, a smoothness covered in very fine almost invisible fuzz. It was so slight Martin doubted she even knew the fuzz existed.

What would happen to the hair at death? he wondered. Hair was supposed to be dead anyway. Maybe nothing happened at all.

He'd read everything he could about the history of death rituals. How the Neanderthals attempted to cure it by surrounding corpses with thistles, cornflower, grape hyacinths, and hollyhocks—all medicinal more than decorative flowers. How bears, perhaps because of their ritual hibernation, figured significantly into early resting places. One bear skull was found with a thigh bone thrust through its eye socket.

Martin wondered at the body, some called it the temple of the holy ghost. He nor Lilly had been particularly religious, but Billy, their only child, had become so in college.

Billy would pray for his mother no doubt, and want to anoint her with oil—on her skin not in her anus—when he got home. He would expect healing, not drying out. He would chastise them for their lack of faith, and that's why they hadn't called Billy yet.

"If you'll get saved, you'll be born again."

But Martin could only think that being born again would mean having to die again. Once seemed more than enough.

But prayer to Whomever might be listening seemed right enough. He'd been asking for guidance every night for weeks. It was a simple request.

"Please lead us on this journey in the right direction." Sometimes he repeated it. Then, when he discovered that the Latin origin for 'funeral' meant a torchlight procession, a way for the living to help the dead find their way to the next world, he added "and give us light along the way."

He was dozing when he heard the hospice van's brakes. They squawked like a flock of crows. The first time he'd met Betsy she'd apologized and admitted she needed new brakes. Martin had helped her carry the bags of supplies into the house and offered her a coupon from Triple AAA for 20% off a brake job at any participating mechanic. Betsy, not much older than Billy, squealed like she won a lottery and thanked Martin over and over. But two and a half months later her brakes still squeaked. Martin didn't ask, and Betsy never mentioned it again.

Betsy let herself inside. Their policy: Why lock doors when the intruder has already invaded?

And she made her way up the steps as she did each day, bringing a bag of nutrients to be plugged into a vein. The contents looked more like runny vanilla pudding than 2,000 calories of sustenance. The doctors assumed that Lilly wasn't eating. Betsy pushed the bedroom door open.

Martin pointed at Lilly, rhythmically breathing and mouthed "sleeping." Betsy tiptoed over automatically scanning all exposed parts of Lilly. Her arms were a little more swollen today than yesterday but not bad. She was bruising on her neck, a little odd, but her respiration sounded better.

"Has she walked the stairs?" Betsy whispered.

Martin nodded yes. And held up two fingers. Betsy wrote something down in her notebook and opened the portable plastic drawers that Martin had bought at Let's Get Organized. He'd dubbed it Pandora's box.

"Time for the leeches?" Lilly asked.

She didn't move, didn't open her eyes, barely changed her breathing pattern.

"We were trying not to wake you," Betsy said.

"You failed."

"How you feeling?" Betsy readied her pen for more notes.

"My temp's 97.9. I haven't urinated in twelve hours. I'd love a rib-eye but had tequila instead. If I opened my eyes, I'd see four of you." She took a breath and rolled her arm over to expose a vein. "Ready for injection, sir."

Betsy opened the gloves and the needle.

"Oh," Lilly added, "and the neck—it's a hickey, not edemic bruising."

Betsy laughed out loud at this. "Shall I double the vitamins or add a bottle of ginseng?"

"No," Martin said, crossing himself. "Unless you give me some Viagra. I can hardly keep up now."

Betsy did her nurse thing, draining Lilly's bladder and feeding her. She took some measurements and made more notes. Martin nor Lilly moved. "Same time, same place tomorrow?" Betsy asked on her way out.

"What are my other choices?"

"I could be early. We could do you on the sofa. Or maybe the recliner."

"Stop. Stop. You're exciting me."

"I do what I can." Betsy winked. "Why don't you see if you can get your wife to pee?" The brakes squawked their way out of the driveway.

Martin had a test that afternoon: embalming 101, the first real hands-on draining experience. He ticked off some facts that might be on the written portion of the exam:

1. Embalming table—stainless or porcelain. Lay body out, strip, return valuables, if any, to family.

2. Disinfect—spray or spread solution over the body to kill insects maggots, mites. Also reduces odor.

3. Nasal suction—a-sucking we will go, a-sucking we will go, hi ho embalming-o, a-sucking we will go. Lilly laughed at this.

4. Lift head. Glue fingers together. Wash and dress hair. Remove blood spots. Lilly was surprised at the glue.

5. Must have mouth formers, trocar buttons to fill body holes, eye caps, and trocar needles to remove body fluid, and inject embalming fluid.

6. Sew mouth closed, may use barbed wire in gums if necessary.

7. Types of embalming fluid— a.) Arterial for blood vessels b.) Cavity, abdomen and chest c.) Hypodermic under skin d.) Surface.

"**You** should ace the test," Lilly said.

She held up her hand for Martin to help her out of bed. "I think I'll change into something without spots."

"Need help?"

Lilly hated needing help. Why did he have to ask. Why couldn't he just help her without giving her a choice?

"No, I'll do it. It'll give me something to do this afternoon. The way I feel, it may take the rest of the day to change. I think you wore me out.

Maybe I'll have enough energy to fill the suet boxes. Have you noticed that scraggily cardinal has come into his own now that I've added some fat to the suet? He's all plump and a deeper crimson than the others."

Martin pulled her close and kissed her forehead. Inside was the brain, not worth preserving according to the ancient Egyptians, like the liver and heart were.

He wanted to ask what she was thinking. Was she getting scared? How much of her act was forced bravado? Did she really want him to embalm her? Should he call Billy now?

Instead he lifted her off her feet. "When I get back, I'll make you a nice little chemo cocktail. If you're a good girl, I'll put a fancy little umbrella in it."

Lilly had agreed to the chemotherapy because it was a way for researchers to monitor the rate her organs were melting. Not any other kind of cancer melted the internal organs like wax. But she was lucky enough to come down with that particular kind. That and the fact that this type of chemo wouldn't make her lose her hair were the reasons she agreed to it. Dying should not be done bald.

She went outside into the autumn air, still wearing her robe. The temperature was seventy-something, somewhat pleasant even in next to nothing. The leaves were shifting to reds and oranges. She'd never known the names of all the trees in her own back yard. She knew the pecan and pines, and that mimosa back at the edge by the fence, but the large oak-looking one was a mystery. She wasn't far enough south for live oaks. But somehow a live oak dripping with moss seemed like it belonged in her back yard. She hadn't noticed the dogwood until now. It was a flaming red as though each leaf had burst and was bleeding from the inside. She wasn't red, but she was oozing from the inside out.

She pulled a leaf from it and rolled it between her fingers. It would've fallen eventually, she reasoned. It was surprisingly tender, slightly cool. She put it in her pocket and walked around to the front yard.

She got the mail from the box. Billy wrote once a week from Johannesburg, and his tales of his Peace Corps work always excited Lilly. This time he noted the hospital had been completed and that he met a girl whose appendix had burst. "She's got the greenest eyes I've ever seen," he said. He wished both Lilly and Martin well, and promised to see them over Christmas break if possible. He might bring the green-eyed girl.

Dying wasn't exactly the best time to meet people. What would Lilly say? I usually don't look this way. I'm not at my best? And you thought death warmed over was bad, but see how bad death warming up looks? But still, I'm so pleased to meet you. You look lovely, so alive.

She started to write back, but the pen felt heavy and she couldn't focus for long enough anyway. Maybe she could do it tomorrow. If there was a tomorrow. Or she would get Martin to when he got home. Billy was her son, her only child. She loved him more than anything in the world and yet she couldn't write to him now. She wondered why sometimes, and sometimes she didn't wonder at all. She was growing tired of wondering things. And tired of trying to milk each moment in frenzied desperation.

Time, she scribbled, *comes from a place inside, an unseen river flowing out. Some say it is measured by the heart. Some say by the clock, some say the rhythms of the moon. But no one thinks to measure the weight of time, the leaden ways each day fills our bodies with life's heavy breath that we must exhale to make room for the next.*

She drew a line through it and started again. These words were coming without having to focus and without effort.

She continued. *In the sea, waves lap themselves into foamy oblivion, not worrying about land or depth or sky. And this is where time ends, but like the sea we don't know where it starts.* She began to scratch through this, too, but shivered. Her bladder was filling. She should try and pee. She ripped the paper to shreds and dropped them in the toilet before she sat down. The white turned to blue as the ink bled. She steadied herself and sat on the toilet for awhile, but nothing came out, only a burning inside.

Her fingernails were bluing around the cuticles. A sign that her oxygen was inefficient. Remediation was easy: some plastic tubing in her nose and a flip of the O$_2$ tank. But today she opted to wait a bit. The blue seemed a pleasant shade after all.

Her breaths grew heavier, like someone sat on her chest, and they sounded weird like a shop vac or something, but they never hurt. She soon grew dizzy and liked the feeling. It was a little like being on the tilt a whirl at the state fair. That's when Martin came in. She was laying on the floor beside the couch.

"My God, Lilly." He screamed, "Lilly! Wake up!" and he made quick work of the oxygen tank and soon everything quit spinning. "What happened? You scared me to death, Lilly."

"Pun intended?" she asked.

And then from nowhere, he slapped her across the face. He had never struck anyone. The blow was hard and jerked Lilly's neck.

Neither could believe it. Afterwards his hand stopped mid-air, as if to jump off his arm and run. Martin wanted to apologize. He wanted to cry. But mostly he wanted to do it again.

He'd dropped the books when he saw her on the sofa, sprawled and white. So he gathered them and put them on the tv.

"I learned about premature burial today. Did you know an 1897 patent featured a tube from the coffin that extended to the ground's surface and was attached to a ball on the supposed corpse's chest? If the person breathed, the chest moved the spring-loaded ball and would be released and let light and air in the coffin. Above ground, a flag would appear, bells would sound, and a lamp would light. Professional mortuaries came about in part due to premature burials. They were holding tanks where living clients had the chance to make themselves known as living before put in the ground."

Lilly rose from the couch. Across her face was a bright red mark. He was rambling. She took Martin's hand, the one he'd hit her with, and kissed it. "Promise me you'll prepare my body for burial?"

It wasn't so much a question as an offer, a trade for absolution. Now he felt he owed her.

"I promise."

"Look at me and say it."

He looked into the same eyes he'd been looking into for 29 years. The red mark seemed to scream "fucking jerk" as it spread across her face. "Bitch" was lolling around in his head and he pushed it away, afraid that he would scream it. Everything seemed to be screaming in the quietness. It made his head hurt. He loved her. More than anything.

"Say it. Say it to me. I haven't asked for anything else. Say it, Martin."

He wanted to say so many things now, but they were things that couldn't be said.

"I promise."

She was staring straight through his eyeball to his brain. She knew him so well.

It made his brain hurt and he began to babble about stuff that she tuned out. She'd gotten what she wanted. Or maybe it wasn't what she wanted so much as what she needed. The noise layered itself in the air like insulation so that Lilly felt cozy. Martin took a breath and then walked out the door. To live in the same house as death was fucking exhausting him. He got in the car, sure that he would never come back. But he didn't turn the key, he just sat there staring at the wheel and seeing her all white and sprawled on the floor. Maybe it wasn't the shadow of death he was having trouble with, but the valley of the shadow of death. This valley went deeper as the shadows lengthened across his understanding of life. It was a depth he feared had no end.

Lilly was in the kitchen. She'd poured two glasses of tequila.

"Here," was all she said when she handed it to him. The next day they hardly spoke. Martin couldn't find any words. He fell asleep on the couch and Lilly didn't wake him when she went to bed. At a time when time was thinning, he lost two whole days. This proved he was a jerk, he told himself. When Betsy came the next day, Martin was still on the couch.

"Lilly upstairs?"

"I guess," he said. "I hit her." He said it while he was looking up at Betsy but not seeing her. Instead he saw himself as she must see him: a pathetic excuse for a man.

She studied his face. There were new lines. "I've been doing this for three years. I see people dying everyday. And I see those that are being left."

"I don't think you heard me. I hit her."

"Muhammad Ali you're not. Don't do it again. But don't beat yourself up either."

Later Lilly went for a walk, and he left for mortuary science. He sat and watched the others with their cadavers. Today he didn't even wear a nose clamp. He could barely feel, much less smell. Everyone knew why he was here. Everyone had agreed it was a tough request to fill, but everyone had volunteered to help when the time came. He could get through it they promised.

The funeral home director, Scott, sat beside him. He had his funeral home suit on and his funeral home smile to match. The smile was meant to be reassuring and peaceful but it always looked evil to Martin.

"I've got a 70 year old woman we picked up today. You want to come back and I'll walk you through a real embalming?" Not only did Martin accept, he found it easy. It wasn't a person; it was a corpse.

"Easy now," Scott said a couple of times. "She's not china, but she's not Tupperware, either." A baby doll seemed more human than a dead human body. It was so easy in fact he found himself enjoying it. Right down to gluing the fingers together and choosing the lipstick color for her. Riveting Red for all eternity.

"Lilly, I did it," he called as he ran in. "I embalmed someone. A real corpse."

Lilly was on the couch with her oxygen. She smiled. "How was it?"

"It wasn't bad. It was okay."

They ordered Chinese to celebrate and Lilly pretended to eat.

"I want to make love," he said. It'd been three days since they had, the longest they'd gone without sex since the diagnosis. Lilly nodded okay and they managed, but this time was tougher. Lilly couldn't get her legs comfortable. They ran out of lubricant. And she gasped until they had to hook her up to the oxygen tank via the plastic tubing. An orgasm for her was out of the question.

They cracked the fortune cookies and set fire to the fortunes.

"Mine probably said, 'Victoria's Secret will add plastic tubing to catalog. Sexiest accessory of the season.'"

God he loved her. He loved her so much he was hating her.

They slept together for a few hours on the couch. When Martin woke, he didn't know anything was wrong. She was warm and he carefully and quietly went into the kitchen without taking her pulse. It was midnight, the edge of another day.

Martin went to bed upstairs and woke to the mid-morning squawking of hospice van brakes.

"Martin," Betsy called. "Martin! It's Lilly."

Martin knew without having to be told. All he could think about was the impending signs of death listed on the hospice pamphlet. She didn't give any signs that she was dying. She seemed fine after sex, restful, so he left her alone so she could sleep. Or maybe he left her alone so he could sleep.

"She's dead," Betsy said as he came down the steps.

"She was breathing okay," he said. "She was socially aware. She was coherent and her vitals were stable." Betsy nodded after each one.

"Why didn't I know it was coming?"

"You knew. You just didn't know when it would arrive. We can't know that, Martin. We can know death's on its way, that it's near, but that's all we can know. Death is a thief and it steals when it chooses to." She sounded wise and stupid at the same time. This felt comforting.

"Have you decided what to do with the body?"

"I've got to contact Billy."

"Then what?" Betsy asked.

Martin sat down to cry but nothing came out.

Betsy began to dump pills down the sink, and mark x's on bottles in boxes, and chart copious notes.

"She wanted a regular funeral, and she wanted me to prepare the body."

Betsy nodded. She knew these things.

She finished the medication disposal. "I've got to call the 1-800 number." She propped a pillow under Lilly's chin to keep her mouth closed. The jaw muscle had let loose already and her mouth was slowly sagging. It was weird to see Lilly's mouth dangle beneath her ears.

Martin picked up Lilly's hand and counted the fingers. "We'll glue 'em you know. Did you know morticians glue the fingers together?"

"I didn't know that. I do know that you've been remarkable through this. You know that don't you?"

The tears finally came.

"She was lucky. She was an incredible woman. You are an incredible man."

"There must've been something else I could've done."

"No, Martin. There comes a time when the only thing you can do is let them go. We have a saying, those of us who do hospice: The living have needs. The dead don't. They don't need a thing, Martin. You, though, you are alive. What do you need?"

He was touching Lilly's lips now. They could be sewn or glued. Probably hot glue would be better. He doubted he'd use barbed wire in her gums.

Betsy went back to packing more stuff up and taking it to her van. She gathered unused Foleys, tubing, needles, gloves, gauze, alcohol preps, suction tips.

"I've got to honor her wishes."

"Martin, what you've got to do is honor yourself. The funeral home will be here soon."

Betsy left, but Martin didn't hear her brakes. He sat beside Lilly. This was too sudden. She didn't give him any warning. How could she not warn him?

They'd load her on the gurney and cover her with a faux fur blanket. Farro Funeral Home would be stitched on the side in gold, and someone, maybe Scott, would be in his suit with his funeral home smile.

Martin took the pillow out from under Lilly's chin and let her mouth fall open. He leaned over and kissed her. Her mouth was surprisingly warm. Bodies drop a degree an hour under regular circumstances. Within eight hours, the post-mortem stain, where the red blood cells sink to the lowest part of the body, would set in. Everything was loose now, muscles, tendons, skin. In two hours, the tightening would start. The cold hardness would follow and the body's autumn would turn to winter. But she wasn't just a corpse. No matter how many facts he spewed, she was Lilly. Cold and dead.

The fat cardinal sang outside the window as the hearse drove up.

"You coming to the home soon?" Scott asked. The fat cardinal wouldn't shut the fuck up.

"Yeah, I've got to call my son and get a few things done. Then I'll be on down."

"I'm so sorry, man. So sorry." He smiled. "But you can do this. We'll help you get through, man." Martin waved bye and then threw his shoe as hard as he could at the birdfeeder. The cardinal flew to the dogwood and seemed to disappear.

Martin prayed again for guidance but before he said amen he knew he would need to pray for forgiveness. He could embalm. He proved that yesterday. He'd promised her he would prepare her, and he hadn't meant to lie. He'd never betrayed Lilly, not once in all the years, and now he was thinking he might. It was an odd feeling, almost like some load had been lifted. He'd vowed 'til death do us part. And he'd meant it. But they were parted now. Part of him was gone. He knew this. But the strange thing was figuring out what part remained.

Perhaps he'd have her cremated and scatter the ashes by the birdfeeder. He retrieved his shoe and went upstairs to get *Book of the Dead*. In it was a slip of yellow paper torn from a legal pad. He imagined finding the words "I forgive you" in her hand writing. But all it said was "Add fat to the suet." He picked up the spotted robe. Maybe she would wear that while she was being cremated. Would they insist she be naked? She would hate that. He'd pay extra for them to keep her clothed. What would she want to wear? He wadded the robe up to bury his face in her smell and found the leaf in the pocket. Surely this meant something. But all Martin knew was he'd never seen anything redder.

Mike Burrell

Making It

"**You're** not gonna make it," he said, looking up from the crinkled folder he held in those soft, stubby fingers of his. He smiled when he saw that I had jumped at the sound of his voice. I wanted to tell him that he didn't scare me. Not this squat little dump of a dude. But the truth was, he did scare me.

He had called me into his office and let me stand behind the chair in front of his desk for what seemed like an hour, but was probably just three or four minutes. It was long enough for me to start itching, and shifting my weight from one foot to the other. Then I rested my hands on the back of a chair, raising up high on my toes while he flipped through the pages in the folder and pretended to ignore me.

He looked pretty busy, thumbing through my folder with jerky little movements, papers scattered across his desk. But after looking at the papers I realized they had been there for a while because they had that kind of a settled in look, like dirty sheets on an unmade bed. The black frames holding the seal of the State of Alabama and the dork's diploma from UAB were all crooked, making me think for a second the room was tilted.

His pale scalp shone between thin strands of graying black hair combed in straight rows and sprayed stiff as wires across his head. A brown spot the size of my thumb peeked through a crease in his comb-over. It was probably just a birthmark or a mole or something, but I was standing there wishing it would move around some when his sharp voice cracked through the hum of the flickering light overhead. "You're not gonna make it." That's why I jumped.

"I hope you weren't expecting some bleeding heart social worker type who tries to sugar-coat everything," he said and then paused, his lower lip wrapping over his upper lip, looking at me with squinty little brown eyes. Then he poked his chest with his stubby thumb. "I'm the kinda guy who believes in telling it like it is.

"You know passing a drug test is a condition of your probation, don't you?"

I nodded, my heart gaining a few beats, remembering that just before court I had eaten the last four Lortabs left over from my recent prescription-writing career.

"I'm gonna let you slide today. One day, when you're sitting around Donaldson Correctional Facility, you'll remember I'm the kinda guy who's tough, but I'm the kinda guy who's fair."

I was aching to tell him I'd always remember him as the kinda guy who likes to tell what kinda guy he is, but he was my probation officer. And even if he was a dork, he had me by the balls.

"Even after I give you every break in the world, you're not gonna make it. You know why?"

"Oh, I'm gonna make it, Mr. Mobley," I said, in my best ass-kissing tone, getting his name from the "A. C. Mobley," carved into a wooden nameplate among the debris on his desk.

"No, a doper like you's not gonna make it through a year of supervised probation. You know why?"

My concentration had shifted to my buzz that was leaving me, so I was a little slow at realizing he just wanted to preach. So I let him preach.

"Values," he said, his voice calming. "You know what values are?"

Now I knew he didn't want an answer, so I shrugged.

"I didn't think so," he said after sucking air through his teeth, pushing back from the desk and settling into the chair. "Everybody's got values. You've got values too—just the wrong goddamn ones. When most people talk about values they talk about faith, patriotism, hard work, honesty. The only things important to people like you are drugs and sex."

I'd been stuck in the waiting area of the probation office for a couple of slow-crawling hours after spending all morning in court. Now I was standing there listening to this pie-faced dork, feeling my buzz shrink like an ice cube in the sun. I had wondered for years where a buzz went when it was over and became convinced it left on my breath. If I didn't have to breathe, the buzz would stay forever. His tight little lips moved, and he was really getting with it, leaning forward, looking me in the eye, pointing to the paper in the file. But all I heard was blah, blah, blah as I held my breath and felt the buzz grow for a moment till I had to breathe again. Then the buzz rushed from my lips, leaving behind a gnawing itch, and a rising fear that I needed to be somewhere else.

"You all right?" he said, watching me gasping for breath.

"I'm O.K.," I said, a little louder than usual, talking over my heartbeat pounding in my ears.

"Sit down," he said. "Damn, you look like you're 'bout to pass out."

"I'll be all right," I said, dropping into the chair.

He studied my face for a moment, then continued his sermon. "There's a lot of reasons why you won't make it. The main reason is, you're stupid. The pharmacist over at Walgreen's was very complimentary, though. She says you write a good-looking prescription, but she started getting suspicious when she saw it was for a hundred Lortabs. 'Course what really raised her eyebrows was when she noticed the doctor on the script was her gynecologist." Then he tilted his head back, sending a volley of cackling laughter toward the ceiling

"No," he said, his eyes now on me, shaking his head, the cackles dissolving into chuckles, then a scowl. "If you don't get caught holding, you'll stop going for testing, and you'll forget to come around here for our regular meetings. If not that, you'll get caught selling stuff that's not yours. Even if by some miracle you pass your drug tests and you don't get busted for stealing, you still won't make it. You know why?"

I was hearing his voice, but at least half of my brain was trying to remember if I still had those ten pills I had wrapped in aluminum foil and stuffed in the pocket of my old jeans at the bottom of my bureau drawer a couple of days ago. If they were still there when I got home, I could get all mellowed out and think this shit through.

He poked his lower lip out and watched me shake my head.

"Hell, you don't believe in working. The last job you had was eight months ago at a dog kennel over in Trussville." He shook his head. "Two years of college and that's the best you can do? Boy your mama must be proud of you."

A few years ago, I would have told him to leave my mama out of it, but I've learned these bastards are going to get their licks in. The more you disagree, the longer it takes. So I sat there, catching my breath, fighting off the urge to scratch while he spelled out the conditions of my probation. "Remember," he said, pointing his finger at the probation order. "You're going to have to get a job. Being the kinda fair guy I am, I'm gonna give you thirty days. If you're not employed within that time I'm gonna recommend the judge revoke you. You know what that means, don't you?"

I nodded. I knew what it meant.

The skinny dude looking down at the blue plastic strip in his hand was shaking his head. "Positive for hydrocodone again, Mr. Clayton," he said, then he jotted something on a form attached to the clipboard in front of him.

Why hadn't I tried to kick? I was asking myself while he studied my face. I was going to, but just thinking about it got my heart racing and made me feel like running somewhere. Hell, there wasn't any sense in rushing it. Besides, guys like this liked it better when you tested positive the first couple of times. He could shake his head and tell me about self-determination, willpower and shit. Willpower. Here he was with a master's degree hanging on the wall, and all he did everyday was wait around for guys like me to come in and piss.

The main reason I hadn't kicked was because I had moved into a little apartment on Birmingham's Southside with Sandra. She was a heavy girl with mousy brown hair and front teeth that wanted to catch on her lower lip when she talked. Just watching her butt straining against the seams of that white uniform as she left the apartment in the mornings made me want to swear off chocolate cake for the rest of my life; but at night I became lost in the folds of her soft warm flesh with the help of an active imagination and the unlimited supply of hydrocodone from the hospital where she worked.

I glanced at the date on my drug test when I walked out of the office. I had been so involved in the full-time job of maintaining my buzz, I had let a month drip by without noticing it. I could put off getting clean, but I just had till tomorrow to get a job. My throat burned as a bitter taste rose in my mouth. What kind of job could I get in one day? The freezing prospect of having to get clean shot through me. Can't do it right now, I thought. I'm under too much pressure. But then my heart thumped as I remembered what Mobley said about violating my probation and the horrible picture of me as the homecoming queen at Donaldson Correctional Facility flashed before my eyes.

Sweat trickled down my forehead as I sat in my car, browsing the employment ads in the newspaper. I looked for something dealing with pets. That was the ideal gig—dump a little food out, scoop a little shit, maybe scrub a mutt down now and then. I could stay high and do that job. No, that was the wrong idea. I had to come up with a clean piss test next time. Besides, there wasn't anything to do with pets in the paper.

Everything required experience. *One year experience as an electrical engineer; Two years of progressive experience in food service management; A minimum of five years experience in pharmaceutical sales.* I looked down where the sweat had rolled off my brow and dotted the paper over an ad announcing, *Automobile sales trainee. No experience necessary. Apply in person. Quality Automotive 9863 Bessemer Superhighway.* They wouldn't hire me, all sweaty and sticky, I thought, taking a quick sniff at my underarms. But I had to try, so I started the car and backed out into the street, making the little whistling sound a boiler makes to relieve pressure.

I drove past a busy intersection with banks, restaurants and a shopping mall that looked like an oasis of prosperity among the ragged signs and used car lots along the Bessemer Superhighway. Not far from there, automobiles lay rusting in piles behind the chain-link fence of a junkyard. There were fast food joints, beer joints, seedy motels, a bowling alley, even a fortuneteller. But automobile sales was the dominant enterprise on the highway, and shiny plastic banners waved over little clusters of used cars on both sides of the road.

Some of the car lots were identified by their owner's name. Some had no names but claimed "We Finance," or offered to "Tote the Note." It looked as though I was in the right place to learn about the values Mobley had talked about; there were "Reliable Motors," "Honest Dave's Used Cars," and "Trustworthy Auto Sales." I turned into the lot with the sign that revered "Quality," parking between the "Cream Puff of the Month" and the "Fire Cracker Special."

The rusting blue trailer anchored in the center of the lot had a glass storm door and two windows in front. A tarnished air conditioner bulged from the window on the right, moaning in the August sun and pouring a stream of condensation from the overflow.

I approached the trailer, climbed the wobbly stacks of cinder block steps, then hesitated for a second on the top stack before swinging open the glass door.

The man facing the door was slumped on a worn couch with his thin legs outstretched, balancing the heels of his brown cowboy boots on the floor. His dingy gray hair was combed back flat against his scalp. Dark glasses were perched on his long nose, and a cigarette dangled from the tight crease of his lips, sending a stream of smoke back into his gaunt weathered face.

The young black man at the other end of the couch had friendly eyes, but his generous lips looked as though they had been formed into a tight sneer to keep from smiling. His head was cocked defiantly under a black baseball cap that he had turned backward. A red T-shirt revealed a slender torso and a pair of lean, muscular arms.

"Is the owner here?" I addressed the black man. The man in the dark glasses didn't appear to be taking any questions.

"Busy," he replied, pointing to the door behind the green metal desk to my right. A toilet flushed, the sound of running water gurgled through the pipes, then the door opened.

The face of the man at the door was flushed a shade darker than the fringe of carrot-colored hair that outlined his bald head. A blue golf shirt stretched across his barrel chest, straining at the seams around his thick shoulders as he walked toward me.

"I'm Doug Whisenant, call me Red." he said, wrapping a broad, freckled hand around mine and pumping like he expected me to rise up off the floor. His grip didn't hurt, but I could feel his strength. His voice was deep and friendly, and his smile was so wide I could see the fillings in his back molars. "That's Hound Dog over there," he said, freeing my hand and pointing to the thin string of a man in the dark glasses. "And that's Junior," he said, pointing to the black man.

"I'm David Clayton," I said. "I'm here about the job you had in the paper."

"Good! Good!," he said, nodding, smiling as though pleased to hear this news. "Have a seat."

"We got a hot one comin', Red," Hound Dog said in voice that sounded like it was being sifted through broken glass.

"Scuse me a minute Dave," Red said.

The storm door banged against the wall and a tall man in a T-shirt and a baseball cap charged through the doorway. "Which one of you is the owner?" he snapped.

"My name's Doug. My friends call me Red," Red said, holding out his hand. "I remember you. Leon, ain't it?"

"Yeah, you the owner?"

"Well, I'm the manager. See, Quality Automotive is a corporation. It's kinda like you go over to U.S. Steel. You ain't gonna find the owner over there. You see what I mean?"

"You were here when this old bastard sold me a car," the man said, pointing an angry finger at Hound Dog.

"Wait just a minute, Leon," Red interrupted. "I got a picture of my mama in my pocket. You wouldn't wonna disrespect a feller's mama with a bunch of cussin' would you?"

"No, sho' wouldn't," Leon said.

"Well set down 'ere, Leon." Red said, dropping into the chair behind his desk, the smile never fading. "When I saw you walk in the door, I said to myself, 'They's somp'm botherin' that feller.'"

"They's something bothering me all right," Leon said, easing into a chair in front of Red's desk.

"See! I been in bidness a long time, and I can tell when somp'm's botherin' a feller. How's that little Dodge Dart you bought from us? Bet you really proud of that thang."

"That's what I come in here for. That man over there," he said pointing to Hound Dog again, "told me it was a local car. That thing was eat up with rust."

"What?" Red bellowed.

Hound Dog stood and walked over to Red's desk. "It was rusty?" he growled.

"All the way through to the door panels," Leon said.

Junior walked into the bathroom.

"This makes me so mad, I could spit," Red said, pounding the desk.

Hound Dog's face was as somber as death. "Who'd we buy that Dodge from, Red?" he asked.

"We bought it from that preacher from Tuscaloosa. He told me that car never been outa Alabama," Red said, shaking his head. "Leon, I want you to know, we at Quality Automotive 'preciate this information. We know now not to ever buy another car from that preacher. If they's ever anythang we can do for you, just come by and see us."

Red stood, but Leon didn't budge. "Anythang else we can do for you?"

"Well," Leon said, "Can't I get my money back?"

Red looked as though his heart had been broken. I thought for a second he was going to cry. "You know, Leon," he said, "I'm just the manager here. I ain't authorized to give nobody money back. Hell, I'm the one got lied to by that preacher. The board of directors probably gonna fire me for buyin' that thang in the first place. Wors'n that, it's the kinda thang makes you lose your faith in mankind. I mean, this hurts. It hurts bad. I just wish they's somp'm somebody could do to help both of us."

"You know, Red," Hound Dog said, easing stiff-legged around the desk, now standing beside Leon. "They's a way we could help Leon, and make all of us feel better at the same time."

"How's that, Hound Dog?"

Hound Dog rested a hand on Leon's shoulder. "We could give ol' Leon a real good deal on some quality transportation."

"You know, Hound Dog, we could do that. Tell you what, you take Leon out there, let him pick out anythang he wants. Twenty-five percent off."

"You mean any car on the lot, Red?" Hound Dog asked, his voice rising, his mouth gaped open.

"Anythang ol' Leon wants. Shoot, I might git in trouble with corporate headquarters, but I always heard you could git forgiveness easier'n you can git permission."

"Let's go on out there, Leon," Hound Dog said, patting Leon's shoulder, "before Red changes his mind."

"I appreciate it, Red." Leon said, walking out the door with Hound Dog.

When the storm door shut, Junior came out of the bathroom laughing.

"Junior, I thought I was gonna hafta kick your ass." Red said, smiling.

"Shit! Dog look over at me, I almost bust. I ain't bullshittin' you."

Red stood at the window, smiling. "Com'ere Dave," he said, crooking his finger.

When I got to the window he put his hand on my shoulder. "Right now Hound Dog's tellin' Leon that I've been hittin' the bottle a little, and he thinks he can git him another ten percent off. Ol' Leon wouldn't know ten percent from a hog's ass."

"You need to cut it out, Red." Junior said, shaking with laughter and wiping tears from his eyes.

Red walked around his desk, sitting down in the ragged swivel chair. "Have a seat, Dave," he said, still smiling. He turned toward Junior, who had settled back down on the couch. "Junior," he said, "I know you need to git up off your dead ass an' quieten that Buick down we got at the sale last night."

Junior stood, scowling.

"You gonna learn a lot about sellin' from Hound Dog, Dave. Ol' Hound Dog can turn 'em loose, can't he Junior?"

Junior walked close to my chair, regarding me with narrowed eyes. "Dog a sellin' mothafucka," he said, giving his head a quick twist, then he turned and strutted toward the door.

Red opened one of the desk drawers, pulled out a pint bottle of whiskey and unscrewed the top. "I ain't bullshittin' you, Dave, that boy right there is a artist with a junk automobile. And he's right about Hound Dog. He can sell ever' car I can drag on this lot. If it looks like a car, Hound Dog'll put it on some sumbitch. Wonna drank?"

"No, I don't drink," I said, still trying to catch my breath from what I'd just seen. "Have I got the job?"

"Yeah," he said. Then he raised the bottle to his lips, sending bubbles gurgling upward. "Whew," he said as he put the top back on the bottle and placed it in the desk drawer. "Tell you the truth, I had that ad in the paper for three months, and you the first one to come by. Ever sold anythang?"

"Some," I said, shrugging.

"How 'bout cars?"

"No," I said. "No cars."

"Cars is different. Even this junk we sell got a big price on it next to most stuff folks buy. Customer takes a look at it, scares him to death. Takes a special feller to unload a car. Takes a better one to unload a bunch of 'em. It'd be good if you could learn to sell a car, but it ain't necessary. Sometimes we have two or three folks on the lot, and as good as Hound Dog is, he can't take care of but one at a time. I'd want you to try to sell 'em, but if you can't sell 'em, hold on to 'em till Hound Dog can git there. Wonna give it a shot?"

"I sure do," I said, thinking I might hold on long enough till I could find a kennel somewhere with an opening.

After a month I was still itching, but it wasn't as bad as before. I took a few hits out of Red's bottle when I got that running feeling too bad, and started keeping a bottle of my own in the car and one at home. Mobley was blown away by my steady employment and clean urine tests—or almost clean. "You showed positive for alcohol," he said. "Hell, I won't sweat that. I have a beer or two myself every now and then. But this won't last," he said, leaning back in the chair. "You'll fuck up. You just don't have it in you to make it all the way."

I was getting nervous over my inability to sell a car. I got along well with the customers who came on the lot, but I just couldn't get one inside the trailer to sign. Red didn't seem to care. "You're doing fine, Dave," he said, patting my shoulder. "You'll catch on to it one of these days."

Red would walk out on the lot to sell a car every now and then, but most of his time was spent trying to find cars. He had cars hauled in from Chicago and New Orleans and attended every auction for miles around, but he could barely keep ahead of Hound Dog, who was selling every one of them. As Red said, he could "turn 'em loose."

Hound Dog would slouch on the end of the couch, his legs straight, supported by the worn heels of the same old brown boots he wore every day. He would rise occasionally to go the bathroom or to the percolator behind Red's desk where he would fill his cup with thick, black coffee that smelled like a burning truck tire. The only sounds he would make for hours would be a hacking cough and the click of his big Zippo as he lit another cigarette.

Hound Dog shook his head at most of the people he saw through his dark glasses. "Goddamn tire kickers," he would growl. But when he saw a prospect, he resembled a cheetah that had spotted a wounded gazelle in the middle of a herd. He would lean forward, his hands resting on his knees, following some movement or expression that years of selling cars had taught him to recognize. When he saw what he was looking for, he would fix a smile on his face and descend upon the lot. In a while, he would return with the customer, talking to him or her as though he had known the person all of his life, and make that customer the proud owner of a Quality Automotive car.

"Gotcha a goodun," he would tell them, patting them on the back. When they left, he would pop a cigarette between his thin lips, light it with a flick of the big Zippo, and resume his place at the end of the couch.

Two weeks into October, the weather became mild enough to turn off the air conditioner and open the windows to the office trailer. The air from the Bessemer Superhighway wasn't fresh, but it was pristine compared to that of Quality Automotive.

Red, Junior and Hound Dog made me feel as though I had been at Quality Automotive forever. Junior had shortened my name to "D." Hound Dog nodded at me in the morning on his way to the coffee pot. "How's it hangin', Hoss?" he would growl, looking at me over the dark glasses.

When Red had time he would lean back in his chair, taking long pulls at the bottle he kept in his desk drawer while lecturing me on the art of selling. "All kindsa thangs can happen after you sell a car, Dave. Believe me, I've seen it all. Had radiators boil over; wheels come off. Had one drive off the lot and the transmission fell out of it, right out there on the highway. Remember that one, Junior?"

"I remember, Red."

Red shook his head. "Had traffic jammed up all the way to Brighton. But you don't worry 'bout none of that, Dave. Your job is to sell. I'll guarant-damn-tee-you, you set around worrying 'bout consequences and you'll never get anywhere in this world. You damn sure won't sell a car."

I nodded, watching him turn the bottle to his lips. When he put the bottle down he said, "Dave, did I tell you 'bout Hound Dog sellin' that little Chevy Malibu to this big sumbitch?"

"I don't believe you did, Red."

"It was beautiful, Dave." he said, his eyes crinkling into little crow's feet at the corners. "When Hound Dog brought him in here to sign the bill of sale an' git the title transferred, he turned to Hound Dog and asked, 'Now, this car don't burn no oil, does it?' Hound Dog can git this serious look on his face. You'd thank he was 'bout to tell you your mama had cancer of the heart or somp'm. Hound Dog looks him in the eye and tells him, 'Mister, I'll drank ever' drop of oil this car'll burn.'

"Next week the big sumbitch come tearin' in here in a pickup truck. Hound Dog saw him comin' and hauled ass out the back. He busted in with a case a oil on his shoulder yellin', 'Where's that old bastard said he'd drank ever' drop of oil that piece a shit he sold me'd burn?' Me an' Junior was 'bout rollin' on the floor, wadn't we, Junior?"

Red and Junior were doubled over, laughing. I found myself joining them, thinking of the stiff old man running for his life.

"**I don't** believe it." Mobley said when he glanced up from my latest drug test report. "Eight negative tests in a row. You still got a job. Come in here wearing a tie. You know, Clayton, you're making some progress here. But you got a long way to go."

I did have a long way to go. I still had the itch every now and then and would catch myself being scared for no reason at all. Deep breaths and a hard slug of vodka seemed to help.

The real problem now was Sandra. I knew as long as I was staying with her I could have Lortabs anytime I wanted. Stealing from the hospital had made her feel guilty at first, but she had gotten used to the extra money I gave her from selling the pills I couldn't eat. Every night or so she would ask, "Could I get you some Lortabs, baby?"

"I'm trying to kick, Sandra," I scolded.

"I'm talking about selling them," she said. "We got oxycontin. You could get some big money for that."

"Goddamn, Sandra," I yelled. "I don't want to get caught holding. I'm under a three year sentence. I get caught blowing my nose wrong, I'm gone."

I'll admit I had just stayed with her because of the dope, but I started getting this raw feeling inside, knowing I had to cut her loose. She had started to lose weight for me and said she could get braces to straighten her teeth if I would sell some more pills. When she lost twenty pounds, she celebrated by buying new clothes.

She danced from the bedroom one day, modeling a pair of jeans. "Look at this," she said, turning with her hands on her shrunken waist, emphasizing the soft curves of her hips. "I haven't worn jeans in years."

"I'm leaving," I said, turning from her before I could change my mind.

It got real ugly, with her calling me a shiftless doper and a sleazy used car salesman, and me saying something about humping a mountain of Jell-O. She was still pissed at me when they caught her the next week leaving the hospital with 500 Lortabs.

"**I'm** sorry about this, Red," I said, feeling like crawling under the couch and curling up with the dust balls when the cops came to the lot for me.

Red put his arm around my shoulder and turned me away from the officers waiting at the door. "Dave," he said, "you got a job at Quality Automotive as long as you want it."

"I appreciate it Red, but it'll probably be a long time before I can come back."

"What makes you say that?"

"Well, I mean, what can I do? I'm sure Sandra's going to say that she stole dope and I sold it."

"Dave, I'll tell you what you can do—deny it."

"Deny it?"

"That's right. If they accuse you of eatin' a horse and you got his tail hangin' out of your mouth—by God, deny it."

The cops let me cool my heels in a cell for a couple of hours. Then they came at me pretty hard, especially the short one in the green T-shirt and the ratty jeans. He had this long brown hair, all slicked back and pulled into a pony-tail with a rubber band. Every time he strutted by the mirrored window on the wall, he would flash a little smile at his reflection and flex his muscles.

"Sure you don't want a lawyer?" he said.

"What do I need a lawyer for? I'd just have to tell him the same thing I'm telling you. I haven't done anything wrong."

"You know Sandra Willis?" he said.

"Yes, sir. I know her. Used to live with her."

"She stole dope for you, didn't she?"

"No, sir!" I said in bullshit surprise. "I don't believe that girl would do such a thing. She's a nurse, you know, at a hospital. She helps people."

"Yeah, she helped you with a shit-load of Lortabs."

"Not me," I said.

"Not you?" he said, chuckling, a smirk twisting his lips. "You didn't think anybody at the hospital ever counted that shit, did you? Listen, Clayton, we been watching you. We know you been slinging Lortabs out of that apartment ever since you hooked up with Miss Tons of Fun."

"If you've been watching me, you've seen me go to work six days a week. You've seen me go for drug-testing every Friday. Officer, I'm a recovering drug addict. I can't even be around that stuff without taking it. I'll take any drug test you want me to take. You'll see I'm clean."

He shook his head, checking his profile in the mirrored window out of the corner of his eye. "Not going to work, Clayton. Not only have we been watching you, but your girl friend ratted you out. She said you got her to steal dope for you. Said she never did anything wrong till she ran into your sorry ass."

"When I broke up with her she took it pretty hard," I said. "She said she was going to do something to hurt me. I didn't think she would go this far. She could go to jail for this, couldn't she?"

They turned me loose about nine that night without charging me. So I stopped off for a couple of beers to celebrate getting out and wound up dragging back to my apartment around three the next morning. I woke to the buzzing of the telephone and looked down at my ankles propped on the arm rest of the couch, the toes of my shoes hiked toward the ceiling. When I swung my legs around and raised up off the couch, I felt the room spin and had to stop for a second before I could reach for the phone.

"D?" Junior's voice danced in my ear. "Shit! Man, I been callin' all over. We thought they still had you up in that jail."

I felt "No," come growling up from my throat. "They let me go."

"You gotta come down here, man," he said.

"What's wrong?"

"I tell you when you get here."

Junior was pacing the floor when I got to the trailer.

"What's wrong, Junior?" I asked.

"The Dog had a heart attack."

"What?"

"He 'bout to sell that little Buick. Customer in the office gonna sign when Dog start grabbin' his chest. The Dog somp'm else. I mean, you shoulda seen him, D. He regular closin' on that mothafucka, same time chokin', turnin' purple and shit. Customer trip out and hauled ass, Dog motionin' for him to come back. Trip me out, too. Shit!"

"How is he?"

"Red say he gon' be all right. I wanna go see him, but we got Millican comin' in with a couple cars from Chicago. Can you stay here and get the keys from Millican, D?"

"Yeah," I said, plopping down in Hound Dog's place on the couch. "I think I can do that. It's about all I can do. Tell the Dog I asked how it was hanging."

Junior smiled and opened the door, then he turned and looked down at me. "Hey D."

"Yeah."

"When you get the keys from Millican, lock up and go home, man," he said, giving me a quick smile. "You look like shit."

I slouched there for a while, legs outstretched, feet resting on my heels, watching the traffic on the highway through the glass door. A white Ford Taurus slowed down and pulled onto the lot.

Mobley got out of the Taurus and had started toward the office when he became distracted by the blue Pontiac Bonneville Junior had dubbed "a major piece of shit." I had heard him tell Hound Dog he would have to sell the car before November because the oil required to keep it from smoking and to silence the valves was so thick the engine wouldn't turn over on a cold day.

Mobley walked around the car, testing the doors and kicking the tires before turning toward the office.

I sat up straight when he pushed the door open.

"I came here to tell you that you came that close to going down the road," he said, holding his finger and thumb close together.

"Somebody was telling lies on me," I said.

"Sure they were. You put that girl up to stealing dope for you. When they corroborate her statement and charge you, the judge'll violate you, and you'll be doing three years, just like that," he said, snapping his fingers.

"I'm sorry you feel that way, Mr. Mobley. I understand, though, with my record and all. You may not believe this, but at times like this, I'm glad you're my probation officer."

"Bullshit," Mobley said, shaking his head.

"Yeah, it's true," I said, pushing myself to my feet. "You're just the kind of probation officer a guy like me needs. I mean you're tough, there's no doubt about that. But I know when all the facts are in, you're going to be fair, give me all the breaks. Somebody outside your office asked me the other day what to expect from you, and I told him you were tough but fair. Those were the exact words I used."

"I am fair," he said, his lips straining against the smile that was trying to form.

"I know you are. I know you say a lot of tough things about how I'm not gonna make it and all. But I believe you hope I do make it."

"I'm always glad to see a guy turn it around," he said, shrugging and glancing toward the floor, a hint of a blush still on his chubby cheeks. "I don't get to see much of that."

"When you told me I wasn't gonna make it, I took it as a challenge. Now that I know you really want me to make it, I'm gonna do everything I can to make sure you don't get disappointed."

"I'll be damned," he said. "You might've learned a few values after all."

"Oh, I have. Learned 'em from you. Speaking of values, I saw you looking over that little Pontiac out there."

"Yeah, my brother-in-law was talking about needing a car. That looks like something he'd be interested in."

"Oh, it's a goodun," I said. "I know how busy you are, but if you've got a few minutes, I could show it to you."

"Why not," he said after looking down at his watch.

I took the key to the Pontiac from the rack and walked with him onto the lot.

"Can I look under the hood?" he said when we got to the car.

"Sure."

I walked around to the driver's side and opened the door. I pulled the release, walked back around the car and opened the hood.

"You must know something about cars," I said.

"I know something about cars, all right," he said, the lip sticking out proudly. "Be all right if I drive it?"

"Drive it as far as you want," I said, tossing him the key. I slammed the hood down and wondered if the car would even make it to the first traffic light. It surprised me when it started. Junior really was an artist, I thought, as Mobley pulled the car out onto the highway.

While he was gone I smiled, thinking about the engine locking up, leaving him stranded in a cloud of smoke. In a while, though, he drove back onto the lot and got out.

He walked around the car, shaking his head. "It's got a few miles on it."

"Well, it's not a new car. But most of those miles are highway miles. We bought it from a preacher outside of Tuscaloosa."

"I'll get my brother-in-law to drive by and take a look at it."

A cool breeze kicked a swarm of dry leaves across the lot. Traffic moaned along the highway. I glanced over my shoulder as though we weren't the only two on the lot. "You know what we could do," I said, now looking straight into the slits of his squinting eyes. "I could cut the price of that car by twenty-five percent. You could sell it to your brother-in-law at a bargain and stick a few bucks in your own pocket."

"Hmm," he said, nodding, dropping his eyes toward the ground.

"Usually they won't let me discount more than ten percent without the manager's OK. But we picked that car up at a bargain last week, and I figure the manager's not here, so I do what I have to to satisfy the customer. Besides," I said giving his arm a pat. "You can always get forgiveness easier than you can get permission. Know what I mean?"

He jabbed the lip out and nodded. "You know, I'm the kinda guy's always on the lookout for an extra buck."

"I thought you were. We'll need to do some paperwork."

I turned toward the trailer, listening to his shoes crunching the gravel behind me.

"Oh, David," he said, in the tone of a doting uncle, touching the back of my arm. "You don't think that car burns any oil, do you?"

I stepped up on the first stack of cinder blocks, then turned to look down into his face. I was towering over him.

"You know, I've learned a lot from you, Mr. Mobley," I said. "And like you, I've become the kind of guy who tells it like it is." He swallowed hard. A little blue vein throbbed under the pale skin of his neck. The lip was poked out, all full and pink, and his eyes had turned soft like those of a doe in a petting zoo. I rested a hand on his shoulder, giving it an affectionate squeeze. "Mr. Mobley, I'll drink every drop of oil that car'll burn."

MARIAN CARCACHE

SHE STOPPED LOVING HIM TODAY

Lenora Lindsey woke up miserable with a sharp crick in her right shoulder and the taste of stale cigarettes and old beer in her mouth. She'd collapsed on the sofa wearing those tight new jeans when she'd come in the night before and they had rubbed her, too.

The television was signing on with "Day of Deliverance" and a too-tall preacher with a little pin head was motioning his arms like Bob Barker saying "Come on down," but the volume on the tv set was off so Lenora couldn't hear what he was saying.

Lenora wished she could wet her mouth and throat with something without tasting or swallowing it. She was afraid she might throw up if she tasted anything right then, so she just said "Shit" out loud, and it felt good. She could count on one hand the number of times she'd actually cussed out loud. She usually said "sh–" but never finished with the "it," or she might say "dang," but she never actually cussed. Once when she had said "dad gum it," Randall had told her that she might as well have said the real thing because God wasn't fooled by the scrambling of the letters.

Lenora is still in love with Randall even though he's spent the last year living with a girl named Sheena who's younger than his and Lenora's daughter Mary Joyce, who herself is living with a potter. Lenora never realized how much Randall contributed to the marriage until he ran off. Their life seemed pretty routine, even dull after Mary Joyce grew up and went off to school. Randall had worked and come home tired; Lenora had fixed his meals and kept his clothes and house clean. They leaned back in the side-by-side Lay-Z-Boys and watched quiz shows and comedies, *20/20*, and an occasional Barbara Walters Special at night. Nothing very exciting—except when Randall got all keyed up to get on one of those quiz shows. But the house sure gets quiet with him gone. And now that Mary Joyce is living with the potter, she never comes home either.

Lenora has highlighted her hair and started cussing every now and then, and drinking Lite beer and smoking Virginia Slim cigarettes—four things she never dreamed she'd do. And last night she gave in and went with Annette, one of the girls from work, to a lounge. Lenora had to get a job after Randall left because, since they weren't divorced, she couldn't get alimony. Annette said when Leonard left her, she'd sued him for everything, which didn't turn out to be much, but Lenora wants Randall back, plus she wants his insurance benefits, so she has gotten a job mornings as a salesclerk and cashier in Cameras and Jewelry at Save Mart discount store. The job takes talent because there are so many different kinds of film and attachments for all those cameras. The jewelry doesn't present much of a problem, none of it being real, but the manager told Lenora the day he hired her that if anybody asked if the pearls were real, she was to say, "They're genuine faux pearls." The thought of doing this made Lenora feel guilty and she told Annette, who is assistant manager in Appliances, how she felt, but Annette said not to feel bad, that Lenora had to do what she had to do, having been left by Randall to root hog or die hungry.

Then Annette invited Lenora to that cocktail lounge. Annette had said, "Lenora, you watch too much tv. I know. I've been there. When I first started working in Appliances after Leonard left me, I watched all those sets going all day at work and then I couldn't be satisfied watching just one when I got home at night. I even started dreaming about tv. There I'd be riding around town with the A-Team or somebody in my sleep. I can see the signs. You're heading for a breakdown if you don't get out of the house and be with real people in the real world." So Lenora went with Annette to a lounge named "Cock of the Walk" and danced with a scrawny little man named Larry who, while they were slow dancing, kept crawling his hand down Lenora's back until it rested on her buttock, and then squeezing and jerking his hand away before she could accuse him of anything. He breathed in her ear on the third dance and told her she turned him on. Lenora jerked away from him and ran into the ladies' room.

That preacher on tv was jerking, too. He seemed to be calling people from the audience to come up on the stage. As the cameras scanned the crowds, Lenora's heart suddenly missed a beat. She could've sworn she saw Randall and that Sheena, their hands raised high above their heads, clapping and mouthing "hallelujah." "Shit," she said again and hit the remote, wondering if all that drinking had made her start seeing things. She had read that science had proven that alcohol killed off brain cells.

The next day, during her break, Lenora told Annette about what she thought she'd seen on tv the morning before, and Annette said, "Honey, you've got that man on the brain. You better start seeing other men and get over him." Annette had already pitched a fit because Lenora still had Randall's picture in her billfold and a framed 8x10 of him sitting in front of what looked like the Swiss Alps, on top of the television set in the den.

Lenora couldn't get over him, though. All day Monday at work she kept making mistakes, ringing up the wrong amount on the register and having to call Mr. Godwin on the green line to come with the key so she could correct the tape. After someone complained at Customer Service that Lenora had looked straight through him without offering to wait on him, Mr. Godwin told her to take Tuesday off and come back acting normal on Wednesday or he'd have to let her go. She decided right there on the spot that she wasn't going out to the lounges anymore. Annette might be able to stay out drinking and dancing and still hold down a job, but Lenora sure couldn't, and she couldn't afford to lose her job either, not after being left high and dry for a dental hygienist with silicon breasts.

On Tuesday morning, Lenora stayed in her gown and Dearfoams. She dragged her blanket and pillow and cup of coffee to the den sofa, and turned on the tv. She had never been one to pile up on the sofa, and had never kept her gown on after getting out of bed, but the fact was that she felt she deserved to lounge around to house after all she'd been through—and she'd seen in the *TV Guide* that *Phil Donahue* was going to be about "Men Who've Left Their Marriages for Younger Women." A panel of three men defended abandoning their families with what Lenora saw as pretty flimsy excuses like "the feeling was just gone," "sometimes I felt like I'd explode," and "I was just a shell watching my life slip past," and on the other side, two former wives took turns crying and then yelling at the men, and an abandoned son told how he became gay because his father left. Phil took the microphone into the studio audience and a woman screamed into it that the men on stage were slimeballs, and Lenora agreed. Then Phil started going around the audience stirring the women up. One woman was really going strong into Phil's mike when, just behind Phil's shoulder, Lenora spotted them: a man that looked just like Randall with a girl as young and skinny as Sheena, sitting up there like they owned the studio audience. She just got a glimpse of them before the camera moved back to the panel of slimeballs and Phil started saying "gotta be quick, out of time." She hit the remote to change the channel, half expecting to find Oprah Winfrey talking to "Girls Who Left Good Homes to Live with Potters."

Lenora hoped Switchboard didn't recognize her voice when she called Save Mart and asked for Appliances, but she had to tell somebody what she had seen. When Annette picked up the receiver, she sounded so professional, "Appliances—Miss Skinner speaking—May I help you?," that Lenora hung up and got furious with Phil Donahue. The very idea of making celebrities out of men who've left their wives for younger women! And when that poor gay boy tried to talk, Phil kept butting in, questioning whether or not the boy really turned gay *because* his daddy left, and then answering his own questions before the boy had a chance to talk. Randall always did that, too. "Why do you think so and so?" he'd ask, and then, before you could open your mouth, he'd say, "Well, I'll tell you why. . . ." But Phil's still with Marlo. He even left his friends in Chicago and moved to New York to satisfy her, whereas Randall left home to live with a floozie with breasts shaped like the Tin Man's hat.

Annette got mad when Lenora told her that she didn't want to go back to the lounges the following weekend. She accused Lenora of enjoying wallowing in her misery. Lenora, before she knew she was going to do it, lied and told Annette that Mary Joyce was coming over for the weekend. Then Annette said she understood and patted Lenora's arm sympathetically.

When Lenora got home that day, she decided to call Mary Joyce and invite her to dinner, to try to turn the lie into truth before she felt any worse about it.

The potter answered the phone and Lenora asked for Mary Joyce. A few seconds later, Mary Joyce picked up an extension and said, "Mama?" Lenora knew that the potter had recognized her voice and clued Mary Joyce in. Lenora also knew that he still had the other phone up, listening to what she had to say to her own daughter. When she invited Mary Joyce home, Lenora heard the suction from palms sliding around on the receivers. Then Mary Joyce said, "We'd feel more comfortable if you had dinner with *us* in *our* home."

What else could Lenora do? She accepted the invitation.

The potter's name was Marcus, and he and Mary Joyce served red wine out of a bottle that had its own little basket woven around it, and into clay goblets that Marcus had made. The goblets didn't match. Mary Joyce said their uniqueness made them art, that anybody could *buy* a set of matching glasses. There were a lot of wine bottles, most of them covered with wax drippings and holding candle nubs, scattered around the house on pieces of furniture made out of tree stumps and decorated with bones and hornet nests and other strange things. The place was clean, though, except for the dirt on the floor around Marcus' wheel which they treated like some kind of god. Lenora thought about the white and gold French Provincial bedroom suite she and Randall had borrowed money from the bank to buy for Mary Joyce. If they'd known the future, they could've just thrown a mattress in a corner of the basement for her and stuck a candle in a Upper 10 bottle for her to see by. Lenora tried not to look at the tapestry-covered waterbed that loomed in the corner of the room like some giant piece of evidence that her daughter was sleeping with a potter, but her eyes kept being drawn in that direction. She was glad she'd worn her new look, her black stirrup pants and boots. She felt liberal, but Mary Joyce seemed to give her outfit a disapproving look.

The second glass of wine had a calming effect on Lenora, and by the third glass, she found herself warming up to the potter and giggling at all his stories about friends he'd gone to college with who'd dropped out to be blacksmiths and weavers and jewelry makers, but who had "sold out" and become bankers and salesmen for I.B.M. The room spun dizzily and Lenora was happy, and when Mary Joyce called from the kitchen, "Mama, we're having Mid-eastern hoppers. Have you ever eaten pita bread?," it struck Lenora's funny bone and she began to giggle. She had to sit down on the waterbed to keep from falling. Mary Joyce came out of the kitchen and stood staring with that puzzled look she inherited from Randall on her face, and her hands on her hips. The puzzled look turned to indignation when Mary Joyce realized that Marcus was laughing, too, and that there was nothing funny unless they were making fun of her. She slung a handful of bean sprouts in Marcus' face, yelled "Shit Face," and stormed out of the house.

"She never could stand not to know what was funny," Lenora said slowly and with difficulty. It felt as though her lips moved without the cooperation of the rest of her face, which was numb. When Marcus didn't answer, she looked toward him and realized that he was sitting on the edge of the waterbed with tears dripping off of his chin. "I'm losing her," he said. "She's leaving me for a tree surgeon named Royce. She's selling out." He switched off the bare bulb that hung from the ceiling, she knew so she wouldn't see his tears, and switched on a funny black fluorescent tube that cast a strange purplish glow over the room and a little lamp that swirled an aqua-colored mucous around inside it. This reminded Lenora of the way her own insides felt, and strangely enough, made her remember the color analyst that had visited Save Mart's cosmetic counter and advised, "When in doubt, wear turquoise. It's everybody's color."

When Lenora felt Marcus sit back down on the waterbed, she pulled him over toward her and cradled his head against her chest, brushing his tear-damp hair back from his eyes and rocking him back and forth on the very waterbed that he'd been keeping house on with her daughter. When his breathing became soft and regular, she knew he had escaped for a few hours into a land where his friends were still blacksmiths and weavers, and where Mary Joyce was not sleeping with a tree surgeon named Royce, and where Mary Joyce's father was not living with a teenager. Hours later, in this land of soft lies, Lenora became Mary Joyce for the potter, and the potter became Randall, and as identities split off, bodies merged, and Lenora awakened to find herself staring over the potter's smooth young shoulders at a glowing obscene poster of entangled bodies, unable to believe what she might have done in the waterbed in this strange, strange lighting with the boy Mary Joyce was leaving for a tree surgeon. She couldn't even tell this to Annette. She was horrified to realize that she was smiling, and relieved to discover that the stirrups on her new stretch pants were still safely strapped across the arches of her feet.

Lenora left a note on a paper towel for Marcus who was still sleeping like an exhausted child, thanking him for a lovely evening—even if she didn't get a crack at those Mid-eastern things—and apologizing for Mary Joyce's behavior and language. She pulled the door to quietly behind her and stepped out into the fresh air. She took a deep breath and realized that she hadn't really breathed since Randall left—until today.

She rolled the Rambler's front windows down and turned the radio up high, tuned in to a country station, and felt good when she joined in at top volume with George Jones singing, "He Stopped Loving Her Today," except that Lenora sang, "She stopped loving him today." When she realized that the man in George's song had died, she stopped singing and shuddered, but it didn't ruin her good mood. She sure wasn't going to have to die to get over Randall. It did make her sad, though, to think that maybe when George was singing that song he was thinking about him and Tammy Wynette. Lenora knew their story; she'd seen it on the movie of the week. But she couldn't let their sad story ruin her good mood, not today.

Lenora wanted to do something different, maybe go to the cafeteria and have the luncheon special and celebrate being over Randall. She'd never be able to explain to Annette or herself exactly when she got over him or why, but somehow, sometime during that strange night of wine and bean sprouts and peculiar lights, she had gotten her mind straight. She shuddered to think how close she'd come to losing it over that worn out shoe named Randall Lindsey—thinking she was seeing him on network tv and all. Lenora decided to go straight home, freshen up, and invite Annette to Morrison's Cafeteria, Lenora's treat.

When Lenora got home and opened the door, there was that 8x10 of Randall grinning at her like an idiot in front of the Swiss Alps on the tv set. "Shit Face," she said as she slammed the picture down so hard that the glass shattered. Then she called Annette who said she'd be ready in fifteen minutes and that she had something important to tell Lenora.

Annette popped on a piece of Juicy Fruit gum excitedly and grinned as Lenora told her every detail of the evening with Marcus—details she had made up her mind not to tell anybody.

They were already in line at Morrison's with their trays and flatware, trying to decide the difference between Watergate salad and Heavenly Hash when Annette said, "I'm real glad about last night getting you over Randall and all 'cause I've been worried about how you might take what I've got to tell you, but I think last night'll make my news easier to take . . ."

"Well what in the world is it?" Lenora asked as she slid her tray past desserts and tried to see down the line to the meats.

"Well, after you couldn't go out to the lounges with me this weekend, I decided to stay in and take it easy, get some rest and watch tv. . . ."

Annette interrupted her story to choose roast beef, and had to have it cut from the middle where the meat was pink. Then she kept changing back and forth between broccoli with cheese sauce and fried okra, and taking her text on Lenora for choosing too many starches: "Dumplings and rice pudding and mashed potatoes! It'll every bit go to those thighs—then see how good you'll look in your new stirrup pants!"

They had gotten through the adding machine and sat down to a table when Annette got back on track, "so I was taking it easy, watching tv, and there was Bob Eubanks with the Newlyweds. They're back on, you know."

Lenora knew before Annette told her. Randall had done it. He had gone and married that girl and gotten on a quiz show on network tv with it for the whole world to see. She wondered if that would qualify as "selling out." She'd probably get some quickie divorce notice when the mail ran Monday.

In an effort to soften the news, Annette told her that they didn't know a thing about each other and only scored 10 points, so all they won was some instant hot chocolate mix, a blow dryer, and a popcorn popper. But Lenora wasn't really thinking about Randall anymore. She was thinking about that George Jones song she'd heard and how she ought to buy the album. When she sang it, she could leave out the part where you learn that the man has died. It was the refrain, her version of it, "She stopped loving him today," that made her feel so good.

"Honey, are you awright?" Annette asked as she looked at herself in a little compact mirror she'd propped against her coffee cup and lined herself some lips in a perfect full bow. "You look 100 miles off. I hope I didn't do the wrong thing to tell you, but I would've wanted you to do the same for me."

"I'm fine," Lenora said with a smile.

"It must be that Marcus then," Annette teased, raising her pencil thin eyebrows and pursing those bow-shaped lips.

Lenora knew Annette wouldn't understand if she told her that it wasn't Marcus—she didn't understand herself—so instead she explained, "I was just thinking about getting my hair done the color of Tammy Wynette's."

Annette was satisfied.

LORETTA COBB

MUSK

Just like every morning, Paula clicks on the computer:

> **Your Personalized Horoscope**
> **Sex and romance are very much on your mind today, Ingrid, though a get-together with a partner may not be possible at this time. Set one up if you can, but if not, go out with friends and enjoy some spirited conversation. You'll need some outlet for that energy that racy novels just won't satisfy! During the day: Stroll through an art gallery, and buy yourself a present at the gift shop. You're in an artistic frame of mind.**
> *Detailed Horoscope*
> *Click here for a more detailed horoscope that includes your rising sign, love scope, Chinese readings and more.*

Paula resists the time-waster. She scampers about the overgrown boundary of the pool, scavenging the plump wild grapes that fall from the vine. They grow too close to the sun for her to pick them. *Hmp. Like Icarus* she thinks. She looks down at the gladiolas that never bloomed this summer, finds three or four grapes still warm from the morning sun.

Paula thinks she's losing it, curses the day she read Allen Tate's poem about muscadines rotting on the vine. Along the edging at the pool deck, she finds more under the wild violets she planted that first spring when she'd started seeing Michael again. She knows her children would laugh at her widow's frugality, hunting grapes like Easter eggs. The same way they assume she's too old for romance. Who did hide these?

The same force that made her laugh at her own fool self this morning. She sat in the dentist's chair, soothed by the sweetness of the boy who's taken over the practice. Like a trick from Olympus, this young Turk with eyes like Michael's had stepped into her life to remind her of grim reality, of facing 60 and worse. The boy shot flirty looks at his pale, willowy assistant whose blue eyes were anything but calm. He exuded a warmth that was irrestible, a sweet concern, a desire to please.

The nearness of him brought flashbacks: the titillation of Michael's arm brushing against her skin. Then the boy was saying, "Open wide. Sorry I know that's a little sensitive. Just bear with me. How does it feel? Do you like it? Is it a little high?

Am I? She titters to herself, takes deep breaths.

Then a girl with dark hair and a voice softer than the Virgin Mary's cleans her up, puts the sucker in her mouth, wipes her tongue, her lips. Paula thinks the girl's touch is maternal or at least she hopes it's that. Otherwise, it's too erotic to stand. Paula wants sex, but she's too busy to take care of it herself or too depressed today. When he asks if she likes her new tooth, Paula smiles, realizing that the soft eyes reflect genuine concern.

Back home, she pops a muscadine in her mouth, decides it's good for her and quicker. When she tries a nap to build up her immune system like the doctor recommended, she can't sleep. She can't think of anything but Michael. *Death's dark vale* runs through her head. Tears slide, then spill down her cheek. She's too old for this. It should be wasted on the young. She doesn't have the sanity to plan two business trips—all the endless decisions: navy or black? Gypsy or Madonna? Grace Kelly look? Jezabel? Maybe jade for her eyes or blue like her mood. She needs to call the hotel, but she can't. Brain's too fuzzy.

Maybe she would do better listening to the voice inside her head that tries to soothe her into letting go, accepting the Grim Reaper's triumph this time. She should get up, but she fantasizes instead.

She would open a Cabernet to let it breathe, its ruby redness like stained glass in the morning light. She'll wear a bustier. Waves crash against the shore when he comes to pick her up for lunch. She opens the door slightly, takes his hand and pulls with all her strength, then slams and locks the door. "Fooled you, didn't I?" she laughs at his startled eyes.

"Please?" she runs her fingers across his lips. "We could just lie in bed and snuggle or maybe make out like we used to. Remember how good my youthful thigh felt against that stiff friend of yours?"

Pain takes over the pleasure smeared across his face, he closes his eyes, thrusts his palms toward the ceiling like a prayerful hostage, "Baby, we got to stop this some time, sooner or later," he tells the ceiling.

"Make it later," she says, tongue in his ear, reaching for his buckle. A willing captive, his hands press her buttocks hard, his lips seeking a nipple. He mumbles, tugging her unclasped hair, "Just one last time, darlin'. Just . . . one . . . oh, God."

Paula stretches like a tired cat, gives up on the nap. "Better than the muscadine," she tells the mirror where a ghost of herself gapes. "What you lookin' at, bitch?" she says, mooning the mirror. "Kiss my skinny white ass. I got work to do." The soft autumn evening and Mars spinning orangely toward Earth while crickets sing are lost in the blur.

JOHN COTTLE

PLAYING BINGO FOR MONEY

Choices.

My life is beset with choices. To be or not to be; straight up or on the rocks; paper or plastic. Beset, befuddled, bedeviled, becudgeled, besmothered, beslobbered, . . . *bethumped* . . . with choices. Choices bedamned, my inner voice bemoans as I enter the parking deck in my Buick LaSabre. The attendant approaches menacingly. I can feel him wielding more choices.

"Gone be leaving before noon or staying all day?"

I freeze momentarily, considering how to respond to this either-or. My mind shuffles the options. I am headed for the Bedford County Courthouse to try . . . or to try to settle . . . the case of Aggie Bingo vs. Holston Trucking Company. Five other cases are set on this morning's docket. Which will the judge call first? If not Aggie's, will he send us away until another day? And there is still the possibility of the oft-maligned courthouse-steps settlement. I could bedone and begone by ten o'clock. But if we start the trial, I'll be here all day. I concoct an ingenious reply, craftily weaving all possibilities into one succinct response that I deliver with casual aplomb.

"Depends."

The attendant's eyes roll backward until I am looking into two globules of eggshell putty. He is either expressing, with theatrical sarcasm, his exasperation with my refusal to choose or experiencing a grand mal seizure. I am hoping for the seizure. Ahh, but the irises reappear.

"Park over there. Between that Lexus and the green Bronco."

He has deliberately assigned me to the narrowest space in the entire deck, one into which my LaSabre cannot possibly fit and still allow room for my exit. I resolve not to accept such shabby treatment from the likes of a parking lot attendant. I am, after all, a lawyer and I don't have to take this belittlement. I know how to forcefully assert my rights.

"Isn't that space a little small for my car?"

"You got room. Pull on in."

I mumble a caustic curse and obey. One must sometimes reserve one's energies in quarrels of this sort. Wisdom and discretion often require the swallowing of pride in order that vital piss and vinegar is not needlessly bespattered upon immaterial conflict. Resolving to conserve my verve for the impending strife of the courtroom, I pull sheepishly into the constricted space, a blood clot entering a clogged artery. I gently open the LaSabre door, being extraordinarily careful not to allow it to touch the luscious, glossy blackness of the virgin Lexus. With my door carefully positioned at its apogee, oversized briefcase in my lap, I gingerly set one foot to the pavement and prepare to stand. Employing all of the coordination and grace of Michael Jordan gliding under the basket for a reverse slam dunk, I catapult myself upward, slamming my chest into the door and sending it crashing into the Lexus at which point it ping-pongs back like a one ton hammer crushing my shin against the LaSabre at which point I quite naturally grab my shin with both hands dropping my briefcase on my foot and yell *"SHIT!"* inadvertently striking the door again, with my shoulder this time, and propelling it smartly back for a second violent encounter with the freshly mangled black paint of the Lexus.

"Sssssheeeit man! What you trying to do?" the attendant politely inquires.

"Tight space you put me in here, sport," I gasp, holding my throbbing shin and checking for broken bones.

"Ssssheeeit man!" he sibilates, noticeably unconcerned for my own well being. "Look what you done to that car."

Controlling my mounting anger at his insensitivity to my searing pain, I astutely conclude that I must quickly defuse this situation. Always thinking like a lawyer, I ingeniously formulate a single rhetorical question that will instantly assuage all of his concerns.

"Ain't *your* car is it?"

His eyes roll backward again as I lock the LaSabre and hobble toward the street. Is it the seizure this time? Apparently not, as I hear his beguiling voice singing in the background.

"I'm telling who done this."

I wave goodbye, choosing not to look back, and thinking what a wonderful start this day has gotten off to. Aggie Bingo is beriddled with luck to have me as her champion.

Entering the courthouse, I queue up behind an eclectic mix of Bedford County citizens, each awaiting their turn to pass under the official Bedford County Metal Detector, a contraption I have detested from the first day the county installed it and have grown to hate even more with each pass I make through its meddlesome threshold. No one can remember the last time a terrorist or a postal worker smuggled a Thompson into the building and wasted a few lawyers and clerks or a judge or two. Nevertheless, the County Commission, in its infinite wisdom (as is oft-said of politicians) decided to take preemptive action lest some Jihad warrior decide that Bedford County, Alabama, would be the perfect place to advance his agenda by taking out a few local citizens and maybe, on a good day, even a couple of big shot lawyers from Montgomery or Birmingham. Hence, the official Bedford County Metal Detector. I know of other counties where they have these things and they always let the lawyers walk right on around them. No special favors here though. In the eyes of the Bedford County Sheriff's Department, we are all potential Jihad postal workers.

No sooner do I step through the annoying monstrosity when it erupts with a series of sharp beeps and flashing lights, identifying me as a possible mass murderer. Three khaki clad deputies look on lazily. If I were a postal worker, I could be on the third floor before they stirred.

"Step over here please," the buxom, blond female of the crew finally orders. One of her overweight colleagues leans against a table and looks on amusedly while he works over a stick of gum, a full one-half of his corpulent ass spread over the tabletop. The uniformed blond comes at me with what looks like an electric charcoal starter and begins probing my personal space. As the probe passes near my genitalia, an alarm goes off.

"Must be that old blue steel," I crack and give her a quick wink. She acts as though she is not amused, but I know she is only acting. The chubby one, however, is laughing from deep in his belly, dangling a stout leg from the table while I disgorge the contents of my pockets.

"Just a false positive," she says dryly. "Nothing dangerous in *these* pants," looking at me as if to say *gotcha*. Chubby begins to laughs louder, the insubstantial tabletop now undulating beneath the pulse of his jovial buttock.

After concluding that my belt buckle is the source of all this merriment, the deputies allow me to pass. As I walk away, I consider whether it might be worth sacrificing a few lawyers, clerks, and judges once every eon or so in order to be rid of that goddamn thing. Before I am out of earshot, I hear it again: *beep, beep, beep* . . . "Step over here please." Ahh, to live in such times as these.

The trial of Bingo vs. Holston Trucking is to be held in the second floor courtroom of the Honorable J. Cavandar Prikle. The Honorable J. Cavandar Prikle has been on the bench a little less than a year, having replaced one of the great jurists in the history of Bedford County, the Honorable Penrose Samuels, affectionately known to the Bedford County bar as Drinkin' Sammy. The difference between the two is like day and night or, as Drinkin' Sammy would have said, God rest his soul, the forces of darkness and the power of enlightenment. Drinkin' Sammy was from an old blue-blooded Bedford County family whose pedigree could be traced back to the earliest settlers of Alabama. A Harvard-educated man, Drinkin' Sammy could quote Shakespeare and scripture all day long and spout off more Latin phrases than a Black's Law Dictionary. He was a man of the people—a judge dedicated to the proposition that no citizen of Bedford County was ever going to sit on the back seat of the bus of justice whenever it rolled through his courtroom. This proved to be a quite pertinent axiom in cases that pitted one of our beloved locals against an out of state insurance company. Drinkin' Sammy's devotion to this particular principle got him into nasty flame wars with some of the hot shot firms in Montgomery and Birmingham who regularly invaded his fiefdom for the sole and sinister purpose of abetting their insurance company clients in denying payment of the honest claims of local residents, the terms "honest" and "local" being synonymous and interchangeable in this context. These disputes often turned vicious and resulted in the spreading of much malicious gossip about Drinkin' Sammy, not to mention several investigations by the state bar. The saddest thing about it all was that the cirrhosis got him before he could clear his name once and for good. Drinkin' Sammy may be gone, but he will never be forgotten. I'll never be able to go into his old courtroom without imagining him up there on his bench in his flowing black robe, peering out innocently from behind the jet-black sunglasses, the two days growth of facial hair casting a dignified shadow over his countenance. He was, let it be said, the very personification of justice.

His replacement (and I hesitate even to use the word) is, to be objective about it, an inexperienced, smooth-faced, blond-haired, wet-behind-the-ears, big-moneyed, right-winged, Christian-Coalition-suck-up, plaintiff-hating, egg-sucking, Republican pissant. It is rumored in some circles that the Honorable J. Cavandar Prikle was actually born at the Country Club but this is obviously untrue and is only repeated by those who do not like him personally. I maintain that he was merely conceived at the Country Club—begotten, as it were, in a sand trap off the eighteenth fairway.

In spite of his many shortcomings, the Honorable J. Cavandar Prickle has his supporters—mainly hot shot insurance defense lawyers, bankers, business executives, and moneyed people who trust him to intervene in the judicial process on their behalf lest a Bedford County jury attempt to redistribute a portion of their wealth to some undeserving crippled, homeless orphan who lost both legs and both parents in a car wreck caused by a drunken insurance executive whose company denies all liability for the accident and, just for good measure, corruptly refuses to pay off on the parents' life insurance policies. These are the same people who so maliciously pursued Drinkin' Sammy. When Drinkin' Sammy passed on to his reward, they celebrated their good fortune by successfully lobbying the governor for the appointment of the Honorable J. Cavandar Prickle as the first Republican Circuit Judge in the history of Bedford County. Now, things will never be the same. Gone from Drinkin' Sammy's old office are the M. C. Escher prints and the faux marble bust of Mark Twain, blasphemously replaced with a wooden plaque of the Ten Commandments and pictures of Ronald Regan. It has been a difficult period of transition.

Those of us in the Plaintiff's bar have also noticed a disturbing show of familiarity between the insurance defense lawyers who supported the Honorable J. Cavandar Prickle and their hero that we find to be unprofessional and downright tawdry. When court is in session, they politely refer to him as Judge Prickle. But in the halls, when they think no one is watching, they slap him on the back and call him Cav. While this is disturbing to us, we have formulated a responsive strategy that appropriately addresses the problem and makes us feel better in the process of its implementation. When we think no one is watching, we slap each other on the back and call him Judge

Prick.

I limp into the pompous wood-paneled courtroom through huge leather-veneered double doors, my overstuffed briefcase in hand, and immediately begin perusing the myriad faces in search of Aggie's. Ever since the day Horace Applebee missed the call of his case from sleeping off a hangover, I have entered the courtroom on trial day with a nervous apprehension that my client won't show. My mind races madly, bestirred with the possibilities. Did I forget to inform them of the trial date? Is this the right day? Am I in the right courtroom? What century is this?

Luckily for Horace, the judge on his case was Drinkin' Sammy who was always understanding about such things. He granted me a postponement for "just cause" over the histrionic and vituperative remonstrations of Clyde Morton, a hot-headed, arm-waving, runt of a lawyer from Montgomery who represented the supermarket where Horace had slipped on a string bean that had somehow found its way to an aisle in the wine section. Clyde bitched and whined like it was his own money at stake. Then he finally did the noble thing and settled with us for a semi-fair sum "just to keep from having to come back before that whisky-logged son of a bitch." (Clyde was never one to put his faith in diplomacy.) When it came to looking out for the abused victims of corporate callousness, Drinkin' Sammy's heart was as warm as a mother's milk. Not so with Judge Prick though. His heart is as cold as a dead Eskimo.

My anxiety eases as I scout over the courtroom and lock onto Billy Strickland, Aggie's live-in boyfriend. He sits there alone in the pew, the garnet and gold Florida State cap perched belligerently atop his head, the dingy unwashed auburn hair dangling to his collar. He is head to toe in faded denim, the jacket concealing the confederate battle flag which I know to be tattooed into his lean, hard forearm. His cavernous nostrils are flared wildly, his face besmeared with unhappy wrinkles as if he were holding a fart in his nose.

Billy and I have had somewhat of a falling out since his last conviction for drunk driving. After successfully dodging justice on two prior occasions, with my expert assistance of course, he finally got nailed. Naturally, he blames me. If only I had done this or that or called this witness or made that objection. Though he basically disgusts me, I resolve to be civil to him today and to greet him with warm friendship. I catch his eye beneath the golden embossment of Chief Osceola's war bonnet that rises aggressively above the bill of the cap.

"Roll Tide, Billy Boy!" I cannot resist a slight jab with the needle.

He mutters something unintelligible. The wrinkles grow angrier.

"Take off that cap in here and try to show a little class. A juror might see you."

More unintelligible grunts as he complies with my suggestion.

"Where's Aggie?"

Again, more garbled muttering.

"Speak up will you!"

"She went to pee," he shouts. The myriad faces all look around.

I canvass the hall for Aggie, lurking just outside the women's restroom. Nondescript people are milling all about, many of them potential jurors. I have stressed to Aggie the importance of employing all of her manners and grace anytime she enters the courthouse. "The next person you encounter could be on *your jury*," I caution. It does not help to advance the plaintiff's case for the plaintiff to push aside a stumbly old blue-haired woman in order to secure the last spot on an elevator stuffed with potential jurors. And experience has taught that it is damned counterproductive when the lawyer doesn't know about the incident until the client mentions it just after the last juror is struck and the blue-hair is seated on the front row of the jury box, beaming malevolent smiles at the Plaintiff and his lawyer. Even Drinkin' Sammy wasn't able to straighten that shit out.

I wait nervously outside the restroom door, nodding smiles at the ladies as they exit. I am concerned about Aggie's appearance. She is, to put it gently, a rather large, roughhewn woman with a penchant for bedraping her ample posterior with insufficient quantities of polyester. But we have discussed this and she has assured me that she will be appropriately attired. As I wait for what seems an inordinately long time, I hear a voice from behind. "Billy said you was looking for me." Turning, I come face to face with my client. I gasp. She is standing there in the hall smiling at me, her brontosaurian form teetering precariously on six-inch stiletto heels. As I greet her, my voice rises involuntarily several decibels and an octave.

"What are you *doing* in those goddamn shoes?"

She is initially dumbstruck by my reaction. When she tries to speak, she tears up. Massive black underscorings of coagulated mascara are in imminent danger of melting. "You . . . you told me to dress nice."

"Aggie! You are here because you sustained a *back injury*. You are supposed to be in *chronic, debilitating pain*. What is the jury going to think when they see you in those . . . those orthopedic nightmares?"

"I . . . I never thought—"

"Get back in the bathroom quick. There's a Pay-Less shoe store two blocks from the courthouse. I'll send Billy after something appropriate. What size do you wear?"

"Either nine-and-a-halfs or tens. Depends on the shoe."

Another choice to be made.

"Get back in there. Don't let anybody that might be on the jury see you."

"How will I know who might be on the jury?"

"How the hell would I know? Just use some common sense for godsakes."

"But how will I know when you're back?"

"I'll send Billy . . . uhhh," I suddenly realize the problem. "I'll . . . I'll . . . Goddammit, I don't know. I'll think of something. Just get in there."

The secret of being a successful Plaintiff's lawyer is maintaining one's calm in the face of impending disaster, of tending to those unanticipated crises that spring forth from nowhere at the ninth hour and handling them with dignified professionalism and a cool head. Lesser attorneys would have folded their hand on this case long ago. Not me. I'm playing this one out to the last card. I am determined, against mounting odds, to achieve justice for Aggie Bingo.

After fronting Billy the money for the shoes together with detailed instructions as to what to buy, and setting him on his way to Pay-Less with great trepidation, I reenter the courtroom to assess the situation. And learn, much to my dismay, that young Judge Prick has already called Aggie's case and is in the process of deputizing a *posse comitatus* to go out searching for me. He sits righteously on the bench in his flowing black robe surrounded by a gaggle of lawyers, all paying appropriate homage, all of whom have cases set for trial today. My eyes fix upon the beguiling, redheaded Mildred Mahorne, the Montgomery lawyer hired by Statewide Indemnity to represent Holston Trucking, the corporate bully that so tragically injured Aggie Bingo. Judge Prick sees me enter and immediately beckons me forward for a high level conference. Wilfred Jacobs, a wiry, crinkled, gray-headed old geezer and veteran of many a courtroom setback, stands by the bench leering out at me through suppressed laughter, his chestnut teeth and liver spots standing out against his pallid skin. There is a glare in young Judge Prick's blue eyes that bespeaks aggression.

"And just *where* have you been?" his prissy voice wants to know. "And just *where* is your client? And are *you* ready to go to trial?"

Which to answer first? More choices.

"Your honor, my client had a minor medical emergency."

"A *minor* medical emergency?" He asks as though my veracity is in question. "And what exactly is a *minor* medical emergency?"

"A problem with her feet, judge. We're on top of it. We'll be ready to go any minute."

"Well I certainly wouldn't want this court's schedule to inconvenience you in the slightest. Just tell us what time you want to start your case and we'll all try to accommodate you." Sarcasm is an art in which many judges are well practiced. It does not, however, become young Judge Prick.

"Give me twenty minutes, judge. Then we'll be ready to rock and roll." I can see immediately from the flush in his cheeks that I have miscalculated the amount of time I should have requested.

"Twenty minutes?" His youthful composure crumbles like a stale soda cracker. "You get this case ready to go in five minutes or I'll dismiss it so fast you'll think it was gone yesterday!"

"Five minutes it is, judge," I concur unruffled, knowing full well that five minutes in this courtroom is the temporal equivalent of a half an hour in real world time. "We'll be ready to go in *five minutes.*"

"Aggie *Bingo*? Seriously, is that her real name?"

"That's it, judge. The one and only."

"Bingo in five minutes then," Judge Prick declares, smiling at the spontaneity of his wit as he fiddles with his watch-stem like a child picking at a scab.

"I never could win nothing at bingo," Wilfred Jacobs wheezes through nicotine seasoned vocal cords. The gaggle laughs politely in broken unison at this asinine remark. *Or anything else either*, I want to say, but suppress the urge. Discipline is the hallmark of a successful plaintiff's lawyer.

I sit across the table from Mildred Mahorne, her delectable red hair bouncing with every movement of her head, exposing flashes of the zillion carat diamond earrings that dangle bewitchingly from her soft lobes. Judge

Prick has ordered us into the conference room with instructions to make one final diligent effort to settle this case while he takes up a motion hearing in a matter he deems to be of greater import. So much for the five minute deadline.

Mildred's penetrating blue eyes look out from under the gentle arches of her deep Bordeaux brows. I am hoping that those eyes did not espy Aggie strutting into the courtroom in her chiropractic calamities. But Mildred is practiced in this routine—her eyes reveal nothing. If she did see the shoes, she will spring it on Aggie during cross-examination. "Didn't I see you in different shoes when you came in this morning? And these shoes you have on now, you purchased them just minutes ago? And at the direction of your *LAWYER*? And the spiked heels are *GONE*? And you got rid of them at the direction of your *LAWYER*?" Mildred is a merciless dynamo with a take-no-prisoners mentality. Aggie figures not to fare too well under her withering questioning.

"I'm going to go ahead and put it all on the table," declares Mildred convincingly. "Five thousand dollars. That's all the settlement authority I've got. That's all the authority I will ever have for this case. That's all the authority I will *ever ask for* in this case." There is an air of finality in her voice. But I am not persuaded.

"I'll take it to her, but I'm not optimistic she'll accept it. Five thousand doesn't go far when you consider a thousand dollars in chiropractic bills, three thousand in time out of work, and then there's my—"

"Don't even *try* to sell me that shit about lost time out of work," she rudely dares me. "She's never even filed a tax return. And all you've got to back up what she says about lost wages is her deadbeat live-in boyfriend saying she felt too bad to go clean houses for ten dollars an hour for people they can't even remember."

I remain unflappable in the face of this outburst. "It may not be the strongest part of my case. But when the jury hears of the months of agony and suffering she went through because your company's callous driver smashed her Pinto into next week with his ten ton monster truck—"

"Scratching her rear bumper to the tune of exactly one hundred thirty-seven dollars and twenty-four cents."

"And viciously twisting her spinal cord leaving her sprained, strained, in spasms—"

"Five thousand dollars is it. Take it or leave it but don't come asking for more."

"I'll talk to her. But don't get your hopes up."

"*My* hopes are that she'll turn it down. I'd *love* to try this case." She stands to indicate the negotiations are over. Then, almost as an afterthought, she pauses to smile directly into my face, her perfidious eyes twinkling. "Since I'm laying it all on the table anyway, I might as well let you see this." She throws a thick file to the table that hits with a splat. "Take a look."

Even before taking up the file, I know instinctively that this cannot be good for us. My premonition is confirmed in spades as I flip through the folder's contents. Page after page of Aggie Bingo's medical records showing "patient complaining of chronic back pain" or "patient is back for re-check of back problems." A dozen doctors and clinics, all treating the same complaints. And all dated *before* the wreck with Holston Trucking. While this evidence would be devastating enough standing alone, its effect is compounded by Aggie's categorical denials, on multiple occasions and under oath, of having any back problem that predated the wreck. I feel my stomach giving way. I am bescrewed. But then, in the nick of time, my survival instinct kicks in. I meet Mildred's blue eyes, my poker face firmly fixed. I hold the file flat above the table for a second, then casually let it fall with a thud.

"So fucking what."

Her eyes roll backward as she shakes her bouncing hair to and fro. I am wondering if she has caught something from the parking lot attendant.

"Five thousand is it. And that's too damn much. Take it or leave it, it doesn't matter to me."

She picks up the file and exits the conference room in confident stride, leaving me alone to contemplate the looming train wreck this case has become. I don't know whether to laugh or cry. But I must stay focused—maintain my composure. Never let 'em see you sweat. Never admit weakness. Keep a cool and easy manner. I can do it. I've been here before. By God, I'm ready for battle. Bring on Mildred Mahorne and Holston Trucking. But first, I need to talk to Aggie.

Back in the courtroom, the Honorable J. Cavandar Prickle in engaged with a trio of lawyers, all still deeply engrossed in the same motion hearing that delayed the commencement of Aggie's case. There will be plenty of time to talk settlement with Aggie.

The courtroom is now full of potential jurors. I survey the assemblage looking for Aggie while trying to assess the faces of the mass. I am looking for sympathetic, merciful faces—faces of people who can relate to Aggie and her mate— that share their values and their social milieu—the faces of ruffians and road hags. There are a few that look promising. I make a mental note.

Aggie and Billy sit near the back of the room and off to one side. I motion them into the conference room and shut the door behind us.

"They've offered five thousand," I inform them.

"Well, I hope you told 'em they could shove that up their ass," Billy declares.

"I think we ought to consider it. We've got big problems with this case. They've got a file three inches thick full of medical records documenting a long history of Aggie's complaints of back pain. All of it *before* this wreck. Which raises the question: *why the hell didn't you tell me about all of that and why did you tell them over and over that you'd never had back pain before?*"

"But that's got nothing to do with this," Aggie pleads. "That was my *upper* back. It was my *lower* back that got hurt in the wreck."

"Aggie, that dog won't hunt," I explain.

"But *why?*"

"Never mind why. Just take my word for it. Mildred Mahorne will crucify you on the stand with those records. She'll have the jury thinking you'd lie when the truth would do better."

She begins tearing up. "This is so unfair. I'm the one who went through all the suffering and now they want to call *me* a liar?"

"It ain't right," Billy chimes in. "She ain't the one on trial here."

"The hell she ain't," I correct him. "This all comes down to credibility and we're going to be *stripped naked* of that when the jury sees that medical file." Looking at Aggie, I immediately regret the use of that figure of speech.

"But I can't settle for five thousand dollars," she whines. "My trailer payments are three months behind. I owe my mother money. I still owe my chiropractor. And then there's your fee. I've got to have *at least* ten thousand."

"Tell 'em we'll take ten thousand or they can shove it up their ass," Billy concurs.

It is not uncommon for my clients to evaluate their cases by looking to what they need to net in order to shore up their own financial situations rather than to what their case is actually worth. I have had much experience dealing with such people and I know well how to explain this matter in the simplest of terms. I begin talking to Aggie about the probabilities of the various outcomes. We will probably get some money from the jury, but it could easily be no more than a thousand dollars. The chances for a verdict of over three thousand are less than fifty-fifty. The chance of getting five thousand is remote. And ten thousand is out of the question. I tell her I completely understand that she *needs* ten thousand but I then go on to painstakingly explain that what she *needs* is irrelevant and must not be considered when evaluating a settlement offer. The object is to get the most money we can possibly get. In this case, all the signs indicate that five thousand is the tops, and if we can get that by settling, we don't need to risk the uncertainty of a jury trial. I lay this all out with lucid, irrefutable logic and wait for her answer. There is a moment of becalmed silence before she replies.

"But I need ten thousand to catch up my trailer payments and pay back mamma and pay you and—"

"Tell 'em it's ten thousand or shove it up their ass," Billy helpfully volunteers.

We are interrupted by a knock at the door. It is Mildred informing us that the Honorable J. Cavandar Prickle is ready to begin the trial. I rise confidently and motion for Aggie and Billy to follow me into the courtroom. My competitive emotions stir. We are going to trial.

The first battle in this war will be fought selecting a jury. Judge Prick has randomly assigned forty of the numerous Bedford County citizens summoned for jury duty to serve on our panel. From these, Mildred and I will each strike one name at a time until we are left with the twelve who will decide Aggie's fate. I reconnoiter their faces with uneasiness. Few of the ruffians and road hags I had identified earlier are on this panel. This is not good. Even worse, the panel appears to be disproportionately loaded with bankers, insurance salesmen, and doctor's wives—the worst possible type of juror for a case like this. I look over at Mildred. There is a smile on her face and a twinkle in her blue eyes.

We begin the *voir dire* of the jury—the process of asking intimate, none-of-your-business type questions to jurors about their personal lives in order to determine what hidden biases they hold that might incline them in our favor. We do this to assure that the jury will be fair and impartial. The term is commonly pronounced *"voy dire"* in the halls of the Bedford County courthouse. But Drinkin' Sammy would always correct us, explaining that the term is actually French, not Latin, and that the correct pronunciation is *"vowaa dear."* Judge Prick has gone back to pronouncing it as *"voy dire"* and could care less which is correct. Just another indication of our backsliding since Drinkin' Sammy's demise.

However you choose to pronounce it, voir dire is a critical part of the trial because it is the best place to slip before the jury the suggestion that the defendant has insurance coverage that will pay off on any verdict they render. The mention of insurance during the trial is strictly forbidden and will result in mistrials, contempt citations, and other sanctions being visited upon the head of any lawyer who even hints at its existence. During voir dire, however, there is some leeway for the skillful lawyer to plant the idea of insurance in the jury's mind. When Drinkin' Sammy was on the bench, there was a lot of leeway. "Now Mr. Juror, have you ever been in a car wreck? And did you have **insurance**? And did the other driver have **insurance**? And who was your **insurance** with? And did your **insurance** pay off on the claim?" And on and on while the other lawyer ranted and raved and objected and raised all manner of hell about "this line of questioning," all to no avail. Drinkin' Sammy would just smile and bang down his gavel and shout *"objection overruled."* Not so, however, with young Judge Prick. One must now be very delicate and subtle with this issue. There is a good deal more artistry involved with the practice of law in Judge Prick's court.

By eleven-thirty, we have selected a jury. We have a doctor's wife, an accountant, and several blue collar workers, one of whom has been involved in his own nasty dispute with an insurance company. Not the best jury I've ever seen for a plaintiff, but not the worst either. Judge Prick elects to break for lunch once the jury is seated. I decide to dine with Aggie and Billy so that we can review a few last minute details. As we leave the courthouse, Billy reiterates our negotiating position, just in case it is not clear in my mind by now.

"Tell 'em if they won't pay ten thousand they can shove it up their ass."

I don't even want to know what it is they are supposed to shove.

The trial proceeds rapidly. It actually comes together much better than I had anticipated. Aggie proves to be a more compelling than expected witness, describing her horrific injuries in a firm and husky baritone. There are even a few well-timed tears as she recounts the months of agony when she hurt too bad to clean houses and fell behind on her trailer payments. Of course, Mildred beats up on her pretty good with the piles of medical records showing the prior back problems, but the damage seems fairly contained. The chiropractor, whom I have paid five hundred dollars for a one-hour appearance, turns in a sterling performance, deftly explaining, with the aid of a rubber replica of the spine, how the impact of the truck caused a "subluxation of the lordatic curve." Things are on a roll for us and I have a good feeling about the outcome. Even Judge Prick, try as he might, can't seem to disrupt the flow of our case. Mildred does not bring up the stiletto heels—she obviously didn't see them. Maybe this will be the break that turns the tide our way.

By four-thirty, we have rested our case and I have delivered a scintillating closing argument. Aggie's fate is now with the jury. Mildred and I reciprocally stroke our egos, congratulating each other on a case well tried. If I am not mistaken, her confidence level has ebbed just a mite. Now the nervous waiting begins. We pace the floors, the halls, the restrooms. Billy races back and forth to the front steps to grab breaths of nicotine. "Relax," I tell them, my voice cracking under the rush of my own adrenaline. I am ready for this to be over. It is getting nigh time for my evening dose of Jack Daniels.

At seven o'clock, the Honorable J. Cavandar Prickle emerges from his chamber and mounts the bench. The jury has given no sign that a verdict is near. "What in the hell could they be talking about for all this time?" he asks no one in particular.

I decide to venture a wishful guess. "Must still be adding up the damages."

"I don't understand it. This case is as straightforward as you can get. What are ya'll holding out for anyway?"

"Ten thousand dollars judge, or they can . . ." I catch myself just in time.

"Ten thousand dollars!" his honor erupts. "You don't seriously think that jury is going to give you ten thousand dollars for this case do you?"

"We've offered them five, judge," Mildred shouts, trying to appear reasonable.

"Well hell, that's reasonable," Judge Prick observes. "You ought to counsel your client to take that and let's bring this foolishness to an end."

I look around to Billy who is shaking his head no. I can *feel* him thinking where he wants this proposal filed. "We'll wait for the jury," I say.

"Well," thinks his honor aloud. "We could let the jury go home and come back tomorrow. I'm sure they're all ready for dinner right about now."

"Fine with me, judge," says Mildred.

"Me too," I say, attempting to be agreeable.

"But then, if we let them stay in there, maybe they'll go ahead and finish up." Judge Prick is going to *starve* a verdict out of them.

"Fine with me, judge," I agree.

"Me too," says Mildred.

Finally, at eight-fifteen, the bailiff enters the courtroom to inform us that the jury has reached a verdict. There is a benumbing heaviness to the moment and a rush of emotions as the twelve haggard people file into the courtroom.

"Have you reached a verdict?" Judge Prick thunders.

A demur woman holding a folded piece of paper nods yes. I would never have guessed that she would be the foreperson.

"Pass me the verdict, bailiff," the judge orders. He receives the folded document and fumbles with it for what seems like an eternity. Aggie stands beside me breathing heavily. I can tell she is about to tear up. Finally, Judge Prick unfolds the verdict. He appears to read it over no less than three times. Then his eyes roll backward. Could there be something in the Bedford County water that causes this, I wonder. But then I realize this is probably good news.

"Mr. Bailiff, will you read the verdict." He hands the paper to the bailiff, shaking his head in bemused disbelief.

"We the jury find for the plaintiff and award damages of fifteen thousand dollars."

"There is a God in heaven," screams Aggie.

"Order in the court!" Judge Prick cries, banging his gavel.

Aggie has both arms around me now, squeezing me in a bear hug. Billy is patting me on the back and telling me what a wonderful job I did. I am back in his good graces, at least until his next drunk driving case. I look over at Mildred who is gathering up her files as she shakes her head in disbelief, a wry smile on her lips. I am flooded with a feeling of warm satisfaction. Against overwhelming odds, I have successfully waged war for my client. I have battled a tough-as-jagged-glass, grant-no-quarter defense attorney and a tight-ass, plaintiff-hating judge and prevailed, leaving the diffused residue of injustice in my wake. I float out of the courtroom in a sublime state of consciousness. Bring on the next challenge—I am ready for it. I am supremely confident. The meek will surely be dispossessed of the earth if I get the chance to contest the Will.

Outside, the streets are calm and the traffic is light. Mildred stands on the curb waiting to cross.

"You did a good job," I console her. "Those are the breaks."

"You too," she begrudgingly allows. "You just can't tell about juries."

"Win some, lose some, I guess."

"I guess."

We cross the street toward the parking deck. It is deserted now, except for my LaSabre and the black Lexus beside it. *Oh shit*, I think as we approach our cars, hoping she won't notice her passenger door.

Down the street, the siren of an ambulance echoes between buildings. I pause to orient myself to its direction. It is coming our way. The flashing red lights produce an eerie strobe effect under the low hanging ceiling of the parking deck. I glance at Mildred. She stands by her Lexus, door open, ready to enter, but pausing just a moment to stand there, erect and still. We watch the ambulance speed toward us, the excited energy of its flashing lights and wailing siren building with its approach, then peaking as it passes, then ebbing away like the streamers of a fireworks display melting into the night until there is nothing left of it but the echoes within our heads. Our eyes meet for a second, maybe longer, no expressions, no words, just one brief connection between minds that does not seem to require elaboration. She shoots me a coy smile as we turn to get into our cars.

F. BRETT COX

THE LAST TESTAMENT OF MAJOR LUDLUM

June 20th 1906

By the grace of God, amen. It has been advised by my lawyer Mr.
Doyle & others that I, Major Ludlum, put in writing a last will & testament
so that my worldly possessions may be disbursed after I am gone. I am
however profoundly certain that as everything else has been taken out of
my hands since the Rev. Mr. Rabon's passing with no regard for my wishes
nor the truth, that this most sorry practice will in fact continue after my
death & that Sarah Williamson & the good citizens of Kingston will carve
up my possessions as they see fit, & so to hell with them. As I have no wife
or children nor relations who have meaning it is of no consequent to myself what becomes of my property. So in the stead of a will I shall make this
document the final & true statement of the events leading up to my wrong-
ful arrest & condemnation. Posterity & the vigilance of Almighty God in
whom my faith is sorely tried but ultimately unshaken will witness to the
righteousness of my claim & blast the rest.

It is two days now from when it is said that I am finally to be hanged, as
my lawyer Mr. Doyle informed me that his meeting with the governor was
of no good & is why I have been removed back to Kingston jail to await the
payment of the debt it is claimed I owe. I owe no debt for I did not shoot
the Rev. Mr. Rabon & so owe not one thing any more than I owed the Rev.
payment on his rotten lumber, which is why I suppose I am here in the 1st
place, that along with the business of Sarah which was nobody's fault but

my own as well as the sorry judgment of the community.

They have said that there was malice between myself & the Rev. Mr. Rabon as if this was proof enough that I did the crime. That this malice existed is a fact I have admitted freely both before my trial & during as well as after, & that this foresaid malice existed for good reason. I had contracted with the Rev. in November of the year of our Lord 1904 to purchase a quantity of timber for the shoring up of my barn which was in a state of lamentable disrepair & sundry other improvements on my property. Which timber I signed for in good faith only to find when I received said timber that it was in fact rotted & in generally poor condition with holes & soft places in it so as to make it worthless for my or any other purposes. I refused to pay & rightly so but the Rev. insisted on payment claiming I signed for the property & so owed him payment.

It was said during the proceedings of my trial that I was a rough man who lived outside the laws of man & God & that it was no wonder that I would not hesitate to take a human life. Perhaps I have failed to be a good Christian for which failing my Lord & Savior will judge me these two days hence but I have never taken human life, not the Rev.'s nor anybody's unless the two niggers I shot for crossing the Dead Line count as the prosecution seemed to think they did ignoring the fact that I was merely keeping the standards of the community which has been ordained by tradition in that no nigger shall come north of the Dead Line to live or to work. The prosecution & the good citizens of Kingston seemed to have ignored that fact besides which one of the niggers fell in a ditch & crawled out & away & was not seen no more & so may or may not have died.

But even as I have not taken human life so I have always paid all debts which are truly mine & I so informed the Rev. when he tried to charge me for the rotted lumber. I told him that his lumber was no good as any damn fool could see & so I needn't to pay for it or any other damaged goods. I told him so reasonable & calm which I know I did as I had not anything to drink that day excepting water at my own well. The Rev. informed me in a loud voice so that all his workers both white & nigger turned to look at us (for we were standing in his lumber yard at the time) that he weren't to be talked back to by a poorbucker like myself & that I had signed for the lumber & so owed him the money & that the few holes that was in the lumber was of no account & would in any case probably be an improvement on whatever I had in the first place. Not wanting to be stared at by the niggers or the trash he had in his employ I said in also as loud a voice as possible that I did not understand why the Presbyterians of Kingston could not afford to have a full-time preacher as rather a preacher & lumberman & that for the spiritual good of the community I hoped that he was better at the first than at the last for his lumber was rotten & I would not pay for it, & so turned & walked away.

It is of no import to detail here what followed in later days & weeks, for my time draws nigh & while my jailer has sworn to provide me with as much paper as necessary to my avowed purpose I do not trust the white trash who imprison me to be faithful to the truth any more than the high & mighty citizens who condemned me. Suffice it to say that after a powerful weight of discourse between the Rev. & myself that the following month the same Sheriff Hamacker who will I am told escort me to the gallows found that I was in the right & that as the timber was "demonstrably faulty" as he showed when he broke a four-inch thick board with both hands & little effort I owed the Rev. no money. I thanked him soundly & went about my business.

From that day on the wrath of the Rev. Mr. Rabon was directed at me. His sermons, I am told, begun to weigh heavy in their attacks upon the unrighteous & the unchurched & the flouters of God's law with most specific reference to some of those who existed outside the limits of the town of Kingston like they also lived outside the limits of the City of God. A man told me that the Rev. even cited my name as an example of the ignorant damned once but I have not in truth ever been able to confirm this.

Now I am used to the scorn of those who were born in town & fancy theirselves of higher station than the rest of us who do their work oftentimes & are no better than niggers in their eyes. I say I am most used to it & it does not bother me one bit. I am not ignorant no matter what they say as I know for my schoolteacher Miss Sessions once told me that I had a powerful fluency with my language & should control & develop it which I never done until now as until now I had no need or desire of writing more than my name when necessary. I am neither ignorant in the ways of the world of men & know for a fact that the Rev. Mr. Rabon was mightily angry at me for having been made a fool of by a poorbucker & nothing he said or did would surprise me.

It did not even surprise me when he began to publicly stain Sarah Williamson & myself. I was aware when I took up with Sarah that the community at large would more than likely as not scorn us for we were not lawfully man & wife & thus sinners. Yet as the community at large has never seemed at all anxious to acknowledge me as other than rough & ill-bred & away from the center of their world it has not seemed necessary for me to do other than see after my own affairs & farm what I can & provide for myself & be left alone, occasionally to do the citizens a service by taking out their niggers when they stray across the Line which I would do anyway as they have no business up here. So if I choose to provide myself with a woman who pleases me I do not see where it is any business of the community of Kingston or the Rev. Mr. Rabon. Admittedly also it was known to me that Sarah was still in the eyes of the law married to Mr. Williamson but it was also known to all folks around & to Almighty God as well that he was a drunk who was unable to provide for her or satisfy her in a husbandly way & cared not what she did. It is said in the Holy Bible that King David partook freely of his handmaidens & if a king can do that with many women I do not see why a simple man as myself should not have an abandoned white woman of some comeliness & no use to anyone else.

& Sarah & I took up & I must witness here as God is watching & the gallows loom that I took care of her, good & proper. I saw to her needs & provided for her & never beat her except that she was ever showing me disrespect or refused to come to me when I wanted her as the Holy Scripture ordains woman to obey man. This never did her no harm & besides if she did not come to me & I beat her she more likely came to me the quicker & with enthusiasm. & as Sarah did washing & odd chores for the high & mighty citizens of Kingston she was able to tell me tales of them that amused me, not the least of which was that the Rev. Mr. Rabon's wife would meet Sarah regular to give her washing & have marks & sundry bruises on her face & elsewhere & claimed she had fell or some such when it was plain to anyone with eyes that she had been beat. Sarah would lay in my arms & tell me these things which pleased me near as much as the smell & touch of her herself.

Yet the Rev. maintained his persecution, & as I said this did not surprise me none too greatly. But it would be less than the truth which above all as God knows I want hard to convey if I did not say that it did surprise me when the Rev. appeared on my doorstep having driven in his mule & wagon all the way up from Kingston for the purpose of reading me scripture & to threaten swearing out a warrant against Sarah & myself on grounds of adultery. This was on July 18th 1905 & as the Rev. read the scripture the sweat poured from his brow from the heat & perhaps also as I have thought since from his nerves as he was right farther from town than he usually strayed & if he had been a nigger I could have shot him.

At this point I must as I am before God & posterity affirm that I was indeed drunk when the Rev. appeared, having just bought a jug of good corn & been sharing it with Sarah, who was also right drunken inside. When he told me the Savior's words that whosoever looketh at a woman with lust in his heart has committed adultery with that woman I laughed & asked the Rev. if he remembered what it looked like. He then became abusive & began to threaten me with the warrant, & I did shout back at him, & then Sarah came stumbling out the door to see what the shouting was about. She was as I have said prior drunk & only partially clothed, & I have after much powerful thought the thin satisfaction of knowing that the Rev. defied his Savior as he stared at my woman. But at the time in my drunkenness it enraged me & I struck him & shoved him off my porch, & then turned & hit Sarah & shoved her inside with my foot. & then I did turn to the Rev. Mr. Rabon & say that if he bothered me more I would kill him.

I have thought of those words often in the time that has passed since then & regretted them heartily, & if there was some way to unsay them I would. Yet I cannot lie now & say that I did not say them for I did. Yet I am not neither lying when I swear before Almighty God that I never did act on those words.

For it was not until the following evening when Sheriff Hamacker & his men came to arrest me & Sarah that I learned of the Rev.'s death. It was not until their questioning begun that I learned of the circumstance. That the Rev. was plowing in his field that morning & that he was shot in the back while plowing, that he fell on his plow & remained so for the afternoon so that a young high & mighty driving by in her horse & buggy thought he had fallen asleep at work, that when the Sheriff & his men finally arrived the sun had worked so on the body to where it was so hot they thought the Rev. still lived.

It is of no consequent to detail the events which followed our arrest as they are well known to all. Despite my protests of innocence & lack of direct evidence, Sarah & myself were in fact brought to trial & were both convicted. The prosecutor made much of us before the good citizens of Kingston & cited the business of the warrant for adultery besides which was all in all enough to convince twelve good men & true. My lawyer Mr. Doyle, who moved here from other parts & has confided in me as we have grown closer throughout the weeks & months that he feels as much of an outsider as any poorbucker, fought good & proper for me but failed before the justice of Kingston. That is one thing I wish to note about the trial.

The other being that as Sarah sat on the stand & was questioned by the prosecutor as to did I in fact threaten to kill the Rev. Mr. Rabon she said "Yes he did" which I would expect no more as it is the truth & I had already admitted as much. But when she was asked if I was capable of carrying out such a vicious deed she stared into the stifling air of the court & said "Yes he is" & no more. Nothing in my defense.

My lawyer Mr. Doyle informs me that this is why Sarah was convicted but with mercy & not sentenced to hang. I say she also is no better than the rest.

Of the appeals which followed & which my lawyer Mr. Doyle so heroically pursued I will not relate neither as it has been a full day since the beginning of this my testament & I prefer to spend my last hours on this earth in contemplation of my fate & my God who awaits me rather than scratching on this paper. Suffice it to say it has none of it been to no use & I will die tomorrow. Only two things remain.

One is that my lawyer Mr. Doyle has been of great service to me, even to having me removed elsewhere for a time so that the Rev.'s kinfolk might not get me, & it is not his fault that I have come to this end. When he last visited me yesterday as I was writing this he embraced me & left with tears in his eyes. I have scorned such from men in the past but am moved by it now.

The second thing being that before my lawyer Mr. Doyle came in yesterday I was visited by the Rev. Mr. Rabon's widow. She was & is an ugly woman & no better than the rest but I was curious that she should visit me now & more so that she should stand outside my cell & say nothing, just stare at me. The prosecutor said she did not appear at my trial in that she was too overcome with grief & three witnesses said where she was that morning which was elsewhere than the Rev.'s field. As she turned to leave I noticed that her bruises were almost healed.

I am most grievously sorry for what sins I have committed but do not apologize for those of which I am not guilty & say now what I will witness on the gallows tomorrow: you are hanging an innocent man.

Sarah tears at me. I never left a mark on her.

I trust the Rev. Mr. Rabon is satisfied now & is looking up from hell & laughing. God damn him, & the rest, each & all.

KIRK CURNUTT

THE HISTORY LESSON

"**This** town excretes history."

So says Drew Tennimon, fifty-three, thrice divorced, forty pounds over-weight, one month short of his thirtieth anniversary in the Montgomery, Alabama, public school system. As the trolley car in which he rides turns left onto one of the city's most historic streets, Drew clutches hard at the center pole. He must do this because this morning his center of gravity dangles somewhere just north of his kneecaps. A katzenjammer rages in his head, and his throat is gravel dry so when he speaks his words emerge caked in an unnatural croak. The only moisture in his mouth is from the beer paste stuck to his tongue. To hide his halitosis Drew has been popping breath mints since first period. The gesture's a formality, however. He knows his class knows he's drunk. He knows his colleagues know. He's just glad no one seems to care.

"You kids know what 'excrete' means?"

The eighth graders crowded onto the trolley benches stare blankly back at him.

"Guess not," Drew says. "Look it up in your dictionaries when you get home. You'll catch my drift."

The trolley halts along a northern curb where the road begins to dip downward to expose the mishmash of architectural styles that is the city skyline. Interspersed among the boxy office complexes and humble eight-story skyscrapers are various Acropolis-styled state buildings, their pillared steps and ornate archways grandiose monuments to bureaucratic self-importance. Despite its classical pretensions, there is nothing to Drew's eyes particularly historic, nothing particularly Montgomery about this vista. It exudes a sleek productivity that offends his sense of what his city is all about. The skyline is more metal than wood, pretends to look more to the future than the past, is more anxious to assure observers that something is happening within its many-spired silhouette, that something's getting done. The real Montgomery, Drew believes, is content to laze and drowse, a land that time forgot.

"Over here to your left—" he snaps his fingers for emphasis "—let's pay attention, please—this is the First White House of the Confederacy. Why should you care? Because this was the home, the very home, ladies and gentlemen, in which Jefferson Davis lived during the first months of the Civil War.

"You know Jefferson Davis, I hope. Only the president of the Confederacy. That's why Montgomery to some will always be known as the Cradle of the Confederacy. Because in the hearts of not just a few historians, the Civil War got its formal start here, right here on this street, just blocks up from our backsides, up there by the state capitol. 8 February 1861: delegates from the southeast adopt the Confederate Constitution, in effect telling Abe Lincoln to stuff his Union up his gob. This place—*your* hometown—was the capital of the South . . . at least until they moved it up to Richmond a few months later.

"You know why that happened, kids? Hotels. Virginia had better hotels. As one delegate put it, the only thing in Montgomery that took his mind off the fleas was the flies. That's right. Something as insignificant as fleas and flies can decide history. Now, if that doesn't fascinate you, then I guess—I don't know—you must have a black hole for a brain."

Nobody pays attention. That's by no means an uncommon state of affairs, but at this moment, Drew finds the indifference grating.

"You kids don't appreciate how historical this town is," he tells them. "History's in the blood—history *is* the blood. It bloats this place; constipates it. That's why I say this town excretes history. . . . It's so thick around here that it backs up the sewers. And not just any old history, but the best kind: contradictory history. Paradoxical history. Here's your First White House of the Confederacy. Now go two blocks down the hill and one block over and you got your Dexter Avenue Baptist Church, the church in which the Rev.

Dr. Martin Luther King, Jr. preached.

"Jefferson Davis and Martin Luther King—those are two tent poles of Southern history, kids, and there's evidence of them here, in this town, within yards of each other. Of course, they weren't in Montgomery at the same time. But just the idea that the soil under your feet could give growth to two forces so different in their direction, so opposing. . . . You can't get a better sense of the complexity, the interwoven ways of history than this—"

A hand shoots into the air. Drew closes his eyes, just for a second's rest, for the rumble of the idling trolley is rattling through his head like a spoon in an empty tureen.

"What is it, Goat?"

A fourteen-year-old black kid, his head half-obscured by the hood of a pullover jacket, leans forward in his seat. His name is Randall, but everyone including Drew refers to him as Goat. The first time Drew heard Randall called Goat he was unhip enough to think it an insult. Then it was explained to him that Goat was an acronym for "Greatest Of All Time."

"Mr. Tenny-man," Goat says. "You couldn't pay me to go in that White House right there. I mean, it's a *white* house, yeah? That guy you're talking up, he was all about the slavery. Why I want to know about him? He was down on me and mine. Probably had him eyeholes cut in his pillowcase. No way 'round it, sir. The dude was a cracker. A redneck. I bet he had him his own rope swinging off the poplar tree."

A subterranean hint of laughter rustles the bus. The kids come to life with the urge to cheer on this challenge to Drew's authority, which Drew doesn't consider a challenge at all. He likes Goat, likes it when the kid talks. Goat's questions keep the class attentive.

"See, that right there's the problem, you guys. You have to be objective about history. I'm not asking you to admire Jeff Davis, even though in all likelihood you'll attend a high school named after him—either him or Robert E. Lee. What I'm saying is that you can't take it personally. The Confederacy, the Civil War, the Civil Rights Movement even—they're facts that happened, and you should know them. Why?

"Not because I believe that old humbug about those not knowing history being doomed to repeat it. No, that's cow pie. The point is that the past is a story. Better yet, it's a *mystery* story, and you're the detective. You've got evidence and testimony and multiple versions of events, and it's your job to sort through it all, to weigh and measure and evaluate and then decide what's true and what's not. You'll hear people say that there's no such thing as true history, just conflicting accounts. But if you come to it without bias, with no agenda other than your love for getting to the real magoo, then you're the one that can decide what really happened and what didn't, and that, as you guys would say, is doper than—"

The class has heard this speech before, so by the fifth or sixth word they've returned to chatting about more pressing concerns. Drew hears the whispers about what's on TV nowadays, where to skateboard, who's been caught frenching whom. As he rambles, Drew watches one girl not two feet away stretch her fingers in front of her friend's face. *I'm talking history*, he thinks. *She's talking nail polish.*

"Amber—you listening to me?"

The girl's hand shoots down to her lap as her eyes broaden in embarrassment. That's the worst thing Drew can do to these kids—call on them. They hate being called on because it means they have to participate.

"Amber dear, I asked if you were listening."

"Yes, sir. I was."

Amber resembles every girl who has taken Drew's class over the past thirty years. She's small and cute in a budding-breasts sort of way, but mostly she's memorable for what's she not: interested. In the hall Amber is all giggles and squirms, but sitting in front of Drew's desk she radiates the stoic perseverance of a political prisoner. She does her homework, turns it in on time, but she only does what she has to do to get by. There's no curiosity, no enthusiasm. *Thirty years of her*, Drew thinks. The decades would be a total blur if this girl's name didn't periodically change. When Drew first started teaching she was a Sandy or a Judy. Then came a decade of Kim and Kathy, Melinda and Marcy. Now he lives in an age of Ambers and Ashleys.

"Are you now?" he asks.

"Sir?"

"You listening to me right now?"

"Yes, sir. I'm sorry, sir."

"This very instant?"

Drew takes a step forward. The girl blinks.

"Sir?"

"You don't like history, do you, Amber? The whole force of your being at this moment makes it painfully clear to me that you can't stand to have to learn about the past—but why? That's what I want to know. What's your grudge against history?"

Amber holds her breath, uncertain what her teacher wants her to say.

"Let me guess." Drew goes on, not bothering to wait for the response he knows isn't coming. "You don't like history because . . . *you can't get into it.* Am I right?"

The girl's eyes dart right and then left. She's looking for backup, for someone to rush in with a sarcastic comment and save her from this grilling. Only the class clowns have taken a powder, and the smart asses have headed for the hills. *Why me?* the little look on Amber's little lost-lamb face pleads.

"Come on, come on." Drew's aware that his voice has thickened, that he's no longer joshing the way he does with Goat. The pumping sensation in his head picks up its pace, the throb rising from the bridge of his nose to the center of his forehead. The ache in his shoulders and spine tells him this is a fight he doesn't want to pick. Amber's the kind of girl who'll complain to her parents—her parents who will no doubt accost him in his classroom one morning before first period as he's trying to shake off his dread for the approaching day. "Our daughter says you're picking on her," they'll say. "You ridicule her. You make her feel stupid by asking her questions. Why do you have to ask her all those questions?"

"I just want an honest answer," Drew says. "You don't like history. Message received. But can't you even explain *why* you don't like what you don't like? Amber, please, I beg of you. Enlighten me."

When Amber realizes he isn't going to let up, she shrugs. *Shrugs!* The ambivalence hits Drew like a charley horse. A knot of pain ropes its way down his neck and into his rib cage. He wishes he could go back to bed. *No:* He wishes he could have a drink and *then* go back to bed. That shrug eats him alive. For thirty years Drew's been nothing but a shrug receptacle. He pushes his students to be articulate, to express a kindling of interest in something—anything—that might enliven them, that might relieve the stupor of adolescent detachment. That's his job, dammit, but they don't get it. *Oh well*, they always answer him. *Whatever. I don't know. Yeah, huh, uh.* When the world ends, Drew thinks, it won't be with a whimper, much less a bang. No, the apocalypse is foretold in the annoyingly abbreviated shoulder jerk of every Amber he's ever known.

The girl decides to break her silence.

"It's too old," she announces with a simple declarative pout.

Drew feels his knees buckle. He grips the pole harder, but his palms are sweaty, and the extra weight he carries makes him feel as though he lugs a heavy Santa sack.

"Old? Well, you're right, Amberbamber. History *is* old. I suppose that's kind of the point, don't you think?"

But, no, the real point, Drew thinks, is that *he's* the one that's old. But he won't cop to that. That would be admitting too much. If he's learned nothing over these thirty years, he's learned not to be self-deprecating. Kids seize on self-deprecation. They gut teachers like deer with it. Drew palms his forehead again, hoping to massage away the stagnant bloat, but the feeling only hardens. A glob of sweat slips down the back of his ear and splashes on his shoulder. It doesn't matter. The rest of his shirt is already soaked through from the May humidity.

"Here's the thing, you guys. Here's the thing you just don't get. You *won't* get it. See, it's your misfortune to grow up at a time in which time itself has splintered into meaningless. Used to be that our sense of the here and now was tied to the past. *Tied to it.* There was nothing that happened that couldn't be traced back to some previous consequence. The world was the sum total of everything that had occurred up to that point. But not any more. No more. You guys, you live in this little bubble of a perpetual present, a bubble that floats free and detached, without any sense of where you've been or where you're going. That's why you don't like history. Nothing's attached to anything anymore. Everything's random, conceived immaculately out of thin air. Old's irrelevant, novelty's the false idol, the fatted calf that we dance around as we sharpen our knives in our hungry anticipation for instant gratifica—Hey!"

The shout he lets off sends a new tsunami of pain rippling along the coast of his temples. The trolley grows silent again as the kids stare at Drew's hunched figure. Amazing, he thinks, how he can only hold their undivided attention when he shuts his mouth.

"Terry Clump! Why do you have your nose under your collar?"

In a backbench a roly-poly kid with straight black bangs draping his eyebrows has tucked half his face under his shirt collar. He looks like a Mexican bandit. It takes several seconds for Terry's chin to pop into sight.

"There's exhaust fumes back here, sir. This bus's stinking me up. I'm getting gas poisoned!"

The class bursts out laughing. Drew knows why. On their last field trip Terry Clump executed a rapid round of machine-gun-style farts that doubled kids over like victims of some St. Valentine's Day massacre. As soon as Drew realized that the sounds were authentic—that these raspberries were no mere wet-lips-on-a-dry-palm imitation—he ordered the boy to cease and desist. But Terry just struck a perplexed look, as if he couldn't believe that Drew might not know that the boy's bowels had a mind of their own.

"It's the Cheetos, sir," Terry testified in his own defense. "They come out the way they go in, hot and spicy."

That smart remark had earned him a permanent write-up in his discipline folder, not to mention a principal's conference with his parents. Yet neither punishment had taught the boy to temper his talents.

"Y'all better be laughing about *car* exhaust," Drew says with disgust. He twists sideways to face the driver. Even the damn driver is smiling at Terry's disruption. "Where are we, anyway?"

When Drew looks out the window, he realizes that the bus has looped a block north and now heads east. Thanks to the distractions the Civil Rights memorial he was supposed to show the kids went right by. Unnoticed.

"Pull over here," the teacher tells the driver. The trolley stops beside a glittering brick plaza. Drew points to the corner across the street. "Somebody tell me what happened on this street corner fifty years ago."

No response.

"It's not a trick question, kids. There's a six-million dollar museum right in front of you commemorating it."

Still no response.

"Bethany?—Tiffany?—Stephanie?—Randall?—Marco?—Kendall?—LaKisha?—Malika?—Juanita?—*Steven?*"

They're intentionally keeping quiet now. Drew's convinced of it. The signs are everywhere. Eyes lowered so they don't meet his, blank faces, slouching bodies. *My life,* Drew thinks, *has been a thirty-year piss to the wind.*

"It was on this corner, this very corner, on December 1, 1955, that Mrs. Rosa Parks refused to give up her seat on the Cleveland Avenue bus. Why is that a big deal?"

Nothing. Drew licks his lips, but it's a pointless exercise. His tongue's too dry to relieve the cracking.

"It's a big deal—" he insists "—because that event begat the Montgomery Bus Boycott, which in turn begat Martin Luther King, which in turn begat nine kids as young as yourselves trying to make it past Orval Faubus into the door of the all-white Central High School in Little Rock, which in turn begat the Woolworth's lunch-counter demonstrations in Greensboro, thus begetting the Student Nonviolent Coordinating Committee and the Congress of Racial Equality, which in turn begat the Freedom Riders, which led to Byron De La Beckwith blowing away Medgar Evers, which led to George Wallace shaking his segregationist finger in the schoolhouse door and Bull Connor turning on the hoses in Birmingham, which led to 250,000 people marching on Washington to have a dream with King, which begat the Sixteenth Street Church bombing, which begat Johnson signing the Civil Rights Act of 1964, which kicked off Freedom Summer that culminated in Goodman, Chaney, and Schwerner getting murdered in a Mississippi bog, which in turn begat the Selma to Montgomery march and the confrontation on the Edmund Pettus Bridge, which in turn led Johnson to sign the Voting Rights Act of 1965—"

He's aware that the kids aren't even registering his words, just his rhythm, the insistent, pulverizing rhythm that has his jaws grinding and the ache in his head bulging to its syncopated beat.

"—All of which begat the glorious spectacle of integration that I myself witnessed not last Friday eve while chaperoning the Fall Kick-Off Dance whence I spied *you*, Candy LeBon, on the same dance floor with you, Gabriel Moncrief, both pumping your tail feathers to the uplifting strains of some rapper rhyming *rootie tootie fresh and fruity* with *big fat booty*."

Drew is staring at his feet now, which seem to expand and contract to the pulse of his throbbing brain. The pumping rubs against the back of his eyes, making them feel like soft-boiled eggs squeezed in invisible fists.

"For Christ's sake, it's not even the Civil War or Civil Rights. . . . I wish you could understand that. Maybe you're tired of the black-white thing. Maybe all this race stuff bores you. Well, okay, fine. So be it. But think about this: right there, right there on that corner where Rosa Parks took her stand—there used to be a little theater there, the Empire Theater. It was in that theater that Hank Williams invented country music. Do you understand the significance of that? *Hank Williams* sang here. The man who fused country with the blues, who made the white hillbilly kin to the black bluesman, made them mythic cousins in their folk woes. Hank—who by claiming he was looking for the lost highway and was so lonesome he could die forged honest anguish into art, who—if you know nothing more about

Hank Williams—died from alcohol poisoning in the backseat of a Caddy on the way to the next flea-bag gig, thus inaugurating the tradition of the star whose public self-destruction becomes an entertainment spectacle, thus begetting your Hendrix, your Joplin, your Morrison, your Kurt Cobain. . . . Don't tell me you kids are too young to care about Kurt Cobain!"

Drew's hands are out in front of his face, his fingers spread, as though he's trying to hold everything he knows in his palms for them.

"Twenty thousand people came out for Hank's funeral. *Twenty thou here in Montgomery.* I mean, can you name me one person in this town who could draw that big a crowd in this day and age?"

His eyes are closed. He shakes his head in disbelief, thirty years of disbelief at kids' disinterest. Drew grinds his neck against his shoulder.

"It doesn't even have to be Hank and his jambalaya *oh-me-oh-my-a.* Just one block down, across Lee Street, that's where the Elite Restaurant used to be. You know who used to eat there? Scott and Zelda Fitzgerald ate there, that's who. You know them? Only the greatest, saddest, most *tragic* love story in the history of American writing, and it happened in this city. Do you know how important Montgomery was for Fitzgerald's writing? I mean, he never called it Montgomery when he wrote about this place, but you can feel its atmosphere in his words. The magnolia, the money, the melancholy. Even in *The Great Gatsby.* Daisy Fay, that's Zelda. . . . Did I mention she was *from here?* Went to *Lanier* High School, which happens to be the very building in which we hang our flanks day after day? Fitzgerald may've moved the city a few hundred miles up I-65 to Louisville in *Gatsby* to avoid annoying his in-laws, but it's really this place, *your* place. . . ."

Even the throttle of the trolley seems deafened by Drew's rambling. He grips the pole again for balance, only to realize that the wheels haven't moved. The throb in Drew's head grows to a tympani thump. From his peripheral vision he sees something swish into the air, a movement that three decades of teaching have taught him to dread as much as desire. A kid has raised his hand.

"What do you want, Jimmy?"

Jimmy's a kid who regularly dyes brown leopard spots into his already bleached hair, presumably to distract from the acne that dapples his face. Each day he wears the same outfit: an oversized T-shirt with some smart saying, droopy jeans, and white tennis shoes big and thick enough to pass for plaster casts.

"This Hank Williams guy," Jimmy asks, one eyebrow cocked above a cocky eye. "He any relation to Hank Jr.?"

The laughter this time is so loud that Drew can't even register his own annoyance. The howling, the snorting, the guffawing—they all blend into one sharp nick of sound that sears into his perception like a bandsaw. The noise is enough to set the floor vibrating; Drew feels the shaking shoot up the nerves of his legs and fire down the lengths of his arms, a long shock of electricity out to blow the ailing circuitry of his heart. *I am dying, Montgomery, dying.* He isn't, of course, and Drew knows it, but the class's hacking and rumbling remind him of the spitty ecstasy of vultures snacking on a purpling corpse.

"Take a left here and go up to Jefferson," Drew tells the trolley driver.

As the wheels lurch into motion Drew tugs his shirttails out of his khakis and wipes the sweat from his face. Kids spot the exposed bowl of his pink belly, but Drew doesn't care anymore. He lets them chatter as the Rosa Parks Museum dissolves in a haze of morning heat.

"What we gonna see next, Mr. Tenny-man?" someone calls out.

"Yeah—where we goin' now?" someone else says. "Nothin' back here but fallin' down buildings and stuff."

And stuff.

"My uncle says there's a place back here where homos go."

"How's your uncle know where homos go? He a homo?—"

"—*You* a homo, bitch—"

"Shut up, you guys. You'll make him mad again."

No, Drew thinks as he turns his back to the class. *It's too late for all that.* He stretches his arms above his shoulders. He feels drained but relieved, like waking up from a post-flu nap. He closes his eyes, closing out the squirrely talk. On the few occasions he consents to open them he directs the trolley driver east again, down a row of hollowed-out brick storefronts where only the occasional sign covered in dust hints that life ever bellowed along this block. Drew knows these buildings by heart, knows their genealogy as well as he knows his own family tree. He wishes he knew someone who cared to hear their stories, someone who would actually give a good goddamn about what events they witnessed, what events rubbed their facades raw.

Only Drew doesn't know anyone like that, and so the facts behind those events will be left to lie, stagnating, in the useless bucket of his head.

"Stop here," he orders the driver.

The trolley pulls alongside a gutted building. On the other side of the street is a field of overgrown rye grass. A few blocks back is the bar Drew frequents the nights he teaches adjunct classes at a nearby night school, before and after class. It's not his kind of place: overpriced food, loud music, too many big-haired women getting propositioned by no-haired men. But it's the only place in Montgomery, Alabama, where it's legal to sell draft beer, and draft has a thick immediacy, a heft, that Drew likes.

"What's this place, Mr. Drew? *Dawg.* Nothing here, man, nothing at all."

"Come on, Mr. Tenny-man. Tell us what this lump'a bricks is so we can get back to school. I don't wanna miss lunch. . . . I'm hungry."

Drew motions for the driver to flip open the trolley doors.

"You wanna know what this place is?" His turns around, facing them, his head suddenly clear and light. His shoulders are relaxed, and the discomfort in his chest cavity has miraculously drained away. Drew feels unburdened.

"This roadway along here used to be called Columbus Street, and a hundred and forty-plus years ago, it was one of the most traveled in Montgomery. You know why, kids? It was because in those days, the days of Reconstruction, there were little white plank houses along here—close your eyes and imagine it—and families who couldn't afford to seed their land would bring their daughters here, daughters who were sometimes as old as fourteen. That's right, the same age as you girls. And these families would rent their daughters to the women who ran these white plank houses for the rich men of the city, rich men, who, of course, subscribed to the Southern rule of gentility and thus made themselves invisible, coming here faceless, only under cover of darkness.

"What do you think these daughters did? Did they wash the rich men's linens? Nurse their children? Mend their shirts and darn their socks? Not hardly. See, these white plank houses were *whore*houses. Just think about it, kids—"

Drew sweeps his hand out toward the street as a ringmaster might, grand and ceremonial. "This is street where your great-great-grandmommas came to earn their dollar a lay."

And with that, he steps outside and starts walking. Not a fast walk but a slow, grunting trudge, the hobble of a man lost among forty extraneous pounds of himself. Still, each step is a relief, so within a few strides Drew feels those extra layers stripping away. He likens himself to a rotund apple peeling off the superfluous pulp, skinning itself to a core that it hasn't had contact with in ages. Just a block away—one block closer to the lone place in Montgomery, Alabama, where he can get draft beer—he hears the trolley idling along the curb. He imagines the chaos on board, the confused mumbling, the awkward *whoas* and *whoos*.

Just about every emotion, Drew figures, but a goddamn shrug.

Ben Erickson

COMING ABOUT
(a novel excerpt.)

The screen door had been sticking for months now, but the last week of summer thunderstorms had finally allowed it to make the transition from hard to open to not closing at all. Hanging slightly ajar on sprung hinges, it creaked in the midmorning breeze that was blowing in off the open bay not far away. A fly cruised easily through the inch wide gap between door and frame then paused on the porch to examine the dried up remains in the bottom of a coffee cup.

Unimpressed, the insect glided through the open door to the small house and restlessly circled the room, making several passes at the sleeping figure sprawled across the bed in one corner. It came perilously close to the snoring open mouth—which was only a well timed inhale away—before being diverted by the remaining slice of pizza in an open box on the table. Using a piece of pepperoni as a landing strip, the uninvited guest settled lightly on the cold greasy surface.

Just as things were getting interesting, the phone on the floor by the bed rang, causing the fly to temporarily abandon its feast and take to the air again. The man on the bed groped about blindly for a pillow to cover his head, his hand finding it before the third ring. By the time the answering machine cut in with the opening riff from "Born to be Wild," he had succeeded in burying his head firmly under it.

At the point when the song's vocals should have begun, a sexy female voice on the tape intruded.

"Looking for adventure?" she asked suggestively. "Well then you've come to the right place. Magical Mystery Charters is your ticket to sailing excitement on Mobile Bay."

The sounds of Steppenwolf were replaced by those of The Beatles as the voice continued its seductive spiel.

"Feel the wind in your face and the salt spray in the air. We can provide the perfect outing for everything from that special party to a romantic evening just for two. Yes, Magical Mystery Charters *is* waiting to take you away. And remember, pirate theme birthday parties for the youngsters are just one of our many specialties. Captain Tom is probably out searching for buried treasure at the moment, but if you'll leave your name and number, he'll return your call as soon as possible." The beep that followed had been modified to resemble the deep two-tone bellow of a foghorn.

"*Mr.* Walker," a disdaining voice on the other end of the line began. It required only a small leap of the imagination to envision its owner holding the receiver by thumb and index finger as far away from his ear as possible, as if the connection itself would somehow contaminate him. "This is Mr. Beaufort calling again from The Hotel."

In contrast to his previous note of condescension, the carefully modu-lated Southern accent of the caller took on an almost reverential tone at the mention of his employer. Beaufort allowed a suitable pause for the phone to be picked up. When it wasn't, he continued unabated.

"If you are within the sound of my voice—which I strongly suspect you are—then be advised that several of our distinguished guests have chartered your boat for the afternoon." There was a distinctly derisive em-phasis on the word 'boat.' "While I have done my best to persuade our guests against it, I'm afraid they remain adamant. If you will check the stack of used bar napkins that you insist on calling an appointment book, you will notice that your presence is required in the yacht basin today promptly at four o'clock. Do try and not be late, need I add again?"

There was a pause as the caller thought about hanging up, but he couldn't resist firing a parting shot.

"I'm not quite sure if it is the mystery or magical aspect of your enter-prise that seems to intrigue our clientele, but please refrain from wearing that ridiculous pirate costume and bringing that foulmouthed bird of yours in the lobby again. The cleaning staff is still trying to remove the stains in the carpet from your last visit. And just so we will not have to have this discussion in front of our guests, kindly recall that the Oak Room Pub is reserved for hotel patrons only. Good day."

There was a click followed by the sound of the tape rewinding, then silence.

Taking the pillow off his head, Tom Walker peered out from beneath it cautiously before closing his eyes again. He fumbled for the half-smoked joint and lighter on the table by his bed. Lighting it, he took a deep drag and exhaled slowly.

A smile creased his weathered face at the thought of Beaufort's message. It was almost worth the ten mile sail to the upscale resort across the bay just to see the look on the concierge's face each time he put in an appearance. Plus, the tips usually more than made up for his trouble if he behaved himself and was in the mood to take the crap the guests often enjoyed dishing out.

His eyes gradually adjusted to the light, and the pounding in his head subsided to a gentle roar as the herb took effect. He knew better than to try and keep up with his first mate, Jim. The big man could put away a dozen beers without blinking. But it wasn't often that Irene gave out freebies at The Hole, so while she was in a generous mood, he had made the most of it.

The sign left by the previous owner actually said The Watering Hole, or to be more exact, The Watering Hol, the "e" being a casualty of the last hurricane. But since Irene had taken over the local drinking establishment almost twenty years ago, it had always been just The Hole.

The rundown appearance of the building's exterior was mirrored on the inside with a decor that could best be described as retro-nautical-shabby-chic with a liberal dose of vintage 1950's Formica and dingy paneling thrown in for good measure. Unlike the new upscale place that had opened up last year just down the road, Irene didn't go in for drinks with fancy names and paper umbrellas, and the songs on the old jukebox hadn't changed much since the day she arrived.

Sitting up cautiously in bed, Tom winced as he tried to work the kinks out of his sore back. When Irene's regular Friday beer delivery didn't show up, she had loaded up her empties and driven them into Mobile herself. She returned with her pickup almost dragging the ground just as he and Jim had walked up. It didn't take much to sweet-talk them into lending a hand, especially after she agreed to throw in some free samples as soon as the first keg was tapped.

It never occurred to Jim to wait for a dolly. He just swung a keg up on his shoulder like it was a bag of dirty laundry and lumbered off through the backdoor of the bar.

"Well?" Irene asked, raising an eyebrow in Tom's direction. "You waiting for a formal invitation?"

With his manhood in question, Tom followed Jim's example without thinking, only to feel a stab of pain shoot through his back as he lifted the heavy load. Determined not to give Irene the satisfaction, he managed to keep from wincing as his mind flashed back to that night over twenty years before.

It was hard to believe that so much time had passed since he and Jim played high school football together. During their senior year, they had made it all the way to the state play-offs, thanks in part to Tom's gun of a left arm and Jim's ability to give him the time to use it. He could still hear the crowd and feel the bright lights of Ladd Stadium as they huddled up with just under two minutes left to play in their final game.

When Tom dropped back to pass, he saw an open receiver near the far sideline. Cocking his arm back, he let the ball go in a tight spiral just as what felt like a freight train slammed into him. He never saw the blitzing linebacker that shot untouched through the gap between Jim and the right tackle to blindside him, and it was days before he even knew if his pass had been complete. When he woke up in the hospital, Jim was sitting by his bed with tears running down his cheeks. It was one of only two times he'd ever seen the big man cry, and Tom did his best not to think about the other one. The weeks he spent in the hospital left him with a long scar down his back, and his dreams of a scholarship to play for Alabama had dissipated like a morning fog on Mobile Bay.

While he did his best to hide the pain, he saw Irene give him her patented "you're not as tough as you think you are" look as he turned and followed Jim inside.

Getting up off the bed required a more concerted effort than Tom had anticipated. Once he was on his feet, he hobbled slowly over to the front door clad only in his boxer shorts. Leaning against the open doorway, he looked out over the sluggish river that flowed into the bay while idly scratching himself. The morning sun already bathed the near tropical landscape in its harsh light, and he squinted against the glare off the dark water as it meandered by.

Tom had celebrated his fortieth birthday at The Hole last night, and he expected to celebrate it several more times before the actual date rolled around in October. He had never attached much weight to arbitrary numbers that ended in a zero, but the last few months had found him stiff and sore in places that he never even realized he had before. Maybe there's something to even numbers after all, he conceded as he scratched his stomach and felt a larger bulge there than he remembered.

He stared absently out at the rickety wharf where his sailboat was docked. An old rowboat was pulled up on the shore next to it, and looking at it reminded him of Annie. He had succeeded in blocking her image out for the last two days, a record that had required the input of significant quantities of alcohol to achieve, but the sound of her voice on the answering machine had succeeded in resurrecting her ghost once again.

The message had been her idea. She had gone to the trouble of having it made at a local recording studio and surprising him with it. After her funeral Tom had been meaning to erase it, but almost a year had passed now and somehow he had never gotten around to it. He pressed the palms of his hands over his eyes to try and block out her image, but the sound of her voice came through anyway.

"Slow down, Tom!" he heard her say with a giggle as she looked around him toward the bow of the leaky rowboat.

Dragging one oar, he pulled hard with the other, causing the small boat to veer sharply toward land.

"Tom, watch out!" she yelled as he picked up speed before plowing into the cattails that lined the swampy shore.

Annie shrieked in surprise as a pair of mallards exploded from the reeds in front of them. She buried her head against his shoulder as they whistled by just a few feet away. Turning, they watched the birds wing their way up the river until they disappeared around the bend.

The phone rang again, interrupting Tom's unintended reverie. Walking over to the table, he picked it up on the second ring before the answering machine could cut in.

"Yeah," he said into the receiver, forgoing the usual business formalities since he knew who it was anyway.

"This is your last wakeup call," the concierge told him.

"Why Beaufort," Tom said amiably. "It's good to hear from you. I was just out swabbing down the *Annabel Lee*'s deck and getting her all ship-shape. I hope you haven't been trying to reach me?"

"Mr. Walker—"

"I prefer Captain Tom, if you don't mind."

"Very well, *Captain* Tom," Beaufort said with an almost audible bitter taste in his mouth. "I have left three messages on your answering machine. Why do you bother to own one if you don't ever check it?"

"You're absolutely right, Mr. Beaufort, and I apologize. But things have been a little hectic around here lately."

"I find that hard to believe," he replied, his feigned accent slipping just a little. "I would simply like to establish if you know why I have been calling?"

"Well," Tom answered, "either you have an unnatural fondness for sixties rock music, or you wanted to know if I remembered about this afternoon."

"The latter, I assure you," Beaufort said caustically.

"You want me there around four?"

"Not *around* four, Mr. Walker, but *at* four."

"I'd prefer—"

"I know, Captain Tom," Beaufort injected. "I assure you that if there was anyone else to call, I would. But since yours was the only sailboat for charter on the bay that survived the hurricane, you—as we say—are the only game in town. So if you could manage to be here at the appointed time, it would make my life so much easier."

"That's my sole purpose in life, Mr. Beaufort, to make your time on this earth as pleasant as possible." Tom said, hanging up before Beaufort could get in the last word.

Putting the phone down, Tom walked over to the table and eyed the remaining piece of pizza in the box, trying to remember how long it had been there. Picking it up, he tried unsuccessfully to date it with his nose before biting off a small piece and rolling it cautiously around in his mouth. When there was no adverse reaction, he took another bite. Walking out onto the screened porch—pizza in hand—Tom stood looking out at the water while chewing thoughtfully.

"Looking for adventure, sailor?" the woman's voice from the answering machine said behind him, followed by an appreciative whistle.

"Not today," Tom replied, going over to give the parrot a piece of pizza crust.

The bird squawked loudly as it paced restlessly back and forth on its perch.

"Coming about! Coming about! Watch out for the boom!" The bird said while bobbing its head up and down.

"Don't get your hopes up," Tom said. "Beaufy didn't mince words this time. I'm afraid you've been grounded."

"Walk the plank, landlubber!" the bird commanded as Tom opened the screen door and made his way down the gently sloping hill to the pier. Behind him, the bird reeled off a string of profanity in a voice eerily reminiscent of his own.

The *Annabel Lee* was tied securely to the dock, and Tom ran his hand lovingly along the varnished rail as he passed. Now that Annie was gone, the boat was the only constant in his life, the one thing that he hadn't let slide. Every spring he still pulled the old gaff-rigged wooden ketch out of the water and spent weeks scraping and painting her hull, sanding and varnishing her spars, and polishing the brightwork until it gleamed. What Beaufy didn't realize was that the only reason she had ridden out the hurricane was that Tom had taken the boat as far upriver as he could go and stayed on board throughout the storm, letting her lines out as the water rose and the winds howled.

Everyone thought Tom was crazy when he moved into the isolated house on the Bienville River that his grandfather had left him. Plumb loco. And when he took his share of the money from his grandfather's estate and bought back the senior Walker's boat that had been dry rotting in a corner of Hawkins yard, they just shook their heads and rolled their eyes. Nothing but sixty feet of firewood, John Hawkins had told him when Tom made him an offer. But Tom could tell that the crotchety boatyard owner was secretly pleased at being able to give the ketch a second life.

His grandfather had been a sailor, both by occupation and delight. He had started out as a deckhand and worked his way up the ladder to captain. When he retired from the sea, he had spent all his spare time designing and building the *Annabel Lee*. It had almost killed him when he grew too old to take her out any more, and rather than look at her sitting idly at the end of the wharf, he had sold her to Hawkins. While the boatyard owner had bought her to strip for salvage, he hadn't had the heart to touch her once she was out of the water. So there she had sat, slowly wasting away.

Some of Tom's fondest boyhood memories were centered around his grandfather's boat, so when the chance arose, he didn't have to think twice before taking it. After a year of nights and weekends spent working at Hawkins yard on the neglected vessel, the day had finally arrived when he slid her down the track and into the water. He stayed up all night pumping out the bilge until the wood swelled, and by morning she was sealed up tight.

His grandfather had named the boat after his wife, whose own mother had been reading Edgar Allen Poe when she was born, and Tom had no intention of changing it. Because of this family history, Tom had memorized the poem in elementary school and could still recite it word for word upon request, which he did regularly for his customers. The name was also special because it was Annie's as well. While Tom had seen this as mere coincidence, she had relegated it to the more mysterious category of fate. And the more he thought about it, maybe she was right.

Tom stopped at the end of the dock to chew the last bite of pizza before picking up an inflated inner tube and throwing it as far as he could out into the river. Curling his toes around the edge of the wharf, he dove cleanly into the brackish water that was a mixture of rain runoff and bay water pulled in by the tide. He surfaced next to the inner tube and pulled himself up on it. Paddling out to the middle of the river, he relaxed as the ripples died out.

Behind him, the small house was almost hidden from view by the spreading limbs of two live oaks that had managed to survive the recent hurricane as well as all those that had come before it over the last several hundred years. The knoll it sat on had protected the house from the rising water, but wind from the storm had blown off part of the roof, soaking much of Tom's meager possessions inside. The dock hadn't been as fortunate. The storm surge had scattered it up and down the river, and Tom had spent the better part of a week towing sections of it home behind the rowboat and nailing them back in place.

Rotating the inner tube, he turned to face the other side of the river. Here the bank was lower, resulting in a jungle of marsh and reeds that until recently had been home only to snakes and alligators. But now a quarter mile long bulkhead jutted out into the river and was in the process of being filled in behind it with hauled in dirt.

The heavy rain had left the dump trucks and bulldozers bogged down in the almost liquid quagmire, and the construction site had been blissfully silent for almost a week now. Tom hoped the developer had taken the daily deluges as a sign that the gods were angry and would rain lightning bolts down on them if they dared to return. But in his heart he knew that they would be back any day now, filling the air with the roar of diesel engines and the stink of their exhaust.

By the time the billboard advertising the future home of Paradise Cove Condominiums had appeared on the road that paralleled the bay one morning, the project was already a done deal. Tom had shown up at the zoning board meeting along with some of his neighbors to protest. While the board members had gone through the formal motions of discussing the proposed change, their downturned gazes made it obvious that their inquiry was a forgone conclusion. When he left the meeting, Tom couldn't help but wonder how many of the board members would be receiving a complimentary condo from the developer.

An artist's depiction of the completed complex was splashed across the billboard. It included rows of three story units dotted with palm trees, and a dozen piers with boat slips protruding far out into the water. It wouldn't be long before the tranquil river would be buzzing with Jet Skis and speedboats.

New money, Tom realized, with a sour expression that looked like he had eaten something bad. Otherwise they'd be relaxing at their old family homes on Point Clear rather than moving all the way out here to muddy up *his* river.

His river, he thought. That's a joke. Like everything else in life, it's all relative. While his grandfather had been one of the first ones to build a summer house on the river, back when the roads were little more than one lane ruts covered with oyster shells, the local shrimpers and oystermen had already been living here for generations. At first they had considered him as much of an outsider as Tom did the condo developers today.

With a practiced swirl of his hands and feet in the water, he turned his back on the new construction and examined his side of the river again.

"Beautiful, isn't it," his grandfather said.

The old man stood next to him, his worn canvas boat shoes barely touching the surface of the water.

"It sure is," Tom replied, taking in the almost deserted shoreline.

"You were the only one in the family who could see it," the old man said. "Your grandmother humored me and even accompanied me down here sometimes, but she was always glad to get back to her luncheons and weekly bridge games in Mobile. Your father never did like the outdoors. 'Worthless marsh,' he called this place, 'nothing but wall to wall mosquitoes and snakes.' " The old man shook his head and chuckled. "But you were different," he said crouching down next to Tom and resting a hand on his grandson's shoulder. "You could see what others couldn't."

Tom nodded. "Remember the time I ran away from home and hitch-hiked all the way down here? I couldn't have been more than twelve or thirteen."

"It was the summer you turned twelve," his grandfather informed him.

"You called and told them I was okay. The funny thing was they hadn't even missed me yet. When Dad drove down to get me, you met him in the yard."

" 'He's coming home with me now,' your father said to me, standing there like you were a prize cow that had gotten out of the pasture."

Tom smiled. "I remember you told him that I already *was* home. When he saw you meant business, he got back in his car and drove away, spraying oyster shells until he was out of sight. I stayed here with you for the rest of the summer that year."

"My son and I never did get along," Tom's grandfather replied. "I guess I passed that curse on to you. Well, there's one thing I'll say for you, boy. You always did know what you wanted." The old man told him, and then he was gone.

"Not any more," Tom said to the empty river around him before slowly paddling back to the dock.

JOE FORMICHELLA

TICKETS

He reads *Slaughterhouse Five* to her in bed, after they make love, in the hour or so before he leaves, skipping around mostly, reading a paragraph here, flipping pages, reading another paragraph somewhere else. She protests:

"Why are you jumping all over the place?"

"That's what the book's about."

"But how am I supposed to follow the story?"

"You're not, really."

"Why not? What kind of book is this?"

"There is no why not, Mr. Pilgrim," he starts, damaging a line from the book, before she bites into his shoulder. "It's a love story," he says.

"Right."

"It's our love story, Red. Don't you see? You shouldn't want the book so tidily arranged, following those lines of chronology."

"No. We're bugs in amber, right?"

"Right, right!" he says, dropping the book to the floor. That's another of Kurt's lines.

In the book, Billy Pilgrim, the hero, says that all moments have always existed, always will exist. The Tralfamadorians told him so. They can look at moments, time, all at once, like a range of mountains. "Like the Alps," he says.

"Mountains are nice," she answers.

"Moments are permanent that way, and you can visit any one you want, any time you want." They don't follow one another, Billy Pilgrim learned, like beads on a string, each moment replacing the last and that one gone forever.

Billy Pilgrim has come unstuck in time, that's how the book starts.

She sits up. "What do you mean that's how it starts? I thought it started with the war."

"Says right here on page 22, it begins when Billy Pilgrim has come unstuck in time, and it ends like this—"

"No, don't tell me the ending yet."

"I'm not. I'm just reading what it says here on page 22."

He, Joshua Martin, was born in New York in 1955, works nights at the University Hospital in Mobile, Alabama, is married, but not nearly contented with that any longer. She, Christine Black, is a red-headed medical student who's not too sure she's as excited about that as she has been since the third grade, or at least is not thrilled with the insensate havoc it has created in her life. She was born in Florida in 1963, but their paths were destined to collide, if only at cross-currents—his life descending down the slope of potential diminished, hers still holding the track of potential realizable—he's certain of that, has always been.

"You've always been a part of my life," he tells her, "always will be," buried beneath the blankets of her heirloom iron bed, upstairs in her one bedroom student's apartment.

They're having an affair, though he hates that word.

"We're making moments," he says. "Tickets to the slaughterhouse."

It's a weekday morning. They put double layers of thick bath towels over the windows to block out the light of day, but he keeps his sunglasses on anyway. They let Pink Floyd's *Wish You Were Here* repeat on the stereo, seamlessly, over and over again. They explore and revel in each other until she has to go to school about noon, when he'll go home, sleep a couple of hours, wake up cranky and bitching about not enough sleep when his wife gets home from work and blame it on the phone, or the dogs.

It's an attempt to obliterate time. He wants to believe Vonnegut.

"Why don't you work days?" his wife suggests. "This schedule is killing you."

No, he thinks, the flip-flopping, sleeping nights off, working nights, sleeping in the day, that's what will help him shake off time.

He makes Christine take off her watch every time he meets her, whether it's at her apartment, on campus, in the corridors and elevators of the hospital. He doesn't answer her greetings, just stands there and stares at her wrist until she huffs, maybe even hisses his name, "Joshua!" and unclasps the Timex with her lovely, freckled fingers. He leaves copies of the book everywhere, at work, in her car, under the pillows of her bed, carries one in his lab coat, with little Post-It notes, lots of little Post-It notes marking passages.

Page 87: Joshua looks at the stars at night and tries to imagine seeing them as a Tralfamadorian does, as "rarified luminous spaghetti." He can't begin to fathom what that would actually look like, but likes the idea. Rarified luminous spaghetti. And human beings as great millipedes, with fat little baby legs at one end and wrinkly varicosed legs at the other. He like that too.

As an adult, Joshua hopes that's true, that time is always all there, hence, pretty meaningless, hopes it's like a lazy Susan on the dining room table, and he can just keep turning and turning until he finds what he wants.

As a child, it certainly seemed that way. He guesses that's what makes kids repeat things over and over and over again, asking the same question again and again, behavior parents see as belligerent while they give the same answer again and again, until the whole transaction devolves into a shouting match:

"Why?"

"Because!"

Joshua understands the problem now: The kid isn't living their whole life at the time, like the parent. The kid's living just that moment, and the next moment will be completely different. It's not that the kid isn't listening to the answer; it's the parent not answering the kid's question. Instead of "3:30," according to how the parent would ask the question, the answer might be "red," if the question is taken out of any established context, the way the kid sees the world.

When he's old, Joshua's sure to need it to be true, so that he won't have to think of his life as if it's some greasy slime trail comprised of mostly mediocrity and disappointment. He wants to be able to look forward, from his death-bed—his frail head and shoulders propped up on a stack of pillows—to moments he knows have happened, will always happen.

"What moments would you choose?" he asks Christine.

She's stretched out alongside him on the bed, trailing her fingertips down his chest. He is half sitting against the headrest.

She thinks, noisily, kind of hums before saying, "The cabin."

"The cabin?"

"Our cabin, up in the mountains. We've just gotten there, haven't even unpacked or start start a fire. We open a bottle of wine instead. We're standing out on the back porch, overlooking the lake, watching the sunset. We're real tired from the drive up, there were all those unexpected delays," she says, sliding down his ribs, kissing his hip, looking up at him, smiling.

"That's it?" he asks, pulling on her shoulder.

"No. You say, 'Let's take a swim.' I say, 'Let's go skinny-dipping.' You, of course, have to ask, 'Have you ever been skinny-dipping?' but I don't answer. I've already taken off my clothes and am running down the lawn naked, wading out into the water. We go out deeper and deeper, until neither of us can stand up, have to tread water."

"That's no fun," he says.

"Sure it is. Suspended in the water, we can't use our hands, we can only rub, or use our legs," she says, snaking a thigh across him, massaging him. "It's excruciating." She laughs.

They don't have a cabin. Whenever he asks her that question, she makes up moments. She argues that they're out of time, just like his, "So why not, Mr. Pilgrim?" One time it's a beach house, the next a sailboat, or a mountain cabin.

He picks two moments, both of which have happened. One could've only happened once, so that when he looks upon it, remembers it, it is always the same, the same time of day, the same weather, they're wearing the same clothes, and it lasts for the same amount of time, always. It is contained, defined, by itself, and he can play it over and over again in his mind's eye, like a favorite song, singing along.

It was early in their relationship, before they needed reality to go away so badly. It didn't matter. The stealing a little happiness, whether it was five minutes or five hours, was enough. He had to take some books back to the university library, asked her if she wanted to come along, and she did. It was a small, minor event, but significant, in a way that snuck up on them somehow. As they were leaving the library, walking down the sidewalk to the parking lot, she came running up behind him and hopped up on his back, wrapping her legs around his waist, clenching his neck, until he stumbled and they crashed into the shrubbery. It was as if she had just then decided that they could be a legitimate couple, whenever they wanted to, if he chose.

The other happens again and again, happens almost every time they're together, in fact, whatever any of their other circumstances of life might be. It's the moment she straddles his lap and he first enters her. Her eyes roll up under half-hooded eyelids in a directionless kind of way. It's a moment of pure satisfaction, and he knows how she feels, except it's not an understanding, or even a shared feeling. He is feeling the same thing. He is her.

"It's a perfect pair," he tells her, speaking of the moments, "like Tiresias, perfectly matched halves making up their own mythological one."

They're standing at a short brick wall that overlooks the hospital's heliport. It's three days after Christmas. The hospital census is way down, the emergency room is empty. She's taking weekend call and he doesn't have any work to do in the laboratory. They're drinking coffee, anticipating, as are a few hundred birds scattered in leafless trees in the park across the street, a clear, crisp winter's sunrise.

He is amazed by the birds, always, and tells her again how wonderful it is that they don't seem even remotely phased that it's wintertime.

"In Mobile they still sing in the morning as if there aren't any changes in season," he says. "That's what I love about this place."

"How DID you get to Mobile?" she asks.

"That's another story."

"So tell me a story," she says, à la Montana Wildhack.

"In the book, Billy tells her about the destruction of Dresden, not a story at all, but a gruesome report about the city's firebombing on February 13th, 1945. He tells her about four of the prison guards trying to make sense of the attack, like a grieving barbershop quartet, the massive stock yards missing all their fence posts, about roofs and windows disintegrated; how there were little logs lying around, people caught in the firestorm. He says to Montana it was like the moon.

"'So it goes,'" Joshua quotes.

Joshua thinks that is the moment when Billy Pilgrim first came unstuck in time, when he stepped out of the Slaughterhouse and saw that the beautiful city of Dresden had been transformed into the moon. Time—all the intricate workings of Germany's best clockmakers—had been consumed in the holocaust.

Joshua makes up a story for Christine, the worst kind of story.

"The oldest story going," he tells her. "A sad story of forbidden love."

He starts, "It's the seventeenth floor of the Riverview Plaza Hotel, a room facing southeast, the docks, the shipping canal, the mottled waters of Mobile Bay that blend finally into the blue-green Gulf of Mexico.

"It's dark out, 9 p.m. Sunday night, January. It's thirty-five degrees downtown, with a quarter moon shining clear. David Sanborn is playing jazz on the radio. A couple stands at their hotel window. They'd registered under an assumed name, Mr. and Mrs. Smith, and didn't care what the man behind the desk thought. They were leaving him and the rest of reality behind and wouldn't care until they checked out the next morning. Mr. Smith's just opened the plush, floor-length curtains, exposing them to the night, it to them.

"'Isn't it lovely,' she says, standing arm-in-arm with him at the window.

"'Don't you wish the bed was by the window?' he says, and they both get the idea of moving it at the same time, dragging the king-sized mattress and pillows across the carpeted floor."

Joshua moves behind Christine, standing as close as he can without actually touching her, something they have a hard time resisting in public, at work. He's close enough that they can feel each other across the narrow pocket of air that separates them. He whispers into her thick, wild mane of red hair, slowly, pronouncing each word carefully:

"He supposes that's what makes their moments possible in the first place, their shared subconscious. Their realities are so divergent and incompatible. She's twenty-five, almost through with her PhD in medical science. She's going to do biological research, going to cure diseases. He's old. Older, anyway. Almost forty. He's decided too late that he wants to be a writer. He sometimes thinks he has stories to tell, but more often wonders if he isn't merely telling lies, and if he tells enough of them the truth won't be so obvious, won't be so true.

"She positions him on his back on the mattress, facing the window and undresses him. She stands over him, smiling, and drops her skirt, blouse, and lingerie to the floor. She straddles his lap. Lightly holding her hips he guides her onto him. He can see stars flickering around her as she moves above him, when he looks. Mostly he closes his eyes, where he can see the entire universe, all at once. He told her the first time they made love that he wanted to immortalize her in his stories, regardless of whatever else he'd ever be able to give her, do for her, because that's how she makes him feel each time they're together, immortal, unbound, free."

Christine turns her head to the left, where Joshua stands just beyond that shoulder. She can see the dawn rising around the hospital tower. "The end?" she asks.

"I hope so," he tries to say, but noise from the helicopter's revving turbines drowns him out.

They watch as a nurse and an EMT, dressed in identical navy blue flight suits, jog across the pad, stooping beneath the whirling blades. The helicopter lifts, and then hovers, as if they haven't finished their checklist, or someone's seatbelt is jammed, before tilting and arching around the building, flying towards the sun. In a matter of minutes she'll be helping the trauma team try to piece back together some accident, shooting, or fire victim's body.

She asks, "What makes it sad?"

"Having an ending. That it has to have boundaries at all, has to end."

"Is ALWAYS ending," she says, turning for the hospital entrance, sounding like a Tralfamodorian, "always will."

TOM FRANKLIN

SMONK GETS OUT ALIVE

It had been raining and cold for three days and four nights and there was harmonica music in the air when Eugene Oregon Smonk rode the disputed mule over the railroad tracks to the boardinghouse where the trial would be.

He got off the animal in the mud and told a filthy blond boy holding a balloon to watch the mule, which had an English horse saddle on its back and an embroidered blanket from Bruges Belgium underneath.

In a gun sheath sewn to the saddle stood the polished butt of the Winchester Model '94 repeating rifle with which, not half an hour earlier and from this very mule, Smonk had shot four of an Irishman's goats in their pen because the only thing he despised more than an Irish was a goat.

By way of brand the mule had a fresh .22 bullet hole through its left ear, same as Smonk's horses and cows and hound dogs did, and even his cat.

That mule gits away, he told the boy, I'll brand your balloon.

A squat, troll-shaped War veteran, Smonk slid the rifle from its holder and climbed the steps and creaked over the boardinghouse porch.

He wore a tan duck coat, denim britches and chocolate-colored calf opera boots, now muddy, and along with the Winchester he carried a walking cane with a sword concealed in the shaft.

He wore no hat because he believed that fresh air and skylight fed your brain.

He had a cigar he was chewing on, and he had five other pistols in various places within his clothing including a derringer in his right boot.

He had about two hundred cartridges, clicking in his coat pockets, and a blackjack in his belt. On a cord around his neck hung a jug of splo whiskey stoppered with a cork his daddy had thrown at him from his death-bed.

The feud he'd had with the old fucker had begun at Smonk's birth, when, sliding down the narrow, slimy canal, he'd gotten the umbilical cord tangled around his feet and pulled something or other loose up in his mother's guts. He'd squirted out in a river of blood but never saw Mrs. Smonk alive.

In his watery right socket he had a glass eye that was two sizes too small.

He had four bullet scars in his right shoulder and one in each forearm and another in his left foot.

A long red welt from a knife across his belly.

He had giant yellow teeth that had been getting looser.

He had syphilis sores on his neck.

The silk handkerchief he had in his pants pocket had blood on it from the advanced consumption the doctor had just informed him he had.

You'll die from it, the doctor had said.

When? asked Smonk.

One of these days, said the doctor.

At the boardinghouse door he paused and glanced around at the muddy street behind him, men and women and children in their town clothes and hats, all shadowed beneath their umbrellas.

All watching him until they saw him looking.

Inside the boardinghouse the bailiff, who'd been playing the harmonica, put it away and said it was no guns allowed in a courtroom.

This ain't a courtroom, Smonk said.

It is today, said the bailiff.

Smonk handed over the rifle, barrel first, and as he laid one heavy revolver and then another on the whiskey barrel the bailiff had for a desk, he looked at the man, who was sitting on a wooden crate, the sideboard behind him jumbled with firearms.

Have I seen you before?

You could say you have, all right, said the bailiff. You foreclosed on my land two years ago. House and barn and ever thing me and my boy had. Ever blessed thing.

I don't recall if I did or not, Smonk said.

Well, I do recall. I recall real good. It's like somebody drawed me a picture of it and I can unfold it and look at it when air I want. Open up your coat and show me inside there.

Smonk did.

The bailiff pointed with the rifle. That 'n too, he said.

Smonk licked his long tongue over his lips and pulled from his waistband a forty-one caliber Colt Navy pistol and laid it on the surface between them.

Keep these instruments safe, boy. Mebbe I'll tip you a penny if you look after 'em good.

I wouldn't take no penny from you, Mr. Smonk, if it was the last penny minted in this land. If it was to come a copper blight over this whole county and a penny was selling for a dollar and a half and I hadn't eat a bite of meat in a month and my boy was starving, I wouldn't take no penny from you. Not even if you paid me a whole nother penny to take it.

Smonk had turned away.

I'll be back directly, he said. After we have our farce in yonder.

Carrying his walking cane, he went on into the hot, smoky diningroom where the eating tables had been pushed against the walls and stacked surface to surface, two-high, the legs of the ones on top in the air like dead livestock.

Several lawyers and farmers and merchants and the newspaper writer and two federal marshals and an army captain with his arm in a sling looked at him when he came in.

The talking had hushed.

The nine ball rolling across the billiard table in the corner didn't quite make its hole and snicked off the four and stopped on the felt.

Smonk coughed into his handkerchief and dabbed his lips and folded the silk cloth away, satisfied no one saw what had come up from the deep black reefs of his lungs.

As he leaned against the wall to get his wind, the conversation resumed.

He uncorked his jug and drank from it.

When he'd got word that his daddy was finally succumbing to cancer of the throat, he had killed three horses riding home from Wyoming to witness it.

The door at the opposite end of the room opened and in walked the circuit judge, a Democrat and Mason equally renowned for his fairness and his mutton chops.

He acknowledged no other man as he excused his way through them and stepped up onto the wooden dais erected for this occasion and seated himself behind the table set up for him, a glass of water there and a notepad and quill and ink bottle.

He wore a black suit and hat like a preacher and for a gavel used the butt end of a new Colt Peacemaker, bought with Smonk's money.

Bribing him had cost Smonk five hundred dollars and his last box of Havanas.

His last box.

Order now, order, the judge called, removing his hat. Be seated, gentlemen. He put on a pair of round spectacles.

The men scuffed into their chairs or leaned against the billiard table or sat on the hearth.

They took off their hats.

In the rear of the room, Smonk kept standing.

For once he wished he wore a hat so he could leave it on.

A sombrero, say.

He cleared his throat, and as he readied himself to strut forward to the defendant's table, he saw that all the faces in the room were looking back at him.

But a shadow had come over them.

That farmer glaring at him wasn't the same farmer Smonk had cheated at dice.

That clerk wasn't the one he'd slapped down in the street.

That other fellow wasn't the one whose dog he'd kicked.

That man there wasn't the storekeeper whose daughter he had won in a card game and taken into the musty feed room in the back.

That one there wasn't the trapper he'd swindled out of seventy-five acres of bottomland including a creek with gold, possibly, in it.

That gimp wasn't the fellow he'd shot in the foot.

That tall one rising now wasn't the ex-marshal he'd had discharged from duty because the man hadn't voted the way Smonk had said.

They were all other faces, other men.

He didn't know them. He didn't know them.

The bailiff wasn't a bailiff now but another man altogether.

But whoever they were, they knew Smonk.

Whoever they were, they were scuffling to their feet as the judge banged his pistol so hard on the table the ink bottle bounced off.

Order, he called. God damn it, I said order!

But there was no order left here.

What there was were nooses and fire pokers and riding crops.

There were bricks and belts and letter openers and knots of kindling.

There was a pump handle.

There were cue sticks and billiard balls.

There were table legs with nails crooked and curved as fangs.

Every hasty weapon to be made from a splintered chair, here it was.

Well have at it, you hongry bitches, Smonk said, grinning.

Those men closest to him saw his bloody teeth and bloody lips.

Smonk coughed hard and his eye popped out into the air and the once-bailiff caught it like a marble.

He looked down in his palm and yelped.

When he looked up Smonk had a derringer in one hand and a sword in the other and he was halfway to the sideboard where the lined-up rifles and pistols lay gleaming.

Outside, the rain had about quit.

The blond boy had tied his balloon in the raw hole in the mule's ear and was climbing into the saddle.

Seated, he wiggled his behind in luxury and slapped the mule across its withers.

Let's git on, he said, and they began to walk, and then trot, not looking back despite the volleys of gunfire, the balloon floating and bobbing above them like thoughts the mule was having, empty of history.

JIM GILBERT

COMING TO PIECES

The dog lay curled up, in the cargo bay of the Land Cruiser. Doug, his hands cupped to form a view-finder around his eyes, peered down at it through the rear window. Nothing, no movement. He flattened his hands against the glass and pushed, rocking the vehicle gently. Still nothing. So he popped the handle of the rear door and swung it open. Most dogs, at that point, would raise a head, roll out a tongue, jump up, bark maybe. But this one didn't.

Doug made a fist and gave the dog an encouraging, or at least experimental, push with his knuckles. The animal itself did not stir, but as though he'd activated some kind of booby trap, evoked some ancient curse, there arose from the dog's matted fur a stench that knocked him back, gagging, stumbling backwards across the backyard. The door to the Land Cruiser creaked and banged shut.

Breathing in uneven, desperate gulps, Doug crab-crawled until he was well into the backyard and crouched in the middle of the grid of withered pine saplings he had planted last December. A cold day, yes, but according to the Old Farmer's Almanac, the right day. The ground had not been frozen. Sap had been down. Rain had come later. So there was no excuse for these damn things to be so dead. They resisted fertilizer, they resisted water, they resisted sunlight. It looked like a damn pipecleaner farm. Doug eyeballed a particularly scrawny specimen at the head of a row. No aphids, no fungus, just brown needles shaking loose in the breeze. Just determination towards slow-motion failure. He grasped the tip of the tree between his thumb and forefinger and tugged, lightly. It came up with a sprinkle of dirt, easy as a weed.

"Pluto's Comet," Pearl had warned from the back porch while he had worked the hoe, hands on her hips, absolutely no help while he ran east-west plumb lines so the trees would grow in unnaturally straight but aesthetically pleasing avenues; calculated the perfect distance between each tree to allow for maximum sunlight; patted dirt gingerly around the slender young trunks. She stood there moaning about the comet—how it was skidding through the stratosphere, spreading cosmic debris. Not a good time to plant.

Pluto's Comet—probably something she'd read about in the back of the *Enquirer*, next to the Nostradamus Horoscopes. Doug wiped his mouth with the back of his hand. Comet, all right, Comet laced with gasoline was what she was pouring over these trees, late at night and while he was away at work, just to prove herself right. She'd be out here in another minute, tip-toeing, still in her terrycloth bathrobe, watering can in hand, sprinkling her homemade Agent-X over the tops of his trees, grinning as they steamed and hissed.

She would do that, soon as she heard him leave. For now, she was discreetly sleeping it off, or pretending to. He'd paused in the hallway a moment ago, listening to the snore-puffs wafting up from under her bed-room door, trying to figure if he was listening to one person snore, or to two.

So he would leave. Doug took a deep breath, yanked open the driver's-side door of the Cruiser and jumped in the front seat, jammed the keys into the ignition, slammed the Cruiser door as hard and loud as he could, gunned the engine three times and peeled out of the yard, cutting double ruts at the edge of the clay driveway. All without exhaling, or, more importantly, inhal-ing any of the fumes coming off that dog. Once out on the highway, he rolled down the window and drove with his head sticking into the wind.

Last night she had been seated caddy-corner from him at the other end of Zonkers' U-shaped pinewood bar, beneath the Red Dog clock. When he noticed her, the neon hands were edging up to midnight. Pumpkin time. That much he had been able to take, nursing one Corona after another, the two of them in this weird Mexican Stare-off, but when Skyler Jones and his Pre-Colombian Dancing Dogs launched into that medley of late-70's Paul McCartney tunes, she, Darlene Douglas, though she now went by "Pearl," had been compelled to dance, this time with Grady the Lugnut Salesman from Fruitvale Hardware. Of all people. His mother and Grady.

It was as if Dad's death had been a quickie divorce, expected. Or wanted. I'm fine, she would say, and I should get on. And so should you, Doug, she would sometimes add (Doug could swear she had once called him Dave, his father's name, during one of these recitations but he'd been half asleep at the time, catching it seconds-too-late, and she would only deny it or not remember if confronted.)

He had been at school at the time, at Pemberton in Georgia, linked back to home by a dorm hallway pay-phone she had decided not to use. "It was right before your finals," she explained when he came home for Christmas, "I didn't want to upset your concentration."

She was in shock, of course; this is what Doug told himself over and over. She and Dad had been married thirty-two years. Doug decided to sit out the rest of the school year, which she didn't understand, chiding him for "deserting his post in a time of crisis" as he moved back into his old room— and he got a job proofreading at the Turpin Post-Horn, which she didn't appreciate. "It's not as if he ever took you fishing or anything." Lunch breaks, he went to sulk in the cemetery, at the edge of his father's still unmarked grave. The rectangular spot was outlined in sand, like a spellcaster's border, marking an area over which Doug could not pass.

He had never understood the extent of his father's work for Xenodyne, the contracted company working within the Turpin Range, never bothered to ask, believing one day it would be revealed to him, through an action or an accident, the way all adult knowledge was supposed to unfold. "He worked with chemicals," she said, trying to explain his sudden cancer, "or radiation."

Pearl became increasingly comfortable with this twist in her life, began to hang out where he hung out, at Zonkers and at Mother Hubbards. She began courting the Jeep-and-Motorcycle crowd, a beer dangling from one hand. Laughing, dancing with them. Worse yet they'd taken her in, as if they'd been expecting her all along. There's a normal period of grief, he would insist. I've skipped it, she would say, and that, with a raised eyebrow and a crease in her over-applied make-up, would be that.

So last night, after attempting to cut in on Grady and instigate another of these pointless confrontations, he found himself careening on two wheels out of Zonkers' parking lot. Driving always helped to sober him up, so taking not the direct route home but some hitherto unknown long way, around the perimeters of Go Junction, looping through Central, down along the outskirts of Fruitvale and Bywater, then back onto Highway 32, he had made nearly a complete circuit of the county when the dog, the god-damned thing, an earnest black, had come hitching out of the darkness, darting back and forth in the goofy, cockeyed glare of the Cruiser's unaimed headlights until being critically pinned, too late. Doug had visualized, in the splitting second, the dog tumbling paws over spine, hitting front axle, then rear, thump thump, then flying free into the night, finished, dead.

It had taken some time to find it in the long grass and the shadows of the ditch. But there had been no question that he would save the body for this afternoon and this ritual, however unfamiliar, he somehow knew would come.

Driving now, Doug turned the radio all the way up, hoping the noise would distract him from the stench. But this failed—it worked its way around him, into him, channeled through passageways other than his nostrils, until he could actually see it—everything tinted a dark forest green, the color those trees should be.

He aimed the Cruiser off the highway and onto a red clay path, still fecally slick from the recent rain, passing a simple whitewashed marker: Fruitvale Pet Cemetery. The path, which soon disappeared beneath layered pinestraw, led to a series of clearings where the ground was heavily bowed, lumpy treeless hillocks, the green of the ground vegetation coming and going in unhealthy thatches—lush avocado grasses dissolving into asymmetrical bald patches of crusty dirt, like signals meant to be read from the air.

Atop the chief hillock Doug could see the gnarly shape of Wendell, the town idiot, using a pickaxe against the dead heart of a mesquite tree-stump. Wendell would heave and wheel the blade of the axe firmly into the stump, then spend long moments grunting, trying to work it loose again. Leaning against a nearby tree was Wendell's green Schwinn with its swollen-looking beach tires. The handlebar basket contained a paper Safeway bag brimming with crushed aluminum cans, the lacquered metals reflecting bright sparks of light. These had undoubtedly been collected earlier this morning on Wendell's regular route, down by Echo Lake, along the strand nearest the Pier, as quickly as they were discarded by sunning teenagers and beached windsurfers. It was what Wendell did, along with odd jobs like this, stump-busting.

Doug gunned the engine, wondering if Pearl had ever danced a slow dance with Wendell during a last call at Zonkers, then killed it, only now realizing, in the shadow of Wendell's axe, that he hadn't thought to bring along a shovel—though he had thought to bring along a garbage bag.

Doug got out, walked around and swung the rear hatch open; the dog had rolled during transit, and now a bar of cold sunlight revealed the left foreleg, sticking up as if to say *Eureka!* Doug grabbed the animal's collar, noting the name Schroeder on the rabies tag, and tugged the swelling body towards the loose mouth of the black thirty-gallon trash bag. Damp shiny clumps of fur came away in his fingers. Flies were already clustering; Doug had to wheel an arm to keep the insects at bay, which left him with no good way to hold the bag open. The rear door kept banging against the small of his back. He soon discovered that the louder he swore, the more of the dog he was able to slip into the bag. With the head and forelegs tucked inside, he tried to tump the rest of the body out of the Cruiser and into the sack. This almost worked. Doug miscalculated the weight, and the body went heavily against one side of the bag, causing the plastic where his fingers gripped it to thin and come apart. He dropped the bag and the dog rolled, the stiff foreleg popping out of the new hole, followed by a trail of what appeared to be wet pink yarn.

The mouth of the bag retreated into a tight pucker as he pulled the drawstrings and then, by the strings, hefted it and slung it over his shoulder, like some wicked Santa Claus. Out of the corner of his eye, he could see the dog's leg pointing out the hole, over his shoulder.

Wendell met him half-way down the hill. He reached around and thumped the stomach of the dog through the thin black plastic, as if testing a melon for ripeness. "That your dog?"

"No."

"You look sleepy. Sleepy?"

"Hung over," Doug answered. Wendell smelled powerfully of peanut butter. *Choosy mothers choose Jif.* Doug held out his hand and Wendell surrendered the pickaxe.

"Head's loose on that thing. Gotta swing it fast, okay, swing it fast or it'll come down on you. Gotta keep it swinging." He pinwheeled his arms to demonstrate.

"Okay."

"Whose dog is that?"

Doug didn't know whose dog it was. Or had been. Nor was he about to ask. Those questions would have been for last night; today was for this task, and this task alone. He dug into his pocket for a wadded five dollar bill, and paid Wendell for the axe. "I need to bury him deep."

Wendell nodded. The creases around his eyes and mouth were dark, and full of motion. "That way." He pointed with his middle finger.

Doug nodded, hoisted the bag and moved over the indicated rise, then over three more, deeper into the woods until he arrived at a slender curve in Fonder's River, near one of the many places where it rose out of the ground. It flowed from a cave in one of these hillocks; there were stories he knew from childhood, about worm creatures who slithered out of that cave at night and crawled around in the dark places between the hills, looking for fresh meat. The dead animal flesh they found in the ground only teased their hunger, made them more irritable. They preferred living meat, humans, small children.

Doug released the bag, took five steps, and heaving the pickaxe, began to assemble the grave. This was difficult digging. The tool was long and pointed on one side, curved and flat on the other, sharp at both ends. The long pointy end made only stupid puncture marks in the ground, like a giant vampire tooth. The flat end disturbed more earth but didn't bring any of it out; when he had turned one layer to the consistency of oatmeal he had to go down on his knees to shovel it out with his hands.

So he worked, the dead dog lying in the growing shadows of a nearby oak, and the afternoon moved around him, the sky overhead trying to form rainclouds.

Waist-deep in the earth, skin and hair and clothes covered in dirt, Doug didn't notice the arrival of the Teller widow until she started tossing rocks into the stream. The surface water was smooth, and the ripples made by the sinking stones rolled apart lazily. He turned toward her, raised his eyebrows in Hello but she did not respond. Doug tried to remember her exact first name before he actually said something; it was either Judy or Jane. Or possibly Lisa. She crouched at the base of the oak, a long white t-shirt tied in a knot at her hip, bare legs bunched beneath her. Still young, not quite forty. Her face was pretty, but hard, like it was carved from wax.

Doug leaned against the handle of the axe, examining her, wondering if she recognized him, too. "I hope this isn't too far down."

She was the owner of this packet of land, by the default of her husband Billy Teller's sudden death, a while back. Doug remembered hearing about it at the time. Teller had been making his ranch rounds near the base of Rook Mountain when something happened to him. It had been a while before they found his body and the wording in the paper didn't allow for drawn conclusions. The public consensus was of an encounter with a drunken hunter who had fled the scene. Other murmurings were more sinister, more theatric, some involved Xenodyne. But dead, by Doug's reasoning, was dead. So Judy/Jane was left holding the Teller Taters potato dynasty, ragged though it was these days. The land seemed worn out, producing spuds only the size of a baby's fist, and hard.

She looked up, training her chin at a point above his shoulder, but casting her eyes down. When she spoke, her lips barely moved. "No. That's a big dog. You'll need to go deeper than that."

Doug looked from her to the bottom of the hole at his feet, back to her. "Oh, no. I mean I hope I'm not too close to the river. It's just, this is where I stopped. I hope it's not too far."

"Whatever." She leaned back against the tree. "You'll need a deeper hole."

"I'll bury him deep." Doug winked like he'd told a joke but Judy/Jane ignored him, continued casting occasional stones to the river. There was a gravity to her presence which annoyed him. He went back to hacking at the ground, pausing intermittently, for her sake, to glance toward the dog, calculating.

He dug and scooped until he was down to his armpits, then paused to catch his breath. The ground was getting softer; his hands were chocolate brown, his fingernails black. He stared up at the sun, trying to estimate the time, and heard her shuffle behind him.

She was standing now, leaning against the tree with one petite sneakered foot propped on a risen root. Doug remembered having seen her, a couple weeks back, on one of his later nights down at Zonkers. She had been drifting from one crooked end of the place to the other and back again; it never occurred to him that she was on the hunt, not until she made her mark. The gentleman she chose was a scrawny sort, not a guy Doug had a name for, but a familiar face. Doug watched as he bought her a beer and they hunched over one of the tiny square tables, drinking and smoking and moving their mouths every-so-often. Doug sat cracking pistachios at the bar, half-eyeing the Stars game on the TV above.

Eventually they made their exit. Through the wide front window Doug watched them walk to the outer edge of the parking lot, to her shiny Explorer. She unlocked and opened the backseat door and entered and Romeo scooted in behind her and the door closed. Doug ordered another beer and watched the Explorer. His stomach and loins tingled, his physical guesses as to what was happening behind the tinted glass of the windows. He lined up his sight against a light pole and tried to gauge any shuffling movements the vehicle might make. The band kicked into their third set. The Stars lost 2-0 to the Sharks and Doug had another beer.

He was engrossed in Sportscenter when Romeo re-entered, alone. The guy just appeared at his shoulder, flagged down Jimmy-Dale, ordered a Budweiser, then went back to the group from which he had come, all still flocking within the greasy yellow light that marked the perimeters of the pool table. He melded into them as if he had never been away. She, however, was nowhere; Doug scanned back and forth until it occurred to him to look in the parking lot, where her Explorer had left a dark, empty spot over the tarmac.

His head above the edge of the hole, for all the world like an expectant crocodile, Doug realized that he was staring. But then, Judy/Jane was staring back, unblinking, perhaps in silent reciprocity. A moment passed, like a shadow, and Doug, without taking his gaze from her, set his hands on the outer ground, and prepared to climb out.

"Not yet," she said. "Finish digging first."

So he went back to work, loosening and tossing huge chunks of dirt and clay. He was head-level with the ground when he decided enough was enough. He looked up and when he did not see her at the base of the tree he at first assumed she had deserted him, again. But with a shock Doug realized she was behind him, standing over him, staring down into the hole with her slick, white face aimed right at him.

"Deep enough now, you think?" He wiped his brow with the back of his hand, to show her he was tired, he had done good work, he was finished digging.

She touched her throat and looked away, eastward, to the river. "Billy used to love to come way out here, this end of the property. In the spring we'd have picnics. In the fall we'd build campfires. He'd make shadow-puppets against the full moon. Or we'd tell each other ghost stories. But after a while, I got to know all his ghosts, you know? I guess he knew all of mine, too."

Now she looked the other way, west, as if to see if anyone else were coming over the rise. "I guess that's the way it has to be, sometimes. In light of everything, this was the least I could do for him. He really did love it here."

Doug gave the pickaxe one more heave. Something just below the surface of the dirt made an acute snapping sound.

"I think," he muttered quietly, "this is deep enough."

Roy Hoffman

THE LAND OF COTTON
(Chapter 1 of *Chicken Dreaming Corn*)

Mobile, Al, 1916

Down the stairs from the bedrooms to the floor of his store, past the blouses and pants under dust covers waiting for day to begin, Morris Kleinman made his way to the front door thanking God, blessed be His name, for a regular night's sleep, his devoted Miriam, four healthy children, and strength enough, after a nagging cold, to be the first one up on Upper Dauphin Street wielding his broom against the walk in preparation for the Confederate Veteran's parade.

Above him the swallows looped their crazy script against the chalky Mobile sky. They circled above the Lebanese clothing store and Syrian pressing shop, turned and soared above the Greek bakery where Matranga was baking his New York twist bread that would sell, in today's busy crowd, for a nickel a loaf. As the Holy Cathedral bell gonged six times Father O'Connor scraped his way on one good leg toward the church steps, calling out to Morris, "May peace be with you," to which Morris called back, thinking of the silent, glaring Orthodox priest of his Romanian village, "Good morning, Monsignor, and *shalom* to you."

Horse hair, wood shavings, tobacco, goat droppings, melon rind, ashes, a lone shoelace—his broom whisked away last night's debris onto the wood-brick street. He reached down into the gutter and retrieved the shoelace, slipping it into his pocket for Miriam's scrap box; yesterday she'd kissed him when he salvaged an ivory button.

As he wheeled out the clothes racks he looked down the street, past the red-brick and stained-glass Cathedral, past the tattered Star Theater marquee and the humble mercantile storefronts of Habeeb and Zoghby and Kalifeh, toward Lower Dauphin where the likes of prosperous Greenbaum and Leinkauf were nowhere yet to be seen. *Oh*, he shook his head, the German Jewish merchants still blithely asleep in their canopied beds.

The ritual morning prayers humming at his lips, he turned to go back in, eyeing a crate to be opened. Facing east, *tallit* over his shoulders, he laced the prayer straps through his fingers and intoned the Hebrew, rocking gently, trying not to think about the work pants he'd ordered from Schwartz in Memphis or the dresses from Besser in New Orleans, *landsmen* with their own ties to the Carpathian vistas of Romania. The sun fanned out like palmetto leaves across the storefronts where cedar bread boxes awaited Smith's Bakery deliveries and, in the doorway of the Norwegian Seamen's Hall, men curled hoping for day jobs cleaning stables or lugging bananas from the docks. As Father O'Connor said his first "amen" in the incensed recesses of Holy Cathedral, Morris said his last "*o main*" standing behind the cash register of his store. He added a prayer for safekeeping of Papa, dwelling still with sister Golda, so far away. 'You will join us here in Alabama," he vowed. "Soon."

He folded away his prayer shawl, picked up a crowbar and faced the shoulder-high crate: *Besser Fashions. New Orleans*. Thinking of his sons curled in a lazy cocoon, he went back upstairs.

In the front room, his own, Miriam lay curled in their bed before the French doors half-opened to the balcony. The collar of her embroidered gown came high on the neck, her dark hair coiled in a bun. Without turning she raised her hand to signal she was awake: the eyes and ears of the house even as she dozed in reverie, he knew, of the village lanes and kitchen tables of her Romanian home.

He passed his daughter's room. Lillian had kicked off the covers, her twelve-year-old legs sprawled to the far corners of the mattress, her gown twisted up to beyond her knees. The color was robust in her face, blessed be His Name, but after her rheumatic fever—three years ago, this day of the Confederates—who could ever be sure? He stole in and draped the sheet back over her.

He turned into the front room where baby Hannah snored in her bed. Just the other side of a muslin curtain dividing the room, ten-year-old

Abraham and eight-year-old Herman lay elbow to shoulder, mouths open like fish. He leaned over and stroked the back of his hand over Abe's cheek; his son groaned. He wiggled his fingertip on the peach fuzz over the boy's upper lip; Abe brushed away the finger.

"*Gutte morgen, mein boychik*," Morris whispered.

"Mornin', " Abe moaned back.

"*Langer loksh*," he exhorted, using the nickname, "long legs," for his lanky son.

"No school today, Daddy."

"Up!"

"Sun's not even up."

"This son is the first who will make good at Barton?"

"Hm, mm."

"Who will make a good marriage to a nice *shayna madele*?"

He nodded in the pillow.

"Who will help his Papa in the store?"

He was answered with a rising snore.

Morris laid his hand on the boy's shoulder and belted, "*Avraham!*"

The boy bolted upright, but Herman was already on his feet, slipping on his pants, dancing from side to side and bunching his fists like a boxer.

Miriam called out, "You will wake Hannah!"

"Abe will hush her," Morris answered.

"Oh, Daddy!" Abe protested, climbing out now, but Morris instructed, "Stay, you, with the baby."

Abe flopped back down and hugged on his pillow.

On the first landing, with Herman padding behind, Morris fingered up a cigar butt he'd stuck into an ash tray and chomped down on it.

"Daddy, are we Rebels?" Herman asked as they came to the crate.

"Today? Yes, we are Rebels."

Morris jockeyed the box out of the corner and wedged the crowbar into a crevice. Herman reached up and grabbed hold of the bar and lifted his feet off the group. The boards groaned apart.

Morris lifted out the skirts one by one: pretty pale blues and checkered reds. "Besser," he addressed the spirit of his supplier in New Orleans, "now, you are making good business."

From in the back he pulled a skirt soiled on the side. Holding it close, he eyed the brown stain. "Besser," he fumed, "you try to sell to me this *drek?*"

"Daddy!"

From deep inside the crate came scratching and scuffling. Feathers flashed brightly, then exploded into wings.

"Gall durn bird!" Herman cried. "Shoo." A starling wove toward the eaves.

Morris found the bag of old shoes and brought one out, hurling it upwards. The starling dove away, arcing across overalls.

"Small blessings," Morris muttered as bird droppings missed the table and splashed against the floor. The starling turned back over his head and flew up the steps. Herman raced behind.

Into Lillian's room, back through Abe's and Herman's, the bird coursed. Herman grabbed up a broomstick and jumped onto the bed, dancing around Abe's pillow.

Abe sat up blearily. "What are you doing?"

"Is this fun!"

"Not fair."

"You're the one didn't get up." Herman poked wildly at the air.

"Daddy wouldn't let me!"

"In bed like a bum!" Morris yelled at him.

The bird swooped back into the dining room, veering by Morris's head, who cursed Besser like he was in the next room.

"Y'all leave Abe alone," Lillian said, coming from her room, jaw dropping at the spectacle of Daddy waving his arms in the air and turning in circles.

Morris ran toward the front of the apartment, throwing open the French doors. The starling looped back, veered toward Herman who shouted, *"Go on, git!"* before it banked and hurtled into the calm, bluing Alabama sky.

After drinking his black coffee and eating a bowl of *mamaligi* that Miriam had fixed—he still preferred to pasty Southern grits this hearty Romanian dish of cornmeal boiled down to yellow porridge—Morris hurried back down to the walk.

Waiting for the parade to assemble, two boys leaned against a hitching post in front of the Lyric Theater, practicing their drums. Their rolls and rimshots climbed the walls of the popular vaudeville venue, by the marquee reading, *Al Jolson May 5*, and *Alabama Minstrels Tonight*, moving like a prowler up the French grille balconies.

Most, this early, just wanted to converse about that bloody conflict he'd heard called "the Civil War" up North but here was "the War Between the States," or "the Cause." When this subject came up, anywhere in America, he kept his mouth shut. Fifty years had passed since the Yankees had come steaming into Mobile Bay and Admiral Farragut had cried, "Damn the torpedoes, full speed ahead," but it was as if the Jackal had appeared yesterday. Morris had learned, soon after stepping off the train here in 1907, that mention of "Grant" or "Sherman" started a fight. Even in school in Romania, he had heard of the great president named Lincoln, but to repeat his name here, except among the Negroes, was to risk a bloody nose.

Besides, with every holiday there were sales to be made. Fourth of July—bathing attire. Christmas—children's dresses. Last month had been the celebration called Mardi Gras. He had no evening dress to sell—not like Hammel's, run by German Jews, where blue-blooded city dwellers, whatever their origins, spent a pretty penny to outfit themselves elegantly for the occasion.

He watched Donnie McCall saunter in now, Panama hat pushed back, red-faced and jowly. Beneath McCall's eyes were always deep circles, like his own Papa's. McCall, an Irishman he called himself, like Papa also had black-black eyes. A better customer there never was.

McCall nodded to his scuffed-up shoes. "Need a new pair, Mr. Morris. Something respectable for today's doings, not too fancy. The colored look up to a man with smart shoes."

Morris fetched two-tone lace-ups while McCall settled into a chair. Kneeling at his feet, Morris asked about the funeral insurance business as he shoehorned on the first pair.

"One thing folks got to do is die. And when they do, God rest their souls"—McCall stood, peering down—"they want to make sure their funeral's a send-off the likes of which"—he wriggled his toes—"has never been witnessed before. Too small." He sat.

"These better will fit."

McCall stood again, rocked back and forth. "Got my name on 'em, don't you think?"

"Right here." Morris patted the tips. "I can interest you in a new Panama hat?"

"Could be tomorrow."

"I will put in the back one with your name just in case."

McCall paid for the shoes and said good-day. A tall man shambled in and plopped down in a chair.

"Got these suckers from you a while ago," the man said, tugging off his muddy boots. "Name's Jackson."

"A good price I remember, Mr. Jackson."

The clammy odor of Jackson's feet rose up. "Don't want 'em."

"Is not possible."

"You make it possible."

"How can I take back old shoes?"

"I paid $2.95 for these durnb boots! They hurt my feet!"

Morris broke into a sweat. "Come, the wife she does not like when I do this, but"—he coaxed the man to the display case—"if she does not see." He handed him a bottle of 25¢ ointment.

The man turned it back and forth. "What's it say?"

"Dr. Zigorsky's Foot Elixir. A medicine, but for you a blessing. Worth many dollars."

"Cost me nothin'?"

Morris shook his head. "Hurry, before the wife, she sees."

"Got you a deal," said the man, who dragged his boots back on and hobbled out the store.

By eight o'clock the walks of Dauphin Street began to fill with people and Morris positioned Herman on a stool near the door to keep an eye out for passersby with sticky fingers. Some paused before the outdoor racks of M. Kleinman & Sons looking over the newest hats and boulevard ties.

A willowy, red-haired young woman turned into the store with easy gait, heading to the fancy ladies' section in the rear. Lillian came from the back office to greet her.

As they went down the rows, the woman selected a blue cotton dress and Lillian directed her to the dressing curtain which she drew around her. A moment later she rolled open the curtain and walked to the floor-length mirror.

"What do you think?" she asked Lillian.

"You look," Lillian surmised, "like a nice spring day."

"What an enterprising girl!" The young woman turned to Morris. "Now for a gentleman's opinion?"

He saw again the rich hair and pale eyes of the Romanian girl, Theodora Eminescu, turning to him in the window long ago. Her shoulders rose from her gown, the lantern glow bathing her skin.

"We call this, a *shayna klayde*. A pretty dress."

"But how do I look in it?"

"In this *shayna klayde* you are"—he hesitated, not wanting to sound fresh—"a *shayna madele*." He felt himself blush.

"By the look on your face, it must be good. Reckon I'll take it."

Morris quickly turned his attention to the register.

Before long the sidewalk was lined with Mobilians craning their necks for sight of the marchers, the Kleinman children among them. There were squeals and shouts as, far off, the full complement of drums sounded, buzzing along M. Kleinman & Sons' street-front panes. The tattoo of cornets charged the air. The first marchers arrived.

No matter their look—one man was rigid, another bent—or their size—one was tall like a youth, another once tall but shrunk in old age—the men carried themselves with the same tired, but defiant bearing. At ages sixty-five and seventy, seventy-five and eighty, they puffed their chests out against their gray jackets, feeble but cocksure.

"The *alter kockers*," Sam Lutchnik, a Polish Jew down the street, had said of the marchers, "the old men, still fighting their war."

It was a war that lived still from regiment to regiment, in the trudging boots, the gray coats buttoned tight around the sloping bellies of men who years before, lean and quick, thundered across the fields of Shiloh and Manassas, that town, Morris had heard, named for a Jew.

Two men passed, aided by young cadets—the first was missing his left leg, his stump wagging as he hopped on crutches, the second on crutches with no right foot. Behind them walked a veteran with a cane, tap-tapping on the street. With his free hand he waved at the crowd, his ruined eyes cocked toward the sky.

Some veteran groups had banners: the Raphael Semmes Division, honoring a man, Morris had been told, who had stood at the helm of a big warship called Alabama and was buried at the old Catholic cemetery a few miles away, and the George E. Dixon Division, memorializing a poor boy from Mobile who had gone under the water in Charleston Harbor in a hand-cranked submarine called the Hunley to blast a hole in a Union ship, and was entombed in those waters.

The music rose, a tune called "Bonnie Blue Flag." It changed to a melody Morris knew well.

It was not a song that belonged to him like the Yiddish melodies he loved to hum from deep in his boyhood, or the religious songs like the soaring "Aveinu Malkeinu" of Rosh Hashanah, or the stirring "Kol Nidre" chanted at Yom Kippur. But these piccolos playing out the spirited melody gave him goosebumps. "Dixie," it was called. The song piped its sad merriment through the streets, where the onlookers clapped and stomped.

Behind the last division of men followed a crowd of marching ladies: A-frame dresses sweeping the street, silver hair up in buns or down in thin gray tresses reminiscent of the days they had waited for their young Johnny Rebs to return from the battlefields. Many had waited, and waited, their faces caught still in that moment fifty years ago when an emissary stepped onto the porch and announced, with deep consolation, that Jack Mayfield or Curtis Kellogg or Ira Glasser would never be returning, sweet Jesus be with you in this time of great need.

Among these women Morris saw Ira's widow, Dolores, who'd later married Joseph Levy, a German Jew who himself had died the year before. Today, though, Joseph was forgotten: Dolores walked mourning her bright, Confederate youth.

Young women now passed who smiled and waved in the modern way. These were the Daughters of the Confederacy: Spring Hill Chapter, Oakleigh Chapter, Saraland Chapter, Bay Minette Chapter. Girls no older than Ira must have been when the word came back that the young man's life had bled out of him at Chickamauga.

Behind a drum and fife corps filed the cadets of Mobile Military Academy, grave-faced adolescents restless for President Wilson to make a declaration of war, allowing them to jump into trenches alongside the Frenchmen and the Brits, having at the dirty Huns. Some had already found action with General Pershing on the Mexican border, chasing the wily Pancho Villa back to his desert lair; the heroic tales they brought back had ignited their friends. The way they stamped their feet reminded Morris of Cossacks, rifles locked on their shoulders. Abe put two fingers to his lips and shrieked a whistle.

A towering lout bumped into Morris and veered into the store.

"I can help you, sir?" Morris asked, following behind.

The man wove toward the rack of hats, reached for a Stetson and knocked several hats to the floor. He stepped back, tottering.

The smell of corn whiskey soured the air.

Miriam looked in from the street. "*Shikker*," Morris said to her.

"What did you say about me?" The man wove toward the counter, steadying himself on the cash register.

"I said you are drunk."

"Don't talk *Yid* talk."

"Out of the store, mister."

"I can do what I Goddamn please!"

"Do not curse the Lord God in here."

"*You're* telling *me* about . . . ?" The man gazed up blearily at the ceiling, then back down to Morris. "What business you people got hoopin' and hollerin' today?"

"Leave this store."

"This ain't your war."

Miriam had disappeared from the door; a band played a weary dirge.

"Passed by a woman here," said Morris, "Dolores Glasser, who lost a husband in this War. How old was he? Only a boy, fighting in Chickamauga. I have seen the place, such a sadness. Passed Molly Friedman, her brother today walks with two crutches and no legs, boom. Fighting for a Jew named Proskauer, I have seen his picture. A proud man from Mobile, too, with a fancy beard. He was not like you, not a horse's behind, not a *putz* making trouble in an honest man's store."

The man fell back from the cash register and glared at Morris. "You're a scrappy cuss, ain't you?" He took a step closer.

Morris picked up the crowbar.

Miriam came hurrying in with Officer Flynn, who gripped the troublemaker's collar and shook him. "You giving Mr. Morris trouble? I got a hole at the jail for a stinkin' mongrel to sleep in."

The man looked helplessly at Morris. Abe and Herman had appeared. Morris shook his head. "No, he will not bother us again."

The man nodded dumbly as they went outside. When Flynn had gone his way, the man said, "You ain't such a bad Joe," and brought out a flask of whiskey.

Morris grasped it, took a swig, and, as the man stumbled away, spat it out behind him on the walk.

"Ach, my shoulder." Morris spoke to himself, sitting in the rocking chair near the door as a lull came in the procession. The sky had clouded over and rain threatened the day. Wearily he rubbed at his shoulder. Since the November night he'd first slept on those feed sacks in the Eminescu barn, he'd felt the Romanian cold haunting his body, like a sliver of ice deep in his wing. He ceased rubbing, wishing he had swallowed that hooligan's whiskey now, a nice elixir to ease his shoulder's ache.

Sheeted men with hoods over their faces trod silently by, on the shoulders of one a large, rugged cross. The Klan members were met with polite, steady, applause. Morris had learned it was prudent, when Klansmen passed, to look straight ahead, nodding, while revealing no emotion at all. What bone to pick anyway, could they have with him? Wilder enthusiasm greeted the wagonloads of farmers who waved Confederate battle flags and hollered and whistled back at the crowd.

At the same time as the children went cavorting down the street going *bang bang* at enemy soldiers there was the crack of real rifles from the direction of Magnolia Cemetery. The sharp report came again in salute to the Confederate dead, scattering swallows from the telegraph wires down Dauphin, igniting a spark in the feet of the children.

Morris rocked back, looking up at the pressed tin ceiling of his store, seeing the brocade of ice on the window of his room as a boy with his brothers and sister close by, hearing the blast of rifles again in the frozen night. Under the blanket next to him stirred Chaim, who burrowed down deeper against the shattering noise. There was another volley of shots and, from the adjacent bed, Ben leapt up and came to join him at the window. Frantically they rubbed their palms across the thick, muted glass, trying to see. Golda began to cry in the next room.

Everywhere snow swirled through darkness, hiding the rattle of steel and the pounding of hooves, hiding the screams until it drew back like a veil revealing a man sunk down into the drifts and another alongside, tugging him up, and a horse, like a black ghost flying. Voices, shouts, villagers emerging from doorways running toward the figures in the snow. Another horse crowded the darkness, then another came thundering, and the door of Morris's own house opened as Papa, night shirt flying, headed toward the courtyard, and Mama was at the door of their room holding Golda, putting her finger to her lips, exhorting, "*Sha shtil, kinder,* be quiet, children, do as Papa has asked and pray to the Almighty."

The night stilled a moment, then held sobbing and angry, rising voices. Morris and his brothers rubbed busily at the window, wiping away their own curtains of breath, watching the men disperse, hearing the sobbing fall away and the voices receding into houses across the *shtetl* square.

Papa's face was long and dark when he came back in, and the next day when he went off to work at his distillery, and when he returned; and the next day and next, when sitting by the fire, prayer book open on his lap, he gazed off at the dancing flames. He said nothing until that night he came home, eyes sunk into deep moons, and told them the soldiers had visited him with swords and guns, a law, they said, barring Jews from this business, as others had been barred from being doctors and men of the courts. Who knew, they said, what mischief Jews might perform on grains and yeast and water; on the magic liquor they sold to the good Christians of Piatra Neamt? How much money the Jews had accumulated, they complained, at the expense of the good people of the village! As Papa spoke, his face darkened still, as though wanting to let loose tears like those that had come when they marched to the cemetery with his own father and tossed the dirt onto the casket and sat solemnly for days until the black veils were lifted from the chairs.

But he held back the tears, and sat one week, and then another, with prayer book open while gazing only at the fire. He called Morris to him and explained there was little money left for the family, and word had come throughout the region of Moldavia, from Dorohoi to Iasi, that others had businesses that were being closed down. He told Morris that he must leave school and go to work at a farmhouse on the edge of the Romanian plain; that he had contacted a grain farmer he knew through the distillery, Stefan Eminescu, a good Christian man with a son and two daughters, who could use a boy with good hands and a strong back.

Mama's hand rested on Morris's shoulder. "Azril," she said, "don't be so hard on him, tell him more gently," and he nodded and said her name, "Shayna Blema," *pretty rose*. "Pretty rose," Morris repeated, reaching up to touch her slender, soft hand. She started to walk away, but he held her hand firmly now; "*gai nisht*, Mama," he whispered, *don't go*, feeling the floor drop away.

"Morris?" Miriam's voice was exhorting him. Her hand jiggled his shoulder. "Chicken dreaming corn?"

He shook his head. "Not so good."

"The parade is over, and more customers will be coming soon." She moved away toward the cash register to go over the morning's receipts.

He stood from the rocking chair, the floor still dropping away, and stepped outdoors to steady himself, breathing in Mobile streets.

SUZANNE HUDSON

LOOKING FOR JOHN DAVID VINES

Christy Ann Logan let her gaze reconnoiter across the dim interior of
the Palomino Lounge outside Columbus, Mississippi, as she and her best
friend Malia took up residence at a wobbly round table on the perimeter of
the room. The crowd was sparse; it was not yet mid-afternoon, the click and
soft roll of pool balls, the thud of cue heels against the concrete floor
punctuating muted country hits. She inventoried the scattered knots of faces.
No JD. But then, she had figured he would not be here, not at their first
stop. That would be too lucky. Still, she was not sure what he was driving
today, so maybe . . . she searched through the scattered wisps of smoke and
hazy light from Christmas strings stapled to the ceiling, trying not to let her
disappointment show when his face did not materialize.

She waved at Miller Sams, the bartender. "Send us two Bud Lights,"
she half-hollered. She had dated Miller five years earlier and liked to believe
he was still not over her, liked to believe that none of them ever really got
over her, intoxicating as her effect upon men was known to be.

Malia fidgeted and squirmed her broadening ass into an armed chair
with a curved back. She had crossed into the territory of her thirties with a
surrendering nod to her saddlebag thighs and fat-dimpled butt that Christy
could not fathom. Malia was married, though, and happily, or so it seemed.
Sometimes Malia's husband, Dewey, joined them at the clubs, but mostly he
stayed in front of the TV rigging his rods and reels when he wasn't running
the feed shed. And he never seemed to mind that his wife went out with

Christy to the bars. Most married men would raise a fuss about that. Maybe he figured no one would find his wife attractive enough to hit on, especially with Christy around to draw the men to her instead; or maybe he really did trust his wife to keep her vows.

Christy herself was twenty-nine, just beginning to steel her ego against her own foray into the next decade of her young life, suddenly a-panic that she was once again singular as opposed to plural, an "I" rather than a "we," and she secretly envied her friend in that regard. Thirty was a terrifying place for a young woman who had come to rely upon her looks not just a little, but for everything.

Malia lit a cigarette, a Capri Menthol Light 120, her sculpted nails like red patent leather under the pointed bits of light. Her frosty-blonde high-lights winked back at the Christmas strings above and she exhaled a rushing cloud of smoke. "Well," she said, smirking, "I had to shave Dewey's butt last night."

"Did not!" Christy drew her nose into a deep crinkle of disgust.

"Oh, honey, yeah," Malia said. "And I'm here to tell you that is one hairy man."

"God!" Christy shuddered. Malia's stories of her devotion to such a disgusting creature as Dewey Dixon was a weekly source of amazement to Christy, especially in the face of her own sense of romance.

"Took a pile of hair off that man's ass this high." She held her palm four inches above the tabletop. "I'm 'on start calling him Sasquatch."

"Gag me one time, why don't you," Christy said, reiterating the nose crinkle.

"Well, shit, it was the only way I could get at those carbuncles. He's got three of the damn things scattered all over his butt. Has to sit on a ring of foam rubber like he's got hemorrhoids or something."

"Does he?"

"Does he what?"

"Have hemorrhoids? Cause that would be just too damn much for me to take," Christy said.

"No, he does not have hemorrhoids. Just carbuncles and a bad case of the dandruff."

"Well that's what you get for marrying a man fifteen years older than you."

"It ain't no big deal." Malia blew a curling cloud of cigarette smoke and studied her sculpted nails.

"God, I couldn't be married again, all the time having to be doing gross shit like doctoring on butt carbuncles and stuff," Christy said, reappraising her rush at the altar, then, just as quickly, gathering up speed for another run at it. After all, Dewey was old, prone to disgusting maladies. JD was different, young, would never have a zit, let alone butt carbuncles. JD was the man of her young dreams, broad-shouldered and blonde, with strong, strong arms and a desk job at the car lot. JD was too handsome and polished to need his butt shaved, ever.

"Aaah." Malia flipped the back of her hand and shrugged as Vicky, the waitress, set two beers down on the table.

"How y'all doing," Vicky said.

"Just barely," Malia said.

Christy leaned forward, waiting to seize an opportunity to ask about him. The door to the outside opened, and a white blast of November sunshine betrayed the light-muted interior of the Palomino Lounge.

"Lord, here she comes," Vicky sneered, as a forty-something woman with spilling cleavage and salon-whitened hair took a seat at the bar. "Old paste-eating whore."

"Uh-huh," Malia said.

Christy knew her, too. Everyone did. Susie Dawson was a fixture at the clubs of a Saturday afternoon, coming out long before most of the women patrons, who arrived way after dark, freshly moussed and perfumed. Susie posted herself at the bar while the men were thick, the competition thin. She usually latched on to a man by six or seven o'clock, usually ended up at the Shoulder Motel on Highway 17 or in the parking lot in the back seat of his car, rocking the undercarriage. She had been married two times and busted up at least three marriages in her years as a bar chick; it was simply what she did. She had been pretty, once upon a time, but now her skin had the sun-leathered, cigarette-cured wrinkling that told on her, her voice a raspy, harsh-toned vessel for emotional cynicism.

"Lord," Christy said. "Wouldn't you hate to be known as the number one bar skank in the county? But, hell, she don't give a shit," Christy said, studying the way Susie leaned over to accept a light from Miller, then reached up to pinch his cheek like a grandma courting a little boy.

"Not *even*," Malia concurred.

"Them men better take cover," Vicky said. "I seen her leave with Melinda

Wallace's old man last night and he's a born again Baptist. Without the teeto-taling part."

"Well, they don't call her 'Screwsie' for nothing," Malia said. "And I know my husband ain't allowed within fifty feet of her, else he knows he ain't getting none from me for a solid month."

"Speaking of, where is that crazy husband of yours?" Vicky asked.

"Hell," Malia drew on her skinny little cigarette. "He's laid up at the house, shit all swole up with the gout."

"I thought it was the carbuncles had him down," Christy said.

"Honey, no. The other day he says, 'Baby my foots is hurting me,'" and he went on being all pitiful like he does, till I got to where I was calling him 'Ol' Foots.' So on top of the carbuncles, Ol' Foots is flat laid out on the bed with his shit swole up."

"Gross," Christy said, wishing the dialogue would turn toward her own concerns. "Talk about a old-man disease."

"No duh," said Vicky.

"Hell, tell it. That man is a train wreck," Malia said. "Just a pile of writhing misery."

"And I see you ain't at home a-holding his hand none," Vicky said.

"Are you serious?" Malia said. "Cause you know I don't give up my nights out for nobody's misery. I'd probably skip my own mama's funeral, but folks would really run me down behind such as that."

"Girl, you are bad," Vicky laughed.

"No, honey. See, I *did* tell Ol' Foots that he could just as easy set his ass on that foam rubber ring and prop his legs up in a bar as he could at home, so I tried to get his ass to come out the house. But do you think he even considered it? Hell, no. See, sometimes he just likes to be miserable. But, hey, that don't mean I got to be."

"Ain't you even going to cook him no dinner this evening?" Vicky asked.

Christy peeled at the Bud Light label, growing antsy and impatient with the conversation. Sometimes Malia was exasperating, what with her mouth and her tendency to run it.

"Shit," Malia said. "I asked him what did he want and I'd go to the store and get it. And I would. Hell, I'd do anything for that man, God love him. I would of cooked him a pile of chicken or a steak, anything, cause that man will eat anything. Well, except English peas—says they're too ugly to eat. But, anyway, he was just so fucking busy, being all pitiful and puny, trying to get me to feel sorry for him, said he didn't want nothing but some Popsicles. 'That's okay, baby,' he says. 'I'll just lay up in here and suck on a old Popsicle or something.' Ain't that fucked up? So I showed his ass. I went to the Food Tiger, got four goddamn boxes of fucking Popsicles, shoved them in the freezer, throwed two damn Popsicles up in the bed with him, and went on my merry-ass way. Now ain't that just some flat-out fucked up shit?"

Vicky was doubled-over, snort-laughing. Finally she managed, "But if he's got the gout, how—"

"Hey Vicky," Christy interjected. "You seen JD this afternoon?"

Vicky's laughter went dead and her left eyebrow twitched upward. "Careful, honey."

"Come on," Christy said. "Has he been by here?"

"No, he ain't. Sorry," Vicky said. "Or, hell, maybe I ain't sorry. You ought to give that man a wide way to go. Hell, let Screwsie have him."

"As if," Christy spat back, quick as an angry cat. "Anyway, did I ask your opinion?"

"Okay, okay. Just remember who said it. Let me get back to damn work. Y'all keep it in the road, okay?" She carried the round wooden tray back over to the bar.

"See," Malia said. "Somebody else agrees with me. John David Vines is a womanizing son of a bitch and ain't *even* about to leave his wife."

"What the hell do you know about it?"

"Just what any fool knows. Hell, he's had four or five girlfriends since he got married."

"Shut up! Don't nobody know what's between us. Nobody. It's a history. We got a deep history together. I ain't just a girlfriend." Christy let her green eyes toss out the quintessential bitch gaze she had perfected as she grew into her twenties. It was a look that had sent more than one man into a blundering marathon of ass-kissing apologies and more than one woman into a fetal, tear-infested restroom retreat. And it had its desired effect upon Malia Dixon.

"So are we going to stay here?" Malia asked.

"Long enough for this beer. Then we'll try some other bars."

"And he said for sure he'd meet you?"

"I told you already what he said. He said he'd do his best to get out this afternoon, that he'd borrow a car so his wife couldn't find him, that he'd run by the usual places. Said he might have to leave and carry his kids out to eat, but—"

"Just his kids?"

"He said 'kids.' Said he might have to take his kids out to the strip and feed them supper, but he'd probably for sure be out after that."

"Don't sound like a promise to me. Lord, I never would of thought you'd get mixed up with a married man."

"Not just any married man. And not for long married."

"How can you think he's not for long married?"

"Cause he said we'd talk about things."

"Things," Malia echoed.

"Yeah, things. Important things. Which can only mean he's fixing to leave her." Christy took a long swallow of beer and belief in what she was telling herself. She could still have any man she wanted and JD was that man.

"Fixing to get ready to begin to start thinking about it is about as far as that man is going to go," Malia said.

Christy fired up the bitch glare again, eliciting an eye-rolling smirk from her best friend. Malia just did not understand real romance, mired as she was in her life as a toenail-clipping, butt-shaving, gout-nursing old man lover. Christy, though, wallowed in romance, had men always vying to have her. Her first round of romance with John David Vines in particular was when she was nineteen, working as a teller at the First National Bank during the day, spending weekends at the bars, dancing to honky-tonk rock bands, learning how to use the power she was discovering she had over men. After a wretched, pimply adolescence, she had come to be noticed for her looks, the black-haired, dark-eyed, bold-breasted looks of a bar-girl queen. She was captain of the dance squad her senior year in high school, and, after graduation, was drafted to hand out the trophy every Sunday at the dirt track races, and at the flat track race every Thursday night, a job which lasted until she was twenty-seven, her butt coated with tight denim jeans, breasts spilling from a black satin halter top tied in a big bow at the neck. She gave out the awards at the Watermelon Festival until she was twenty-five, clad in Black cowboy boots, high-angled cutoff jeans and a wife-beater t-shirt. She even ran for Watermelon Queen early on and won in a landslide. When she walked into a bar, just a few short years ago, men hollered her name, bought her drinks, and talked too loud, to impress her; women either maneuvered into her small circle of girlfriends or watched her from across the bar, downing drinks and jealousy, wishing they had some of her magic.

John David Vines was one of the first to get deep into her panties, which was the richest part of their history together. He had a magic of his own. He was four years older, a boy she had watched on the football field when she was a freshman in high school, not yet pushed out at the breasts and hips. JD was golden and blonde, with a bad-boy attitude that drew the attention of the kind of females who liked to taste danger. He never noticed Christy in high school, but when he came back to town after a stint in the Army he could not overlook the hottest girl in any club, and he courted her, ran his tongue along her neck and pulled her red lace underwear aside to touch her with the kind of knowledge the other boys did not begin to have.

She was not a slut, though, did not honor just anyone with that regal warmth between her bronzed thighs. She had lost her virginity to a blundering, knobby-dicked baseball player back in the eleventh grade and decided not to just hand it out to anyone who did not show a plethora of potential. Which made her all the more desirable, since those few males who had that honor bestowed upon them could pass in the knowledge that she had knighted them in recognition of their sexual prowess, and everybody else knew it, too. Other women were intrigued when they heard who was Christy Ann Logan's latest all the way man; consequently, for that chosen man even more pussy became available, increasing exponentially with each score thereafter. It was the strongest reference one could hope for.

She managed to keep herself from giving in to JD for a long time, though, in spite of his practiced fingers. She only let him put it in part way, at first, keeping him fevered and amped up on hormones. She had him where she loved to get men, on the teetering edge of potential ecstasy, where they filled her head with lush words, Mississippi sonnets of desire, and odes to her heart-thudding presence. She feasted on the rush of it all until it played out, most times growing tired of it after a while, moving on to the next man without ever even letting the previous one put it all the way in. But JD had a way with his touch and it was only a matter of time before her long, tanned legs were slung around his back, thighs sliding in a slippery rhythm that snatched all sense of control away from her, leaving her the one wanting more, her sexual compass in pieces on the floor. It was too, too, frightening, and she quickly broke it off, spitting on his heart, scoffing at his pleas to get married and have his babies, moving on to the next rush of power.

Christy rode the wild-child, hot-chick reputation for several years without slipping into slut-dom, but the latter part of her twenties found her reflection in the fluorescent-lit bathroom mirrors more hardened and drawn with precursor wrinkles born of late nights and chain smoking to the buzz of booze and weed. She married briefly, at twenty-seven, to an older man who had a little money and premature ejaculations that left her irritated by his ineptitude, left her spitting disgusted words at him until she realized he wasn't worth what little wealth he had. But she was married long enough to have a baby, a little boy who reminded her too much of his wimp of a daddy, a little boy who was now being raised by her mother. The thing that had grown inside her left scars of stretch marks on her stomach and thighs, gave her breasts too much of a sag to tolerate. She got herself some implants, "store bought titties," Malia called them, thongs in every color with condoms to match, and stepped inch by inch toward a metamorphosis into that which she had resisted up until now, up until she took up with a married man and ex-love named John David Vines. She knew, deep in the back of her head, that if her life did not take a different course, and soon, she might be just before turning into a bar skank her own self. So she grasped at JD and the legitimacy of marriage, knew she would have him, as she had him when she was nineteen. Because she wanted him. End of story.

Christy took the last sip of her beer and set down the bottle, stripped bare of its label, a result of her fidgety nerves these days. She squinted at Malia. "What do you think's the best thing about being married?" she asked. "And what's the worst?"

"Hell, that's easy. The best thing about being married is having him there. Right there. Going to be there every day and every night. A thing to count on."

"And the worst?"

Malia smiled. "Same answer. Having him there. All the goddamned time. Ain't that some fucked up shit?" She laughed. "It's a double-edged sword. You just got to dull down one blade and sharpen up the other, that's all."

When Christy and JD first took up for this, their second go-round, JD was falling all over himself to get back to the Promised Land between her thighs, and she put up little resistance. After all, he had a wife now; all Christy had was some first-rate pussy with which to level the playing field.

She felt an advantage, though, as wives were notoriously asexual, especially after scooting out a few babies, and JD's wife was apparently no exception. He could not get enough of Christy for four months solid, called her at all hours with heavy, warm words, telling her how he wanted to fuck her at the car lot, on the hood of a Lincoln, how he wanted to lick deep down in the crease of her elbow and spin circles around her nipples with his tongue, and she would coax and encourage until his breaths told her he had reached the end of this grab at satisfaction. It gave her a steady fix of power, the guiding force she felt over his orgasms, and it made him even more anxious to find time to be with her. He told her how his wife would only do it face to face, just one position, and then only three or four times a month, so Christy reached into her vast repertoire and showed him what all she had learned since their first run at romance. Front, back, inside out, upside down, she made him yell when she pushed the slick-sweated, supple curve of her body into his. He told her his wife was a complaining bitch, so Christy spoke soft and sweet, careful not to spook him with any criticisms, at least until recent weeks. In recent weeks his promises had waned, and Christy had begun to feel emotionally cornered, had begun to fret and demand.

"You said you loved me," she told him.

"And I do."

"You begged me to marry you, years ago. It should have been us."

"I know."

"Make it right, then. Make it be us."

Silence.

"Are you going to make it right? Are you?"

"It's complicated."

"Well, uncomplicate it, then."

"I will."

"Promise me."

"Hell, I said it, didn't I?"

"But promise."

He sighed. "Alright."

And now Christy was counting on that half-hearted promise.

The crowd at the 45 Club was ushering in the after-five spirit, thick with conversation and music. Christy and Malia had executed brief passes through the Three Pigs, Peggy's, and The S Curve, feeling the growing swell of happy hour with each stop, giggling more easily with the friends and acquaintances they encountered. The 45 Club was beer-buzz animated with loud laughter.

"Y'all know Godzilla Dixon, don't you?" Malia asked a group clustered by the bar. "She's my monster-in-law, Dewey's mama. She hates my guts but she's the one got us together in the first place."

Oakley Starnes and Tim Hillyer, fishing buddies of Dewey's, and Teddar Bumpus, roving sidekick to all, chuckled at the reference.

"That old woman is mean enough to scare the buggers out of a eight-nostriled toad," Tim said, throwing his foot up on a straight chair, leaning his elbow on his knee, giving Christy a wink. He was a good looking man, had always captured her interest, but he was married and therefore out of bounds. Christy had always kept true to that rule, until JD.

"No shit," Malia said. "Still and all, she brung us together. It was back when Dewey was dating this Pentecostal church woman, you know, Babs Elmore. She was one of them walking Elmores that used to walk up and down the highway of a day, walk to town, walk to the next county. Anyway, I reckon she walked to a Pentecostal Church one time, cause she got saved. Then she took up with Dewey, then she left him cause he didn't love the Lord enough, I reckon. And you know what Dewey's mama said?"

"Naw," Oakley said.

"Tell it, then," Tim said.

"Well Dewey was all heartbroke, you know, and he wouldn't even leave the house cause he was so full of grief and misery. And Godzilla said, 'Boy, you need to quit mopin' and moanin' 'round this house, laying all over the sofa eating up the cushions with your butt crack.' She said, 'Son, forget about that church woman and go on out to a bar somewhere and find you a nice woman that'll make you happy.' Ain't that some shit? 'Go out to a bar and find yourself a nice girl.' Hell, he's lucky he didn't get all wadded up with Screwsie Dawson."

Christy let laughter and smoke billow up around her thoughts about JD.

"Old Dewey's stove up, huh?" Teddar asked.

"God, yes," Malia said. "Got the gout and the butt carbuncles, and—I forgot to tell you this, Christy—he's got some seed ticks in his head that's been living there since he went hunting in the woods last Tuesday evening and won't *even* let me pull them out."

"Good God! How do you keep from puking at all the shit you have to do for that man?" Christy said. "And how can you sleep up in the same bed with a man that's got things living on him?"

"It ain't nothing, really," Malia said. "But I admit I like to fell out and fainted when he showed me them seed ticks and said we was going to have to let them suck on his scalp a while till they get big enough to grab a holt of."

"Hell, ain't that man never heard of no tweezers?" Christy said.

"Tweezers don't do much good on them little bitty ones," Tim said, "but I pulled one the size of a big raisin off my wife's pussy not long ago."

"Gag a maggot," Christy said. "What's next? I halfway expect you to go to wiping his ass."

"I'll do anything he needs me to do. I don't want him to have to go to the doctor, ever, and have to say something like, 'Hey, Doc, would you look at this thing back behind my nut sack? Cause my wife won't.'"

Christy let the laughter die down before she attempted to change the subject. "Look here," she said.

"No, you look here," Teddar said. "Come on and dance with me, Christy."

"I ain't in a dancing mood," Christy said. Teddar was a high school friend who had always harbored a crush on her, as did many of the other boys she grew up with. She routinely encouraged them all, smiled up at them while she twirled her hair around her fingers, bit at her lip, enticing them to stay in the electric-charged field of sexual energy surrounding her.

He leaned close to her ear. "One day," he said. "One day you going to let me touch it, ain't you?"

She punched him hard in the arm. "Have any of y'all seen JD?" she asked.

Oakley cleared his throat. Tim looked down at the floor.

"I know y'all have."

"Naw, we ain't. Really," Tim said. "Hell, he ain't no good to you."

"That's the third opinion I got today that I ain't asked for." Again she trotted out the bitch look.

Tim smiled. "Go on and dance with Teddar. Give him a thrill."

"I said I ain't in a dancing mood."

"Hey. Y'all remember the time old Dewey put that bull catfish in the wading pool?" Oakley said.

"Why the hell y'all want to change the damn subject?" Christy whined like she had as a teenager.

"Tell them about it, Lia," Oakley prodded.

"That goddamned bull catfish, now that was some fuuucked uuuup shit," Malia drew the words out long. "Dewey was so fucking proud of that big-ass fish that he blew up this blue plastic wading pool we keep in the shed for our little nephew. Then he called up Bobby Pollins because Bobby had done told him he wasn't no kind of a fisherman and couldn't no decent fish be caught in the dead of the winter besides. Well you know that made Dewey get all drawed up and pissed off, so he just had to show the damn fish to Bobby, you know, so he could make like he had a dick after all."

Christy pushed her nail against the label on the beer bottle, under the gummy-wet side of it, thumb sliding across cold condensation. She worked down the side of the label, then over by millimeters.

"So there's that goddamn monster catfish, a-needing to be skinned and et, you know, just a-swimming around and around in that stupid little pool. Can you imagine what that river-reared fish must have been thinking? So that fish was steady swimming, the living proof that Dewey has a real big old dick, only Bobby didn't come over till the next morning. And see, that fish had done stayed in that little blowed up pool all night, and it was February, you know, and the temperature dropped."

The men laughed, threw their heads back, bent forward in a rhythm of humor. Christy pushed her thumb against the backside of the beer label, wishing they would stop egging Malia on to share those long winded stories they had heard scores of times, knew by heart, with no twists, turns or surprise endings.

"So Dewey got all puffed up, so proud of this big fat dick hanging between his legs, and walked Bobby round back to look at the fish. But the water had done froze and that fish was laid over on its side, stopped right square in mid-swim, with its fin pointed up to heaven, just wall-eyed dead. And I guess poor old Dewey's pecker shriveled up like a old pea hull or something, but all he said was, 'I reckon I need to go on and skin that 'un, don't I?' The poor thing."

The laughter wrapped them all, then, until Christy punched through it, tearing at the label on her beer bottle. "Where the hell did y'all see JD? Huh?"

"To hell with JD," Tim said, grabbing Christy's forearm and pulling her over to the small dance floor near a jukebox that fuzzed out a Randy Travis song.

"Why you want to be grabbing me like that?"

"Cause you make me lose control, baby," he said, laughing.

"Why do y'all change the subject whenever I mention JD?"

He pulled her in to his body and they moved to the slow country rhythm. He leaned his lips close to her ear, sending tickles of air down the flesh of her neck. "I get jealous when I'm trying to impress a woman and all she does is go on about some other man."

"You are full of shit."

He straightened up to look her hard and steady in the eyes, a look ripe with interest, coaxing her intrigue. "Am I?" And he pulled her in again, arms encircling her, tightening, every subtle ripple of muscle against muscle telling her the tide was turning, honky-tonk currents were swirling past, threatening to carry her down under.

She wanted to throw a smart remark in his face, toss her hair back, do her bitch walk away from him, but she equally wanted to finish the dance, nice as it felt to forget about JD, if only for a few minutes. So she let him push his knee between her thighs, breathe into her neck, stroke his palm down her back until it glanced the upper regions of her ass. But when the music ended, the panic set in as never before, so she lifted her eyes to meet his, squinted hard and mean. "You," she said again, "are full of shit." She strode over to the table, gathered up her purse and Malia, and they headed out for the next bar.

The ladies' room at Martin's River House Club had four stalls and a bank of sinks backed by a big mirror. Flushing rushes of water, the clunk-clunk of the paper towel dispenser and gossip-toned conversation echoed against tiled walls.

"This is the nicest john of all the bars," Malia observed as she touched up her makeup. "Too bad the damn club sucks." She had been acting a shade different since they left the 45 Club, close-mouthed, but now she engaged in restroom girl talk.

"You told that right," came from Jennifer Gainus, who was bent over, head down, brushing her thick-curled hair. She straightened up fast, throwing her hair out in a puffy fluff of spiraling waves. "Only reason I come here is to see is anything going on, just in case there is, just to check it off the list and move on, you know?"

Christy contorted her lips into a tight 'o' and re-coated them with frosty bronze lipstick before blotting them with a square of toilet paper. "So have you seen JD?"

Malia rolled her eyes.

"Not lately. I seen him last night at the Playmore," Jennifer said. She crimped and pulled at her hair, bringing it farther out from her head.

"Damn, girl, if your hair gets any bigger you're going to steal the Sasquatch title off of Dewey," Malia said.

Jennifer laughed, then let her voice get fierce and low with the promise of a newsy tidbit. "I have to tell y'all though, what I heard about Tim Hillyer."

Christy's level of interest doubled. "Yeah? We was just with him."

"Well he's on the make, wife or no wife, so be careful. My sister-in-law seen him out back of the Playmore last night, back behind the dumpster, getting himself a blow job from damn Screwsie Dawson."

"Goddamn," Christy breathed. "He ain't just on the make. He's done sunk way the hell down."

"No shit," Malia said. "What I hear is guys go back for more of them Dawson blow jobs cause if she really likes you she takes out her upper plate."

The three of them let squealing laughter echo up the tiled walls. Then Jennifer dug through her purse for a compact. "You better watch JD's wife don't get wind of the two of you, though, Christy."

"Shit," Christy said. "She'll know before long, and she ought to know by now. I been leaving clues behind lately."

Jennifer giggled. "You are crazy, girl."

"Seriously," Christy said.

"What in the holy hell you been leaving?" Malia asked.

"Oh, just little things," Christy said. "A earring here, a Kleenex with my lip color on it there, but she's so dumb she ain't figured it out yet."

"Hell, if you want her to know, just call the bitch up," Jennifer said.

"That'd just make JD mad. No, the clues I'm leaving could be, like, accidental, you know? He couldn't get mad about that," Christy said.

"So she ain't picked up on them clues, huh," Jennifer said.

"Hell no." Christy sighed. "That must be one dumb as dirt woman. Shit, I'd leave one of my thongs in the car but she'd probably just pick it up, take it for a Scrunchy, and put her damn hair up with it."

A fresh wave of giggles bounced from the lavatory walls, as the three women shared more bits of gossip. Malia did an impersonation of Dewey trying to see his butt in the mirror and the giggles were magnified in volume. The three of them chatted, primped, and preened, making ready to move on to the next club, perhaps hoping for another drama or two, perhaps even their own.

The parking lot at the Playmore Lounge was almost full when they turned in around seven-thirty. A Dangerous Thing, one of the local dance bands, would be playing tonight, but not until nine, and would go until one or two. JD always showed up at the Playmore at some point of an evening, just like everyone else who frequented bars on the back side of town. At once it occurred to Christy that JD had never offered to meet her at the Ramada Lounge or the Montclair, or any of the bars where a more upscale, professional crowd gathered. She had frequented those bars fairly regularly before JD, but they only met at the rough-around-the-edges places where he would not be seen by his wife's friends.

Christy glanced over at Malia, who had gone quiet once again—for her, an aberration. A few clusters of folks were scattered about the parking lot. A young couple made out against the passenger's side of a Toyota. Jukeboxed music rode the neon glow lighting the car's interior in a haze of red. "I don't want to get out here yet," Christy said. "Let's just drive around some."

"Alright," Malia sighed. "But I'm a couple of beers into my buzz. Don't let me fuck up in front of a goddamn squad car."

"You're doing fine."

"For now, I guess. Where you want to go? To the bar at Sipsey?"

"Hell, no. You saw the Simms boys' pulpwood truck there and you know JD ain't going nowhere them Simmses are hanging out. Every time he runs into them he breaks a pool cue over somebody's head."

"No shit," Malia laughed. "Them Simmses ain't good for nothin' but the four F's: fuckin', fightin', and fixin' flats." She gave Christy a suspicious sideways glance. "So where you want to go?"

"Drive down the strip, okay?"

Malia looked at her then with a sudden expression Christy had never experienced, so buffeted as she had always been by beauty and desirability. It was an expression of concern, even pity, and it took her breath with its quick intensity. "You don't want to do this, hon."

"Goddamn, don't look at me like that. I just want to see is his car at any of the restaurants on the strip."

"We ain't never gone chasing him down when he was with his family. That's over the line. That ain't right."

Christy slapped the dashboard with her right palm, hard. "I ain't chasing him down. Just go the hell to the strip and drive through the Wendy's and the McDonald's and whatever the hell other burger joints and restaurants you see."

"Okay, okay," Malia said. "But I ain't getting out and neither are you. If you want to make a scene, save it for the Playmore. Not in front of no damn young-uns."

"I ain't stupid."

Malia said nothing. She put the car in drive and turned out of the parking lot, onto the highway back to Columbus.

When Christy had first confronted her reflection in the mirror after the birth of the baby, she had collapsed in a sobbing heap on the hospital floor. It was too much. The dimpled flesh of her stomach hung like the skin from a fat woman's upper arm. Her stomach was supposed to be flat and firm, a backdrop for the sexy emerald navel ring she wore. And her hipbones! They had fanned out, widening her lower body. Her whole skeletal and muscular ecology, it seemed, had been upset. Her breasts were swollen huge and hard with milk that seeped from her nipples, leaving round wet spots on her nightgown. Once emptied, those breasts spilled lower against her chest. It had taken almost a year and a good chunk of money to coax her body back into the kind of shape she could bear to show a man, and just in time for JD. JD told her she was beautiful, that his wife had let herself go after having their two children. JD kissed her stomach, told her stretch marks were a badge of honor, like the scar on his chest from being cut in a bar fight when he was stationed at Ft. Benning. He called her store-bought titties magnificent, reassured her that she was the most lovely, most luscious woman he had ever known or could ever hope to know. Where he had known just the right touches to her flesh in their early romance, he now knew just the right words to say to her flagging, aging ego.

His car was parked at the Mexican Kitchen, his favorite restaurant. Malia had ridden her around the vinyl-lined, playgrounded drive-thrus of every ticky tacky fast food joint on the strip before it occurred to Christy that he might have picked a place he liked better. Malia pulled into the parking lot across the street from the restaurant that was roof-topped with a life-sized team of heavy plastic horses pulling a wagon. One of the horses had fallen over, its white plastic legs stuck sideward, like a carcass ripe with rigor mortis. The stucco building spilled light through two glass doors and a bank of windows on the upper level. Christy and Malia sat smoking Capri cigarettes, like partner cops on a stakeout.

After the second cigarette, Malia sighed. "This is boring. Let's go back to the bar and dance."

The bitch look came across Christy's face with authority.

"Well the plan was to have a good time," Malia said. "Dewey's probably having a better time than we are, him all laid up, even."

"That's his car. It can't be much longer."

"Only a lifetime."

"What kind of a friend says that? How come you want to say things like that to me?" Christy threw her cigarette through the open window, something in her emotional gut telling her she should not have asked.

Malia put both hands on the steering wheel, looked thoughtful for a moment, then turned her face to her friend. "Teddar told me, when you was off dancing with Hillyer, that JD's been avoiding you like crazy."

"You're lying." Christy felt cornered, hemmed in, desperate. "You don't know what's between us."

"Honey, JD ain't worth all this. Teddar said—"

"Teddar said shit. Teddar Bumpus is a dumb-ass redneck from Gordo who—"

She stopped, the parking lot's light hitting her arms as she leaned forward, palms on the dashboard.

JD strolled through the glass door of the Mexican Kitchen and out into the open night air. He was followed by two small boys, dark-haired little boys six and seven years of age; running, rambunctious little boys who wrestled and horse-played their way across the pavement and into their daddy's car. JD leaned against the hood and lit a cigarette, his muscular frame bathed in fluorescence.

Christy reached for the door handle, but Malia leaned all the way across her, taking her wrist. "I ain't letting you do that, honey," she said in a soft voice.

Christy was crying, had not realized it, but now she knew she was crying, watching JD lean against the hood of his car, smoking like a cocky, never-caught thief.

"Let's go." Malia reached for the keys.

"No," Christy said, still watching as a woman approached JD, a plump woman with dark hair, the woman who was his wife, Christy knew. And the plump woman with the dark hair took the cigarette from his lips and thumped it out into the highway. JD laughed and grabbed the woman, twisting her arm playfully behind her back and the woman was laughing, too. Then one of the little boys stuck his head out the back seat window and JD let go of the plump woman and pretended a punch toward the boy, who ducked back inside the car. And before the woman walked around the car she looked up at JD and said something that made him throw his head back and laugh like Christy had never, ever seen him laugh. He was still laughing and shaking his head when the passenger's side door closed.

Malia had her arm around Christy through the whole of the scene in the parking lot, Christy's eyeliner and mascara smudged and smearing as she rubbed at hot tears. Then she stopped, abruptly, bitch-look overtaking vulnerability, overriding it as unacceptable, an effigy giving in to its first real gulp of a bitterness she had barely tasted up until now. "Get me the hell away from here," Christy said, "before I kill his ass."

The Playmore was rocking by the time make-up was refreshed and emotions were packed away. A Dangerous Thing covered songs like "Strokin'" and "Knock on Wood," classic songs that pulled folks onto the dance floor, but the band was taking a break at the moment. Christy and Malia found themselves reunited with Teddar, Oakley and Tim, who had made their way there via Burt's Game Room, where they had seen Joey Taggart and Sonny Sams get into a vicious fist fight in the parking lot, a fight during which Sonny kicked Joey's butt for telling lies on Sonny's girlfriend.

"Good," Malia said. "I never did like Joey Taggart. He ain't nothing but one of them long, tall, raw-boned fellers with a headache for a face."

"Well, it's one messed up face right about now," Tim said. He turned to Christy. "You're mighty quiet, girl,"

She gave him her practiced glare. "I was just thinking," she said.

"About what?"

"About how stupid men are to fight over women, for women, about women."

"Shit," Tim laughed. "We'll do just about anything for pussy. And y'all know it."

"Ain't that the truth," Teddar said. "Hell, Lia said that old man Christy was married to would get so beside hisself he'd water the furrow before he could even go to plowing."

Christy rolled her eyes. "Don't remind me."

"Hey Malia, what about you? Will old Dewey jump through hoops for that good stuff?"

"He's a man, ain't he?" Malia said, and Christy was glad to let her carry the conversation now, now that she had gotten her answer to the question of the evening. Malia went on, holding forth. "Dewey's so horny all I got to do is aim it in his direction and he's all over it. Or he'll say, 'Baby, why don't you put on them "fuck-me" pumps and crawl up in the covers with a tired old man.' Ain't that some shit?"

"He ain't real romantic, huh," Oakley said.

"Dewey Dixon? I'll tell you an example of Dewey's idea of romance. He called me from work one afternoon a couple of weeks ago and said, 'Dust off that ol' puss, Baby, cause I'm coming home for a sardine sammich and then I'm fixing to lay some pipe up in there.' And that man didn't understand why I just went on to the Food Tiger, went on about my business, carried my mama her hormone prescription, didn't give him another thought. Had his bottom lip all run out by the time I got home."

Malia's audience laughed, swapped Stupid Romance Tricks stories while Christy let it all become nothing more than air rushing at her ears, air becoming the angry sound of the ocean, as if she was ear-muffed by two big seashells. She wished the band would start up again. She wanted to dance, to move, to feel as wild and beautiful as she had as a teenager. She wanted to lean her body into Tim Hillyer's and make him want her more than any wife could ever be wanted, and she let her eyes go to his. The group was still talking, laughing, mouths moving soundlessly in the smoky dimness, but Tim's eyes cut to hers more and more frequently, sending her a look she knew. She let herself smile him an answer, then slid her glance away from his.

At the bar, Wendell Mitchell was serving up beer after beer, filling trays for Gail, Jo-Jo, and Katrina, the three Saturday night waitresses. Colored lights danced around the Playmore's huge party room, and the clusters of faces were like photo images of the faces Christy had seen here last week.

It never changed much. Most of the men at the bar had occupied the same barstools for years, and the predictability of their attitudes, of the music and fights and soap operas playing out from night to night, kept fear at bay, for a little while. At the far end of the bar Susie Dawson stood between the legs of Karl Thornton, her palms rubbing his outer thighs. Karl's divorce was final and he was looking to get laid, Christy figured. And it wouldn't be difficult with Screwsie Dawson staking a claim there in the shadow of his crotch.

Somewhere through the padded silence Christy finally heard the electric buzz of a bass guitar, the rattle of drumsticks against a snare and a cymbal as the musicians took their places. There was a picking and tuning of strings, a random strike or two at the drums. Then, finally, a blending of rhythms into a tune and the gentle rock of singing guitars. A slow song, another old dance standard, "My Girl." She had danced with JD a hundred times to that very song and he could go to hell as far as she was concerned. A sting of tears tried to rise up to her closed eyes now, as she pressed against Tim's chest, her cheek against his shoulder, moving with him on the dance floor. She let her arms slide up and around his neck, fingertips brushing the flesh of the back of his neck, and when he pushed his lips against her own neck the warmth of his kisses took her. She would be alright if only she could have another shot at it, and she would go on peeling the labels off beer bottles for however long it took. She squeezed the back of Tim's neck, pushed her hips forward, let her crotch rub a tempo against his thigh. She would try for as long as she had to, beginning with Tim Hillyer. And she didn't care if her fingernails went to nubs from peeling back labels as long as she could have another shot at that which she kept cloaked in fragile power and musky promises, the kind of love she craved and hoarded and inevitably hurled away.

LAURA HUNTER

WAITING FOR THE PINK

Horace Noland was rubbing coal oil into his el bone to fight off the lumbago when he heard the first shot. Just a little pop, not worthy of rising and moving to the window. Too stove up to try. Old scrap of meat throwed over some bones. That's what Willie Mae Blesser allowed ever time she put her thick wide arms round his middle.

The second shot popped popped popped like a repeating cap gun. Lawley, guess he best check out the commotion. Black man peeping out a black window into black night wouldn't be seen. Using his hand to boost his weight off the mattress, he stirred the air round him. When he moved, Horace laughed a high-pitched he-he-he and spoke out loud. "Well, Greenback, so old I don't even know the sound of my own fart. Willie Mae Blesser would of throwed a blue fit. 'Ain't nothing worse than a man who can't keep his own gas, Horace Noland,' she'd've said. Sure enough."

From the door sill a slick green lizard watched as he edged himself off the naked mattress. So bent by age, he slid along with his head down, angled level with the ground, he seemed older than God himself. "Best I bent like a wind-broke tree," he said. "Folk looking straight on at me'd be scared shitless," thinking bout the misplaced dimple deep in his upper lip. "Looks for all truth like I got me a third nose hole to my face," and he chuckled again. "Ain't that the truth?" he said to the lizard. The lizard blinked and looked back.

"Gotta take a leak, Greenback. Get out my way for I mash you flat,"

Horace said. As he rose from the bed, a trickle ran down his thigh and pooled dingy pink pee in his shoe. "Reckon I old. Can't even make it to the edge of the porch, you lizard." He sighed. "Where's that Willie Mae Blesser when I need her?" He dropped back onto the mattress and laid his angles across the bed. His feet, too heavy to lift off the floor, swung like matched pendulums, then stopped. His head pointing to the foot of the bed, his eyes facing the door, he pulled a wool crazy quilt over his arms and slept.

Before midnight, early March rain hit the roof all at once and a night full of acorns bounced like dancers across the tin. Later tiny men in black and white stripes crawled up on his back and, starting at his backbone, moved round to his hips, using steel hammers, and pounded sharp even nails into the flesh of his waist. In his sleep, he twisted and shivered trying to shake them off, but they stayed till they finished, then vanished.

He woke at daybreak, Greenback on the bed next to him, turned brown against a rusty quilt square. The door stood open, either because Horace had forgotten to close it before dark or because the wind came in during the night. Horace didn't remember.

Rolling over to gain leverage for sitting up, Horace groaned. "Done a fine job this time, you slimy old lizard, them chain gang mens. They fill me so full of aches my body done stuck in one place. Hum. Hum. Hum."

Greenback didn't move till Horace slapped the bed before him and said "Scat."

Horace slid over to a sawed off barrel turned upside down to hold the electric eye for cooking. He scraped yesterday's oatmeal out of the black bottomed pot and dumped it on his green plastic plate, then ate, using a knife to cut the oatmeal into chunks, spearing each bite into his mouth with the blade's tip. When he finished, he dropped a glob of cold oatmeal on the floor before the lizard.

Greenback scurried up the wall.

"Don't blame you, old lizard. Looks more like snot than food, I reckon."

A little before noon a white girl appeared in the door, as quiet as if Horace'd conjured her up himself. He'd been waiting for Willie Mae Blesser to come in from the kitchen with greens and corn pone all hot for the eating, so he jerked when she tapped a puny white knock on the door frame.

Dressed in pale pink with glittery yellow hair, he thought she must be an angel, so he didn't speak, thinking his quiet'd make her stay. After a bit, she cocked her head and Horace craned his neck to see if her wings showed. But nothing behind her shifted except a shadow throwed cross the porch by Willie Mae Blesser's dogwood.

When she said "You Mr. Noland?" with a question at the end, he knowed she weren't no angel. No self-respecting angel'd come to earth not knowing what she's about.

"If she ain't no angel, Greenback, she's apt to be a ghost. Lawley. Lawley." He slid across his naked mattress toward the wall, not thinking about lifting his feet.

"No sir," she smiled. "I'm not a ghost, and I'm certainly not an angel. I'm with DHR." She stepped across the sill. "Can I come in?"

"Looks like you are in," he said. Greenback skittered down the wall and hid behind the barrel half.

Seeing the lizard, the girl drew back.

"Ain't nothing but a lizard's all," Horace said. "Come in and set. Willie Mae Blesser ain't in here yet, but she's coming."

"I need to ask you some questions, Mr. Noland. It's reported that you might could use some services." Inside, she glanced at his face and her head fell, her face all at once like everybody else's. Looking not at him, she slipped a black book and pen out of her pink bag.

"Don't reckon I'll be needing no services. Lawley. Now there's a service, so's I's told. Had my fill of services."

Still standing, the girl kept her eyes on her paper. "What's your full name, Mr. Noland?"

"Carver Horace Noland. Most folk round bouts calls me Horace."

"Horse? That's a strange name. Why would your mother name you Horse?" Glancing up, she smiled and shifted her weight to one foot.

Seems a might green to be working in this part of the county, Horace thought. Else she's poking fun. "Don't reckon she did," he said, not sure he liked this girl. "Wouldn't be no stranger than being named letters like you." He scooted himself up to the rim of the mattress so's he could put her out the door, if he saw fit.

"DHR's not my name." She laughed a real laugh this time. "I work for the Department of Human Resources. We can assist you with whatever you need to keep you safe and healthy." For the first time, she raised her eyes, bluer than my Lawley's baby blanket, Horace thought. Looking at him this time, she didn't flinch. "My name's Barbara and most people call me Barb." She offered him her hand.

Putting her pen in the pink bag, she stepped closer, her hand still out, a jingly silver bracelet rattling her wrist.

He looked past her out the door, at Willie Mae Blesser's dogwood. Horace'd knowed eyes like that before, but they hid in dark cracks in his mind, and thinking now don't always let him dig deep into what's real and see what's not like he once done.

"Think you'd be blown away in last night's spring storm?"

He heard a broad smile now.

Without looking, Horace took her hand. It was warm and floppy, like shaking a wet washrag. When Horace didn't answer, she continued. "I'm always skittish in storms myself."

"I ain't scared." He took his hand back, but he kept his face turned, now to the wall. "Some white women's scared to come in here. Scared I be jumping they bones." Horace cut his eyes toward her without looking at her straight on. "That Baptist do-gooder come in here and tacked a white Jesus up on my wall, now she be scared. Jumped like a kitten ever time I moved. You ain't scared?"

Barb walked over to the picture of Jesus, his hands open so everybody could notice his nail marks. "No sir. I'm more scared of that lizard crawling up my leg than I am of you." She laughed a chopped up laugh that had trouble coming out, then turned her back to the picture and faced Horace. Pointing to the lizard, she asked, "What's Miss Willie Mae Blesser think about him staying in here?"

Horace Noland figure'd he'd said enough. When he didn't answer any more of her questions, she left, saying she'd be back.

Judging by the wall calendar, she come by on the second box of ever week, first just talking, bringing him grocery, a jacket for next year's winter, then talking bout moving into town to a senior home. "Old folks home ain't for me," he insisted, and she'd drop it for a spell. Then she come by a cool weather morning catching him rubbing his kerosene, sitting next to his gas heater, and she'd start in again.

It took three boxes for Greenback to cotton up to her. On a day so full of coming summer sun it burned your eyes, Horace spied the lizard moving cross the floor, Barb not noticing but talking like a greased wagon running in sand. When Greenback come nigh on to her slick black shoe, Horace spoke, quiet as the lizard, "Now, don't you shy none, but old lizard Greenback's nosing your toe. Just you be still while he sizes you up."

Without moving her head, Barb spotted the lizard with sidewise eyes. Only her eyes, round as the moon, moved. Horace told she could go ahead and breathe now. "He ain't aiming to hurt you. Lizard he ain't got no teeth. He just like me. All gum." Horace laughed his he-he-he.

Barb let out her breath, reached down and ran her finger across Greenback.

"You finally come to a like-minded house, girl," Horace said with a grin.

Before month's end, she come to him in white. He saw her standing in the swinging door, its glass window cutting down one side, then lost her against the hospital wall. He didn't place her again till she spoke, her voice quiet and gentle, not a single thorn on the vine.

She told him his neighbor had no choice but to call the police when he saw Mr. Noland walking, gun loaded and ready, round and round his house. "Why do that, Mr. Noland? Don't you realize that going around with a loaded gun can get you in jail? Didn't I hear you were at Atmore Prison for a time? Why on earth?" She'd reached the bed by the time she stopped asking questions and put her hand, damp, sticky, soft, against his forehead. "The nurse says you have a serious kidney infection. Passing blood, even. You didn't tell me you needed a doctor. Are you better?"

He watched red and yellow cartoon frogs dancing in and out among trees and green bushes on the television set hanging from the wall.

Barb turned off the television. "Talk to me, Mr. Noland. You want to get back home. Greenback needs you."

"The county they come and say to me cut down that tree." He stopped.

"Go on," she encouraged.

"It's in the way of a wider road, they say." Without thinking what he was doing, he looked directly into her steel blue eyes. "Us chain gangers we built them roads. I know what they takes, and they don't have to take no dogwood tree to make a road." He turned to the wall, talking now more to him own self than to her.

"Willie Mae Blesser she planted that tree out by the road when we's just married. A sign for all to see she prided our home place. Brought it from the old Mrs.'s own yard. 'The Mrs. give them to me, fair and square,' she said, 'for scrubbing her back steps clean. It's two. One white and one pink and I aim to plant it both in the same hole.' And it growed strange, up together then split right down the middle. Like it was two trees with one root. And when it bloomed, one side showed white, white as snow in April. The nother side waited for the white to die off and popped out pink, like it'd been stained by the blood from the death of the white. But my Willie Mae she loved that tree. Waited in season for the blooming. She birthed our Lawley boy the one year the whites stayed on for seeing the pink." Horace rested, gathering energy for carrying on.

"And then some white strangers come on my land and say 'This ain't your land so near the road. This here land's the county's. Say cut down this tree or we'll do it ourself.'"

Her hand rubbed like cream cross his head where it lay flat on the bed.

"Mr. Noland. Mr. Noland." She sounded tired.

"Nobody ain't taking down my Willie Mae's tree. Weren't I sick and abed, I'd be marching my yard still, guarding her tree." He jerked his hand back and wiped his eyes so she couldn't shame him by looking at his sorrow.

"I don't know what to do, Mr. Noland. You concentrate on getting well and we'll see to the tree then."

"You go and set on my porch and see to it that tree ain't cut." He locked her eye and grabbed her hand, gripping it, pulling it to his chest. "You DHR. You come saying you here to help. You go now and do that one thing for my Willie Mae."

"I can't do that. That's breaking the law." She tried pulling her hand away, but he held strong. After a moment, she said, "If they cut your tree, I'll plant you another one. One just like it."

"Ain't nother one like it nowhere." He let go of her hand and turned his face away.

April nigh out of boxes when the blue policeman come in Horace's house without so much as a tap on the door. He took the gun and said, "Time to go, old man."

"Time? I done my time." Horace set on the edge of his naked mattress, staring at the floor. "Done my service. Service in WW Two. Service in Atmore and up and down them asphalt bubble roads. Pulling a chain waist to waist. I done it. Lawley. Lawley." Facing the plank floor, Horace shook his head.

"Yeah. You served well. Now come ahead peaceful." The police took Horace's elbow.

Horace pulled it away and cradled his left arm in his right, as if he held a newborn babe, kneading out the lumbago as best he could without a spot of kerosene.

"Service for twelve. Lawley still a lapbaby, he was. Service for twelve with a silver pie server. Willie Mae Blesser she brung it home. For polishing for old Mrs.'s Christmas party. Cause Lawley sick as a horse and needing his mama near by." Tears, spread out and wide, wet Horace's face, but the blue police had hold of his el bone so he couldn't wipe away the shame.

"What service for twelve, Mr. Noland?" Barb came in from behind the policeman. She kneeled down in front of Horace and smoothed the collar of his shirt, then rested her hand on his shoulder. "What're you doing here?" she asked back at the policeman. Without waiting for an answer, she spoke to Horace, "What're you talking about, Mr. Noland?"

"The Mrs. she say my Willie Mae kept her silver pie server."

"You DHR?" the policeman asked.

"No. Not anymore." She stopped and looked up at the policeman.

"Oh?" the blue police said, hoisting his eyebrow.

"They fired me, if you must know. I just come by." She turned back to Horace. "You want a pie server? I've got one I had since I was little. I'll give it to you," Barb said.

"Fired you, huh? What'd you do, slug this old stubborn coot?"

"Claimed she stole it for me to sell. Medicine for Lawley. That's all we wanted. But she never done it. I never sold none of it. Never seen it." Horace continued, shaking his head with every word.

"What?" Barb spun round to the policeman. Seeing his tobacco grin, she spoke through stretched lips. "No. I wasn't objective enough, it seems," and turned her back on him, squatting still, keeping her face leveled with Horace's.

"Got the medicine by loading the Mr.'s hay. But it never done no good. The Mr. he knowed where the money come from. Promised he'd do whatever it takes to make it right. But he never spoke for me at the courthouse. He set dumb and let me go off to Atmore and not stand by my Willie Mae at our Lawley's service. And he wouldn't speak for me again come time to leave Atmore Pen for my Willie Mae with her dying of a busted heart.

Busted wide open, they says, from grieving so." Horace stared eye to eye at Barb, thinking the Lord he'll strike me dead looking straight on at a white woman and not caring.

"Come on now, Mr. Noland," the policeman said, twisting his arm to see his watch. "It's time for you to move on cross town. They've got you a fine room with a window and good food. You'll be right at home in no time."

"Ain't going." Horace kneaded at the pain in his arm. "Damn el bone. Got chains on my bones."

"What'd he do this time?" Barb asked. "Why're you here?"

"Chained to this house I am. Chained."

"Shooting at the road crew this morning," he answered. "So they's a warrant. Most got that young kid what holds out the stop sign. Kid with green hair."

"Me and my lizard. Waiting for the pink."

"What the hell's he talking about now?" the officer blurted out, then stopped. "Sorry, Miss." Moving toward the door, he said, "Guess I need some air."

Barb lifted her bones off the floor and her and the police walked out on the porch. Horace slid up behind them, counting on Barb to run the blue man off his land.

"It's his tree. The tree by the road," she said. "He's waiting for the pink side to bloom. His wife Willie Mae was buried the second week in April. When pink dogwood flowers. Seems they're late this year."

The blue man nodded.

"White's almost gone now. Leave him here another week." She spoke in an almost whisper. "Once the pink blooms, I'll take him over. I'll do whatever it takes to make things right. I promise."

Horace couldn't see her eyes through the back of her yellow hair, but her words called out to him and told him where he'd knowed them same blue eyes. The courthouse. Her own granddaddy, the old Mr. himself, promising he'd keep Horace and Lawley and Willie Mae safe on they own land. The chain gang mens draped a log chain round his neck, this time so heavy he couldn't look up.

Greenback skittered toward the door. When he passed Horace, Horace lifted a heavy foot and, knowing he'd have to stand by his own self this time, mashed the lizard flat. "Don't blame you none, old lizard."

Passing the yellow-haired girl and the blue police, he gathered up a chunk of rusted chain off the porch and drug it, creeping along in a slow moving slant, leaving a spotted trail of bright red pee. When he reached the split dogwood, Horace grasped the gray trunk, now grave with branches weighted heavy in Willie Mae's pink, buds waiting to open. Lowering his own self to the ground, he looped the rough chain round his old weary bones and Willie Mae Blesser's tree and snapped shut the lock.

MICHAEL KNIGHT

FIREWORKS

Evan Butter found *hotbush.com* on the internet the day after Christmas. He'd talked his parents into getting him a computer and an on-line hookup for his room. School work, he said. It's the only thing I want this year, he said, hinting that if there wasn't a computer under the tree they'd have a deeply unhappy twelve year old on their hands and he knew they remembered how he sulked two years ago when they got him a three speed instead of the mountain bike he asked for. He'd memorized his father's American Express number and had been downloading naked pictures of a woman named Veronica ever since—Veronica on a pool table, Veronica emerging from a hottub, Veronica doubled over and mugging for the camera through her legs.

There were other women on the site—petite Autumn, busty Desiree, long-legged Lorelei—and there were other sites—*bigsluts.com, beavershot.com*— but he was faithful to Veronica. She reminded him of a girl named Lulu Fountain, who went to his school and had acquired both breasts and braces the previous summer. She sat in the next desk over from his in Ms. Frietag's class, smelled faintly of maple syrup, as if she had pancakes for breakfast every morning. Just before the holidays, he'd been flipping through his yearbook and come across her picture and circled it in red ink. The picture had been taken before the braces so he sketched them in across her smile. She hardly ever smiled like that anymore, her whole face in it. The emphasis in her features had shifted since the summer. Now, she kept her mouth pinched shut, her eyes open wide like she was constantly in the process of being startled. He looked at her picture for a long time. Then he added a mustache and horns. If asked, he would have been hard pressed to explain what exactly Veronica and Lulu Fountain had in common beyond the most rudimentary physical similarity—brown hair, brown eyes. There was, however, a barely perceptible look of amazement in Veronica's features, as if she was surprised to find herself naked except for hip-high leather boots, the whole world looking on.

Tonight, his mom and dad were off somewhere at a party. He and his little sister, Nicole, were under Miss Anita's care. Miss Anita was the housekeeper. She was old and black and could be counted on to have no plans for New Year's Eve. She had children of her own—now and then, Evan heard his mother asking her about them—but they were grown, didn't need looking after anymore. Right now, Miss Anita was watching TV in the living room with Nicole, one of the New Year's countdown shows. Evan could hear music drifting up the stairs and under his locked door. He'd been masturbating pretty much nonstop since dinner. He was a little sore and more than a little bored but refused to admit it to himself. It didn't seem possible that such a wonder as Veronica could ever lose her charm.

hotbush.com offered a link called the VIP Room where for the *LOW, LOW PRICE OF $9.99 PER MINUTE* he could chat in person with the girl of his choice while perusing her *PRIVATE PORTFOLIO—HOT! HOT! HOT! BUSH AVAILABLE ONLY TO PREFERRED CUSTORMERS.* Evan wondered if he qualified. His cursor had been hovering around the link for half an hour when the doorknob rattled. He heard Miss Anita say, "Whatchu doing in there you need to lock a body out?"

Evan got his jeans organized in a hurry, brought a video game called *Lucifer's Gate* up onto the screen.

Miss Anita said, "Boy?"

"What?" His voice was high-pitched, constricted. He wiped his face with his shirt tail. He was sweating like a boxer all of a sudden. He said, "I'm not doing anything."

Miss Anita said, "You just sitting in there, hunh? All quiet. You just looking at the wall?"

"I'm playing a computer game."

Miss Anita laughed—huh huh huh—her soft old black lady laugh. He pictured her in her housedress and her step-ins, her black fat forearms, her round black face, her black ankles thick as knees. "Un-hunh," she said.

"It's *Lucifer's Gate*," he said.

"Lucifer," she said and she was quiet for a moment. "Well—why not give old Lucifer a rest—" He was sure he heard amusement in her voice, felt certain she was mocking him somehow—"and come watch the TV with your sister. We gone pop some popcorn in a minute."

"No thanks," he said.

Miss Anita said, "Un-hunh."

Evan decided to take a break from the computer. He stretched out on his bed, pushed his hand into his pants, tugged idly, half-heartedly at himself. He thought about Veronica. He thought about Lulu Fountain. He thought of the woman on the toothpaste commercial. He thought about the tormented damsels in *Lucifer's Gate*. He thought about Veronica again, wondered what he would say to her given the chance, wondered how much more private her portfolio could be than the pictures he'd already seen. He thought of these bare-midriffed high school girls he'd followed at the mall last week. He thought about his retarded cousin, Maisie. He thought of the redhead on the show about lawyers. He thought about the ladies in his mother's book club. He thought about the woman in his comic books who could manipulate the weather. Then, against his will, there was Miss Anita in his mind. Evan snapped his eyes open and lurched off of the bed. He felt furious and weird. Who did she think she was? This wasn't her house. He wasn't her child. He was too old for a babysitter anyhow. As if to spite her, he bolted across the room and turned his fingers loose on the computer keyboard, launching himself back into the cyberspace, back to *hotbush.com* and straight into the VIP Room with Veronica.

His computer whirred quietly to itself. Evan considered his father's American Express bill, wondered how long before it would arrive. Then the screen flashed blank and was refilled pixel by pixel with Veronica in the shower, her right foot raised and propped on the soap dish, her left hand at her crotch and the thought of his father's credit card dissolved. Veronica looked vaguely astonished, though not displeased, to find Evan in her bathroom. These words appeared below the image: *I'm in the shower, sexy. I'll be right out. Why don't you tell me what I should wear.*

Evan nearly logged off. He forced himself to concentrate, shut his eyes, tried to imagine what a man in his position ought to want from a woman like Veronica. The only man he could think at the moment was his father. He pictured the photo of his parents hanging in the hall outside his room.

A wedding dress.

Kinky. What's your name?

Evan.

How's this, Evan?

The shower scene vanished. In its place appeared Veronica in long white veil and white pumps and that was all. She was smearing cake icing on her breasts.

I'm so hot. I want your big hot cock.

OK.

Where do you want to put your big hot cock?

Blink, blink, blink went Evan's cursor.

Where would you like me to put it?

I want it in my mouth. I want to suck your big hot cock.

The image shifted this time to Veronica on all fours, her backside looming. She was looking bug-eyed at the camera over her shoulder. There was a peeled banana in her mouth.

It's so big and hot and hard.

Between his legs, however, Evan could only manage half a wood. He jerked himself with his free hand to no avail. He worried that he'd worn himself out for good, wondered if it meant there was something wrong with him that he couldn't keep it up for a woman like Veronica.

Tell me what you want, Evan.

Blink, blink, blink.

Do you want Veronica on top?

Veronica appeared on screen astride a saddle. She was pinching her nipples. The saddle was on a marble floor in front of a blazing fireplace.

I'm riding you. Make me cum.

Evan stroked himself wildly, felt the pressure of frustration building in his chest. He was red-faced, panting. He was limp now as a sock. He went at it a minute longer—*That's it, Evan. Give it to me, Evan*—then bounced himself off of *hotbush.com* and back into his room. He could see his face reflected in the monitor. His hair was mussed like he'd been asleep, damp with sweat at his temples and his brow. He waited to catch his breath. From downstairs, he could smell the familiar, fake butter smell of microwave popcorn and it made him hungry. But he didn't want to go down there yet. Instead, he booted up *Lucifer's Gate* and disemboweled the devil's minions for a while.

Miss Anita was sprawled on the couch with her heels in Nicole's lap. Nicole was massaging her arches. Miss Anita's feet were fat as hams, the color of chocolate on top, caramel on bottom, her toenails hard-looking, yellow, shot through with cracks. Nicole didn't seem to mind. She pressed her thumbs into Miss Anita's flesh and Miss Anita moaned. The popcorn was in a ceramic bowl on the coffee table but Evan had lost his appetite.

"You got it now, baby girl," Miss Anita said.

Her eyes were squeezed shut and though she did not open them at his approach, Miss Anita turned her head slightly when Evan dropped into his father's leather chair.

"How's Lucifer?" she said.

Evan said, "Dead."

Miss Anita popped her right eye open.

"Praise Jesus."

Evan looked at the TV. Times Square. The milling, roaring masses. There was a rock band playing on a raised platform. The crowd moved like wind-licked trees. Evan felt a blush rising in his cheeks. You didn't actually get to do battle with Lucifer until the seventh circle of hell and he'd only made it to the third, where he'd been beheaded by a demon called Asmodeus. There had been a maiden in a tattered dress chained to the wall in the chamber where he died.

Nicole said, "Miss Anita is letting me stay up to watch the ball drop." Nicole was eight years old, blonde, her hair chopped into a pageboy. Her hands kept moving over Miss Anita's feet. "She said I could if I gave her a massage."

"That was sposed to be our secret," Miss Anita said. She didn't sound particularly concerned.

Evan said, "Mom won't like you up til midnight."

"You either," Miss Anita said. "We all in this together. Or we all in bed at ten o'clock."

Nicole jerked her knees and slapped the bottom of Miss Anita's foot. "But you promised. You said if I rubbed your arches I could stay up. That's what you said, Miss Anita."

"And you said you wouldn't tell nobody. Now look."

Nicole gazed at Evan with pleading eyes, her fist closed tight around Miss Anita's toes as if she'd forgotten what was in her lap.

"Evan. Please."

Miss Anita did a sleepy, slit-eyed smile. "How 'bout it, big brother?"

Evan glared at her a moment, turned his attention back to the TV. Beside the bowl of popcorn, there were four tiny, empty liquor bottles, the kind his father drank on airplanes. He knew his parents wouldn't like that either. He was thinking of a time several years ago when he'd said something smart to Miss Anita—he couldn't remember what it was—and Miss Anita spanked him and he'd gone running to tell his mother and his mother had gotten mad at him instead. She made him write a hundred times, "I will always be polite to Miss Anita." His hand-writing was clumsier and slower and loopier back then and it had taken him two hours and twelve sheets of paper to get it done. Now, he felt trapped. He felt like his skeleton was too big for his skin. On TV, the camera panned in on the vocalist. Her lips and eyes were done in black. Then the camera backed away and she was taking these long, spidery steps, her elbows jacked above her head, hair visible in her armpits. He wanted to head up to his room, log back onto *hotbush.com* but he was afraid his erection would let him down again. He'd seen movies where cancer victims refused to go to the doctor because they didn't want to know about their disease. That was how he felt.

"I'll think about it," Evan said.

Miss Anita groaned and rocked to her feet. She told Nicole, "Don't you go nowhere, baby girl. I got a-whole-nother foot needs some attention." She tottered off in the direction of the bathroom. Her purse, a huge ungainly thing crocheted with roses, was on the floor at her end of the couch. When she was safely out of earshot, Evan slipped across the room and unlatched the clasp.

Nicole said, "You better not."

Evan gave her a look. There were half a dozen airplane bottles in the purse, maybe more, still unopened. He picked one up and read the label. Peppermint Schnapps.

"I'm telling," Nicole said.

"Not if you want to stay up," he said.

The toilet flushed and Evan dropped the bottle back where he had found it. It made a plinking sound. He took another look before refixing the clasp and he would have sworn he saw a pistol, small and black, wedged in the bottom corner, part-hidden by Kleenex packages and paperback books and mittens and hard candy and a keyring that must have held a hundred keys. The sight of it made his scalp itch. Then the slap of Miss Anita's step-ins on the hardwood floor and Evan hustled back to his chair.

"All right, baby girl," Miss Anita said, kicking her shoes off, wiggling her toes. "You ready with those magic fingers?" It took a minute to get herself rearranged on the couch. There was a lot of scooting and sighing and pil-low-smacking before she was satisfied.

Evan didn't know what to do about the pistol or the schnapps so he watched the parade of musicians on the countdown show while Nicole and Miss Anita jabbered about nothing in particular. He considered his evi-dence. He couldn't figure how to let his parents in on what he knew without seeming like a snoop, without getting himself in trouble too. He wasn't even sure of what he'd seen. Miss Anita worked for his mother two days a week and in the afternoons his mother drove her to the bench up on Spring Hill Avenue where Miss Anita met the bus that would take her to her neighbor-hood. Evan didn't know where she lived. He pictured her sitting there at the bus stop, while his mother's car receded. Now, he heard his name and his ears pricked up.

". . . With Lulu Fountain," Nicole said.

"Well, well." Miss Anita's eyelids looked like the tongues of his father's old brown shoes.

"He circled her in his yearbook. I saw it."

"I didn't make that circle," Evan lied. His skull felt huge and molten. "The yearbook was already like that when I got it."

"You love her," Nicole said.

Evan said, "I do not."

Miss Anita said, "Sometimes love don't feel like love." She crossed her ankles. "I didn't much want to love McNeal."

Evan said "Who?" in an irritated voice. He wondered why some people had to go around saying what they thought about everything all the time. It took all his willpower not to blurt out what he knew.

"My babies's father." Miss Anita paused, pinched her lower lip. "He gone."

Evan was struck by that word—gone—by its mystery, its finality, and by the way she said it, like it was familiar on her tongue, but he didn't want her to think he was curious about her life.

"I don't love Harold Flower," Nicole said.

"You don't?" Miss Anita said.

"There's no such person," Evan said. "You made Harold Flower up."

Nicole poked her tongue at Evan. "How could I not be in love with him if I made him up?"

Evan gaped at his sister. That was such a stupid thing to say he could hardly imagine a reply.

Both Evan and Nicole dozed off well before midnight. Evan dreamed, predictably, of Veronica and *Lucifer's Gate*. Except that the circles of hell were not dungeons or chambers of fire but the rooms of this house and the rooms of his school. Except that Veronica wasn't always Veronica. In certain rooms, the school cafeteria, for instance, she was Lulu Fountain—her new braces, the dusting of freckles on her nose, the perpetually embarrassed look on her face. But somehow she was also and always Veronica at the same time. She said the kind of things that Veronica had said. She said *big hot cock* no matter whose face she was wearing. She said *make me cum*. Her dialogue was distracting, made it difficult for Evan to focus his attention on the demons he was supposed to kill. One might expect that these demons took the form of Miss Anita in the dream but this was not the case. They were run-of-the-mill video game demons—horns on their heads and talons on their hands and gaping, fang-thick maws. Dreams are irregular, unreliable things. In Evan's dream, Miss Anita was nowhere to be found.

He woke in his father's leather chair with an erection pressing against his zipper. Miss Anita was shaking his shoulder.

"Wake up, big brother," she was saying. "It's almost midnight. Wake up, boy. Hey."

Evan recoiled, brought one arm up to cover his face, dropped the other into his lap. He was at once relieved and embarrassed by his erection. He wondered if Miss Anita noticed. She straightened up now, put her hands on her hips. Behind her, Evan saw two more empty miniatures on the table.

"The new year has arrived," she said.

He heard distant voices counting backwards—*eight, seven, six*—located them on TV. An old man with dyed black hair was on stage now leading the chant. *Five, four, three*. A glittering golden orb descended a silver pole. Nicole was slumped against the arm of the couch, her jaw hanging open. Evan felt creepy, distant, half-lost in his dream.

"What about Nicole?"

Before the words were out of his mouth, the band cranked up, fireworks lit the TV night.

Miss Anita shook her head. "They been a lot of new years before this one," she said. "They be a whole lot more for her." She chuckled and clapped her hands and did a little shuffle with her feet. Evan thought she was drunk. He'd seen his father after a couple of martinis—wobbly, over-affectionate—but he didn't act like this. "Praise Jesus," Miss Anita said. She snatched up her purse and danced around behind the couch.

"Time don't never stop," she said, high-stepping into the hall. Evan heard the front door open. He looked at Nicole—she was breathing deeply in her sleep. He pushed to his feet and followed Miss Anita, found her on the lawn, glaring at the stars as if they'd offended her somehow.

"Ain't no fireworks out here." Her voice sounded too loud among the pretty houses, the magnolias, the somnolent sedans. Her words took shape, like ghosts, and lifted on the air. Evan shivered. His skin prickled at the cold. "Can't have no New Year without no fireworks," Miss Anita said. She dipped her hand into her purse, rooted around. This time she brought out the pistol—wet-looking in the moonlight.

"What are you doing?" Evan said.

Miss Anita smiled at him over her shoulder. Her eyes were swimming in their sockets. She looked almost sad.

"We alive," she said. "Time don't never stop but we alive."

With that, she raised the pistol over her head and fired three times into the sky. Dogs erupted all over the neighborhood. After a moment, lights began to flick on in nearby windows. "You alive and baby girl alive and my children all alive," she said. She uttered the word—*alive*—in a noisy kind of whisper, like she was afraid of jinxing it by saying it too loud. She fired twice more over her head. "Miss Anita *alive*," she said. She jigged a circle on the lawn. Evan felt suddenly light-headed, his legs nothing but air, his heart loose and throbbing in his chest. He thought of Veronica and of Lulu Fountain. The canopy of trees along the road looked menacing and lovely, denuded branches like women's fingers, like demon arms. Miss Anita fired again and Evan flinched. He doubted that his parents would let her off the hook for this and before too long his father's credit card bill would be arriving in the mail. There would be consequences for both of them. But after that . . . but right now . . . He didn't know if the world looked so peculiar because he was still seeing it through the scrim of his dream. His lips were parted and he could feel the look of wonder on his face.

Norman McMillan

THE WAITING ROOM

After Ted kissed his wife on the cheek as the orderlies rolled her off for knee surgery, he walked down the hall to the outpatient surgery waiting room. On the door he saw a sign: "Only two family members per patient allowed. . . . Children under twelve not permitted." Through the glass in the door, he could see a woman sitting at a desk, and he nodded to her as he entered and took the first seat he came to. On the woman's desk rested a metal sign reading "Volunteer."

The volunteer, a silver-haired woman who seemed to be in her seventies, wore heavy makeup that made her face look exceedingly moist, and she had a fake orchid corsage pinned to her kelly green blazer. "What patient are you with, sir?" she asked cheerily.

"Emily Fallow," he answered, and the volunteer picked up a highlighter and ran it across the page in front of her. "Let's see. Dr. Garville," she said. "What's he doing on your wife?"

"Knee surgery. To repair a torn meniscus."

"A very common operation, very routine," she said reassuringly.

An old black man, very tall and thin, was sitting in the far corner of the room, his head bowed and his eyes closed. On his lap rested a light blue summer cap, and he wore a starched white shirt buttoned at the neck.

Ted opened *The Norton Anthology of English Literature* he had brought with him, and he turned to Pope's "Essay on Man," which was on his syllabus for sophomore English the next day. He took a ball point pen from his shirt pocket so that he could underline important passages, but before he could start reading he looked up to observe a man and woman entering the room. The woman, thin with distinct sharp features, wore a pair of pink knit slacks and a white sweatshirt with a baby's smiling head appliquéd to the front and a caption underneath reading, "Ask me about my grandchild." She was followed by a stocky man, wearing a striped knit shirt over a swollen middle and a pair of very dark blue jeans with a tab on the leg to put a hammer in.

When the volunteer asked what patient they were with, the woman said, "We're here with my mother, Mrs. Ollie Mae Prisoc. From down in Grant County. We drove up here this morning. Had to leave at 5:15."

Ted realized that he was listening as if the woman were actually speaking to him, and he quickly looked back down at his book.

"The muscle that controls Mama's urine has done almost quit working," the woman said, "and Dr. Sartain's gonna do some procedure, I'm not sure exactly what." The woman took a seat across from Ted, and her husband eased down by her side, immediately taking out a pocket knife to clean his nails.

"Would anyone care for fresh coffee?" the volunteer asked, looking at Ted.

"No, thank you," he said at the very same time the sharp-faced woman exclaimed, "I make myself one cup of instant every morning for breakfast and that does me for the rest of the day. Rufus here has done quit drinking it at all, it plays such thunder with his kidneys."

Ted wondered if Rufus could speak for himself as he heard the old black man softly say to the volunteer, "No thank you, ma'am, not for me."

"Well, I guess I'll have to drink alone then," the volunteer said with exaggerated resignation as she went over to the Mr. Coffee and poured herself a cup. Then she walked to the television mounted on the wall, reached up, and turned it on. The announcer was solemnly intoning details about the burial at sea of the ashes of John F. Kennedy, Jr. and his wife.

"It's just so very sad," the volunteer said softly, shaking her head back and forth.

At this point a blonde woman in her late fifties, wearing a fashionable loose-fitting beige dress and sling sandals of the same color, entered the room with great vivacity. She was wearing large designer glasses with lens so thick that her eyes seemed to swim behind them. "Good morning," she said to everyone with a smile. She explained to the volunteer that she was accompanying her sister, who was having a small operation to correct the carpal tunnel syndrome in her left hand.

When she sat down, the sharp-featured woman asked, "What was that you said your sister's got?"

"Carpal tunnel syndrome. It is an extremely painful condition of the hand, an inflammation of the nerve." She held out one hand palm-up and with her pointing finger of the other hand outlined the place the injury affected, a large diamond glittering on her ring finger. "My sister is an executive secretary," she said, "and the condition has been impairing her in her duties, not to mention the extreme pain. The only way she has been able to sleep at night is to dangle her hand off the side of the bed."

To Ted's amazement, the two women seemed to fall immediately into an intimacy. As they chattered away, he tried to read Pope.

Ted looked up to see a tired-looking middle-aged woman leading in a much older woman, her mother perhaps. The younger woman, whose hair was intricately plaited and piled high up on her head, wore no makeup. The old lady, very fat with wisps of gray hair falling around her face, seemed to have come directly from her bed, as her dress resembled nothing so much as a loose white nightgown. She was wearing taupe-colored oxfords without any laces. Her face was expressionless.

The younger woman escorted the old lady to a chair and dropped her large pocketbook in the adjacent chair. She was breathing heavily as she walked to the volunteer's desk and said, "I'm Eunice Sawyer. You may remember me, ma'am. We got Daddy back in here again. You remember they took that cyst off of his neck about two weeks ago. Well, they're taking another'n off this morning. I hope this'll be the last'n."

"Well, I do too. It looks like when it rains it pours," the volunteer said, sipping from her coffee cup.

As Eunice took her seat, Ted was surprised to hear the sharp-faced woman ask her, "Is that your Mama you got with you?"

"Yes, ma'am, it is. She ain't doing too well, though, so I couldn't leave her at home by herself. She's got the Allheimers," Eunice said, shaking her head. "Sometimes—like right now—she don't even know where she is." She fumbled through the magazines on the table next to her.

The sharp-featured woman shook her own head and looked down. The old woman remained without expression.

The news of the burial of John Kennedy continued to come from the television set. The sharp-faced woman watched for a bit, and, when the announcer talked about the bodies having been cremated, she addressed the others in the waiting room: "I've got a question. I don't know about this cremation. I've always heard that they burn the bones, but what I wonder is, do they burn the meat too? Or do they strip the meat from the bones before they burn them?"

Ted, feeling slightly queasy, looked down at his book so as not to be called on for an answer. The vivacious lady, however, answered quickly, "Oh, I should think they burn the flesh too. Otherwise, what would they do with it?"

"I see," the sharp-featured lady said, "but tell me about this urn. I know they put the ashes in the urn when they get through, and I know that they sprinkle the ashes in the water. Well, does this urn have holes in the top of it so you can sprinkle out of it like a big salt shaker? I mean how is it constructed?" She spoke slowly and earnestly as if pleading for the answer to a great mystery.

Ted felt an unexpected giggle trying to come up out of his throat and he dared not look up, pretending to read.

"I should imagine that it does not have holes," the vivacious lady volunteered. "I think it's just a regular urn, like a Grecian urn."

The sharp-faced woman seemed to be satisfied with the answer, and Ted was surprised when her husband Rufus began to speak. "Well, I got a question for all y'all," he said, his voice very loud like he had saved it up so it would be more powerful. "First, they go down there to the bottom of the ocean and bring them bodies up. Then they cremate them. Then they just take them right back down there again. Now does that make sense?"

Ted smiled inwardly and imagined how much fun he would have telling Emily and his colleagues at school about the conversation of these ridiculous people.

"Oh, sir," said the vivacious lady, who had by now clearly established herself as the group's resident authority, "they had to bring them up. There was nothing else to do. Otherwise, those deep-sea photographers would have gone down there and taken their pictures to sell to the tabloids. Privacy means nothing to the press corps." She paused a moment, then added solemnly, "That would have been way too gruesome a thing for the family to have stood. They've stood enough as it is. It's a real American tragedy. I'm just glad that Jackie was not here to suffer this."

"You got a point," Rufus said, "but I got one more question." He narrowed his eyes a bit and asked, "Why wouldn't the Kennedy family let them do a autopsy? Can you answer me that? I personally believe he had drugs in him and they didn't want that to come out."

The authoritative woman had a stumped look on her face, and all she could say was, "That's a very good question."

The old black man began to make an effort to get up. He tried several times before he righted himself. Ted noticed for the first time that he had a large beige woman's purse under his arm. He started toward the door, and as he passed the others he said to no one in particular, "The Lord giveth and the Lord taketh away. Yes, Lord."

Eunice and the sharp-faced lady nodded, and the vivacious woman said, "Isn't it the truth?"

"What I think," said the sharp-faced woman, "is that this is nothing but a case of the sins of the fathers being visited upon their children. I believe it goes all the way back to the old man Kennedy, who got rich selling whiskey and ran around on Rose all the time. And, of course, we all know about JFK."

The old lady in the nightgown, who had not appeared to be listening, began to stir, as if something was bothering her. "What is it, Mama? Are you hurting anywhere?" Eunice said.

The old woman focused slowly on her daughter. She took in some air slowly, then said, "These people don't know shit. That nigger don't know shit, and these white people don't know shit."

Shocked by the comment, Ted looked around at the others. The sharp-faced woman looked as if she had been shot with a stun gun. The vivacious woman looked a little pale. The old black man, who had come back into the room, seemed not to have heard.

Eunice's weary face turned a bright red, and she said, "Why, Mama, how rude of you to say something like that." Then she addressed the others, "Y'all don't pay her no attention. She don't even know she's in the world."

It seemed to Ted that Eunice had looked at everyone in the room but him as she tried to explain her mother's comments, and he felt vaguely excluded.

"She don't never say bad words like that, y'all," the daughter continued.

"It's the Allheimers that's done it. It's eating out what mind she has left."

The old lady seemed not to hear her.

After an awkward pause, the vivacious lady murmured, "No apologies required, I'm sure."

"It don't bother me a-tall," said the sharp-faced woman, who had regained her composure. "I been around old people all my life, and it don't bother me a-tall."

Rufus stopped cleaning his nails and leaned over toward Eunice and said, a slight look of mischief playing in his eyes, "But you know, ma'am," he said slowly, "your mama might have herself a point." Then he laughed loudly, but not one of the ladies did.

As for Ted, he did his laughing inwardly, but shortly thereafter he fell to wondering about how everyone else, other than the old woman, seemed to have formed a community, a community to which he did not belong. *Am I really so different?* he asked himself. He didn't know how cremation was done either, and the man's question about bringing up the bodies of John-John Kennedy and his wife had a certain logic to it, he thought. The old black man's assertion about the Lord giving and taking away was the kind of vacuous piety that had long since ceased offending him. Nevertheless, he felt separated from the others, and he was shaken slightly when it occurred to him that he might have more in common with the old woman afflicted with Alzheimers than with anyone else in the room.

The room fell silent except for the sound of the television, and Ted began to think of how rare it was for him to be in the company of such people as these. And it seemed to him that everybody he associated with would have been equally out of place. As he thought of his world of cocktail parties and concerts, plays and lectures, and even the Saturday night poker games with his colleagues, he became acutely aware of how rarefied his world was.

The phone rang on the volunteer's desk, and she told the vivacious woman that she could now see her sister's doctor. The woman grabbed up her purse and, smiling broadly, said a cheery goodbye to the others as she walked out.

As soon as she was out of the room, Rufus cupped his hand to the side of his mouth and said in a loud whisper, obviously intended for the benefit of everyone in the room, "Goodbye, Miss Know-it-all."

His wife said, "Shh," as she stifled a chuckle, and there was scattered laughter in the room.

A man and woman wearing identical western shirts, jeans, and cowboy boots entered the waiting room and told the volunteer that they were there with his mother, who was having gallstones removed. They sat down and began whispering to each other, after which the man got up and motioned to someone in the hall. An extremely skinny boy of about sixteen came through the door, wearing cowboy boots, a neatly pressed plaid western shirt, and tight jeans. Behind him slowly came a fat little girl of eight or ten wearing shorts and a halter and flipflops, her eyes wide, as if she expected to be stopped.

Ted expected her to be stopped too. But the volunteer did not say a word, though she did cast a knowing look at Ted, as if to let him know that part of her job was putting up with people who couldn't follow rules. He averted his face, not acknowledging the raised eyebrows.

At once, the girl began to hang on her father's neck. "I'm hungry," she whined.

"You're always hungry, fatso," her brother said.

The man reached in his pocket and took out a handful of change. "See what that'll get you," he said. "You know where to go?"

"She knows where every vending machine is in Cherokee County," her brother said. "She don't enter a building without casing it out."

As his sister left, the boy spotted a telephone on the wall, and he got up and went over to it. He dialed a number and after a moment said, "Shirlene, this is Ricky. . . .Yeah, I knew sure as the world you wouldn't be at school today. . . .Yeah, we're here at the hospital with Meemaw. Mama let us skip school to be here. . . .Yeah, I'm gonna come see you tonight. . . .Yeah, yeah, I'm gonna bring you something good." Ricky talked as if there was no one else in the room.

The little girl returned, one hand holding a Mountain Dew and the other clasping two candy bars. She sat in her chair and began pulling the paper back off of a Baby Ruth and eating it quickly.

"Slow down, sister," her father said, "you don't have to inhale that thing."

The volunteer looked at Ted again, and this time she shook her head. Ted did not want to be taken into her confidence, but he gave her a very slight nod, looking back down to his book. He was still on the first page of "The Essay on Man" and had not underlined anything.

The phone on the volunteer's desk rang again, and after a short conversation she announced, "Members of Mrs. Prisoc's family may go to meet with the doctor."

As the couple got up and left, the wife walked over to Eunice and said softly, "I'll be praying for you and your mama, honey." Rufus nodded at the woman.

Ted looked back at his book, but before he could begin to concentrate on it there entered six of the grimmest looking people he had seen in some time—three couples, all in their sixties it seemed to him and all well-dressed, the women in nicely-pressed blouses and skirts and the men in khakis, plaid shirts, and very clean running shoes. They found their seats without a word and stared out in front of them. The volunteer finally asked what patient they were with, and a tall thin man, whose face shone bright with cleanliness, got up, walked over to her desk, and began speaking in a whispery voice to the volunteer. Ted found himself straining to hear what the man was saying, and he was disappointed when he was unable to make out a word. As the man went back to his seat, Ted wondered why the patient needed all six of them—four more than the rules allowed.

"I want some potato chips," the fat little girl said, and her mother began rummaging in her pocketbook for some change.

"Now this is the last thing you can eat before lunch, Bambi," the mother said. "I'm gonna have to put you on a diet anyway."

Bambi took the money and skipped out of the room. Ricky continued to talk to Shirlene. "Naw," he said, "I'm not going to get no Camaro. I'm gonna get a Grand Prix with glass packs."

The father, who sat with his arms folded in front of him, looked around at the others in the room and said, "Huh. He ain't gonna get anything unless he gets a part-time job to pay the insurance. You wouldn't believe what the insurance is on a sixteen year old."

Bambi skipped back in, already eating from the open bag of chips. Just behind her came a well-dressed black woman, who looked to be in her early thirties. Her teal blue suit was nicely tailored, and she had a very fine black leather bag thrown over her shoulder. She hurried over to the old man in the corner, leaning over and kissing him quickly. "Dad," she said, "I'm sorry I couldn't get here earlier, but we had a small emergency at the office. Have you heard from Mama?"

"No. Not yet. But we should hear soon. The way they do that eye surgery now don't take too long."

The daughter sat down and opened her purse, pulling out a compact and looking into it. She patted her red hair on one side. Then she put back the compact and pulled a cell phone from her purse and punched some numbers. "Roberta," she said, "would you cancel my luncheon date at noon? . . . It's on my calendar. Do you see it? . . . Thanks. I just wanted to be here when my mother gets out of surgery. . . . Bye, now."

"You didn't need to do that, Gwendolyn. Your mother's gonna be all right. It's a simple operation."

"It's okay. I really didn't want to see that client anyway. Now I have an excuse."

Bambi was staring at the black woman intently. "She's pretty. Ain't she, Mama?" she said.

"Yes she is," she answered, then looked over at the woman, who had surely heard the little girl's comment herself. "My girl here said she thinks you're pretty."

"That's very kind of her." It seemed to Ted that Gwendolyn was casting around for some way to extend the conversation, and, smiling weakly, she asked, "What's your name, honey?"

"Fatso," her brother shouted, having finally gotten off the phone.

"Shut up, Ricky," his mother said. "Her name is Bambi. Like the deer."

"That's a very sweet name." Gwendolyn paused for a moment and said the name again. Then she opened her purse and pulled out the cell phone again.

"Excuse me, Dad," she said, "but I have to call my broker." Staring down at the floor, she talked to someone about something she called an IPO, which was a new acronym for Ted, and she discussed other stocks, asking the broker about their betas and p/e ratios, terms Ted was only slightly familiar with. Finally she said, "Go on and buy a hundred shares then," punching off the cell phone and dropping it back in her purse.

The volunteer, like Ted, was listening to the woman, and she looked over at Ted again and rolled her eyes upwards, he assumed to imply that she thought the young black woman was putting on airs. Ted himself wasn't sure whether Gwendolyn was showing off, but he chose to believe she was not.

When the phone on the volunteer's desk rang again, she listened for a moment, then turned to the old woman and Eunice, who looked as if she might fall asleep any minute. "Y'all can go see the doctor now, honey," she said. The daughter stood up and pulled her mother to her feet. As the two walked out of the room, the old woman's eye caught Ted's for a moment, with what he thought was a knowing look.

The three couples continued to sit there morosely, still not speaking at all. Ted looked from face to face trying to discover one hint of expression, but there was none. They paid no attention to the television, which continued its coverage of the Kennedy burial, and they seemed to take no interest in the exchange between the black woman and the family in western clothes or to Gwendolyn's telephone calls.

"Have you been watching the Kennedy burial on television?" Gwendolyn asked her father.

"I been listening to it."

"It's sad, isn't it?" she said. "So sad."

"Yeah, it's sad. But I wonder if that boy really knew how to drive that airplane. It was night and the sky was sort of hazy-like, and I speck he got confused and didn't know which way he was going, up or down."

"But we don't know yet whether it was pilot error or whether the plane malfunctioned," Gwendolyn said, her voice very precise.

"It's true, Gwendolyn, we don't know. And we probably won't never know."

"Oh, the National Transportation Safety Board is investigating the accident very carefully and will make a full report," Gwendolyn said.

"Yeah, they're investigating, and they'll come up with an answer," the father said, "but we still won't know. That's how it always is. Like they investigated and said Oswald shot President Kennedy, but I don't believe it. That was a easy way out. I believe them Cubans did it."

"Well, you may be right," Gwendolyn said as she smoothed her skirt. "What you say reminds me of a philosophy class I took at Vanderbilt. My professor was always saying, 'All truth is provisional.'"

"All truth is what?"

"Provisional. You know, true for the time being. Open to change."

The old man seemed to mull over what his daughter said for a short while. "Well, the way I see it," he said, "if it's the truth, it's not open to change. We need another word for it. It's a theory, maybe, but it ain't the truth."

"Gee, Dad," the daughter said, laughing, "you're turning into a regular philosopher yourself." She patted him on the back affectionately.

"Ain't turning into nothing. I been knowing that since I was a kid."

Ted liked the old man's manner very much, and he liked his ideas. He was curious about his life—where he came from, what his education was, what he had done for a living. But he knew very well that he would never ask him anything.

The phone rang again, and the volunteer turned to Ted and said that he could go talk with the doctor now. He was surprised by a strange sense of regret coming over him, a feeling like having to leave a play before it ended. More than he would like to admit, he wanted to see how things turned out. There was still too much he didn't know. Would old Mrs. Prisoc be able to urinate properly again? Would the executive secretary be able to stop dangling her left arm off the bed? Had they got the last cyst from the husband of the woman with Alzheimer's? What would Ricky take that night to Shirlene? Would Fatso be put on a diet? Would the three silent couples ever speak? What was the profession of the old black man's daughter?

Ted closed his book and stood up to leave. It hit him that Aristotle was wrong. Drama doesn't really have a beginning, middle, and end. This pageant he had been witnessing would have no grand conclusion. It struck him powerfully that, while everyone waits for his own exit, the crowd of waiters goes on and on forever.

Ted thanked the volunteer, who smiled at him, and he looked around the room at the others. They seemed to be paying him no attention at all. As he left, he heard the television commentator saying that the Kennedy family were noted for stoically bearing their grief in silence and that it was most appropriate that the services on the USS Briscoe should be held in private. Walking out the door, Ted glanced up at the television and could see the ship off in the distance, far away from the prying world, sitting placidly on the silvery sea.

Janet Mauney

Riding the Waves

Monday morning a crash wakes me up. Mama emptying her purse on the kitchen table. Pennies and lipstick hit the floor, scattering like they're scared. "Where's my pills?" she says. "Papa took them," I answer, standing in the doorway still wearing yesterday's clothes. I don't tell her he flushed them down the toilet. She picks up the phone. Pushes the numbers. She's wearing shorts and is barefooted. Hair wet. The smooth tanned skin on her arms and legs shines against her white face. Her voice goes sweet while she asks to speak to Larry, waits and drums her fingers, gets this look on her face like she's tripped and is not sure whether she'll stand or fall. "No message," she says. "I'll call back." She hangs up the phone. "Fuck you," she says to the dead phone and pours herself a cup of coffee. Her hand is steady, but she rubs her forehead and takes two aspirin. She looks at me and asks about breakfast. I get a box of Cocoa Puffs, but she says no, she wants to make French toast, and she gets a bowl and starts cracking eggs like she's mad at them. Papa is a property appraiser with First National Bank and he can be hard to locate. "Go wake up DeeAnn," she says.

DeeAnn is already awake and we eat about a dozen pieces of toast with Mama getting on my case about our dirty feet and asking why I didn't put pajamas on DeeAnn before we went to bed last night, although we never really went to bed, but slept in our sleeping bags in front of the television. DeeAnn's only seven. Mama gets happier while we eat because she likes it when we eat a lot. It has something to do with her growing up on a farm where her father raised their own food, and they ate it to see if it was any good. He took it personally if they didn't like something. Now she doesn't eat anything, just sits and smokes while she drinks a glass of tomato juice. She sneezes a couple of times and takes a little red pill. "We're going to the beach today," she says. "Katy, go wake up Sharon." DeeAnn's eyes meet mine. We both remember the last trip. Ever since we moved to Panama City in June, going to the beach is Mama's favorite thing to do. Mama blows her nose and tells us to get a move on before she changes her mind. She's already putting Gatorade, potato chips and crackerjacks into a paper bag.

Sharon's fourteen and wants to move out of our house only nobody'll give her a job doing anything but babysitting, which she doesn't like. I'm almost twelve. While we're in Sharon's room, I hear Mama going through the kitchen cabinets. "Son of a bitch," she says.

We're brushing our teeth when she comes in the bathroom, starts tossing dirty clothes out of the hamper, and finds a half-full bottle of vodka wrapped in a towel. "Ha!"

She goes back to the kitchen. By the time we're ready, she's wearing big sunglasses and has the car packed with beach chairs, towels, a cooler, styrofoam boogey boards, straw hats and a bottle of sunscreen which she tells us to put on each other on the drive out. She's drinking another glass of tomato juice.

DeeAnn rubs lotion on my back and shoulders while I keep an eye on Mama's driving, then we change places. Sharon sits like a stone all the way to the beach. Eyes closed. Doesn't even open them when Mama stops at a 7-11 to pick up a six pack. I get worried. Last time we went to the beach, Sharon drove us home because Mama wasn't feeling good. When I tell her to wake up, she says, "Leave me alone," and pushes a sharp elbow in my side.

As soon as we're at the beach, Sharon stretches out on a towel and goes back to sleep while Mama sits in a folding chair under an umbrella, opens a beer and says, "The ocean is so relaxing. We should do this every day." I'm curious about what time Sharon got home last night. She went to the movies with two of her girlfriends who do a lot of big talking about picking up boys, riding motorcycles and drinking beer.

The water is choppy from the summer storms. DeeAnn and I paddle the boogey boards out as far as we dare and ride the waves back in. Seaweed tangles around our legs. Each time we go out a little farther. We put on our plastic scuba masks and hang our faces in the water to watch the fish, but can't see much because the water is filled with sand. A lifeguard blows his whistle and motions us to come back. As he wades towards us in knee deep water, he points to a blanket of flannel clouds that looks pretty far away to me, but he tells us to stay close to shore.

The beach is full of people hunting for sea shells. Two little boys poke a stick at the insides of a dead fish. Sharon sits up and brushes her hair. Mama is reading a magazine. We pull and beg them to come on in the water, but they say "go away" just as a group of surfboarders runs past, hooting at the big waves. DeeAnn and I follow them back into the water.

After awhile, Sharon stands skinny-legged at the edge of the ocean in her little bikini swimsuit with her sunglasses on, her hair blowing into her face. We ride over to her. "Come on," we say together. She folds her arms the way Mama does when she's about to say "no" but Sharon wades in and hangs on to DeeAnn's board with her.

We've just gone far enough out to turn around and ride the waves when the lifeguard blows his whistle and hollers through a megaphone for everyone to get out of the water. Black clouds have covered the sun and in the distance, we see dancing shoots of lightning. The waves are suddenly bigger. I feel myself rising higher and higher when a wave breaks and turns me over like a pancake, so quick my boogey board slips away and disappears. My swimsuit fills with water and sand, the straps tugging at my shoulders. The bottom washes out from beneath my feet. When I surface, I blow out a mouthful of bitter water. Sharon and DeeAnn are way ahead of me, kicking their legs and paddling their arms fast trying get to shore. By the time I make it to the beach, it's beginning to rain and they're gathering up the beach towels, taking things to the car, which is locked. Mama nowhere in sight. The rain peppers us hard. We shove everything under the car, grab some towels and head for the closest restaurant, a Ramada Inn.

Mama is sitting inside at the bar eating oysters and drinking beer. She smiles when she sees us. "Hey girls! You three look shipwrecked. Come on over and get some food." It's dark and damp with low lights and music that is nothing I've heard before, but Mama hums a little, tapping her sandal against the bar. Overhead, bamboo is on the ceiling and the walls are mirrors covered with painted leaves that are supposed to make us think we're in a grass hut. There's only one other person in the room and he's talking in a low voice, except no one's with him. ". . . and I told her, but she wouldn't listen, so I said now you'd better listen to me . . .and I told her, but she wouldn't listen. . . ."

The same thing over and over. Mama says for us not to pester him, he's got enough problems quarreling with someone who's not there.

Wrapped in our beach towels, we climb up on the barstools next to her and order hamburgers. DeeAnn whines to go to the bathroom and Mama says, "Take her, Katy," while Sharon sits with her head propped on her hand, not looking at us because she knows it's double trouble to take a wet bathing suit off DeeAnn. Doing a slow burn, I go down the hall with DeeAnn and push her just a little until she starts crying and makes me feel bad, so I talk nice and help her out of her suit which is filled with sand so she doesn't want to put it back on. I rinse her bathing suit out in the sink and hold it under the hot air dryer fifteen times. A lady in an apron comes in and tells me to quit messing around. She has a skull head on a long skinny neck and gives me that look that I've seen before. We're a nuisance and she won't leave until we get out of there. DeeAnn's hiding in a stall, and I have to go in with her to put her suit on because she doesn't want the lady to see her naked.

When we get back our hamburgers are waiting. Mama's got another order of oysters and forks one out of the shell, dips it in hot sauce before she swallows it. Sharon says, "Aren't you allergic to seafood, Mama?"

"No. Besides, this is shellfish," she answers.

"I don't want any tomato," says DeeAnn. I take it off her hamburger and put it on Sharon's plate. Sharon flings it on my plate and I put it on a napkin on the bar. DeeAnn takes the pickle off her hamburger and put it on the napkin, then says Mama's oysters look like a ball of spit. Mama laughs, digs out another oyster, holds it way above her mouth, then lets it drop in, acts like she's choking, then grins at DeeAnn. The man across the bar stops talking and claps his hands. Mama gives a little bow and orders a margarita. Her gold loop earrings dance in the dim light. The man says, ". . . I told her, but she wouldn't listen and I said..." There's nobody watching, not even the waitress, but my face is burning. I want Mama to act normal. DeeAnn claps her hands. Sharon stares at her plate.

The rain slows down and DeeAnn and I go over to the window to write our names in the steam until a waitress tells us to stop. We mess around with the game machines, but Mama's out of quarters so we can't play. DeeAnn yawns. Complains that she's cold. Sharon is trying to get Mama to come on and go home while the weather's clear. She has her hand on Mama's arm, but Mama pushes her away. "I can get down by myself," she says, stepping off the stool and falling on her knees. "Get real," says Sharon as she puts her hands under Mama's armpits, but Mama tells her to get away and gives all of us that look like she's going to hit someone. Slowly, she stands up and walks out of the restaurant to the car by herself with us dancing around her, skinny arms out like we're guards on a basketball team. With a crooked smile she says, "And you girls thought I wouldn't make it." Like she's won a race or something.

It takes her awhile to find the key, then we have to load the car with all our soggy beach equipment. Sharon wants to drive, but Mama says it's okay, she's okay, everything is okay. That's not a good sign. She slides behind the wheel and won't move. Sharon tells us to fasten our seat belts. Mama gives her a squinty look before she closes her eyes and sits like she's fallen asleep. DeeAnn says, "I want to go home." I shake Mama's shoulder and ask her to let Sharon drive, it's time to go home. She opens her eyes. Starts the car. It springs out onto the beach highway like a jumping horse, slides through a big sheet of water, and spins halfway around, stopping sideways across the road. Mama bursts out laughing. "Damn! Did you see that?" she says while another car is honking its horn for us to move out of the way. DeeAnn whimpers. Sharon makes the sign of the cross. I yell, "Mama, get out of the road," while my heart flies around and beats against the inside of my chest.

She backs the car up, straightens it out, shoots a bird at the other driver and heads in the right direction, only she's going twenty miles an hour, and she steers from one side of the road to the other, trying to avoid big puddles of water. Sharon folds her hands and starts saying the Lord's prayer. Mama loses it. "Shut up," she says. "Goddammit! You sound like your father. Always preaching at me." She pounds the steering wheel and steps on the gas, speeding through dips, yahooing like she's lost her mind.

I don't know how long the policeman was behind us. Sharon sees him first. "Pull over, Mama," she says, but Mama pays no attention until the flashing red lights are beside us and he's motioning for her to stop. She does. DeeAnn's crying and won't stop.

I put my arm around her and hold on tight to keep from shaking. Sharon's face has gone white.

The policeman tries to get Mama out of the car, but she won't move.

"Have you been drinking, lady?" he asks. She tells him hell no it's her allergy medicine that makes her groggy. Before our eyes, she breaks out in hives, big shiny welts, one after the other all over her face and arms. "I'm trying to get to the emergency room," she says, "I'm having an allergic reaction." With that, her head drops and she falls asleep right there in front of the cop.

"Oysters," says Sharon in a voice that doesn't sound like she believes it. He bends over and looks at all of us. No expression on his face, just this camera-eyed look like he's registering our descriptions for a wanted poster. He asks Sharon to find Mama's driver's license. She goes into Mama's purse and gets it for him. He walks to his car and talks into his car radio, but we can't hear what he's saying. I watch his mouth, trying to lip read. "Are we going to jail?" asks DeeAnn in a whisper. "Don't talk silly," says Sharon.

The patrolman's partner moves to the driver's seat of the police car, while the first policeman walks back to our car. He moves Mama over against Sharon and drives us to the hospital while the other car leads the way with its lights flashing. We go right up to the back door of the emergency room. Two men come out with a little bed on wheels, get Mama out of the car and take her inside. We run along with them, trying to touch her. Mama is limp and breathing heavy. A doctor shines a light into her eyes and moves her into another room, closing the door so we can't see.

We all start crying, even Sharon, but nobody notices us. The policeman comes out of the room and wants to know how he can get in touch with our father. "Is she dead?" whispers Sharon, and she cries so hard, he has to wait for her to calm down to answer. "No. She'll be okay, but we need to talk to your father. Somebody has to take you girls home."

I give the patrolman Papa's office number, and I listen while he talks on the telephone because he might have lied to us. Nobody wants to tell children their mother has died. But he tells Papa the same thing he told us only a lot more about DUI and an invalid driver's license. I figure she is still alive, but I want to see for myself, so I try to push the door open. A nurse says, "You can't come in here," and rushes over to shove me out, but not before I get a quick look. Mama is wrestling with another nurse who is trying to get a hospital gown on her. Something rips.

We sit in a waiting room for a long time. Someone brings us a brown paper bag with Mama's clothes in it. Finally Papa comes rushing in and just has time to say "hello" before a doctor takes him away to talk. When he comes back, we cluster around him, all chattering at once. I ask him if we can tell Mama goodbye before we leave, but he won't let us see her. "When can she come home?" asks DeeAnn. "We'll see," he answers.

"Can we visit tomorrow?" asks Sharon. "No," he says, "she's going into detox for a week, then maybe . . . depends on what happens."

"What's detox?" I ask. He never answers. Maybe he's sad because mother can't come home, because he gets quiet and doesn't say much more. He takes us to McDonald's for dinner. I try to tell him about the big waves, the monsoon storm, and the Ramada Inn, but Sharon interrupts and says to quit being so melodramatic. "You're not my mother." I snap back, but we all get quiet and eat our dinner. Papa takes us home and says he has to go back to the office to finish up two appraisals that he was working on when the policeman phoned. It won't take long. Sharon is in charge.

Inside, our house is sweltering and smells moldy after being closed all day. We shut the curtains and turn on the window air conditioners. The place rumbles like a refrigerator. Sharon locks herself in her room and talks on the phone to her buddies. DeeAnn and I wash our feet and put on our pajamas. We take our sleeping bags and pillows into the living room and turn off the overhead lights to watch the Bill Cosby Show. Dee Ann makes a run for the sofa, while I spread out on the floor and count out six chocolate chip cookies before passing her the bag of Chips Ahoy. Dr. Huxtable tells his son Theo that he can't buy an expensive shirt just to go on a date with a new girlfriend he wants to impress. It sounds serious. Theo is pretty intense. His sister Denise sews him a shirt that looks like she put it together all wrong, but the girlfriend thinks it's cool and everybody ends up happy. DeeAnn falls asleep with half a cookie still in her hand.

A beam from the streetlight outside comes through an opening in the curtains and shines across the floor and up the wall in a long bending slice. I watch television alone until Jay Leno comes on, and Sharon walks in with a blanket and pillow to curl up beside me. Every time I close my eyes, I can feel the big wave lifting me up and turning me upside down. We don't talk, we just eat cookies and wait for Papa to come on home.

PATRICIA MAYER

CORRIGAN'S OMENS

My name's Corrigan and I was the best traveling salesman in the history of Southeastern Pipe and Joint. I made my home on the road, a different bed and bedmate every night, but these days, I find myself in a closet in Babylon, Alabama, sharing the space with another old man. They call this storeroom a retirement home, but it's really just a warehouse with a staff, a geriatric cupboard where old relics like us are put out of sight.

In my case, it was self-commitment. Any lines of kindred, cousins or aunts or uncles, ran off the spool a long time ago. When you're ninety and you've got nowhere else to go, the closet will do. We're like old mangy dogs at the pound and any day could be gassing day but we try to ignore it, as though we're going to be the exception. They should tear all these places down and salt the ground.

Some of the people around here grieve with homesickness and bend any available ear with stale reconstructed lore, but I don't. I can't miss the home I walked out of when I was eighteen and never passed my shadow through again. For years I lived the suitcase life in damp hotel rooms, keeping sales appointments in cluttered offices that reeked of funk and diesel, neon cafes for supper alone, and the rented indulgence of indifferent female impact. The other salesmen used to remark that I sold pipe in the daytime and laid pipe at night. I just let them talk because I got the collisions I paid for. I always enjoyed the wildwood flowers I plucked on the road.

The salesmen I knew were a superstitious lot and we all had our little rituals to help business along. It might've been an article of clothing we wore or a charm carried in a pocket. It was different for every guy because, on the road, luck was the only thing that stood between us and rejection by a shop boss in sweaty, salt-ringed coveralls. When we were desperate to make a sale, we'd fall back on a trick or two. It was all part of the sales game, and after a while, it ran our lives.

I've lived a long time. I owe my longevity to my ability to read the signs and omens, and it's probably the same for a lot of the other relics who call this crypt their home. Retirement communities are the last strongholds of superstition. Young people these days, they don't believe in it. They don't understand that it's a talent, a craft, if you will. I call it *my intuition for the impending event*. There are signs and omens everywhere, coming at us like diving bees, if we only know how to look and how to see.

I've got a roommate in this joint, a fellow named McNeeley, and he's a pretty decent sort. On the day I lost McNeeley, I'd already seen a couple of definite omens and I picked up on them, snatched them out of the air like grabbing houseflies, and held them buzzing in my fist. I knew right away that something big was about to happen.

Early that morning, I snagged the first omen. We were suffering through one of those damn family visiting days and the staff was getting the dayroom ready for the relatives to come in. Somebody opened the door to the outside and a wild bird flew into the dayroom. A wild bird in the house is a powerful sign. The poor thing almost beat itself to death in panic, flying against the window glass. The bird couldn't understand how something could be so bright and clear, hardly there at all, and still be a dead end.

A group of us stood watching like spectators at an air show while the bird beat itself against those window panes. Finally, one of the orderlies put a stop to it. He rigged up a make-shift slingshot out of rubber bands and brought the bird down with a paperclip. I was rubbernecking the show like everybody else and the bird fell dead directly at my feet. I scooped it up, warm and soft and floppy-necked, and handed it to the orderly and he threw it out on the lawn for the ants to eat. The bird was mighty small to have made such a big fuss. It hardly weighed anything at all in my hand.

Later that morning, McNeeley and I were playing cards and I kept dabbing at my face with a napkin, sweating like a whore at High Mass, and he said, "What's the matter with you?"

I said, "That was a bad omen. A wild bird in the house means somebody's going to die soon."

McNeeley said, "This is an old peoples' home, you damn fool, of course somebody's going to die soon."

"But it fell right at my feet. I don't like the odds."

McNeeley said, "Shut up and play."

I shuffled the cards and while I was dealing, Mrs. Wilson keeled over her walker, dead as a Christmas goose and I breathed a sigh of relief.

"See, I told you it was a sign," I said to McNeeley.

He gave me a disgusted look. McNeeley was never good at reading the signs. He'd better watch out, is all I've got to say.

The staff hustled to glaze over Mrs. Wilson's unsightly demise and all the families went on obliviously, visiting and raising all kinds of ruckus in the day room. Of course, nobody ever came to see McNeeley and me, so we always passed the time with rummy at a vacant table away from the crowd.

McNeeley had somebody on the outside, for all the good it did him. There was a grandson, Buster by name, but the boy took off for California, which wasn't such a bad thing for me. When Buster left, it freed McNeeley up for rummy on family days. We created a passably pleasant time for ourselves, especially when the game deepened enough to shut out the noise of the brat grandchildren and the annoying chatter. I have to admit that rummy with McNeeley was my salvation on those days, until everything changed for him and I was left alone.

The bird was the first omen that day and the second omen happened while we were at our usual table away from the babble. McNeeley dropped an ace of clubs on the discard stack and I picked it up. It made three aces for me, waiting for the fourth and I'd be out with a sweet little set. I discarded and McNeeley drew and discarded another ace of clubs. I got gooseflesh when I saw it.

"What the hell is that?" I asked and tapped my old scaly fingernail on the card.

"Ace of clubs," McNeeley said. "You blind?"

"But you just discarded an ace of clubs. Here it is right here, you idiot." I pulled it out of my hand and flung it on the table.

McNeeley studied the card I'd thrown down. Then he considered the card he'd just laid on top of the discard stack. The way he looked them over, you'd have thought it was one of those naked lady decks instead of plain old Bicycle brand.

"That's odd," he finally remarked.

"Odd? *Odd?* That's all you've got to say? You shuffled this deck. Didn't you notice there was something wrong with it? Don't you know it's bad luck to have two of the same card in a deck?"

McNeeley got snippy. "I counted it first. Fifty-two, just like it's suppose' to be." He started scratching the age spots on the back of his hand, like he does when he's cornered. I don't put it past him to cheat.

"Yeah, but *which* fifty-two? You must have mixed up two decks, you dolt."

He set into pouting and whining and said, "There's no need to be testy about it. I can't help it if the cards got mixed up. You know those old women play canasta with these decks. They didn't put them back correctly, so blame them, not me. What's it mean, anyway?"

"It means a dangerous stranger is going to come calling."

McNeely shook his head in puzzlement. "What do you mean by *danger-ous?*"

I was half listening by that time because something happened that made me forget the cards. I was looking past McNeeley, focusing on a young gal who'd walked into the day room and was glancing around. She was a real doozie—a looker. Red hair, tight skirt, a pound of lipstick. Legs. Long legs. No lumpy, purple veins in them. We don't get that kind around here very often. She reminded me of my younger days on the road, a phone call, a knock on the hotel door, and then, *Oh, Mama.*

"Take a gander at that," I told McNeeley and pointed with my chin as I gathered up the cards.

He shuffled with his felt slippers and worked his way around in his seat and that's when she spied him and started strolling toward our table.

"Oh geez, she's coming over," he said, flustered.

"Great," I said, and meant it. I was up for a closer look.

She stopped at McNeeley's elbow and he looked up at her, all shaky and shy. "Mr. McNeeley? My name's Tiffany. Can I speak with you a minute?" She eyed me up and down like I was a tick on her dog. "In private."

McNeeley studied her with bleary eyes. "Do I know you?"

"I'm a friend of Buster's."

He gave his head a small shake and continued to stare with owl eyes through his thick lenses and his glaucoma.

"Your grandson," she added with her red, impatient mouth.

McNeeley's puzzlement cleared. "Ooooh. Okay. Let's go over there." He gestured toward the fake-rattan seating arrangement, olive green, piss-stained.

He struggled to his shaky feet and tottered towards the chairs. The girl shuffled along behind. I got up and followed them. We all took seats.

"I said I wanted a word in private." Tiffany glared at me through the caked mascara flaking down on her cheekbones.

"I want to hear this, too," I said.

McNeeley made a dismissing sweep in my direction with his arthritic hand. "Ignore Corrigan. He's deaf as a door jamb."

Tiffany scowled at me while she thought it over, then shrugged. McNeeley asked, "How is Buster doing?"

She pressed her purse against her bosom with both hands, deepening her cleavage, and I stopped breathing. She said, "I dunno. He left me."

"He left me, too," said McNeeley.

Tiffany said, "The fact is, now I'm pregnant."

"Don't look at me," McNeeley said.

I chuckled. McNeeley has his moments.

Tiffany's eyes watered up. I hate it when women do that. "It's your grandson's baby, Mr. McNeeley. Buster's. But he took off and now I need money."

McNeeley let it soak in, then he asked, "Does Buster know about the baby?"

"Of course. Why do you think he took off?"

"Are you sure he's the father?" I asked, just stirring the pot a bit.

Tiffany shot daggers at me and hugged that purse and didn't answer.

McNeeley studied the linoleum as the minutes dragged out. Finally, he narrowed his eyes at the girl. "What do you need money for?"

"You know." She blushed and looked away.

"I'm afraid I do. Come back tomorrow, will you? Let me think about this." He was using that same flustered look he wears when a favorite memory of his has slipped just beyond recollection.

Tiffany agreed to return the following day. We watched her walk away, backside twitching. Man, oh man. She was non-brand trailer trash, of course, but luscious, the type of female who has five peak years, tops. I've seen them roosting on a stool at the end of the bar, swigging lite beer from a bottle, hoisting it with a flash of stubbly armpit, a foot propped on the next stool to favor the room with a shadowy glimpse of inner thigh. Lordy, those used to be my favorite preambles.

McNeeley sighed as Tiffany gained distance on her way to the door. She drew the attention of various male visiting relatives to such a degree that their wives seemed about to cuff them on the back of the head. McNeeley said, "Now, at least I understand why Buster left town. I thought it was to get away from me."

"Just give her the money for the abortion and be done with it," I urged with practicality.

McNeeley didn't answer. He was unusually quiet the rest of the day and he passed on cards after supper. I heard him tossing most of the night. Little did I know that that the old fool was going to buy himself a whole new family.

The next day, McNeeley dressed and groomed ceremoniously. So did I, for that matter. Salesmen are a dapper lot, and I never lost the habit. When everything you own is in a suitcase and you're wearing your home on your back, you tend to make the best of it. I looked fine that day, but McNeeley had outdone himself. We sat together in the dayroom, fidgeting and reeking of spray starch and that brand of aftershave favored by stock car drivers.

Tiffany made an impressive entrance on those legs of hers and drew the attention of several orderlies. She and McNeeley put their heads together and he told her that he wouldn't finance an abortion, but he consented to bankroll the pregnancy. He agreed to pay the medical expenses and said he'd give her two hundred dollars a week to come by for an hour's visit every Sunday. After the baby was born, she was to bring it along as well and when the hour was up, he said, he'd hand her a check each time. Tiffany said two hundred a week would pay her expenses, so she agreed to go along with it.

Of course, I was thoroughly disappointed and left out. Now McNeeley had somebody on the outside again and I was losing my rummy partner and I wondered how I'd pass the time on visiting days without him.

True to her word, Tiffany showed up the following Sunday and every Sunday after that, looking a little rounder and rosier each time. At first, she and McNeeley visited awkwardly, but they got used to each other, and she did most of the talking, the way women do, about her new trailer, McNeeley told me, and what she'd bought off the home shopping network.

After a few weeks of solitaire, I started sitting in on the visits, raining attention on her, just like McNeeley did. We brought Tiffany cups of punch and napkins of cookies off the refreshment table and listened to her chatter and we taught her how to play rummy. The time went by pretty fast because she gave us the hour each week and not a minute more.

We got a call from a nurse on the day of the birth. Tiffany asked her to let McNeeley know. It was a boy and the old fool was so proud, you'd have thought he'd done the dirty deed. He was intolerable for days. As soon as Tiffany was out of the hospital, she brought the brat by and picked up her weekly check. McNeeley even held the squirmy thing. It vomited on him. I laughed and McNeeley reeked. He didn't mind.

Everything I just told you happened about two years ago and Tiffany still comes around with the damn kid every Sunday and gets a check. It's the highlight of McNeeley's pitiful life. He's got a wallet full of pictures of the brat in various stages of growth, grinning through the cellophane pockets with an aggressive display of baby teeth. The old fool talks about the boy constantly. I'm so sick of the grandfatherly discussions, I could vomit, myself. And to think of the money he's shelled out. Pretty much all his savings, I understand. They made a deal and he lived up to it, but he's just about broke now. He can't even afford to smoke anymore and those Lucky Strikes were the biggest joy in his life, next to the kid.

Tiffany's dating a construction worker and they're talking about getting married and moving to Texas. She brings the burly beast around and he communicates mainly by grunts and shrugs and crotch scratching and it seemed to me that Tiffany's baby favors him unduly; looks enough like him, I think, to void the warranty. I've never pointed the resemblance out to McNeeley, even though he's half-blind and goes on about how the baby's a carbon copy of Buster, down to every snaggly grin and gas-pain grimace. Last week, when McNeeley held out the check, the brute was the one who took it out of his hand.

McNeeley's in a substantial panic over the potential marriage. Poor old guy actually cried the other day after the three of them left. And he's not sleeping because of the worry. Oh well, if they move away and take the kid, McNeeley'll get over it in time, and there's always rummy.

Besides, there's been another omen. I was gumming my way through a hamburger pattie (around here they call it "chopped steak," but it's plain old hamburger. I ought to know because I ate enough of it in diners on the road), when I bit down on a hard object and reached into my mouth and pulled out a wedding ring with bits of ground beef still stuck to it. The staff said it came off somebody's finger while they were handling the hamburger, but I know an omen when I see it, and finding a stranger's finery in your meat is a genuine sign, I promise you. I went on about that little circular harbinger so long that McNeeley sighed and asked me what the wedding ring omen meant. I answered, "It means there's going to be a wedding, of course, you moron. What else?"

He looked at me, alarmed for a few seconds, then he got hold of himself and said, "Maybe you should propose to Mrs. Finkley, now that you've got a ring. But you'd better hurry because she doesn't look very well lately."

"No way. Mrs. Finkley's a sorry lay."

McNeeley gaped. "My God! How do you know that?"

"You remember the lawn party last spring? She gave me a quickie behind a camellia bush." I showered McNeeley with a bevy of winks and eyebrow archings. Of course, I was just trying to cheer him up. The old fool's up to his prosthetic hip joints in denial and refused to see that the hamburger jewelry's probably an omen that Tiffany's going to marry her brute if he can grunt out an intelligible "I do." Let McNeeley find out about it when it happens. That way, he'll be easier to live with until then.

Well, they did it. They eloped and found a justice of the peace who conducted a ceremony in primate vernacular for the groom's sake and that same day the three of them headed out for Texas just like she said they would.

Poor old McNeeley's heartbroken. I thought I'd feel better about getting my rummy partner back full time, but, strangely, I don't. Hell, I even miss the little booger, myself. It wasn't so bad, watching him grow and change over the months. McNeeley and me, we're back to rummy on visiting days, but our hearts aren't in it now.

Another wild bird flew into the dayroom this morning. They say it's the big glass windows that attract them. They're fooled into believing they see another bird, a reflection of themselves, a small version of what they are, and they mindlessly go for it and become trapped by the very clarity of what they can't see—the big glass box of the visiting room. If this new bird omen holds true, I suppose there'll be another death around here. McNeeley's so despondent, I don't think he'll mind if it's him and I know how he feels. I'm tired of this place and at this point, it would be okay if it was me. Then, my waiting for nothing to happen would be over.

We might even croak together, McNeeley and me, and neither one of us would be left alone to fill the time on visiting days. If that happens, we'll stroll through the pearly gates arm in arm like we own the joint and find a table in a corner of the clouds and smoke Lucky Strikes and play cards up in the wild blue yonder. We could even play rummy with a naked lady deck. Hell, why not? It's heaven, ain't it?

In the meantime, we've been mulling over a plan. An escape plot, actually. I'm getting an itch for the road again and I think McNeeley's caught it from me. We're thinking about blowing off this joint, escaping from the big glass box and flying off somewhere, maybe out west. Maybe Texas.

JANET NODAR

THE GREEN WOMAN

One night Lisa dreamed that her short, well-groomed, rather fly-away hair began to pump out of her scalp and thicken and twist like wisteria vines around the mattress, the pillows, the bedposts. Her fingernails and toenails burst forth from her feet and fingers. They hooked across the carpet and up the drapes with little snaffling tendrils. Her hands and feet burned. Her shaved armpits burned. The cleft between her legs burned. She was cinched into the bed like a gnat in a web. Lisa knew she was only dreaming, but her heart beat against her ribs like a fist. Her husband, Jack, snored beside her.

She must have fallen back asleep, though, because when the alarm went off at 6:15 the room was cool and dark, the jaquard bedspread only mildly disturbed. Jack was whistling in the shower. Lisa made pancakes for breakfast and then helped her son review for a chemistry exam. She glanced at herself occasionally in the mirror over the sideboard. She looked much as usual. A tinny mental residue, like the after-taste of diet cola, was all that remained of the dream.

At her desk later that morning Lisa thought her fingers looked green under the office lights. She went outside to double-check in daylight. It was only her imagination. Fluorescent lights made everything look green. To be safe, though, Lisa asked the opinion of a co-worker smoking nearby. He agreed. Fluorescent lights. They could not be trusted. She thanked him and he nodded, white smoke curling out of his nose. Glad to help. She looked at her hands. Somehow it all seemed like a trick.

That was all for that day.

On Saturday, Lisa dozed off in a wicker chair in the back yard. When she woke up she couldn't move. The sun burned on her nose and arms and made her eyes water. She strained to shift her feet. Roots had sprouted from her heels and knitted her into the ground. A stroke? Was she now a statue, soft and frozen? Who could have done this to her? But no—her children called for her (*Mom? Mom, where are you?*) and their voices seemed to plug her back together. She stretched gratefully.

Lisa put all her house plants—wandering jew, philodendron, coleus—outside and let the caterpillars eat them. The lawn was as green as lime KoolAid. She lay in bed at night and listened for it, simmering outside her window, breathing like a person. In the Southwest, where she had once lived, lots of people didn't bother with lawns. They just burned off the weeds once a year and spread sparkling gravel in their yards. Jack was a little irritated when she mentioned this a second time. No one had a sparkling gravel yard in Mobile, Alabama. Besides, he enjoyed his riding lawn mower. Lisa bought a twenty-pound sack of salt, and when Jack wasn't home she sprinkled handfuls of it over the lawn and in the flower beds. The hydrangeas shriveled. The lawn turned gray and brown. Poisoned. Serves you right, she thought.

One day her daughter suggested that Lisa get a check up. Better safe than sorry, she said. So Lisa made an appointment. The doctor tapped and listened and took samples. She was fine. Just for fun, she made an appointment with a psychiatrist. She wrote up some preliminary notes: *My parents were kind and patient people. We lived in a pleasant, tree-shaded suburb. The ribbed sidewalks buzzed under my bike tires. I watched the same cartoons as everyone else. I was a Camp Fire Girl. I kissed Bobby Wexler when I was fifteen.* Lisa had never been unusual. The psychiatrist would see that there was no sensible explanation. They spoke politely to one another. She answered his questions and pondered his deck of pictures. He rubbed his dimpled chin and wrote her a prescription. Lisa realized sadly that she had not made her point.

The medicine made her feel stupid, as if her skull was stuffed with cottage cheese. She took it seven times and then buried the pills in the spot where the roses had been. That seemed to help. Her concerns lifted for a time. Her son became engaged to a charming girl, and her daughter was awarded a scholarship to a prestigious college. As a test, Lisa put an African violet in her bedroom. She never watered it, and the room was always dim, but it flourished anyway. Then one morning Lisa parted her hair and saw that her scalp was covered with a faint, sinuous pattern, a tribal tattoo, of leaves and stems and purple flowers. She dropped the comb. What an enemy she had! It almost pleased her, the slyness of her foe. She imagined her autopsy, the pathologists cutting her open and marveling. She snipped the African violet to pieces with her kitchen shears. She pruned her hair down to her skull. By Friday, the tattoo pattern was gone.

The next day, Jack had a heart attack while fretting over his gardening catalogues. They decided to move to a condominium and sold the house for a handsome profit in spite of the ruined lawn. Lisa painted all of the condo's rooms white. She really wanted to move somewhere flat and cold where nothing grew and she could see all the way to the horizon, but she knew her husband wouldn't do it and she didn't want to go alone.

Lisa drove back and forth to work, averting her eyes from the trees. She generally covered her stubbly head with a scarf. She thought it best not to let her hair grow back. After awhile, Jack quit asking her why. He told people she was a terrorist. Strangers spoke to her gently, assuming she had cancer. Although she didn't correct them, she didn't feel that she was cheating. After all, something treacherous multiplied in her. A moment's carelessness, and what green riot would ensue?

MICHELLE RICHMOND

OCEAN BEACH
(a novel excerpt.)

A cool Gulf Coast afternoon, waiting for the storm. Three p.m. and
the sky was dark as evening. Hurricane Frederick was on its way, and my
mother had sent me and my sister Annabel to Delchamps for supplies. Our
cart was filled with gallons of distilled water, cans of Campbell's Soup and
Starkist tuna, bottles of Gatorade, two new flashlights and a dozen batter-
ies. The shelves had been ravaged, and the aisles were bustling with customers in that giddy pre-hurricane state. The check-out line stretched all the
way to the meat counter in the back of the store. The guy in front of us,
whose cart was filled with ramen noodles, Heineken, several rolls of silver
duct tape, and a box of tapered white candles, turned and smiled at me. He
had black hair, cut very short, and was wearing a University of Arizona T-
shirt.

"Excited?" he said.

"About what?"

"The hurricane."

Annabel rolled her eyes and pinched me on the elbow. I shrugged my
shoulders. "Not so much."

"My first," he said. "Just moved here from the desert." He kept glancing down at my legs, and I knew he was old enough that he shouldn't be
looking at me that way. "Got any advice?"

"Boards," I said, "not duct tape."

He looked confused.

"For the windows," Annabel chimed in, in a tone that was clearly meant to indicate that he was the dumbest guy in the world.

"You put plywood on all the windows," I explained. "Duct tape's just a short-cut."

He shifted his weight to one foot, and as he did so his T-shirt raised slightly, revealing a patch of hair sliding in a straight line down his belly, into the waistband of his jeans. He caught me looking, grinned. "Anything else?"

My face felt hot, but I didn't care; I was enjoying the game. I plucked the box of candles from his basket. "What's this for, a romantic dinner?"

He winked. "You fishing for an invitation?"

"You offering?"

Annabel crossed her arms over her chest. "Please," she said, snapping her gum.

"Seriously," he said, leaning in close to me. "What's wrong with the candles?"

"It's no picnic when the lights go out. You want hurricane lamps and flashlights." I dropped the candles back into his cart and picked up his only jug of water. "And you'll need more than this unless you're planning on drinking out of the neighbor's pool. Last time, we had no water for nine days."

The line moved. He bumped his cart forward with his hip. "I'm clearly unprepared," he said. "What I need is a personal hurricane coach."

"How much does it pay?"

"That's negotiable," he said, laying his warm hand on my shoulder, allowing one finger to slip beneath the skinny strap of my tank top.

"God," Annabel said. "She's not even fucking legal."

"Don't pay attention to my sister," I said. "She worships Satan."

A few minutes later he was standing by the station wagon, helping me load bags into the back, while Annabel stood off to the side, arms crossed, glaring at both of us. Above the parking lot, birds careened in confused circles, while the traffic lights on Hillcrest Road snapped back and forth in the wind. When all the bags were in the car he shut the door and held out his hand. "Ramon."

"Abigail." I shook his hand, feeling awkward and businesslike. His hand was hot, and it swallowed mine up entirely. He held on tight for a couple of seconds before letting go.

"So," he said, "can I go to jail for asking for your phone number?"

Annabel held her stomach, bent over in mock agony, and pretended to vomit.

"Why don't you give me yours instead?" I knew that if he called my house, my parents would have questions I wouldn't be able to answer.

He reached into the back pocket of his jeans and pulled out a leather wallet, from which he extracted a business card. *Ramon Gutierrez*, the card said. *Portrait and art photography*. I slid the card into my pocket and opened the driver's side door.

"Get in the car," I said to Annabel, who looked like she was about to haul off and punch him.

She flipped him off one last time and said, "I've got two words for you, mister. Jail bait."

Ramon ignored her. He waited until Annabel was in the car before he rubbed a spot of oil on the ground with the toe of his boot and said, quietly, "You'll call?"

"Yes."

I did not understand then that I was at the beginning of something, that each choice leads to some other choice, and another, and another, so that a single, seemingly meaningless decision reverberates through an entire life. I did not know it was a moment in time that would help to shape the course of my life, that would determine the nature of my relationships with men.

"You cannot step in the same river twice," Heraclitus said. Since the composition of the river changes from one moment to the next, it is never the same river. Everything in the universe is in a constant state of flux. Everything changes. Nothing stays the same.

Once a moment has passed, it is gone. Any choice you could have made has already been made. The choice is no longer yours, a different response to that moment is not possible. I want to step again into the river. I want it back—the time, the choice, the tiny, irretrievable seconds.

KATHLEEN THOMPSON

LIVING LIKE THE LILIES

Perhaps *she would not write about hummingbirds at all. She stared at her newest nail color, Peru-B-Ruby, as she tapped her forefingers lightly on the keyboard, tap, tap, tap, tap. . . . She started over: "Redbirds usually feed on sunflower seeds; this one is trying to eat glass. He pecks repeatedly at my French windows, as persistent as a jazz drummer." She pondered the mating habits of the redbird as she typed in a new title, "Mating for Life." He was just returning from the next room where the printer was located. He held a few printed pages. Just the sight of him made her have to think again about how to breathe, the process. She knew she needed to draw some air into her lungs first, but when to let it go was not always clear. Her rhythm was off. She bit her lip, afraid of inadvertently huffing, like a woman practicing natural childbirth. He leaned over and whispered, "Ready for lunch, Lib?" Fast and furious little wings fanned in her chest. She nodded yes, unable to make a sound.*

* * *

At first lilies were not Lib's idea, but Mattie's. Mattie wanted her baby sister to have something of everything from her yard. She wanted Lib to know her plants and her family history. Only rich woods dirt could be used in repotting her leather-leaf ferns—ferns first sprouted by Granny Josephine, then passed on to her daughter, Aunt Belle, and then to Imogene, one of Aunt Belle's daughters. Granny Josephine brought the ferns back home to Fayette after Grandpa John died over in Pine Bluff, Arkansas, with brain fever. Aunt Belle pampered the ferns until she ended up in the nursing home. Imogene inherited them and started that big patch in the shady part of the cemetery at Phillips Chapel. Mattie's sprouts came from there.

Mattie and her husband had arrived at Lib's one Wednesday with their old gray Chevy truck loaded down with plants. He had on his denim overalls, unbuttoned and flapped open on each side at the waist. A dingy white baseball hat with a red *A* fit snugly on his head and shaded his eyes. Mattie was wearing one of her classic house dresses, a burst of orange tropical flowers with green bamboo shoots that you might have worn in Hawaii, indoors, or if you were pregnant. She had to constantly grip a wad of the skirt in her hand to keep it from hanging up under her walker.

"Unload the wheelbarrow first," she directed her husband.

He unlatched the back of the truck bed and lowered it. Then he grappled with the wheelbarrow that was running over with plants. It was red, but pocked with rust spots. After he rolled the wheelbarrow near the largest bed, he stood in back of the truck and handed Lib the plants one by one in an assortment of aged pots and kitchen containers—large plastic pots that looked like faded terra cotta, black flimsy ones with white stains ringing the bottom, some commercial kitchen pots in dented stainless steel, and one or two speckled aluminum stock pots with holes rusted through.

Then Mattie's husband began to prepare the bed. He lifted the wooden handles of the post hole diggers up until the metal ends were about to his knees. Then he plunged them downward, hacking into the ground over and over again, rotating the sharp rounded ends until there was enough loosened clay for him to bite up a diggerful by swinging the handles apart.

He muttered, "Damned builder. Ain't two good inches of topsoil here. No wonder your shrubs died."

Lib had come to the same conclusion last Mother's Day when she planted a yellow rose. Her son perceived she was in a yellow phase in this new house and bought a fancy hybrid with a metal tag. A tea rose. Peace. Her husband might never notice one of her phases, yet she depended on him the way migrating birds do the stars. Home only on weekends since he had taken the engineering consulting job, he faithfully and dutifully dug the big hole. She filled the hole with topsoil, added the requisite bone meal and rose food. But at the end of the long growing season, the rose was still just a stub. What few new leaves had emerged during the summer had made a thorny salad for a hungry deer. Twice. She could understand a deer's desire for pansies. She wouldn't plant those again. But prickly roses?

* * *

Her *mouth was so close to his smooth cheek she could smell the flavor of her own breath mint. She felt like a rose petal, floating among the handfuls flung above the heads of newlyweds. She hovered there like a hummingbird for a moment. She could have kissed his cheek. She could have run her hungry tongue along his jaw line, tasted his boyish ear lobe. She could hardly breathe. She had forgotten how. She cleared her throat and whispered, "Do you know why this computer won't let me print?"*

*   *   *

Mattie, six years older than Lib, was like a mother sending a child off to summer camp. She had dutifully educated Lib about periods and body parts.

"What if it starts at school?"

"Just go to the Home Ec room. They keep pads there," Mattie said. "Or carry one with you in your purse."

"What if somebody sees it?"

"So what if they see it. They know what it is."

"What if it gets on my skirt?"

"My Lord, Lib, if it gets on your skirt, just go to the restroom and wash it out. Either that or just lock yourself in a stall and don't ever come out. If you don't show up for seventh grade next year, I'll come looking for you."

Mattie's husband had been working topsoil and cow manure into Lib's bed, showing Lib how to wiggle the rake through loose soil like a stiff row of earthworms. He stood now propped on the rake. He threw his Winston butt down and ground it into the dirt. He had become Mattie's gardening proxy since her last back surgery.

"You know if you'd spend the time working cow manure into the topsoil that you do propped on that rake pulling on cigarettes, Lib'd have a Garden of Eden here," lamented Mattie. She steadied herself with the walker and kicked at a mound of topsoil.

Her husband didn't answer. He wasn't much of a talker. He was from South Alabama and had some Cherokee in him. He lit another cigarette and let it hang from the corner of his mouth as he raked.

"Mattie, if anybody can transform this clay hole into a lush garden spot, I'd like to ask him for a few more miracles," said Lib, hoping to lessen the possibility for tension.

"Ah, you still got some of the miraculous in you, ain't you babe?" Mattie said, patting her husband on the rump.

"Still put up with you, don't I?" He rolled a row of smoke rings out of his mouth toward her.

It was obvious they had an understanding, just as Lib and Mattie always had. Mattie knew both their limits. And even though Lib resented giving up a day of writing short stories to struggle with clay and cow manure, she knew she would lap up the outcome, the blossoms and their colors, just the way she did pear preserves.

In the laborious project of preservation that Mattie insisted they tackle each fall, Lib relished the task of picking the fruit. Lib liked the slight snap it took to break a pear from its branch, the way a pear completely filled her palm. She liked to arrange a bowlful of pears to look at. Considering how she might sketch the curve of a single pear could keep her occupied all morning. At least until Mattie began her lecture of the grasshopper and ant again.

"Chip your pear off the core in little pieces. Then pour a good amount of sugar over the cut up pears. Wash and scald your fruit jars while the sugar dissolves. When you start cooking the pears, look for teensy weensy bubbles to start. Wait until then to take your preserves off the heat, or they won't be thick enough."

Dutifully following instructions, Lib would return to the boiling pot of pears, stirring, waiting for big bubbles to grow small.

* * *

He picked up her green briefcase from the table to move her over to the next computer. Their fingers met as she took the briefcase. She thought he might have whispered something as he tugged at the leg of his jeans, shifting tight faded denim. Had she imagined it, or had his hand slowed over hers just by an eyelash, just by a thread? Her senses were as keen as a palm reader's, staring, touching, listening for the very tiniest of intended gestures, and, yes, his long fingers had definitely paused. He pushed a button and the computer started to whir. Her heart thought itself a tread-mill. Its pounding strained against the mother-of-pearl buttons on her blouse. She eased herself into the chair in front of the computer.

* * *

Like an adolescent weary of a mother's advice, Mattie's husband did the best he could. He was always reminding Mattie that he only knew about vegetable gardens. Mattie stood by on her walker, huffing and puffing, or-dering and pointing in between little groans of pain to what needed to be pruned, weeded, mulched, or fertilized.

Lib winced each time Mattie groaned. She suspected that this magnanimous gift of plants was not just generosity, but that it came from her sister's need in some way to become eternal. Mattie had no children. She never wanted to talk about it, but she let it slip once that she knew nothing about birth control. Mattie had always adored Lib's son, even when he had been a bratty teenager.

Mattie gave the same kind of attention to the old timey plants, her offspring—the English Dogwood, the Grancy Graybeard, the Lemon Drops, the Snow Ball bush and the Confederate Rose. Mama's favorites, too, Mattie said. The most important thing was that these old ones would stay put. If you gave one a bed space from the start, you could count on its being right there next year, perhaps a little wider and taller, but in its space.

"These lilies can make you lose control easy. You can forget who gave what. They multiply like rabbits, taking over the beds."

It was the lilies that intrigued Lib. She was moving toward expansion in a writing program, learning to think as freely as if she were using a pseudonym in life. Meanwhile Mattie had become increasingly more restricted. First Mattie gave up her Tuesday morning sewing circle because all they ever talked about was grandkids. Then she refused to go to the Piggly Wiggly, but sent her husband with a list. It wasn't worth it. She hardly cooked at all anymore, not even the fried apple pies she was known for. She had a retort: "Sara Lee's not bad." Then there was the back surgery. Lib was feeling a twinge of guilt already that she would be away in Louisville the fifth Sunday in April. She would be too busy preparing for the ten-day writing residency to help Mattie with Decoration Day. It was not just a matter of cooking lunch for the "dinner on the ground," at Phillips Chapel, but cleaning off Mama and Daddy's graves and shopping for flowers. Lib hated artificial flowers, but Mattie insisted on silk because "real ones won't last a day in that heat."

The writing program was a small sign, for sure, that Lib might be moving out of the monochromatic yellow phase. This phase did not seem to have the staying power of the blue period of her mid-forties. At that time a glimpse of the Williamsburg blue backsplash behind the kitchen sink had had an effect on Lib that could only be equaled now with a fresh estrogen patch.

Surveying this truckload of lilies stirred something inside Lib she sensed might be hormonal. She was partial to the whites, pinks, and purples in lilies, although she knew that was as apt to change as her bird choices did in her stories.

"These little babies need shade," said Mattie, cuddling one of the purple blossoms. "Fool them with a lot of water so they'll think they're still down by the river."

Lilies could grow anywhere from eleven inches to four feet tall, and these grew waist-high and wild with tiny blooms. Mattie had instructed her husband to hunt those up on his fishing trip to Sipsey Swamp. They brought them to Lib's in large clumps.

"Let's group these bad boys by color," said Mattie, pointing to the canna lilies.

Their wide leaves suggested already they might be the amazons. The folds of the leaves emerging from the stems reminded Lib of an O'Keeffe she'd seen once.

"They'll chug-a-lug water like elephant ears during a drought," Mattie insisted. "There's a good spot," she said, waving vaguely toward the back yard. "Set them out in threes—reds and oranges and yellows—by the back porch down where the sprinkler system drains."

Mattie quickly took a deep breath.

"And listen here, Lib, these Milk and Wine Lilies are regular steel magnolias. Don't crowd them. They'll have the biggest blooms you'll ever see. Mine get this tall," Mattie said, holding her hand above her waist.

Mattie pointed to one of the large speckled pots. "Fourteen lilies on every single bloom. They're a pale pink. I know how you like pink, Lib. You'll be tempted to cut a bouquet for your table, but they're way too milky. They'll spot your tablecloth every time. Table, too. Spots just as sticky as linoleum with sweet tea dribbled on it. So if you can't resist, better have your mayonnaise remedy ready. How about that open space outside your kitchen window? I'm telling you, these gals will spread like perfume. Take my advice. . . ."

Mattie's monologue, suddenly pained, broke off. "Oh, Lordy mercy," she groaned as she pressed against her lower back with both hands. She stopped to gasp for air, but she would not be bested. She eased her walker along the lawn toward the driveway. Her husband followed behind with the shovel.

She sputtered, "Better just keep—just keep those outside—for the public."

*   *   *

Public. *This computer lab was definitely too public. The attendant at the front desk was staring at the two of them like a spinster librarian. Maybe trying to guess her age. Her gray hair confused people, even in its new French cut. She had the urge to shock the attendant, to stand up on the table and rip open her pearl buttons, swing her blouse over her head a few times like a lasso. Her face flushed at that thought as if she had just had a mild acid peel. "Sorry," she mouthed to the attendant. She zipped open a pocket on the briefcase as quietly as possible. A zipper could be so loud.*

She motioned for him to come closer. His pants zipper curved as he bent.

"I have been thinking about living like the lilies that blow in the fields," she whispered to him.

His brown eyes formed a question.

"Mary Oliver. The poet. It's a poem I clipped for my journal a long time ago."

*   *   *

"**Plant** these others anywhere," Mattie said, sweeping her hand across the lilies. "I can't call their names. With Plumbago I have to think of the disease first, Lumbago. You probably never heard of it. You learn these things when you've got a bad back. She's a frilly jezebel. Lavender blue. Mine froze out this winter."

Mattie's husband had added about fifty bags of topsoil to the beds and a "good saturation" of cow manure; yet the roots would still have to snake their way through clay, Mattie warned.

"Not to worry, though. Lilies could probably live in solid rock," she said. "Plant them on a bare hillside. In an empty pocket of a bed. All you need to do is to add a handful of sand at the roots to guard against slugs. A few pieces of peat if you have it. Lilies will spread like fire in sage grass. You'll have so many lilies you won't miss the few that the deer eat. Lilies thrive on being let go, left to just wave in the wind and feed the humming-birds."

*   *   *

She *thought when she returned home from this writing residency, she would rethink the colors in her home. Right now the kitchen was Lemon Meringue and the hall and den were Butter. Clean crisp colors.*

Next year her lilies would be in full bloom. She had looked up the names of the lilies. Sometimes she simply uttered the names aloud like a litany: spider lilies; daylil-ies—the lemon lily, the tawny lily; star gazers; zephyr or Easter lilies; agapanthus

*lilies, ginger lilies—not to mention all the ones that would have already bloomed—
amaryllis, hyacinths, buttercups, daffodils.*

*She could fairly float in the sounds of the daylilies that grew in this area, page
after page of names so opulent they rivaled nail colors—Egytian Queen, Rick
Rack Ruffles, Awakening Dream, Shady Lady, Riviera Rapture, Paper Butterfly,
Peach Magnolia, Eloquent Silence. . . .*

*She read extensively about lilies and their propagation, how their underground
tubers and rhizomes reproduce rapidly and with ease. Just as Mattie had said, she'd
have a truckload of color.*

Mattie's husband had stopped raking and cocked his good ear toward
the wooded edge of the yard.

"Sweet-sweet, where-where, here-here, see it-see it."

A dazzling turquoise blue flutter. *Passerina cyanea.* The first Indigo Bunting
Lib ever saw was not blue. Not one in the small flock was. Brownish, nondescript, really, compared to the flamboyant pair of toucans nearby. Her
husband had an assignment in the Misiones Province, and she was touring
at Iguazu Falls. Their guide to the Jesuit ruins was astounded that the indi-
gos had migrated this far south. The guide was impatient with her assistant
who was translating.

"Look for this one back home," the guide said, pointing beyond a tree-
sized cactus. "The male won't be brown or silent in the states. He assumes
an alter ego when he migrates south."

Mattie's husband shaded his eyes to search through the top of the tall
oaks.

"Man's got a song that sweet, he ought to be traveling with a woman,"
he muttered.

"Not just one," said Lib. "He'll have four or five females over the
season—a different one for every clutch more or less."

Mattie's husband looked at Mattie and winked, and laughed out loud
for the first time that day. Mattie was close enough she took a big swing to
slap him, but he dodged, and his baseball hat went sailing off.

* * *

*Lib quickly backspaced through the title and typed in "From Silence to Song,"
saved it, and switched off the computer. He was gathering up his backpack.*

*Lib could sense the new color phase coming on. A decorator had once suggested a
purple Victorian loveseat for Lib's living room. Now she could imagine it there with*

its fringed velvet skirt, a shade darker than Spiritual Corridor, an orchid and lavender daylily. Maybe she'd sprinkle in some bright Kosta Boda crystal pieces, or add a splash of cobalt blue, perhaps a Chihuly basket the color of an Indigo Bunting.

Mattie would not approve. She was the absolutist Lib once was. Mattie's kitchen appliances were still avocado. Lib wondered whether stoves and refrigerators came in primary colors. A red stove? She tried to outline it, imagine it nestled in beside her white refrigerator and dishwasher. Lib glanced up at him. Right now she was ravenous—for lunch.

Sidney Thompson

A CLASSICAL EDUCATION

I didn't doubt Father when he told me he would kill Mr. Carr. "Come with me," he said. And I followed him onto the path worn into the woods behind our pasture. He carried the .22 rifle. I carried the shovel.

"This does not make us niggers, you understand." He spoke without turning, without breaking his stride or spitting. "We are still black, Son. Don't forget that."

Father's right trouser pocket bulged with cartridges. He never walked with a loaded gun. He said it wasn't safe.

"Niggers are cowards. Their violence is selfish and misdirected. Never allow a white man to call you a nigger."

"I won't," I said.

"You will be entering high school next year."

"I'm ready."

"You will be assigned to read more of the moral literature and none which argues for the natural state of man. They fear murder without guilt and retribution."

"I know."

"*All's Well That Ends Well?*" he asked.

"Shakespeare," I answered.

"*Samson Agonistes?*"

"Milton."

"*Back to Methuselah?*"

"Shaw."

"Sophocles?" he said.

I said, "*Oedipus Rex.*"

"What else?" he said. Father was a very demanding teacher, and by demanding I mean constant, always reinforcing my memory of titles and authors and characters and themes.

"*Antigone* and *Oedipus at Colonus,*" I said.

" 'Rex' means?" he asked, and I answered, and he said, "Very good," still without turning. "How could you or anyone else ever doubt that you are *not* a nigger?"

Instead of continuing on the main path, Father turned on Primrose Path—as he liked to refer to our minds' pleasure—which was less traveled and so less distinct than the central one which had no name except the Path. Neither of us spoke until we reached the bench, a tree Father had felled and debarked and shellacked the summer following my graduation from grammar school. Since then we had built fires in the dirt before the bench, and he had read to me from books he cherished, while usually a couple of squirrels, sometimes a rabbit, we had hunted that day roasted on the skewer he had improvised out of wire coat hangers. He forbade discussion during our supper. "Consider only the taste," he had said, before our campfires and our behaviors had become ritual and automatic. "The life we killed deserves that." And when the squirrels or the rabbit had been eaten, he would explain what he had read.

Father sat on the bench, and I sat down beside him.

"Who would have condemned the man who assassinated Hitler, if there had been such a brave and rational man?"

"No one," I said.

"Who would cry if someone murdered James Earl Ray in his jail cell tonight?"

"No one rational."

"Do you honestly agree?"

"Yes, sir," I said.

"Is man more righteous than other animals?"

"No, sir."

He put his arm around me. "This is your soul speaking?"

"Yes, Father."

He smiled, nodding his head. He looked down at his hands, still nodding. Father thought members of the black race were as much afraid of literacy as we were about the underside of our hands and feet. On my first day of grammar school, just before I boarded the bus, Father told me the myth his father had passed down to him from his father, that the white man had mocked us by bleaching our hands with his cotton and our feet with his shoes. "But it is different for us now," Father said. "Let the turning of pages bleach your hands." He said, "Do not worry about your feet. You do not have to touch the earth to be of the earth. Look straight ahead."

Father continued to nod and to examine his hands. I wanted to say something to make him proud.

"Sport hunting is legal," I said.

"Yes, it is," he said.

"But it isn't ethical."

"What about the guilty?" He was looking at me. "What happens if we hunt those who are guilty of harming our souls?"

"We go to jail."

"If—" he said.

"If," I said, "we get caught."

Father withdrew the pouch of tobacco from his pocket. He chewed a moment and spat and said, not looking at his hands but downward, "Do you know why I want to kill Russell?"

"No, sir," I said, but I knew he would not do it without good reason.

He began retelling the story of how his father and Mr. Carr's father had worked together running gin in Memphis during prohibition until they had earned enough money to walk away from the whole dirty scene to buy fifty acres of Mississippi farmland, which they divided and cleared and nurtured for crops, except for four acres of woods and two acres for their homes, which the two men built themselves.

"Russell has taken advantage of this family trust. He has stained my honor and your honor and your little brother's honor and, sadly, your mother's honor. He has crippled my soul. And I hope I don't cripple yours by sharing this with you." He put his hand on my shoulder. "Russell," he said, withdrawing his hand, "has disrupted my marriage.

"You understand the implication, do you not?"

I nodded.

"Your mother has cried when we are together, alone at night," he said. "From where does the guilt come if she no longer loves me? She knows whatever exists between us can heal. She has known all along, when we hug and kiss and criticize each other, it is not the end or the beginning of anything, rather the middle of something extraordinary."

He stood up. He walked around the remains of our fire from the week earlier, when he had read from Plato's *Republic*. Father faced away, in the direction of home, but you could not see home from where we were.

"Clarissa refused to tell me why she was crying. I talked to Russell about it. I confided in him. I always confided in him. His first loyalty, his first investment was in our friendship. I deserve more from Russell than what he has offered, what he is, now I know, capable of offering. Clarissa does not need such a . . . Grendel. What can the world gain by allowing him to pillage?"

"Not a goddamned thing," I said.

He turned and joined me on the bench. "You are right," he said. "Not a thing. But, please, Son," he said, "do not curse."

"Yes, sir," I said.

"Now," he said, "get the shovel and dig a hole in the center of those ashes."

He stood up and walked toward the trees beyond the clearing.

"We need a hole two feet by two feet by two feet," he said.

"For what?" I asked.

"While you do that, I will hunt firewood."

I felt I was disturbing sacred ground as I dug into the remains of no less than a hundred fires. The first foot in depth consisted mostly of ash and cinders. Then gradually the earth became more clay than soil or ash and more red than fire itself.

Father returned with an armload of branches and dry leaves as I finished digging the queer grave. He dropped the load near the hole, picked up the rifle and said, "Leave the shovel and come with me."

"Father?"

"Yes?" he said, without stopping, without turning to face me. We were following Primrose again, back toward the Path.

"Does Mr. Carr know that you know?"

"No," he said.

"Does Mother?"

"No. And she must never know. Virgil, do you understand?"

"Yes, sir."

"As far as anyone knows," he said, as I watched his feet but thought of his face, his thin lips, "I have no motive. And you are my alibi. Who would ever suspect a man, even a black man, of committing murder with his son along as a witness?"

"Father?" I said.

"Yes?" he said.

"How did you get Mr. Carr's rifle?"

"581, Son," he said, "Maxim 581."

I was well familiar with Father's favorite maxim by Publilius Syrus: "It is not every question that deserves an answer."

He stopped at the edge of the woods behind a tree to load the single chamber of the bolt-action. He spat out his plug of tobacco.

"I am returning his rifle," he said, holding the rifle upright against his shoulder military fashion. "Are you ready?"

"Father," I said, "you are positive about Mother and Mr. Carr?"

"Without a doubt." He put his hand on my head. "Would you rather stay behind?"

"No, sir."

"The virtuous act is chosen," he said.

"I choose to continue."

"I respect any choice you make."

"I choose to continue," I said.

Father removed his hand from my head. He bent down so that his eyes were level with mine. I didn't see anything but his seeing. He looked into my eyes as a doctor examines a throat and as quickly, and as if he had found what he was looking for, his seeing perhaps, he moved his eyes away and kissed me. It was the first time we had ever touched lips. He turned and walked out of the woods into Russell's cornfield, and I followed.

Every Saturday Mother visited her sister, and Horace, my younger brother by five years, always joined her because his best friend was our cousin Quinctius. Mr. Carr lived alone. And on Saturdays he stayed home to watch television. Approaching the porch steps with Father, I thought, No one will hear except Father and myself and Mr. Carr, of course, and Mr. Carr will hear it forever.

Father held the handle of Mr. Carr's screen door without pulling it open. Without turning, he said, "All men are mortal. Socrates is a man."

"Therefore, Socrates is mortal," I answered, and Father opened the door and called out Mr. Carr's name.

"In here, Gerald," said Mr. Carr.

Mr. Carr was the only person I knew who still called Father by his real name. Even Father's siblings called him Job. Father named me and my brother and our cousin, and before I was born he renamed himself because, he said, Job converted him into a thinking man and, therefore, into a man, and he believed his new self deserved recognition.

Mr. Carr was sitting in his recliner in front of the television watching wrestling and eating from a can of pork and beans.

I sat down on the bench across the room from Mr. Carr. Father stood, leaning in the doorway with the rifle in the crook of his arm pointing the barrel at the floor.

"I didn't hear any shots," said Mr. Carr, still looking at the television. "Y'all didn't see anything?"

"We saw not one squirrel," said Father.

"Did you try over near Buckman's land?"

"No, we did not try."

"You need to go over there," Mr. Carr said. "I popped four there, you know, last time."

"I do not feel much like hunting anyway. Do you, Son?"

"No, sir," I said. "Not for squirrel."

"I'm watching wrestling if y'all want to join me. There's some cookies in there, Virg."

"No, thank you," I said.

"We are not going to stay long," said Father. "We did not come here to practice our social graces. I am returning your rifle because it does not belong to me. However, the cartridge in the chamber is mine, and, of course, it is the same brand that you buy."

Mr. Carr turned to me and was, I think, about to ask what had gotten my father's goat when Father raised the rifle and shot Mr. Carr in the foot.

He dropped his can of beans and began screaming, holding his foot. When the blood started to run out of the hole in his shoe, he started shouting: "What the hell? My God! What the hell?"

On the television a man parading in make-up and bleached hair flexed his muscles and was hollering about his omnipotence and insensitivity.

Mr. Carr continued to shout, and Father told him to silence himself, while he pulled a handkerchief from his pocket and ejected the hot casing into it. He looked at me while he wiped the casing. "Son, always erase the signs of design." He dropped the casing on the floor and bolted another cartridge into the chamber.

Mr. Carr began calling Father's name.

"'The gods are deaf to the one who turns to crime.'" Father turned to me. "Who wrote that?"

I shook my head.

"'Justice turns the balance scales, sees that we suffer and we suffer and we learn'?"

"That's in *Agamemnon*."

"Which character's words?"

"The Chorus."

"Is that a character?" he asked.

"The character of truth," I said.

"Author?" he asked.

"Aeschylus."

"Very good, don't you think, Russell?" But Mr. Carr was moaning and begging Father not to hurt him any more.

"I asked you a question, Russell. Russell, don't you think my son is extraordinary?"

"Yeah, Gerald, yeah," he said. "Please, Gerald, what're you doing?"

"Call me Job," Father demanded.

"Okay, Job," Mr. Carr said.

"I have allowed you to show me disrespect for too long."

"Job, I'm sorry, please, Job."

"And Mr. Carr," I said, standing, my arms crossed in front of my chest, "call me Ishmael."

"Bravo!" said Father. "Bravo!" He held the rifle under his arm so he could clap. I sat down and smiled with victory. He turned to Mr. Carr. "My son has just paid us a compliment. I will accept with gratitude the reference of hero in this analogy, but you—you are not so mysterious, are you? You are not so complex."

Mr. Carr was only slightly wounded but he already looked like he was dying, shaking his head, shaking all over and beginning to cry. "I don't know what you're talking about," he said.

"Are you suffering?" Father asked.

"My God, Job, can't you see I am? What're you doing?"

"You tell me."

"I don't know."

"We suffer and we learn." Father shot him in the other foot.

Mr. Carr began screaming as before, but instead of screaming noise, he mouthed a word that ended in the interesting sound of flesh in pain.

Father turned to me. "Did you notice he called out for God in vain?"

"Yes, sir, I did," I said.

"Russell!" said Father. "Russell, if you want us to leave you alone, you better participate."

Mr. Carr forced himself to a whimper and then forced himself further until his sounds of pain and protest were drowned out by the wrestling announcer's screaming—about a chain and unsportsmanlike conduct and the unfortunate loss of a respected referee.

"Look what has happened, Son, when we took the games from the lions and gave them to the Christians."

"Pitiful," I said.

"Turn off that Christian trash. With your elbow," he said, and I hit the power button with my elbow.

"Now that I have your attention, Russell, tell me why I would come here this day and shoot you."

"Job, we're best friends. We've known each other all our lives. Our fathers were like brothers. We're like brothers."

"Like cousins that makes us, you imbecile."

Mr. Carr looked at me. "Please, Virg," he said.

"He told you to call him Ishmael," demanded Father. He ejected the empty casing from the rifle into his handkerchief, rubbed the casing as before, dropped it and inserted another cartridge. He raised the barrel at Mr. Carr's face.

"Okay, okay, Ishmael," said Mr. Carr, "I'll call him Ishmael, and you're Job."

"I will for certain kill you if you do not admit what you know. I want you to tell us why we seek justice." Father backed away and sat down beside me on the bench.

"We are waiting," said Father.

Mr. Carr, with a leaking foot in each hand, looked like a crude rocking horse.

"What's Clarissa told you?"

"What would Clarissa have to tell me?" asked Father.

"Job, I didn't go to her," he said, forgetting his pain. He took his red hands from his feet to motion with them as he spoke. He brought his hands to his stout chest. He said, "She came to me. I swear, Job. I swear to God I didn't go to her. I didn't make the first move."

"You're a liar!" I shouted, suddenly standing.

Father put his hand on my arm. "Calm yourself."

"He's lying, Father."

"Perhaps," he said, "but sit down."

"What'd she tell you?" asked Mr. Carr.

"What she has told me makes no difference," said Father. "Should what *you* tell me?"

"It just happened," said Mr. Carr. "By accident. I didn't plan it. She came to me. I ain't lying, I swear."

"Russell," said Father, standing up, "do you remember that night years ago, years ago before I was married," Father was pacing between me on the bench and Mr. Carr in his recliner, "when you cried for me?"

He hesitated. He seemed to fear admitting his forgetfulness. "No," his voice wavered.

"Russell, you cried for me because I told you I was an atheist."

"Yeah, I remember," he said. "I remember."

"You told me you hated to see me go to hell when you knew you were going to heaven."

"You'll go to hell for sure if you kill me."

Father looked at me. "Virgil—" He smiled, "May I call you Virgil?"

"Yes, sir," I said, "but he must call me Ishmael."

He laughed. "Did you hear that, Russell?"

Mr. Carr wasn't laughing. He had remembered his feet and was holding them again. "Yeah," he said.

"Do you remember *The Clouds?*"

"Yes, Father. Aristophanes."

"Russell thinks of me as a sophist," said Father, still pacing.

"I do not," said Mr. Carr.

"Silence!" Father told him. He turned toward me. "He doesn't understand our language."

"No, sir," I said. "He's a nigger."

"Right you are, Son." Father stopped pacing. He stood in the doorway, leaning against the facing, looking at me but pointing the rifle at Mr. Carr. "Aristophanes mocked Socrates for being an atheist, a sophist, an independent thinker, for believing, 'Zeus is dead.' How outrageous!" said Father. "And do not the believers mock Nietzsche for saying, 'God is dead'?"

"They do," I said.

"But who today still mocks Socrates for not believing in Zeus?"

"No one," I answered.

Father pointed at Mr. Carr. "Do you think you are better than Socrates and Nietzsche?"

"I don't know who you're talking about," he said. "Believe me, I never meant to hurt you."

Father leveled the rifle and shot him in the arm. "You are the worst kind of sophist." While Mr. Carr held his new wound, Father wiped the casing and threw it in the corner of the room behind Mr. Carr's recliner and turned to face me while reloading.

"Let the police try to reason that," he said.

Mr. Carr lunged at Father before I was aware he had risen from his chair. Father turned and swung the butt of the rifle into Mr. Carr's face, and Mr. Carr fell backward into the recliner.

"Tell him, Son, what Plautus says concerning patience."

"Patience," I said, "'is the best remedy for every trouble.'"

"Did you hear that, Russell?" said Father. "There is no need to hurry us. You will die soon enough."

"You think you're so smart," said Mr. Carr without wiping away the noseblood running into his mouth. He rested his arms on the arms of the chair as if he, while fearing pain, no longer felt pain.

"I suppose a man deserves an opportunity to defend himself as a man," said Father. He laid the rifle on the floor. "Tell me, Russell, explain to us with logic your right to exist."

"My God, you're crazy. What do you mean, explain? I don't have to explain. You're breaking the law." He looked at me. "You'll both go to jail."

Father laughed. "Russell, our ancestors were slaves by law." He looked at the ceiling, his arms out with palms open, as if he were checking for rain. He said, "This house was built with illegal funds."

"God," said Mr. Carr. "I know you don't believe, but Jesus died for us, and you'll be judged, Gerald."

"You son of a bitch!" I said. I was ready to jump up again and really hit him that time.

"Watch your mouth," said Father. "I'll take you over my knee right here."

"He doesn't address you with proper respect."

"Let him speak," Father said. "Speak," he told Mr. Carr. "Continue."

"That's your name—*Gerald.* You ain't so different than me. We grew up together. We played the same games, slept in the same beds."

I leaped up at that, but Father caught me.

"Sit down, Virgil."

I tested my strength against his by pushing forward, but he threw me backward.

"Virgil!" Father shouted.

"I'm sorry," I said.

"You know what I meant," said Mr. Carr. "Forgive and forget, Gerald. Forgive and forget."

"Who said that?"

"What?"

"Who popularized the saying that you just misquoted as 'forgive and forget'? If you can answer, I won't kill you. My word on that."

"What does it matter who said it first?"

"If a man cannot successfully articulate a defense for his life, he has a sad, sad life." Father shook his head. "I would not allow a dog to suffer. Now answer my question."

Mr. Carr began to cry again.

"It appears in *King Lear,*" said Father.

"Who the fuck is King Lear?" said Mr. Carr.

Father looked at me. "Do you hear this pitiful excuse for a man? The wisdom of forty-six years has spoken. Russell, King Lear, the character, says, 'Pray you now, forget and forgive,' and that is said in *King Lear,* by William Shakespeare. Son, to whom does Lear speak?"

"His daughter Cordelia," I said.

"Thank you, Virgil."

"You're welcome, Father."

"Why are you alive?" Father asked. I knew the answer, but he was looking at Mr. Carr. He ignored Father. He looked down, weeping, I think, without making sound.

"What makes man distinctly man?" asked Father. Again, Mr. Carr refused to speak.

"You do believe in God?" said Father. Mr. Carr couldn't ignore God. But he did. He said nothing, made no motion or nod of head. He seemed to have resigned himself completely to his fate, hibernating inside himself.

Father was standing beside the rifle on the floor. He still looked at Mr. Carr, even though Mr. Carr was still looking at himself.

"Russell, what would we say of a spider that denies its ability to spin webs?" Still Mr. Carr refused to speak, but Father continued, "What would we say of an elephant that refuses to use its trunk?" Mr. Carr was no more alive than dead.

"If you saw an elephant that did not eat or drink or bathe with its trunk," said Father, "could you correctly call it an elephant?" Father turned toward me and shrugged. "Man is the only animal that chooses to deny his essence."

I had to force myself to listen. My body wanted to lunge at the rifle.

"If he does not think, is he a man?"

I couldn't answer.

"Virgil, does he have a name? Is he an *am*? Is he a man?"

"No way!" My words burst out without forethought.

"Russell," he said, "you better pray Plato was correct when he said you will be wiser in reincarnation. You better pray the Hindus are not correct, or you will return as a silverfish."

Mr. Carr lifted his head. His face was red and wet from crying, but he was no longer crying. "I have prayed," he said, looking at Father. "I have prayed," he said, looking at me. He looked back at Father. "I'm forgiven." He raised his hands to point at each of us. "I'm forgiven."

Father began to shake his head in disappointment. "'The soul takes nothing with her education and culture; and these, it is said, are of the greatest service or of the greatest injury to the dead man, at the very beginning of his journey thither'—Plato. I am sorry to say, Russell, you need not bother packing."

He bent down to pick up the rifle. But I reached the rifle before Father. I sprung back in case he wanted to take the gun away from me. But he didn't move.

I stepped toward Mr. Carr.

"Don't react," said Father.

I aimed the rifle at Mr. Carr's forehead, and the tranquility of faith on his face disappeared with the closure of his eyes and the opening of his mouth as he screamed.

"Not out of emotion," said Father, without trying to stop me. "Act from the mind."

I tried to listen to Father.

The ugly scent of Mr. Carr's sweat was too intense in my mouth. Then I spoke: "'Beauty is truth.'"

"No, Virgil!" Father screamed.

Mr. Carr's head jolted backward as if he had been kicked by a horse. "'Bold Lover,'" I said, still quoting, "'never, never canst thou,'" but I could not continue. The spectacle of blood spouting from the burnt hole in his forehead and the smell of gunpowder oozing into my mouth and down my throat made it difficult for me to speak.

Father walked up without looking at me and took the rifle and put an arm around my shoulders. "Son," he said, "you need not feel guilty for killing a man who intentionally harmed your soul, but neither should you enjoy killing him. You do it only if you feel your soul and the soul of the world can improve without such a person. You do it, and you respect yourself for your honor and courage and rationality. But never enjoy it."

I swallowed. "Yes, Father."

"If you start killing without reason, you may begin harming the souls of those who do not deserve such treatment. Do you understand, Son?"

"I'm sorry, Father."

"You scared me when you cited Keats."

"Father," I said, shaking under his arm, "I'm afraid I may be a romanticist."

"We will work on it, Virgil."

Father removed his arm from around me to eject the casing from the .22. He wiped it clean and tossed it on the floor, then wiped the fingerprints from the rifle and laid the rifle on the floor. With arms free and open, he approached.

I stared at the hole in Mr. Carr's forehead as Father held me, as blood now rolled gently down and was covering Mr. Carr's eyes and face and neck. His secret symphony of heart and blood had come to a finale and was not so secretive any more.

I laughed suddenly. "Father," I said, regaining myself, my mind, and I motioned toward Mr. Carr, "he looks like a Cyclops, doesn't he?" Father laughed and slapped me on the back.

"Bravo, Son. You are not hopeless, yet." He walked to Mr. Carr's body. "Help me throw him around," he said.

I picked Mr. Carr up under one arm as Father picked him up under his bleeding one.

"Into the table," he said, and we threw Mr. Carr, and the table fell over, breaking the lamp that was sitting on it. "Good," Father said. "Now grab onto one of his legs." Each of us held a leg and pulled him around the room, knocking over furniture. After Father forced Mr. Carr's fingerprints on the barrel of the rifle and on the base of the broken lamp, Father and I left the room to Mr. Carr's bedroom.

Father opened Mr. Carr's box of .22 cartridges which was lying on his dresser and emptied the cartridges on the bed. He removed the case from one of the pillows.

"Don't touch anything," he said. "Just follow and observe." And he filled the pillowcase with loose change and jewelry. We walked back into the living room, and Father removed Mr. Carr's watch and took his wallet and threw them into the pillowcase, then set it on the floor. He unplugged the television and carried it to the back door and dropped it, and the plastic casing cracked and a glass tube inside broke. He wiped his prints from its side and from the plug. "They had to leave in a hurry," he said. He opened the back door with his hand in the handkerchief. "They entered through this door because Russell never locked his doors, and they found his rifle in his bedroom. They surprised him, but he struggled with them, and we heard the shots and thought he was hunting, and when we came up here to see what he had shot, the burglars heard us and left this television behind."

"Bravo, Father." I patted him on the back.

"Thank you, Son."

I followed him back into the living room. He picked up the pillowcase of loot and looked at Mr. Carr on the floor on his back. Father smiled. I smiled, too. I was proud for him.

"A masterpiece." He turned to me, still smiling. "You have learned a great deal today."

"Yes, sir, I have."

"Let's go," he said.

Neither of us spoke as we hurried back through the cornfield, into the woods, along Primrose to our clearing. Father dropped the pillowcase in the hole and began stripping and tossing the bloodied clothes and shoes in the hole. "You, too," he said.

Father covered the hole with the pile of clay and ash and cinders and added to the top a fresh fire, burning the branches and leaves he had gathered earlier while I made the hole that the fire now made invisible. We stepped back to watch it blaze. The heat was intense to our uncovered bodies.

"We heard the shots," he said, "and we took it upon ourselves to prepare the pit for his game, but when he did not appear, we walked up to his house and found him dead. Can you remember that?"

"Yes, sir. Father?"

"Yes?"

"Would Mother admit to the police she was having an affair with him?"

"Why would she do that?"

"If she suspected you."

"Do you think she would admit to you, to Horace, to her parents and to the entire community that she had behaved like a strumpet?" I shook my head. He said, "How would she support herself without me? Would she evict herself with two children?" We shook our heads in unison. "She would not risk losing everything she has. Our alibis rely on the testimony of the other, and that would mean her risking you. For the sake of that ass? Never. I know she loves us." He put his hand on my head, then moved his hand down and rubbed my neck.

"Don't worry about the police either, Virgil. They hate us. They hate blacks and niggers alike. The justice in this county is blinded by ignorance and prejudice, and that means on this occasion they will be on our side. They will do the usual minimal investigation. They will take one look at Russell and say to themselves, 'Thank God. Thank God. There's one we didn't have to kill ourselves.'"

He patted my back. "We have to shower before we call the police." He turned, then called out to me without slowing, "Bring the shovel." It was stirring to see him move through the trees like an animal of the woods, his muscles and hair and dark skin revealed. As I followed his agility with awkwardness and weakness, still no more than a student at best—the shovel clumsy in my hands like a musical instrument I hadn't yet learned to play— he was to me and to the world at that moment and all proceeding moments no less than Pan—Pan indeed, if Pan could be mortal and rational and still be Pan.

He did not stop moving until he reached the steps to the back door of our house. As I approached, he told me to push the shovel into the ground of the flower bed. I left it standing like a mutant hollowless reed among the irises.

Father waited for me before opening the door. But suddenly, I felt an urge to quote Rouseau.

"'It is reason that runs man back on himself and that separates him from all that annoys and afflicts him.'" I continued urgently, "'It is philosophy that isolates him; it is philosophy that allows him to say privately, at he sight of a suffering man: "Perish if you will, I am safe." '"

Father analyzed my solemn expression with his own.

"Do you agree?" he asked.

"Most certainly," I said. "But we intellects need not be ashamed."

He smiled. "We have set the house in order once for all."

Before he had a chance to form his question, I said, "You paraphrased Clytaemnestra."

"Very good, Son." He held the door open for me to enter, "Very good."

Brad Watson

INTERMISSION

Her scent blossomed in the car like heavenly polecat, like flowers manufactured in a tire plant, something dusky and nostrilstinging, like perfumed coaldust, nasturtium on hot oilgrimed engine blocks. She smacked her Spearmint in something like meditation and I didn't know if we'd make it to the old theater or not. We drove down the near-empty wide lanes of 22nd Avenue, over the bridge, the heavy, sooted freights chugging by underneath, into the heart of town—silent and thrumming like hummingbirds, our hearts. Or maybe it was just me. I turned onto 8th and pulled up beneath the marquee, the bright light slashing through the windshield, cutting her body in half. She pursed her glossy, strawberry lips, leaned toward me and took my hand. I was trembling. Ever have a woman kiss the palm of your hand? No, she didn't. She closed my fingers over the little ball of gum. Toss that out the window for me, baby. Okay? I wish she hadn't looked up right then. Her eyes, between sticky spiked lashes, some kind of deep neon green. Her hair smelled of exotic salts at the roots. Her tongue like a blind, hairless, nursing mammal in my mouth.

The car was rolling, I don't know. Horns blaring, that bending sound going by. I was bent into Mona, I could feel the back of my leg against the wheel, steering somehow, I don't know where. Folks shouting. It was like church. She was kicking, with those wild pointed shoes, big holes in the headboard. She made sounds like a peacock crying, Aye! Aye! Aye!

I don't know how far we idled down 8ᵗʰ. I don't know how many folks we ran up over the curb. I don't know how many cops they called out to run down the '62 Bonneville driving itself down the road. I don't know, the jailer said one cop called over the radio, Look like it's being drove by a big hairy ass to me.

I don't know how long I'll be in here. I can see all that from the top of the county jail, the long stretch of 8ᵗʰ Street, west. I can see the flickering sign of the Davis Grill, where I was going to take her to eat. I can see the marquee on the old Theater there. I think I can see her sometimes, that plump-legged, kind of pigeon-toed waddle, her nylons going whish-whish, see her actually make it inside the place with some more restrained type of guy. I can see all the way south to Bonita, where her little white house sits on top of the hill. I see other cars pull in there and, the next morning, leave. I can see the lights go on in the hallway, the kitchen, the bedroom, and out.

JAKE ADAM YORK

LEAVING ALABAMA

Think of everyone you hate—the fourth-grade bully you kicked in the face, the cheerleaders who turned you down, classmates who laughed at you reading then later asked for help, the beer-swilling crowd on Senior Skip Day watching the quarterback fuck the fat girl in the river. Zip your bags, nestle your breakables in the twelve-year-old car, and check your route once again. Chattanooga, Hagerstown, Philly.

Think of everything you hate—librarians' eyebrows, Baptist deacons' hair, a bookshelf of Bibles and nothing else. Walk through your room once again, checking under the bed, the desk, in all the dresser drawers. Say goodbye to your swimming trophies, academic certificates, and family photos. Avoid the one of you as the high school mascot held aloft by your two beer-swilling Senior Skip Day friends. And the one of the girl who will open her goodbye today.

Think of everything you hate as you walk back to the car, unclip the hood and pull the dipstick along one of your father's blue automotive cloths. Ignore the way the dark fluid slips off the metal the way the river pulls along the far shore at Minnesota Bend. Ignore the way the dipstick dives into the check tube as if it were a current pool, the deepest channel in the county. Ignore the falling feeling, the weightless sense of freedom, your heart rising into your throat, the air trailing from your lungs, this terrible relax.

Take a deep breath and think of everything you hate—how you haven't been to church in two years but everyone's still asking when you're coming back, the terrible, grainy grape juice, and the post-Skip Day rededications, the promises to say goodbye to the bottle till Friday night. Try to ignore the smell of bacon wafting from the kitchen, the coffee perking up, nearly ready, and the dank of your great grandmother's skillet about to bid farewell to its fourth generation, the dank that rhymes with the warm-metal smell your father wears home from the plant.

Try not to realize that this damp-morning smell through which breakfast wafts is the river's, the way it washes everything, the way you wear it on your skin. Try not to think that this will be gone. Ignore the wren's little Charlie Parker by the pool and the high cackle of the yellowhammer and the mockingbird's speaking in tongues like he just believes again.

Think of everything you hate.

Think of a bookstore. Think of a record store. A town with more restaurants than churches. A town where football's not the only entertainment. Whose newspaper has more than just the one page.

Don't think how everything you own fits in this one little car. How your whole life could be erased if you wrecked in just the right place. Every CD melted down, every book of poems burned. The little note your grandmother's put inside the envelope with $300 you won't find in your duffel for three weeks yet. The plane ticket home your mom's tucked in the First Aid beneath the driver's seat. That fist of steel your father gave you years ago, the only thing he's ever said about work, that you should never have to do this, the fist he's wrapped in cloth and settled in the hub of the spare tire in the trunk. The little grains of river sand, little bits of slag and clay you can never wash from the carpet. Your father's Thermos.

Don't drive past the cemetery or your grandparents' house. Avoid the school where your Skip Day buddies are sharing biscuits on someone's hood. Drive one last time along the river, and don't think how the morning sun lights it till it looks like molten steel that time you snuck in to see your father's work. Don't look over the bridge where your best friend killed himself, shallow diving, where the girl in the photo will sit crying tonight.

Look straight ahead. Adjust the rearview mirror. Adjust the rearview mirror. Feel it warm beneath your hand, its box of river and sun and steel and shadow. Ignore your heart rising to your throat, this terrible relapse.

Think of everything you hate. Everything. Then pull the mirror down.

Biographical Notes

Marlin Barton: I was born and raised in the Alabama Black Belt and have spent most of my life there, either in Montgomery or rural Greene County. And it is the Black Belt that has helped to give life to the people and places in my short stories and my novel, *A Broken Thing*. I hope, though, that my fiction, while grounded in the specifics of place, ultimately has some sense of universal appeal.

Armond "Beaux" Boudreaux grew up in Thomasville, Alabama. He has worked as a reporter for *The Thomasville Times* (a job which led to the inspiration for "Baptism" and other stories). He holds a Bachelor's degree in English from UWA, where he served as the editor of the *The Sucarnochee Review* and co-feature editor of *The Life*. In Fall of '04, he will begin work on an M.A. in creative writing at the University of Southern Mississippi.

Sonny Brewer owns Over the Transom Bookstore in Fairhope, Alabama, and it is "just around the corner from where you are" on-line at www.overthetransombooks.com. He is the editor of *Stories from the Blue Moon Cafe*, volumes I, II, and III. Sonny's first novel, *The Poet of Tolstoy Park,* is set for Spring, 2005 release from Random House. You can read the first 30 pages at overthetransombooks.com.

Wendy Reed Bruce received the Lincoln Unity Award in Media, Public Affairs/Social Issues Reporting Category, for her documentary A Closer Look: The Alabama Institute for the Deaf and Blind and a fellowship from the Alabama State Council on the Arts for Literature. Her publications and /or awards also include New Letters, New Millennium Writing, Kalliope, Dogwood, Writing Today, and George Mason University. All Out of Faith: Southern Women on Spirituality co-edited with Jennifer Horne is due out from UA Press next year. She is a doctoral student at The University of Alabama where she works at The Center for Public TV and Radio(neither of which have anything to do with embalming). She lives in Birmingham with her three children.

Mike Burrell is a native of Valley Head, Alabama and a graduate of Jacksonville State University. No one who observed him during his school days would have forecast that he would ever aspire to become a writer. In fact when "Making It" was chosen to be included in this anthology, Mike said that he heard an eerie rumbling in the distance that he suspects was one of his old English teachers rolling over in her grave. A file cabinet in Mike's home contains a healthy stack of rejection letters, yet he keeps on writing, revising and submitting. Several of his short stories are now floating around in the mail system somewhere or in a garbled embryonic state within his brain. He has completed a novel, *'Til the Whistle Blows*, which has been described by a member of his writing group as an Alabama cocktail because of its mixture of race, politics and college football. It is now being considered for publication. He practices law in Bessemer, Alabama and lives in Vestavia Hills with his wife, Debra, who has mysteriously stayed with him despite his propensity to daydream and his insistence upon defending the David Claytons of the world.

Marian Carcache's fiction has appeared in several journals including Shenandoah, Chattahoochee Review, and Appalachian Heritage. One of her short stories was made into an opera, for which she wrote the libretto, and appeared on PBS stations nationwide. It was nominated for a regional Emmy Award and was a finalist in the New York Festivals. Her stories have been anthologized in Due South, Belles Lettres, Crossroads: Tales of the Southern Fantastic (Tor Books, August 2004), and, most recently, Climbing Mt. Cheaha: Emerging Alabama Writers (LivingstonPress, October 2004). She is the 2003-04 recipient of the Alabama StateCouncil on the Arts' Fellowship for ficition. She lives in Auburn with her son and five dogs, parakeet, and sugar glider. In addition to writing fiction, she is studying Traditional Chinese Medicine and is an assistant in an acupuncture clinic.

Loretta Cobb is Founder and Director Emeritus of The Harbert Writing Center at the University of Montevallo. She has published academic essays and poetry, and she has done a series of travel pieces for *The Birmingham News* as well as a regular column for several years. A graduate with honors of the University of Montevallo and Bread Loaf School of English in Vermont, she has written corporate histories, profiles for *Contemporary Novelists* and has edited several published books. "Seeing It Through," in *Belle's Letters*, was her first published fiction, after which she completed a collection of short stories, *The Ocean Was Salt*, published by Livingston Press. She is also at work on her first novel, *How Can I Keep From Singing?* Loretta Cobb lives in Montevallo with her novelist husband William Cobb, very near their two grandchildren. Her greatest joy in life was the birth of her daughter, Susan Meredith Smith.

If you really want to hear about it, the first thing you'll probably want to know (skipping over childhood turmoil and all that David Copperfield kind of crap) is that **John Cottle** is a small town lawyer who spends his spare time reading and writing fiction and playing with his GrandGirls, McKenzie and Sydney. He lives on Lake Martin in central Alabama with his wife and number one editor, Nancy. Blame her for any mistakes you find in his work. He has won several awards for his short fiction, including three Hackneys and an Alabama Writers' Conclave prize. Go figure. A collection of his short stories, *The Blessings of Hard-Used Angels* (Texas Review Press) won the 2003 George Garrett Fiction Prize. His creditors would be mighty pleased for you to purchase a copy. Visit his web site at www.johncottle.net

F. Brett Cox's fiction, essays, and reviews have appeared in *Century, Black Gate, The North Carolina Literary Review, Carriage House Review, Lady Churchill's Rose-bud Wristlet, The New England Quarterly, The New York Review of Science Fiction, Paradoxa, First Draft,* and numerous other publications. He is co-editor, with Andy Duncan, of *Crossroads: Tales of the Southern Literary Fantastic* (Tor Books, 2004). A native of North Carolina and former resident of southern Alabama, Brett is Assistant Professor of English at Norwich University in Northfield, Vermont. He lives in Northfield with his wife, playwright Jeanne Beckwith.

Kirk Curnutt is professor and chair of English at Troy University Montgomery. He is the author of a story collection, "Baby, Let's Make a Baby," and has recently completed a novel entitled "Aphrodite and Dad." He has also published five scholarly books and remains an ardent admirer of all things F. Scott Fitzgerald.

Ben Erickson grew up in Mobile and graduated from the University of South Alabama. His first novel, *A Parting Gift*, was published by Warner Books in 2000. Set on Mobile Bay, it was originally written as a high school graduation present for his son. Since its publication *A Parting Gift* has been required reading in high schools and colleges across the country and was chosen by The American Booksellers Association as a *Book Sense 76* selection. It has been published in several foreign translations including Chinese and Korean. Ben has written numerous articles and reviews for woodworking magazines as well as contributing to several books on the subject. An article he wrote about writing appeared in the fall 2001 issue of *First Draft* magazine. His short story, "Jubilee," was selected for the anthology *Literary Mobile* and also appeared as "Floundering" in *Stories from the Blue Moon Café II*. He has completed a second novel and is working on a third, from which "Coming About" is the first chapter.

Joe Formichella's "Tickets" was the 1993 Hackney Literary Award for short fiction. Shortly thereafter he stopped serious writing until the occasion of the 2002 Southern Writers Reading, hosted by Sonny Brewer and Over the Transom Bookstore. It was Brewer, in fact, who sought him out and encouraged him to write again. Thanks immeasurably to Sonny's efforts, Formichella's *The Wreck of the Twilight Limited*, was published in July, 2004, by MacAdam/Cage, to be followed by *Here's to you, Jackie Robinson* in May, 2005, based, in part, on interviews conducted back in 1993. His work has also recently appeared in *Stories from the Blue Moon Cafe*, and *Yalobusha Review*. In that other time, a distant, fuzzy memory now, he wrote freelance for *Mobile Bay Monthly*, and published pieces in *Grasslands Review* and *Red Bluff Review*. He lives and works in Fairhope, Alabama.

Tom Franklin grew up in Dickinson, Alabama. His family moved to Mobile in 1981, where Franklin attended the University of South Alabama. In 1994, he moved to Fayetteville, Arkansas, where he earned an MFA in fiction. He has published two books, Poachers: Stories, and Hell at the Breech, a novel, both from William Morrow. His work has appeared in The Georgia Review, The Southern Review, The Oxford American, New Stories from the South, and elsewhere. In 2001 Franklin held the John and Renee Grisham Chair at Ole Miss and was awarded a Guggenheim Fellowship. Currently writer-in-residence at Ole Miss, he lives in Oxford and is married to poet Beth Ann Fennelly, and they have a daughter, Claire. "Smonk Gets out Alive," originally a short story, is now the opening chapter of a new novel, The Book of Smonk.

Jim Gilbert lives on the Alabama Gulf Coast, where he scribes rambling essays described as book reviews for the *Mobile Register*. He does not own a single pair of khaki pants.

Roy Hoffman is author of the novel, *Almost Family*, winner of the Lillian Smith Award for fiction, and the nonfiction collection *Back Home: Journeys Through Mobile*. A native of Mobile, he worked in New York City for twenty years as a journalist, speechwriter, and teacher before returning to Alabama as staff writer at the Mobile Register with a special interest in the diverse cultures of the South.

Hoffman's reviews and essays have appeared in the *New York Times, Fortune, Southern Living* and other publications. He currently resides with his wife Nancy and daughter Meredith in Fairhope, Al., and periodically visits Louisville, Ky., where he teaches in the Brief Residency MFA in Writing Program at Spalding University.

As a graduate student in creative writing in 1977, **Suzanne Hudson** won an international prize for short fiction in a contest judged by the likes of Kurt Vonnegut, Jr., and Toni Morrison, then withdrew from the publishing world. Over twenty years later, however, a short story collection, *Opposable Thumbs*, was published by Livingston Press and was a finalist for the John Gardner Fiction Book Award. Her short fiction has been included in *Stories from the Blue Moon Café*, volumes I and II, as well as *The Alumni Grille*, the companion anthology out this year. Her first novel, *In a Temple of Trees*, a dark tale inspired by a real life murder near her hometown of Brewton, Alabama, debuted in September of 2003 to critical praise and will be released in paperback in January, 2005. A second novel, *In the Dark of the Moon*, is also due out in January, 2005. Hudson is a resident of Fairhope, Alabama where she is a middle school guidance counselor and creative writing teacher.

Laura Hunter, born in the Alabama hill country of Walker County, currently lives outside Northport, Alabama, with her husband Tom. Throughout her life she has lived nowhere other than Alabama, never wanted to live anywhere else. She retired from an education career teaching on the high school and college level and began another at the local senior center, trading one set of "seniors" for another. Raised on a rise surrounded by broom sedge and thrust early in life into the religion of noisy clapboard churches ringed by century-old headstones, she didn't begin writing until her mid-50's, for writing, a "frivolous pastime," was not considered an option for a country girl. Since she began writing stories and poetry, all of which reflect the perseverance of Alabama downtrodden and those who refuse to give up, even against extreme odds, her work has appeared in numerous journals and collections, as well as in *Belles' Letters*. Several of her stories and poems have won awards on state, national, and international levels. "Waiting for the Pink" is her second publication in 2004.

Michael Knight is the author of a novel, *Divining Rod*, and two collections of short fiction, *Dogfight and Other Stories* and *Goodnight Nobody*. His stories have appeared in *Esquire, The New Yorker*, and *Paris Review*, among other places, and have been selected three times for *New Stories from the South: The Year's Best*. He teaches writing at the University of Tennessee.

Janet Mauney is a writer and artist living in Auburn, Alabama. Her stories and novel excerpts have been published in *Sundog, The Apalachee Review, Woodrider, Q Magazine, Belles' Letters,* and she has published many art reviews in *Art Papers* and *The Florida Flambeau.* "Riding the Waves" won an Honorable Mention in the Hemingway Days Short Story Contest in Key West, Florida.

Patricia Mayer lives in Mobile with her husband and son in a house called Spider Alley, and digs in her garden while wearing floppy hats. Late at night when she can't sleep, she writes. She recently completed her second novel, and her short fiction occasionally crops up in periodicals and anthologies. Her work has been nominated for a Pushcart Prize. Of the characters in "Corrigan's Omens" she says, "Corrigan is like so many of the patients I had when I worked in the field of psychiatry. He's a cynic who trusts in nothing except his own web of superstitions and blames his wasted life on bad luck. In contrast, his gentle friend McNeeley believes anything as long as it makes him happy. Corrigan can't find his own contentment so he taps into McNeeley's. By the way, the omens in the story are authentic and I learned them as a child growing up in the South."

Norman McMillan, Professor Emeritus of English at the University of Montevallo, is the author of a memoir, *Distant Son: An Alabama Boyhood,* and of a play, *Truman Capote: Against a Copper Sky.* Currently he is working on a play commissioned by The Weil Family Endowment for Eminence in the Arts and Humanities in the School of Liberal Arts at Auburn University in Montgomery. Entitled *Ashes of Roses,* the play is based on stories of the prize-winning Alabama author, Mary Ward Brown. McMillan lives in Montevallo with his wife Joan. He particularly enjoys theater, fishing, travel, and four grandchildren.

Janet Nodar: When I was eight, I wrote a thrilling story in which two sets of identical twins discovered several skeletons buried in their basement. I believe there was also some pirate treasure involved. And, yes: I had been reading the Bobbsey twins. (Remember them?) Well, I was eight a long long long time ago, but I'm still writing thrilling (ahem) stories. I'm also teaching English and raising children. Go figure. I recently completed a novel and am looking for an agent. I expect I'll just keep on writing. It doesn't pay well, God knows, but I am unable to imagine myself without the word "writer" after my name.

Michelle Richmond grew up in Mobile and currently lives in Northern California with her husband and son. Her books include the novel *Dream of the Blue Room* and the story collection *The Girl in the Fall-Away Dress*, which won the Associated Writing Programs Award for Short Fiction. Her stories and essays have appeared in *Glimmer Train, Other Voices, Gulf Coast, Alabama Bound, Stories from the Blue Moon Cafe*, Salon.com, and elsewhere. She teaches writing at the University of San Francisco, edits the online literary journal Fiction Attic, and serves on the advisory board of the Isherwood Foundation. She earned a BA from the University of Alabama and an MFA from the University of Miami, where she was a James Michener Fellow. Her major obsessions are Krispy Kreme doughnuts, dark chocolate, single-malt Scotch, and globe-trotting. "Ocean Beach" is excerpted from her novel-in-progress.

Kathleen Thompson's story, "Living Like the Lilies," was a finalist in the Writers@Work Fiction competition, 2004. She has published fiction, nonfiction, and poetry in various magazines and journals, most recently, poetry in *Sou'wester, Birmingham Poetry Review*, and in *Oracle*, as the winner of the Vivian Smallwood Poetry Award, Eugene Walter Writers Festival, 2004, University of South Alabama. She has published a chapbook of poetry, *Searching for Ambergris*. A former teacher of high school English with a BS from the University of Alabama, she is a recent graduate of the MFA in Writing program at Spalding University. She lives in Birmingham, AL, where her searches continue—for plots, eternally, and for a publisher for her collection of stories and the novel-in-progress.

Sidney Thompson: "A Classical Education" was conceived when I was driving through the Mississippi Delta thinking of the poor people living there who weren't as fortunate as my father, who grew up poor in the Delta himself but who grew up white and in the 1940s and therefore received a classical education in the public schools, thanks to the aristocratic cotton planters who demanded it at that time for their own children. Readers sometimes wonder why I chose to make the characters black (since I am white), so here you are: 1) to make the story more contemporary, by reflecting the Delta's current population and its political and ethical concerns; 2) to make the story more mythical, by using the oldest race of people; and 3) to make the story more challenging, or unsettling, hopefully causing some to question their expectations of whites and blacks, whether rich or poor, educated or uneducated. My short stories have appeared in such publications as *The*

Southern Review, The Carolina Quarterly, Louisiana Literature, and *Stories From The Blue Moon Cafe, Volumes 1 & 2* (MacAdam/Cage). I live in Fairhope, Alabama, with my wife, author Jennifer Paddock.

Jake York: I haven't published a short story since 1994 and I have never published a book of short stories at all. I have published over 80 poems since 1994, some in journals including *Shenandoah, Greensboro Review, The Southern Review, Quarterly West,* and *Crab Orchard Review,* and Routledge will publish my academic study *The Architecture of Address: The monument and Public Speech in American Poetry* in 2004. I have been a Colorado Council on the Arts fellow in poetry, and my work has been nominated for a Pushcart Prize.

Brad Watson received an MFA in creative writing and American literature from the University of Alabama. He worked as a newspaper reporter and editor on the Alabama Gulf Coast and in Montgomery, Alabama, where he was State Editor for The Montgomery Advertiser. He returned to UA to teach in 1988. In 1997, he received a five-year appointment to teach fiction writing at Harvard University. Since then he has been a visiting writer-in-residence at The University of West Florida and The University of Alabama at Birmingham. In 2004-05 he will be the John and Renee Grisham Writer-in-Residence at The University of Mississippi. Watson's work has has been anthologized in *Best American Mystery Stories, Walking on Water, Stories from the Blue Moon Café,* and *The Norton Anthology of Literature.* His books are a collection of short stories, *Last Days of the Dog-Men,* which received the Sue Kaufman Prize for First Fiction from the American Academy of Arts and Letters; and a novel, *The Heaven of Mercury,* which was a finalist for the 2002 National Book Award in Fiction. In 2004 he received a grant from the National Endowment for the Arts. When not teaching, he lives on the Alabama Gulf Coast, and is the father of two sons: Owen, a musician, writer, and fabulist who in his spare time attends fifth grade; and Jason, a forester, avid reader, marathon runner, and raconteur par excellence living and working with his wife, Katie, in Columbia, South Carolina.

photo courtesy of Alabama Public TV

Don Noble has hosted over 125 episodes of his literary interview show *Bookmark* on Alabama Public Television and has reviewed over one hundred books for his weekly segment, *Alabama Bound*, on Alabama Public Radio. He is the editor of *Hemingway: A Revaluation*, *The Steinbeck Question: New Essays in Criticism*, *The Rising South* (with Joab L. Thomas), *A Century Hence* (by George Tucker), and *Zelda and Scott/Scott and Zelda: Essays on the Fitzgeralds' Life, Work and Times*. His reviews, essays, and interviews have appeared in numerous periodicals over the past thirty-five years. He serves on the board of directors of the Alabama Humanities Foundation and the Alabama Writers' Forum. Noble holds the Ph.D. from UNC-Chapel Hill and is Professor Emeritus of English and Adjunct Professor of Journalism at the University of Alabama.